Pearl

A Historical Novel by
Cynthia Jordan

Emerald Eagle Publishing 2013
ISBN: 978-0-9886578-0-9

Published by
Emerald Eagle Publishing
2137 Office Park Dr. Suite A
San Angelo, TX 76904

©2013 by Cynthia Jordan All rights reserved
Printed in the United States of America

This is a work of fiction. While, in all fiction the literary perceptions and insights are based on experience, the Lady Pearl's names are products of the author's imagination. No reference to any real person is intended or should be inferred.

This story is based on historical facts. References include: Karen Abbot, "The Concho Country" by Gus Clemens; Old San Angelo and "Come Into My Parlor," by Charles Washborn." Most research references were provided by Wikipedia and the Bible. A special thank you to the people of San Angelo for telling stories of their city's colorful past.

Photos of the "Lady Pearls," Beth, Rosey and Aunt Katherine were created in the 1920's by Alfred Cheney Johnston (with the exception of Texas Katie). Special thanks to Doctor David and Janet Harvey who generously allowed us to photograph their home as Miss Pearl's Parlor and to Lee Pflueger for the beautiful photos of his Clear Creek Ranch in Menard County, Texas. Miss Victoria Pearl's photographs are of the great Edwardian actress, Lily Elsie.

ISBN: 978-0-9886578-0-9

*To my mother Margaret Jordan
who once told me,
"It's like walking into a field of flowers
that all open up at once."*

Forward

"The God of Love lives in a state of need."
~ Plato

Her full name was Victoria Pearl McDougal McKnight. She was like hard candy on the surface and marshmallow cream inside. Pearl was in the business of *selling love,* or at least that is what some people called it. When a man wanted a woman he would go see Pearl; however, not just anyone could be a patron at Miss Pearl's Parlor. Membership into this circle of society was a privilege to be earned and a status to be enjoyed by only the most affluent men. To qualify as a patron, a man must first be a gentleman and have the ability to appreciate her girls like a fine wine or decadent dessert – a lesson Victoria learned in Chicago from her teachers, Ada and Minna Everleigh, who employed her during her younger years.

From 1900 to 1911, the Everleigh Club was the most elegant place in Chicago for a man to find female companionship. Like the *Geishas of Japan* and the *Courtesans of Venice*, the girls were elegant, smart, gorgeous, and extremely masterful in giving sexual pleasure. An exclusive club with a select clientele, the Everleigh Club was only available to men whom Ada and Minna knew or to those who possessed a letter of introduction. Men of wealth and status bragged to their colleagues, "I am going to get Everleighed this evening," thus; the term "going to get laid" was born. It was here that, in three short years, Victoria Pearl learned her life lessons that would prepare her for a most adventurous life.

The intention of the Everleigh women was never to steal husbands or entrap men with pregnancy. That would be deceitful and dishonest. The Everleigh girls made an honest living with all parties knowing exactly what to expect. They were there to provide a service, and they did it better than any of the other 500 businesses of its kind in Chicago. The Everleigh girls were playful and skilled in the art of sexual satisfaction. For this reason, the ladies made an excellent living which in today's market could be compared to $400,000 a year. This included expensive gifts as well as bonus gratuities for services rendered.

Fate had brought Victoria Pearl to live in West Texas. In 1921, she opened Pearl's Parlor, incorporating her experiences in Chicago, along with the knowledge she had learned about men, business, and "making happy, satisfied customers."

Victoria Pearl saw many changes in her lifetime but nothing as drastic as the changes for American women after World War I. For decades the Victorian Age dominated society in a formal, conservative fashion. In 1920, the 19th Amendment gave women the right to vote, inspiring a culture soon to be known as *The New Woman*. Skirts and hairstyles became shorter, and the music of the Jazz Age promoted a new sensuous attitude of sexuality. The term "flapper" was created from the idea that women were becoming free to flap their wings and more and more women were graduating with a college education.

Before the 1920's, only prostitutes smoked, drank liquor, revealed too much leg, and wore make-up. When the automobile came on the scene, young women were no longer under the constant watch of their families and were discovering a new kind of independence. In 1923 the United States Attorney General declared that women could wear trousers. Although birth control was not made legal until 1965, by the 1920's condoms were becoming more available, especially to soldiers, with the intention of preventing disease. More and more young women were breaking free from the conservative mindset of the Victorian Age.

With the onset of prohibition, San Angelo, Texas had 63 pharmacies that sold booze by prescription. All you had to do was pick up your preference of liquor written on a piece of paper from a basket as you walked into the store and take it to the counter. The Roaring Twenties were on fire, and San Angelo was a fun place to be.

Victoria Pearl was a successful entrepreneur in San Angelo, Texas. She bought a mansion on the Concho River where she opened a business she called Miss Pearl's Parlor. Everyone who patronized the Parlor knew her as "Miss Pearl." The girls called her "Mother," and San Angelo knew her as "Madame." Like many women in her business, she liked to maintain a professional mystique; and name changing was common to accomplish just that. Miss Pearl was adamant that her girls be educated and current with the latest news in politics and trends. Her experience, working as a courtesan at the Everleigh House in Chicago, taught her well. She had learned from Ada and Minna Everleigh the importance of etiquette, knowledge, and how a woman should conduct herself in the most lady-like fashion. Life had taught her many lessons, and Pearl felt a strong need to pass the knowledge on to her girls.

At the beginning of the 20th century, New Orleans was creating a new sound called *jazz*. Some speculate the word came from jasmine perfume, a popular fragrance of the sporting women in Storyville. Blues, boogies, and burlesque music were the new rage and had become enormously popular. The style was a perfect combination of African and European traditional music. The slow sexy rhythms of the blues and the smooth, deep sounds of woodwind instruments such as the saxophone were stirring up deep primordial sexuality in young Americans everywhere.

In 1923, West Texas began prospering from oil exploration and San Angelo was at the heart of the boom. It all began May 28, when the Santa Rita oil well finally began producing crude oil in the Permian Basin. San Angelo was ideally located and had already been established as a major trading center. With an elevation of 2300 feet above sea level, San Angelo boasted weather pleasant most of the year with an arid climate and bright, blue skies. The gentle flow of the Concho River's teal green waters along serene riverbanks make a picturesque setting through the middle of town. Victoria Pearl had fallen in love with San Angelo and found it to be a perfect place to run her business.

Although they were not necessarily among the wealthiest of men, Pearl was especially fond of cowboys. She considered them incredibly sexy and loved the way they talked with their smooth western drawls. Those who could behave like gentlemen were welcome at Miss Pearl's Parlor. Because they were ruggedly handsome, muscular, and for the most part a lot of fun, cowboys were good for morale. The *Lady Pearls,* as their patrons affectionately called them, loved it when the cowboys came to town!

Throughout the years several girls came and left Miss Pearl's Parlor. Our story will focus on how in May of 1923, thirteen ladies, including Victoria Pearl, became part of Miss Pearl's Parlor. Together they had learned how to prosper and survive in a time when there were very few job options for single women and one sexual experience put a girl in the category of "a fallen woman." Their friendships developed into a sisterhood, and together they created a family. Pearl was passionately protective of all of her girls and for this reason many times the girls referred to her as "Mother Pearl." Her experience at the Everleigh Club had made her a master at understanding human nature.

When they were little girls, the women at Pearl's Parlor never had the dream, *"One day I want to be a prostitute."* They all preferred the *"One day my prince will come and take me away to his castle"* story. It is important to understand that sometimes on life's journey circumstances can cause people to lose hope. Every girl at Miss Pearl's had a story that brought her to San Angelo. It was there they found a family, love and protection from the challenges presented to women of that time.

Running through the center of San Angelo is the Concho River, home to a unique mussel that produces lavender-pink fresh water pearls. In fact, San Angelo was called The Queen City of the Concho Rivers. Because of the lustrous rare beauty of the Concho Pearl, Victoria Pearl took it as a sign that San Angelo was where she belonged.

On the day she was born, Pearl's mother named her Victoria Pearl. "All women are like beautiful pearls, Victoria," her mother said one day. "A pearl is formed when a grain of sand has entered the tightness of the fresh water shell and then irritates the mussel inside. The longer the process the more beautiful and lustrous the pearl becomes with layers and layers of iridescent radiance. Finally when it is opened, a beautiful treasure is discovered inside."

Women are capable of taking a man into uncharted realms of exciting adventures of mystery and universal understanding. Like the discovery of a lustrous pearl, when a woman is appreciated and adored she will open herself up to reveal the sacred treasures and gifts she holds deep within her heart. Her soul is love, and her true beauty is the generous light radiating within her heart. In her story, Miss Pearl teaches us that the human experience is fascinating and nothing on earth can compare to the deep love we are all capable of giving.

At the foundation of Pearl's Parlor was the understanding that sexuality is a natural instinct. Females can get pregnant and have a baby only once a year whereas males are capable of procreating hundreds of times a year. Females look for strong providers and protectors in a mate, whereas males are simply looking. Pearl often said, "Men have a physical need to get their pipes cleaned. My girls simply provide a service."

Sex can be like a sporting event, and in fact, women who worked in brothels many times were referred to as *sporting women*. As one girl put it, "A good romp in the hay can be fun and physically satisfying like a good tennis match." In a world where any kind of expressed sexuality was considered unacceptable behavior, the young women who worked at Pearl's Parlor had permission to be sexy.

For two people in love, sex is a beautiful gift from our Creator to express affection, thus the term "making love." This kind of sexuality enables the participants to experience the universal feeling of oneness. Making love can be a spiritual experience that satisfies the soul with a sense of complete satisfaction and peace.

Miss Pearl's philosophy was simple. *"To be in denial of our human sexual desires is simply unnatural!"*

The historical facts in this book are true and the stories are real. The names have been changed to protect the innocent and the guilty.

Emma Grace - Prologue

Friday, May 25, 1923: Creative sexuality was not the only talent the friendly ladies at Miss Pearl's Parlor possessed. Daily reading was mandatory because Miss Pearl wanted her girls to be interesting conversationalists.

Pearl had exceptionally high standards for intelligence, beauty, and grace. These qualities were appreciated and seemed to attract a more sophisticated clientele with money to spend; after all, she was running a business. Pearl was extremely strict and required her girls to act like ladies. She learned the trade from Ada and Minna Everleigh in Chicago. The sisters had made a fortune catering to wealthy gentlemen.

At the turn of the century, Victoria Pearl had worked as an Everleigh "butterfly" in Chicago for several years. Every day the sisters gave lessons on how to be a lady and demanded the girls read and know about current events. This was practiced by the very famous Venetian Courtesans centuries before. In fact the courtesans were the only women allowed in the libraries. Victoria liked the fact that San Angelo had been named after Saint Angela Merici, a nun who started a school for girls in the 16th century when learning to read and write was not readily available to young women. Angela attended Saint Afra Church every day. Ironically, Afra ran a brothel in the Temple of Venus and later converted to Christianity. Refusing to participate in pagan rituals, she was martyred in 304 A.D. Later the church named her, "the patron saint of concubines".

Pearl exercised the same standards at Miss Pearl's Parlor. "Pretty is as pretty does," Miss Pearl liked to say. This made for a better product and better profits. "In order to appeal to a gentleman you must first be a lady. Remember girls, this profession is only temporary. You must always demand respect and keep your eyes set on the future. Save your money, and be independent in your thoughts and actions. The world is changing, and each one of you is capable of achieving great things!"

The sun was warm as the clouds cleared to reveal a beautiful bright blue sky. The air smelled clean from the pleasant rainfall that had just quenched the dusty West Texas town of San Angelo. Ten stunning women were sitting on the porch that wrapped around the three story stately mansion known as *Miss Pearl's Parlor*. Their names were Katie, Annabelle, Ginger, Betsy, Maggie, Sarah, Heather, Lucy, Redbird, Harmony and Miss Pearl Each of the girls was reading a different book with the exception of Harmony, who was strumming her guitar.

Maggie had chosen a book of poetry written by Veronica Franco, a celebrated Venetian poet and courtesan of the 16th century. Accused of casting spells and having too much power over men, Veronica had been tried by the Spanish Inquisition for the fatally punishable crime of witchcraft. At her trial, she was redeemed by the efforts of the noblemen who knew her.

"Listen to this everyone!" Maggie exclaimed. *"So sweet and delicious do I become, when I am in bed with a man who, I sense, loves and enjoys me, that the pleasure I bring excels all delight, so the knot of love, however tight it seemed before, is tied tighter still."*

With that Maggie whimsically held the collection of poems to her heart, closed her eyes and smiled. "Isn't that beautiful?"

"Maggie, sounds like you're reading fairy tales," Ginger sighed. "Knot of love is a bit of a stretch, don't you think?" Ginger had wavy flaxen hair that shimmered in the sun.

"Don't mind her," Redbird defended with a sweet smile. "I know what Veronica means. It's about appreciation. I have not known many, but when you get a man who *really* knows how to make love to a woman, it can be like a beautiful dance and quite delightful indeed," she sighed.

Miss Pearl had been quietly listening to the conversation among her girls. She slowly took a sip of mint tea, then spoke, "Indeed you are quite correct, Redbird. When a man really knows how to enjoy a woman and appreciate her many gifts, the memory of that experience can live in her heart forever. This is because a woman completely gives with her heart, mind and soul when she is appreciated. Sounds to me like Veronica Franco enjoyed her life as a courtesan."

"Sounds to me like she had some good lovers," Heather giggled.

"I agree," Lucy chimed in. Lucy was known for her fun-loving attitude, and she was especially creative in her work. Men loved Lucy's wit and charm, and it seemed as if she was always smiling which made her popular, especially with men.

With that, Harmony, the parlor's muse, picked up her guitar that had been leaning on the wall. "*Put your arms around me honey, hold me tight, cuddle up, and cuddle up with all your might…*" she sang.

Ginger looked at Harmony and rolled her eyes. "You're in the same fairytale as Maggie!" she exclaimed with a smirk.

Texas Kate loved to tell stories and spoke up loudly, "I remember my Daddy told me his daddy used to say, 'If you love what makes your living, you will never work a day in your life.' If I could do anything, I would choose to become a Texas Ranger but that will never happen. I think Daddy always wished I'd been a boy. He taught me how to shoot. Sure do miss him."

Betsy suddenly became melancholy. "I miss my Daddy too. He's probably setting tobacco and planting corn right about now."

"I, for one, can say I love working here. I know I won't be here forever, but it seems like the best choice for now. I have to say the money is much better than any kind of job I could find," Heather commented.

Sarah was sitting at the end of the porch totally oblivious to the conversation at hand. She was engrossed in reading poetry by D.H Lawrence. "What do you think of this one, Ginger? *A woman unsatisfied must have luxuries; but a woman who loves a man would sleep on a board.*"

Ginger grinned. "It is true. I do have expensive taste." She stood up and began dancing around the porch. "I admit I do love French perfume and the feeling of silks and satins on my skin. As far as love… Lord knows I've heard the word plenty of times, but no one I would sleep on a board for!"

Annabelle, the quiet one of the group offered her opinion. "I was in love once, and I would surely sleep on a board if I could be with him now. In fact, I think I would do just about anything if I could be with him again. The smell of rain always takes me to our magical day on the lake together."

"I know how you feel, Annabelle." Pearl smiled. "I believe true love comes once in a lifetime."

"I think I'm going to take Rusty for a walk by the river," Katie announced. "C'mon boy."

From the front porch of Miss Pearl's Parlor, there was a peaceful view of the Concho River gently flowing, with tall Texas pecan trees standing along its banks. Mozella came outside to straighten the chairs and sweep the porch, singing one of her favorite spirituals.

Mozella was Miss Pearl's best friend and Pearl trusted her with her life. It was Mozella's job to make sure life at the parlor ran smoothly. She was in charge of the house cleaning staff, food preparation and keeping the grounds manicured. Mozella also collected the money. She was best known to the girls for her knowledge of Bible scripture.

"*Psalm 147: Who covers the heavens with clouds, who prepares rain for the earth, who makes grass grow on the mountains,*" Mozella expressed, admiring her clean porch.

"Why do you always quote the Bible?" Maggie asked.

"My grandmother named me Mozella after Moses himself. Every day she used to quote the Bible to me. I suppose I'm just carrying on the family tradition."

Ginger turned and pointed to the east. "Look, Miss Pearl, someone's walking toward the house."

A young woman wearing a simple peach colored cotton dress and carrying a brown suitcase and an overcoat was making her way to the mansion. She was slender and medium in height. Her clear light skin had just a touch of sun, making her look as if she were blushing. The young woman looked up at the women on the porch with soft round greenish-blue eyes, revealing her childlike innocence and lack of worldly knowledge. It was obvious she was a little fearful and unsure of herself.

Miss Pearl stood up from her chair. She always had an eye for a pretty face. It was good for business.

"Excuse me, Ma'am, are you Miss Pearl?" the young woman called from the gate in front of the house.

"Yes, I am, dear," Miss Pearl answered with a kind smile. She was a graceful woman and treated everyone as if they were important. The young woman pulled a letter from a small leather bag.

"A very nice gentleman, Mr. Swanson, told me to come see you, Miss Pearl. He has written a letter of introduction," she announced, holding an envelope in the air.

Sarah could see the girl was nervous. She smiled at her and waved. "Hello there… I'm Sarah!"

The young woman nodded her head and smiled. "Hello," she replied.

Victoria smiled a warm friendly grin. "I see… Ladies, I believe I would like to have a visit with this young lady. It is Friday night, and the weekend is at hand. You know we are expecting our cowboys to show up tonight! Go into the house now, and start getting ready."

The young women gathered up their books and returned them to the library inside the house. They were talking and giggling with excitement. The girls loved it when the cowboys came to town. Somehow showing them a good time just didn't seem like work. "There is just something special about those cowboys!" Maggie liked to say.

Mozella looked at the young girl standing by the gate and then at Miss Pearl. "She reminds me of a young lady I met in Chicago a few years back," she said to her friend with a wink.

"Come up on the porch, dear," Miss Pearl called from the porch. "Mozella, would you please bring this young lady and me some fresh tea?"

"Yes, Ma'am." She looked at the girl with her intuitive wisdom and then back at Miss Pearl. "*Psalm 104: Some wandered in the wilderness, lost, and homeless,*" she quoted as she strolled back into the house.

"Sit here, dear. You look tired. What is your name, honey?"

"My name is Emma Grace, Ma'am."

"You are quite pretty, Emma Grace."

"Thank you, Ma'am. I've fallen on some hard times, Miss Pearl. I have no place to go, and Mr. Swanson told me I should come and talk to you about a job."

Emma Grace quickly handed her the letter. Pearl opened the envelope, put on her reading glasses, and began reading the letter aloud.

May 23, 1923
Dear Miss Pearl,

I hope this letter finds you well. My purpose for writing is to introduce you to Emma Grace. Her father was a "lunger," and they came to West Texas when he became ill. Unfortunately, her father died of tuberculosis in Carlsbad last week. He was a good man and strong in character. I recommended that Emma Grace contact you as I personally hold her in good standing.

With kind regards,
Mr. Charles J. Swanson

"Good old Charlie," Miss Pearl commented shaking her head. "He always has had an eye for a pretty girl. Well, Emma Grace, tell me about yourself."

"Mother died when I was born, and Daddy and I came to San Angelo several weeks ago. He had tuberculosis. They called him a 'lunger', and he has been in the Sanatorium in Carlsbad. I guess it was too late for my Daddy. He died last Thursday. There isn't much money left, and I'm afraid I don't know what to do."

Tears filled Emma's eyes, and she quickly looked down at her hands folded tightly on her lap. "I have nowhere to go Miss Pearl," she murmured quietly. "I have an aunt and uncle back in Missouri, but they have seven children already. I certainly don't want to be a burden."

Mozella walked out on the porch and handed Emma Grace a glass of cold mint tea. As she turned to go back into the house, she raised her eyebrows at Pearl and smiled.

"Thank you, Mozella." Pearl turned to Emma Grace. "You are quite lovely, Emma Grace. Did Charlie, I mean Mr. Swanson, tell you about what we do here?"

"Yes Ma'am. I know," Emma whispered softly. Then she looked up into Miss Pearl's face with all the courage she could muster. "Miss Pearl," she stammered. "I… uhm, well I… Miss Pearl, I have never been with a man before."

Pearl was taken by Emma's sweetness and charm. "Somehow I knew that, dear," she stated with a kindly tone.

"But I'm sure I can learn!" Emma forced the words from her mouth with some hesitation.

Pearl liked her. "I have an idea. Mozella could use some help with some domestic chores. Can you cook?"

"Oh, yes, Ma'am! I have been cooking for my Daddy my whole life," Emma Grace exclaimed with some relief.

"Well, at least you won't go hungry and we can put a roof over your head. Another pretty face at the parlor is always advantageous. Emma Grace, I believe you could do well in my business. However, I do not want you doing anything you are not ready to do. We can give it a few weeks and see what happens. Come on in the house, honey. Mozella will be happy to have that extra help right now. It's Friday night, and the girls are bubbling over with excitement. We are expecting cowboys tonight!"

It is the spring of 1923. Fate has brought 13 women together to work at Miss Pearl's Parlor in San Angelo, Texas. These are their stories.

Victoria Pearl

The fiddler performed cheerfully as Brian McDougal watched his fellow passengers dance and sing on the deck of the massive sailing ship headed to America. Every evening at dusk the musician would begin playing traditional songs from the homeland. He was devoted to keeping up the spirits of his fellow Irishmen on their long journey to the unknown. At night the people sang folk songs and danced to Irish reels. One evening, when the old man finally laid down his fiddle, Brian asked him, "Why do you think a violin is shaped like a woman?"

The fiddler looked at Brian, pointed his finger in the air and grinned. "Aye me boy, it might be on account of the fact a violin is just like a woman. When a violin is tuned well, and you play it with respect, passion and grace, she can make your soul sing and produce the most beautiful music in the world," he answered with a wink.

The year was 1876. Dreams of prosperity and the courage to explore new opportunities found Brian McDougal and Molly O'Connor with hundreds of other Irish immigrants boarding a ship headed to the untamed lands of America. Brian first saw Molly the day the ship set sail for the New World and her smile instantly captured his heart. Day after day they spent their time on the deck of the ship talking about days to come as they watched the vast waters of the deep blue Atlantic Ocean and  listened to the music of her ancient song. Several weeks passed, and by the time they finally saw land again, Molly and Brian were in love, and engaged to be married. Within a week after setting ashore, the happy Irish couple became man and wife.

In 1878 Victoria was Queen of England, the first telephones were being installed, and Thomas Edison presented a new invention he named the "phonograph" that could record sound. That same year little Victoria Pearl was born to Brian and Molly McDougal in Aurora, Illinois. Victoria was a beautiful baby, and when her father first laid eyes on her, he was smitten. "Oh, Molly, me love. What a lovely wee one we have. She looks just like a little peach."

Aurora, Illinois, was an up and coming community on the Fox River near Chicago. Brian's cousin, Michael Kelly, had arranged a job for Brian as a foreman for the Chicago, Burlington and Quincy Railroad in the roundhouse and locomotive shop. Molly found a position teaching English literature at the new high school for girls. From the time she was a baby, Victoria learned Irish folk songs from Molly, and by the time she was 2, the little girl was singing along with her mother. As she grew older, Victoria learned dances and how to make Irish lace.

Her mother told tales of Irish folklore including stories of fairies and leprechauns with pots of gold at the end of the rainbow. Molly taught Victoria to read before she was six years old. "A woman who can read can travel through time and visit faraway places anytime she wants," her mother would often say. Victoria especially loved Hans Christian Andersen, and her favorite story was, *The Ugly Duckling.*

Molly was well educated and taught Victoria the etiquette of being a lady. "Pretty is as pretty does" was a common phrase she used. Going to Chicago on the train with her mother was always a special event. Because of her father's work, the family was able to obtain free passes to travel for the day to the big city 40 miles away. They visited libraries, churches, and wonderful parks. When Victoria was 14 years old, Chicago held the World's Columbian Exposition to celebrate the 400th anniversary of Christopher Columbus's arrival to  the New World in 1492. The family visited the expo several times and together they rode the first Ferris wheel ever made. Standing at 264 feet, it took twenty minutes to complete a revolution and was built especially for the event. "So this is what the birds see," Brian McDougal said to his girls when they stopped at the top. It was a memory Victoria would hold dear in her heart all of her life.

Victoria grew up to be a stunning young lady, tall and shapely with long, reddish, dark blonde hair and expressive blue-green eyes that twinkled when she laughed. Victoria's laugh alone sometimes made even perfect strangers smile. One afternoon Molly, gazing at her daughter, thought of how exceptionally lovely her daughter had become. "All women are like beautiful pearls, Victoria. A pearl is formed when a grain of sand has entered the tightness of the fresh water shell and then irritates the mussel inside. The longer the process the more beautiful and lustrous the pearl becomes with layers and layers of iridescent radiance. Finally when it is opened a beautiful treasure is discovered inside. True beauty comes from within, Victoria. Kindness is the light that illuminates from the soul."

When Victoria was 19, Molly McDougal caught a fever and died of pneumonia. Victoria was devastated at the loss of her mother. A year later, Molly's beloved husband, Brian, died of a broken heart. Alone and depressed, Victoria fell in love with Ian O'Donnell, a handsome young man from "the old country." He was fun and charming, but his favorite pastime was to drink too much ale and sing silly songs and limericks in the pub. He made Victoria laugh, and for a short time, she forgot about her sadness.

One evening, under a starry, moonlit night, Ian told Victoria he loved her and wanted to marry her. Victoria said "Yes" and was overjoyed with happiness. Ian had brought some spirits and convinced Victoria to drink with him to celebrate their future. Ian kissed her deeply like she had never been kissed before, and when he did, it sent a thrill throughout her body. Between the ale and the kiss, Victoria was carried away into the fantasy of becoming Ian's wife. She had only known the love her parents had for each other and believed in that moment that she was now going to have Ian forever, loving and adoring her just as her father had loved her mother. All the passions of youth and virility swept through Ian and Victoria, and in the heat of physical desire, Ian was insistent that Victoria give him her precious virginity. "I love you with all of my heart, Victoria. We can begin forever right now. I want you so desperately, and I want to spend the rest of my life with you. In my soul I'm already married to you."

Victoria's body was feeling new sensations she had never known. She believed Ian's convincing words of love and devotion. Victoria was in a state of complete surrender and did not protest when Ian lifted her skirt and entered her womanhood. In that moment, she felt alive with a new awareness of giving herself completely. As Ian released his seed, he made a moaning sound so loud she thought he was in pain. Victoria, on the other hand, was full of different feelings and emotions. Although she felt a subtle physical pain, in a strange way, Victoria felt fulfilled as a woman and content in knowing she had satisfied the desires of the man she loved. After that evening, everything changed. Ian's words were different, and although he was polite, his demeanor was also different. He became less available to her, and she noticed he was becoming friendlier with other women. Ian had ceased talking about marriage all together, and it was not too long before Victoria realized she was with child. When she told Ian about the baby, he promised to marry her in a secret ceremony. Within a week, Ian left town.

Victoria was brokenhearted and completely lost her will to live. She was sick every morning and had no appetite at all. Victoria went into deep depression and slept through most of the day. When she was awake, she cried. Two months after Ian left, the baby miscarried. No one was with her as she cleaned herself up and retrieved the small, lifeless tissue that had been living inside her. Victoria wrapped the tiny fetus in a lacey doily her mother had made and put it in a wooden box. Quietly she prayed as she buried her baby in the rose garden. "Go to the angels, my little one. Your grandparents are there waiting for you." After losing her child, Victoria became even more depressed. She was left alone and felt ashamed.

Aurora ceased to be the joyful home Victoria had known as a child. After her experiences with Ian, she harbored too many painful memories, and missed her family enormously. Many times her mother told her, "Victoria means Victory! Follow your dreams, my dear. There is nothing you cannot do!" With that, Victoria got on a train to Chicago and never looked back. She found a job as a librarian and a room to call *home* in a modest but clean boarding house with several other young women. She preferred her privacy and kept to herself most of the time. She liked working at the library because she loved books. Molly McDougal often told her daughter, "Reading can take you to another world, Victoria. God made human beings because God loves a good story." Reading romantic novels took Victoria away into new worlds full of fantasy and love. Victoria was in love with love, the kind she saw between her parents, Brian and Molly McDougal. She, on the other hand, felt soiled and used. By now, Victoria had surrendered herself to the idea that true love only happens to other people.

Victoria was stunning, and men looked at her with lustful eyes. One time, while checking out some books on philosophy, an older gentleman winked at her, smiled, and said, "If I looked like you, I would certainly be a wealthy man. You are sitting on a million dollars, young lady." Victoria blushed and wondered, "What in the world was he talking about?" Somehow it made her feel uncomfortable. Twenty-one years old and beautiful, Victoria had grown bored with young men and felt like none of them could be trusted. Her bitterness and obvious disinterest only enticed men more. Victoria's indifference intrigued a lot of men. There was always some young stud coming around to the library trying to court her. It was in times like these that she really missed her mother. She felt she had no one to talk to or to give her the advice young women so desperately need. Victoria wondered how differently her life would be if her parents were still alive.

It was September of 1899. The first days of autumn brought crisp cool weather and colorful foliage to Chicago's Grant Park by the shores of Lake Michigan. Victoria was sitting on a bench reading Emily Bronte's, *Wuthering Heights*. For a moment, she glanced up from her book and saw two attractive young women walking along the path in front of her. One was redheaded, and the other had dark blonde hair. Both were wearing elegant clothes and expensive jewelry. They stopped for a moment and looked at her. After a brief conversation between them, the two women walked toward the bench where Victoria was sitting. They smiled a friendly smile and said, "Hello." Victoria smiled back.

"You are reading one of my favorite books," one of them said. "Catherine and Heathcliff are two of my favorite characters."

"Alas, a story of unrequited love," Victoria sighed. "I have read it before."

"Unfortunately, sometimes love just does not work out," the other woman quipped in a songful Southern accent.

"I have had my own disappointments when it comes to love," Victoria said. "My parents were in love, but sometimes I think they were just a fairy tale. Both of them are gone now. I have not had much luck with men."

The two women looked at each other. The blonde haired woman raised her eyebrows, and the other eagerly pulled out a calling card. "My name is Minna, and this is my sister Ada. We would like to invite you to tea next Saturday. Ada and I are opening a new business in a few months, you might be interested in. We shall serve at 4 o'clock. What is your name, dear?"

"My name is Victoria Pearl," she answered politely as she took the card. Pink roses framed a cream colored background and the lettering was done with gold engraving.

It read:
Minna and Ada Everleigh
2131 South Dearborn Street
Chicago, Illinois

"Where do you work, if I may ask?" Minna inquired.

"I am a librarian," Victoria answered. "My mother taught me to read when I was six years old, and I have been in love with books ever since."

"Victoria Pearl, a refined, intelligent woman with beauty like yours can become quite wealthy. Come see us," Minna said with a warm yet businesslike tone. With that, the two sisters bid Victoria a good day and walked away.

That was the same remark the man made at the library. Somehow it sounded different when a woman said it. Victoria was full of curiosity. She was not sure what the women had in mind. Losing herself in books and romantic literature had brought her comfort and offered an escape, but she was not well educated in the ways of the world. Victoria opened her book and read for another hour. It seemed she was often drawn to the theme of unrequited love, and *Wuthering Heights* was one of her favorites. In the story, Catherine is passionately in love with a young man named Heathcliff who is sent away. Heathcliff returns three years later successful, and very rich. Because of her desire for social advancement, Catherine marries a wealthy man, shortly before his return. Tragically Catherine dies from a broken heart. "What a waste," Victoria thought.

When Victoria was a little girl, Molly McDougal sometimes raced her to the front porch. "Victorious Victoria wins again!" her mother exclaimed, and they both clapped their hands, laughing. As she contemplated the invitation, she felt a surging sense of adventure just as her parents did when they climbed aboard that ship to explore their dreams of living in America.

"I wonder what it would be like to be wealthy," Victoria thought. Her journey was about to begin.

Tea with Ada and Minna

Victoria was more than a little surprised that her invitation for tea was in the Levee, a neighborhood known as the center of prostitution in Chicago. Her first instinct was to ignore the invitation completely. However, she could not get over the fact that the Everleigh sisters had such impeccable etiquette and seemed so prim and proper. Their Southern accent was most charming, and for days, she heard Minna's words repeat over and over in her head, "Victoria Pearl, a refined, intelligent woman with beauty like yours can become quite wealthy." Curiosity and a sense of adventure got the best of her, and now she found herself in a place she had never been before, the Levee District of Chicago.

The cab left Victoria standing in front of the two mansions at 2131 Dearborn Street. She was smartly dressed and her hair was pinned up neatly beneath a modest sized hat decorated with dark purple and green flowers. It was a glorious autumn day, and the trees were beginning to lose their leaves after weeks of displaying their brilliant colors. Victoria was 15 minutes early for her appointment and decided to wait outside until it was appropriate to approach the door. Her mother always told her it was rude to arrive early to a lady's invitation. "You never know what last minute preparations might be made," she had said. The Everleigh sisters said 4 o'clock, so 4 o'clock it would be.

Just then Victoria saw a woman in one of the windows, the curtain moved to the side. It looked like Minna. A minute later, a friendly black woman wearing domestic clothes and a crisp white apron appeared on the top of the steps of the mansion. "Miss Minna said for you to come in, Miss Victoria."

"Thank you. How did you know my name?"

"The ladies are expecting you Ma'am," she answered with a big smile. "Looking forward to it."

"What is your name?" Victoria asked.

"My name is Mozella, Ma'am. Just follow me, and I will show you where to go."

Victoria slowly strolled down the most exquisite hallway she had ever seen. On her left, she saw a small brick fireplace with Italian ceramic vases on each side. There were two colorful oriental rugs on the floor, and the paneling on the walls was made of dark mahogany. On her right was a large mirror. Victoria looked at her reflection and stopped for a moment to straighten  her hat. "What have you gotten yourself into, young lady?" she asked the young woman in the mirror. These were the same words her mother had said when Victoria did anything out of character.

Mozella led Victoria into a beautiful room where an elegant table with fine china was set for tea. "Miss Minna and Miss Ada will be with you shortly, Miss Victoria. May I take your jacket?"

"Yes, thank you Mozella. This is a lovely room."

"Make yourself comfortable. You can sit over here," Mozella said as she laid her hands on the back of a cherry wood chair with a gold and powder blue brocade covering.

At exactly 4 o'clock Minna and Ada, well dressed wearing an excess of diamonds and pearls presented themselves. Both women were wearing an exquisite diamond brooch shaped like a butterfly. They seemed sincerely happy to see Victoria again. Victoria stood up from her chair.

Minna had a genuine, big smile, and although her sister was also smiling, Ada seemed a little more reserved. "Welcome, Victoria. Thank you for coming; Ada and I are delighted you are here," Minna declared in her sweet Southern drawl. "Please sit down, dear."

Mozella walked into the room with a tray of tea biscuits, dainty cakes, and a china teapot filled with hot tea. "That will be all for now, Mozella. Thank you so much," Ada said in a kindly voice.

"Tell us about yourself, Victoria," Minna inquired as she poured the tea.

"There is really not much to tell. I grew up about 40 miles from here in Aurora. My parents were Irish immigrants who met on the boat that brought them to America. They fell in love and were married within a week after they set shore. Mother died of pneumonia a few years ago, and my father passed away soon afterward. When my father died I became depressed, and decided to come to Chicago. Mother brought me here often, and I fell in love with the city. Now I am a librarian and live in a boarding house full of women."

"Why did you choose to be a librarian?" Ada asked.

"I love to read. I love the way books can take me to places and times I have never been before. Sometimes when I read I feel like I am experiencing another life," Victoria responded.

Ada seemed especially impressed. "What kinds of books do you like, Victoria?"

"I mostly enjoy historic adventure and some romantic novels, but as far as authors, I love to read Charles Dickens. He can make my senses come alive with his descriptions and make a story so real I forget it is only just a book. There are some books I wish would never end."

"You sound like a passionate woman," Ada commented.

Minna decided it was time to address the purpose of the meeting. "Victoria, I am sure that by now you understand the nature of our business. It is our intention to open and operate the finest parlor in America! To do this, we are looking for poised, intelligent lovely ladies like you."

"I am flattered. If you do not mind my saying so, I would never guess you and your sister are involved in this kind of profession. May I ask what made you decide to start a business of this kind?"

"Quite simply, my dear; we like nice things," Ada answered.

"Our father made sure we attended the finest finishing schools in Kentucky. My sister, Ada, and I were married to brothers from a good family, at least we thought, with the last name Lester," Minna explained. "Just about every evening, including our wedding night, my husband put his hands around my throat and said, 'This is to remind you who is in charge, and then he forced me to agree that women are a pain in the neck.'" Grimacing, Minna delicately touched her throat. Ada gently patted her sister's hand.

"When I heard Minna had left her husband, I joined her. I too had become discouraged with love and did not adhere to the philosophy, 'You've made your bed now lie in it.' We joined a theatre company and went to Omaha, Nebraska. It was the last year the Trans-Mississippi and International Exposition was being held in the city. We were snubbed by the socialites there. One night one of the girls made the comment, 'Please don't tell my mother I work in the theatre. She thinks I work in a brothel.' It was meant as a joke, but from that one statement, Minna came up with the idea that we should start a business to entertain the wealthy men visiting town. We thought if the wives won't accept us, their husbands certainly would. Minna and I learned quickly that there is a very high profit when sexual services are presented with high class and style. We started with an investment of $35,000 from personal assets we had acquired. Within a few months, we doubled our money. When the Exposition was over, my sister and I went on a quest to find an appropriate location to execute what we had learned in Nebraska."

"After visiting several cities, we went to Washington D.C. where we met a madam by the name of Cleo Maitland," Minna continued. "Cleo told us she had heard Effie Hankins was considering retirement and had a place known as *The House of Mirrors* in the Levee District of Chicago. We came to Chicago and bought her business. Our standards are quite high; therefore, we are basically starting over with new girls and staff."

"Mozella was with us in Nebraska. She was working as our housekeeper, and Minna and I fell in love with her. We insisted she come to Chicago and work for us here. Mozella had moved to Omaha from New Orleans. She has some great stories about that place!"

Victoria was completely captivated. She was being introduced to a new world she knew absolutely nothing about. It was Minna's turn again. "My instincts are quite good, Victoria, and when I saw you reading *Wuthering Heights,* I took it as a sign. Although I usually prefer books on philosophy, *Wuthering Heights* happens to be one of my favorite stories. You are quite lovely, in fact, strikingly so. Ada and I are looking for girls with certain qualities to work for us. They must be beautiful as well as intelligent and have superior communication skills. We called our girls *butterflies* in Nebraska. Just like a butterfly, we see our girls as delicate creatures that dance from flower to flower."

Victoria's head was spinning. She could feel many kinds of different emotions running up and down her spine. She had always thought that *ladies of the evening* were the dregs of society, but the Everleigh sisters were painting quite a different picture.

"We will be paying our girls $100 a week," Ada expressed in a business like tone. "You will live at the Everleigh Club, and we will provide healthy meals for you. Our clientele will be only wealthy gentlemen; therefore, our standards are very high. The men will be paying a high price, but in return, they will have the classiest, most beautiful women in Chicago. Your job will be to be a lady and become a *love goddess,* a kind of fantasy girl. We will take care of everything else." Watching for a reaction, both sisters stopped talking.

Victoria looked around the room. She had never been surrounded with such elegance. It was a lifestyle she had never known before. Victoria liked Minna and Ada. Somehow she knew she would never have an opportunity quite like this again.

For a few moments Victoria did not know what to say. Finally she spoke. "It all seems interesting, but honestly, I have never considered this type of employment before."

Minna's tone was gentle but firm. "We plan to open the first of February. Right now we are renovating, painting, and interviewing musicians, domestics, chefs, and, of course, lovely young ladies. We would like to invite you to move into the mansion close to Christmas. It will be a good time for us to bond and an opportunity for our *butterflies* to become friends. Every day we will be holding lessons on charm and etiquette. It is mandatory that our girls have impeccable manners."

"The money and elaborate lifestyle sounds wonderful. If you do not mind, I would like a few days to think about it."

Minna was very direct. "Are you a virgin, my dear?"

Victoria's eyes welled up with tears. "No! I am not!" Tears flooded down her face.

Ada quickly handed her a handkerchief and patted her hand. "There, there, dear. It will be all right. We will look after you."

Victoria had never shared her secret before. She had told Father Anthony in confession, and he told her to pray for forgiveness. Besides him, only Ian knew the truth, and Lord knows whatever happened to him.

"Normally we insist our butterflies have experience. However, Minna and I both agreed you are a good candidate for the job when we saw you reading at the park. Call it instinct. You are quite lovely, Victoria."

It was a quarter-to-5. Darkness was quickly falling onto the Levee. "We have called you a cab, my dear," Ada said tenderly. Victoria was still wiping her eyes. "A lady like you is not safe on the Levee after dark. Please get back to us as soon as you can one way or the other. Minna and I have been interviewing girls for weeks and already we have quite a waiting list. We are extremely selective with our young women."

Mozella was at the doorway holding Victoria's jacket. "Your cab is here, Miss Victoria."

Victoria stood up and hugged both sisters. "Goodbye, dear ladies. Somehow I feel better than I did before I walked into the Everleigh Club."

"Goodbye, Victoria," Minna said.

"Goodbye, dear," Ada echoed and kissed her on the cheek.

Mozella helped her with her jacket. "Thank you, Mozella."

As she walked down the hallway toward the door, again Victoria looked at her reflection in the mirror. It seemed a different woman was looking back at her. Victoria's secret was out and spoken in an environment where there was no judgment for what she had done. For this she felt free and even empowered.

Victoria straightened her hat and smiled at the familiar, yet somehow different woman looking back at her. "You can do anything you want. You are Victorious Victoria! Thank you, Mama. I am going to be wealthy. I am going to be a fine lady!"

"Goodbye, Mozella! I will be seeing you soon."

Mozella smiled. "Goodbye, Miss Victoria. I will be happy to see you again." Then she waved from the top of the porch until she saw Victoria safely ride away.

A New Life

Until now, Victoria had never had a high opinion of women who made a living selling their sexuality and had even equated it to selling their souls to the devil. However, she could not help but think about the beautiful décor of the Everleigh mansions and the formal elegance the sisters had demonstrated in attitude, speech, and appearance. Chicago was unfriendly toward Irish Catholics. That, coupled with the fact she was a soiled woman, also made the invitation to work in the Levee more attractive. She already had two strikes against her. Why not? $100 a week compared to the $5 she was making now was an appealing offer. Living in a fancy mansion and wearing beautiful gowns were things she had only read about. Fate had challenged her to participate in a new world she had never known before.

Victoria responded in favor of the Everleigh sisters' business proposition a few days after the meeting. The sisters were actually pleased that she had not responded too eagerly. This quality impressed the women, and they saw Victoria as having sound judgment and contemplation of matters at hand. They knew this type of characteristic would suit their clientele nicely. After all, many of them were self-made men who knew the importance of contemplation and investigation but, at the same time, knew all about taking risks.

The day before Victoria accepted the Everleigh sisters' invitation to work for them, she decided to take a walk on the north side of town where there were stately mansions that displayed wealth and opulence to anyone who dared to be in their presence.

She remembered a day she took that same walk with her mother. "Are rich people happy, Mother?"

At that Molly McDougal put her arm around Victoria and gave her a squeeze. "Every human being on this great earth has a story, Victoria. Some are happy like your father and me, and some are so very sad. Remember love is the only thing that brings true happiness."

Minna and Ada invited Victoria to make the Everleigh Club her permanent residence in December. There were other girls who were invited to do the same. Victoria spent the month of November working for the library, settling business affairs, and saying goodbye to what soon would be a past life. The most difficult was saying goodbye to the children. Victoria always encouraged children to read and praised them when they returned a book. She would ask her young friends questions about the story and have them describe their favorite character. Sometimes they made her wonder what her life would be like if her child had lived.

It was December 20th, 1899 when Victoria moved into the Everleigh mansion. Chicago was hustling and bustling with the sounds and smells of Christmas. Groups of harmonious carolers filled the winter air with holiday songs and joy. Her room was simple and elegantly decorated in a mauve, gold, and white motif. The curtains were made of white lace, and the large four poster bed was filled with lovely brocade pillows.

On Christmas Eve, the Everleigh sisters bought four Christmas trees for the girls to decorate. There were angels, white doves, and golden ribbons on the tree in the Everleigh library. Beautiful ornaments and red and green ribbons decorated the trees in two of the parlors. The main room had a spectacular ten foot tree decorated with china ornaments, silver bells, and sparkling white ribbons draped with perfect symmetry. Mozella and her staff filled the house with the aroma of warm baked goods and plum puddings. The girls drank hot cider flavored with cinnamon and nutmeg. Ada and Minna gave each of the girls an elegant new gown, shoes, and a string of pearls to wear on opening night.

A part of Victoria felt she was in some kind of dream where she had walked through the looking glass into a world filled with elegance and style. However, the new lifestyle was in direct conflict with her Irish Catholic upbringing. It seemed that there was another small voice trying to reason with her fantasy, trying to remind her, "Everything comes with a price." She chose to ignore her conscience for now.

Ada and Minna intentionally wanted the girls to bond in a kind of sisterhood. This appealed to Victoria since she had no family at all in America. Any kind of competitive undermining would not be tolerated and was grounds for termination. The sisters understood the importance of evoking a harmonious atmosphere and had strict rules and high standards of behavior. The more pleasant the experience of attending the Everleigh Club, the better the chance men would spend money and keep coming back for more. Victoria had a passion for life and until now vicariously enjoyed love and drama through the characters in the books she read. Now her interest in stories had changed. Victoria had found a book of poetry written by Veronica Franco, a courtesan who lived in Venice in the 16th century. Veronica offered a kind of perspective that suited Victoria's understanding of the type of profession she was about to enter.

The Everleigh sisters had recommended that Victoria read about Geisha girls. She also discovered a book on the Kama Sutra. Because Victoria loved to read, she found the material fascinating and much different from the attitudes of Queen Victoria, whose influence had blanketed women in the Western world in the last several decades.

On New Year's Eve, the "butterflies" as the sisters called them, entered the twentieth century with chilled champagne, courtesy of Ada and Minna Everleigh. As Victoria felt the bubbles float down, she smiled. In just a few weeks, the Club would be open for business. The other girls were more experienced than Victoria, and some had already been engaged in the business for quite some time. All of them were beautiful.

Victoria's heartbreaking experience with the handsome and charming Ian had scarred her for life. She believed him when he told her he loved her, and in that one evening, she had surrendered her body and soul completely. She was now soiled, and the thought of sharing that truth with any potential suitor was painful, indeed. Victoria felt it would be unfair to lie about her tainted virtue to any possible marriage proposal, especially someone whom she loved and knew loved her completely. It was easier to not think about a relationship with a man and instead get lost in her books where she could vicariously live a life of fantasy.

Victoria Pearl had come to the conclusion that she would probably never find a love like her parents had. To her, men were not to be trusted. Because Victoria did not come from an affluent family, working as a "lady of the evening" seemed like her only option to acquire any kind of wealth. Although Victoria loved the luxury of her new life style at the Everleigh mansion, the thought of having sex with a stranger was wearing on her deeply. Her journey to the unknown made for sleepless nights, and there were many mornings she wanted to leave. That is until the day she made friends with Madeline. Everyone called her "Maddie," and it was rare anyone ever saw Maddie without a smile on her face. Maddie was from England, and her accent was charming. She could really pour on the "la dee dah."

It was a cold January afternoon. The two women were sitting by a fire when Victoria confided in Madeline that she had almost no experience and had major concerns for opening night. "Maddie, I have only been with a man one time. I must admit, I do not know what to do. I do not even know what a, a man's… a man's, well, you know, what a man's thing looks like. All I know is Ian was suddenly inside of me, and I became pregnant. When he found out, he left town, and I lost the baby."

"Oh, my dear, that is terrible," Maddie said. "I am so very sorry for you. You might as well be a virgin."

"I am nervous, Maddie, and even a little afraid."

Maddie reached over and patted Victoria's hand. "There's nothing to be afraid of, dear! Men are wonderful creatures! In fact, sex can be enjoyable anytime if you have a good attitude. Think of yourself as a sex goddess much like Venus herself: beautiful, sensuous, and powerful. We are the sacred feminine, Victoria, full of mystery and magic. This is because it is within women that life begins and is then nurtured and sustained." Victoria was fascinated. "The Celts saw sex as sacred and performed various acts in religious ceremonies. In olden times, the tribe would form a circle in a sacred oak grove and place a young man and woman in the center. They believed that the orgasm was strong, powerful energy. The woman would perform the sacred sexual rite on the young man, and when he finally released that powerful, sexual energy, the tribe would use it as a prayer for better crops or, in times of war, a victory on the battle field." Victoria had read many a book, but this was the first time she had ever heard sex explained in such a fashion.

"I had a wonderful friend and teacher in England," Maddie continued. "She knew of the old ways and taught me to look at what we do as what she called, *the erotic ritual honoring the bearer of the seed*. The Greeks called it, *the divine gift*. When the woman puts herself in charge, the experience can last much longer and be much more interesting and even more enjoyable to the man. There are so many different ways to satisfy a man's sexual needs without lying on a bed and letting him have his way with you. In fact, that can only bring you problems worrying about pregnancy or some kind of disease. Not only that, but many times after a man has had his way, he quickly loses interest. Over the years I have studied the ways of the Venetian courtesans and their secrets of sexual pleasure, and it has brought me quite a good living, if I should say so myself. Much more than I could ever hope for trying to find a job working 80 hours a week in a factory or even as a clerk."

"Do tell, Maddie," Victoria expressed, peaked with interest.

"Technically, Victoria, a man's, oh, let's just call it a 'happy-stick,' is not what I would call a pretty thing, and they vary in shape and size just like the nose on someone's face. However, if you see it as the seed bearer, the staff of life, the rod of creation, it can look quite different and even glorious. It is all about perspective. Most men are extremely proud of their happy-sticks; some will even give them a name! I certainly have heard some doozies! Brutus, the Gladiator and even Oliver, quickly come to mind," Maddie laughed.

"Satisfying a man can be quite fun if you make it like a game. Let him see your lovely feminine curves. Tell him you are there to serve, and let him know that your pleasure is his pleasure. Whatever happens, do not let him inside of you. If you do, the mystery will disappear, and you will relinquish all control. Men always love a good hunt. Your goal is to simply create a fountain of pleasure. In other words, your job is to simply clean out his pipes!" Maddie sang in her funny English accent.

Victoria had never heard talk like this before. She was completely captivated with Maddie and her attitude about sex.

"When you enter the room, the first thing you should do is make sure he is comfortable. Let him know all he needs to do is to lay back and enjoy himself. Then slowly allow your gown to fall loose, and tell your client you want to do all of the work. Do not get completely naked, or the mystery is gone. Make him ask for the privilege of viewing your womanly gifts, and then reveal your body slowly and sensuously as you look straight into his eyes. Ask the gentleman's permission to simply look at his manhood. No matter what it looks like hold it gently in your hands, and for several minutes, lightly stroke it, and tell him it is the most gorgeous thing you have ever laid your eyes on! Then as it becomes firm, stroke the underside very lightly with your fingers. In some cases, that is all you will ever have to do!"

Victoria was surprised. "Really?"

"Yes really! Some men require more. You can skillfully use your hands with oil or lotions. Remember the longer he can sustain the more powerful his orgasm. The more experience you have, the more you will know when to stroke it slowly, stop for a few seconds, and then stroke it a little more quickly, each time bringing him higher and higher into his ecstasy. Be playful and encouraging. Most of all, remember what is most important, is that you be sensuous and even playful." Maddie's eyes were gleaming with delight.

"There is another technique to pleasure a man much like enjoying a delicious stick of peppermint. We can talk about that another time. You are going to be fine Victoria. The Everleigh sisters are brilliant women. The men who come here will be paying an exorbitant price for a beautiful woman to act as their sexual goddess and pleasurable fantasy. Many of our clients will be married. When a courtesan performs sexual rituals like I described on a married man, somehow he can justify it in his mind and honestly say, *'I never had sex with that woman!'* Of course, if he were to finish the sentence, he would probably say, *'she had sex with me.'* Men are funny that way," she laughed.

From that day on, Maddie and Victoria became trusted friends. They went on outings together, and it seemed like every day Maddie, a great teacher, had a new story about the clients she had known in the past. Her carefree approach to sex and educational demonstrations on how to please a man put Victoria more at ease. Maddie had succeeded in awakening Victoria's curiosity to the point she was actually looking forward to opening night.

Being a librarian had been predictable and manageable. Those days were gone. Victoria was on the threshold of a new life she knew nothing about. The next few weeks were like a rollercoaster of emotions. She was feeling excited, and at the same time she had a fear of the unknown. Victoria felt like the main character of a novel, and she was writing the story. "Once upon a time, there was a lovely librarian who loved to read. She found that stories helped to satisfy a passionate hunger she so longed for. One day while reading *Wuthering Heights* at the park, she was approached by two sisters who invited her to tea…"

By the middle of January, over 25 girls had been employed by Ada and Minna Everleigh. Finishing touches were being made in what was formerly known as "The House of Mirrors." The double brownstone mansion had been built in 1890 by a black woman named Lizzie Allen for $125,000, cash! Only recently it had been leased to Madam Effie Hawkins. The sisters knew there were wealthy men who lived or did business in Chicago. It seemed like the perfect place for the madams to open shop. There were 50 rooms in all in the Everleigh mansions, and no expenses were spared. The $15,000 gold leaf piano (equivalent to $370,000 today) was placed in the Music Room. Some of the rooms, including the Library still had mirrors on the ceilings. The different rooms were themed and decorated to correspond with the name of the room. Victoria especially loved the quaintness of the Rose Parlor.

The Everleigh sisters provided the girls their meals because they insisted the girls eat a healthy diet to maintain their shapely figures. Daily reading was required, and every afternoon the girls were updated on current events. This made them more interesting to talk to. Minna and Ada insisted the girls conduct themselves in a lady-like fashion. Drugs or excess intoxication were strictly prohibited and subject to instant termination. The girls all knew there were plenty of other young women on a waiting list ready to take their places. According to Ada and Minna, the Everleigh House was going to be known as the most famous, luxurious house of its kind in America. They were competing with over 500 other businesses like theirs in Chicago. For this to happen the sisters knew the young women needed to be classy and beautiful.

Minna and Ada Everleigh were very wise women. "The first thing you must always remember," Ada said, "is to forget why you are here! Be charming, and have a good time. Men are wired differently than women. They have physical needs as well as a longing for female companionship. Here at the Everleigh House, we have a service to fulfill both with grace and elegance. This is how we will compete with any other brothels in Chicago. If a man just wants sex, he can go down the street and pay less for it. Here, we give them much more."

Minna was much more outspoken than her sister. "You will *not* be lined up like cattle. You will position yourselves in different locations throughout the house. Gentlemen only act as gentlemen when properly introduced to a lady, and remember you are all ladies! You will receive regular examinations by a doctor. All of you are healthy now, and we expect you to stay that way. Men like women to be clean and smelling nicely. Do not be hasty to take anyone upstairs. We require that you spend at least an hour in conversation with any potential clients. This fulfills the male need for companionship. Remember, you are their fantasy girls."

"We want our girls to be masterful and creative with their talents. There are several ways to satisfy a man's needs with no fear of pregnancy or disease. Again, your attitude will provide the excitement he longs for. After a man has reached his climax, your power is gone, and typically his adoring nature will change. The longer he is experiencing your charms, the more erotic his experience will be. This increases the potential that he will return," Ada expressed in a factual tone.

"You will all be paid $100 a week, and you are allowed to receive tips and gifts. You have a beautiful place to live and delicious food to eat. We will be sure you are dressed well. The entry fee for every client is $10 ($300 today). We will charge $50 for dinner, $12 for a bottle of wine, and $50 to spend time with you," Minna told the girls. "Make no mistake, we will soon be known as the finest in Chicago!"

Opening Night

It was the morning of February 1, 1900. After months of planning and teaching the young women lessons on good manners and grace, tonight the Everleigh Club would open for business. Victoria was full of butterflies! Perhaps this is one of the reasons the sisters sometimes referred to their young women as the "butterfly girls." Outside, the Chicago streets were covered with crispy white, new winter snow. The brownstone mansions were heated with steam, and every room with a fireplace had a warm cozy fire lighting the room with a golden glow, much unlike the boarding house where Victoria had resided for the last few years. Tonight she would pay the price for her new life.

Ada and Minna wanted to disassociate from their married name, Lester, and chose to be called, *Everleigh*, instead. They chose the name because the sisters' grandmother, whom they dearly loved, always signed her letters, *"Everly Yours."* They also greatly admired Sir Walter Raleigh, whom Queen Elizabeth had assigned to oversee the colony of Virginia in the 1600s. Legend has it that he gallantly had spread his cloak over a puddle to prevent the queen from getting mud on her shoes. To the sisters, "leigh" meant class and aristocracy, thus the name "Everleigh" was created.

The two adjoining three-story stone mansions at 2131 South Dearborn Street provided 50-rooms and had been renovated and richly furnished. The Everleigh Club had 30 bedrooms, a library, an art gallery, a dining room, and a Turkish ballroom complete with a huge fountain and parquet floor. The sisters created 12 opulent parlors all exquisitely decorated and named with different themes. The parlors were private and sound-proofed. Minna and Ada spared no expense in constructing a sensuous ambience, with the sole purpose of providing an exotic, sexual fantasy for their clients. Three orchestras entertained their guests and rich oil paintings of nude women displaying their sexuality and feminine curves were hung on the wall.

The most famous parlor was the Gold Room which featured gold-rimmed fishbowls and an exquisite miniature piano made of gold. The elegant Rose Room smelled like roses. There was also the Japanese Throne Room, the Silver Room, the Copper Room, the Blue Room, the Red Room and the Green Rooms, the Turkish Room and the Mirror Room. The Egyptian Room had a full-size effigy of Cleopatra; the Moorish Room had overstuffed couches and sweeping draperies. The Chinese Room was a place where gentlemen could set off tiny firecrackers in a huge brass beaker. Each of the rooms had a solid gold spittoon.

Upstairs in the boudoirs the gentlemen found marble-inlaid brass beds, mirrored ceilings, gold bathtubs, fresh cut roses, and push-buttons to ring for champagne. One room had an automatic perfume spray over the bed. Another room had a silver-white spotlight that focused on a divan. For the gentleman with a fantasy of having several wives, the ambience of a Turkish harem was created with rich furnishings.

Minna and Ada had hired all "colored" help. Colored employees with a Southern mistress were a safe bet, a concept Minna had known all along. Mozella, along with the others, knew she belonged to the *front of the house*; the sisters saw them as members of the family. Although the sisters had done so much to prepare for opening night, there was not much fanfare. "That would be tacky," Minna told the girls. "We will build our reputation through word of mouth and, believe me, they will come!"

That day the girls read, ate well, were educated on current events, and took long naps. It was dark when they began getting ready. The butterflies had baths and spent time fixing themselves to look more beautiful. The hair went up, rose oil perfume was applied and each girl was adorned with a beautiful evening gown. All last minute details were addressed, and everyone was ready to go to work.

The Everleigh butterflies were excited about opening night at the Everleigh Club. They looked stunning in their new gowns, and Victoria Pearl looked especially exquisite. Her hair was pinned up in an elegant sweep revealing her long slender neck and perfectly shaped ears. The lavish beaded gown she wore had a heart shaped neckline, accentuating her luscious ivory skin. Victoria felt and looked like Cinderella going to the ball.

For weeks, every afternoon, Minna and Ada Everleigh had taught the girls lessons on etiquette and social graces as if they were attending a highly respected finishing school for ladies. Most of the women who worked at the Everleigh Club came from poor backgrounds. However, because they were pretty, charming and intelligent, they qualified as good candidates for the sisters to work with. In some cases it was a major task to transform a woman who had been brought up with much lower standards into a lady with high esteem. The girls learned that the scent of roses was the scent of the elite. They studied the ways of the Geishas and the infamous courtesans of Venice. Ada assured the girls, "We will be known for having the finest, most elegant ladies in Chicago and, in fact, all of America."

Opium was a common drug used by the women on the Levee. The sisters knew discipline was important, and they had excessively strict rules. "Remember there are many intelligent, pretty women waiting to take your places. Your actions must be impeccable, and drugs will absolutely not be tolerated!"

So many thoughts were running through Victoria's mind. She remembered the night with Ian when he stole her virginity. She thought about those Sunday afternoons when she had seen her mother give her father "the look" and then announce they were going to take a nap before dinner. Molly would walk to his chair and smile as she reached for his hand. Victoria's father would stand up, put his arm around Molly, and together they would walk into their room and close the door.

Minna and Ada were well aware that their beautiful "butterflies" were not girls bred in high society, in fact, quite the opposite. Most of them had come from poor families or some kind of abuse. Some had no family at all. Minna and Ada had their work cut out for them, trying to convince their clients that these women were well-bred ladies.

Minna Everleigh gave her final instructions to the women assembled before her. "Be polite, and forget what you are here for. Remember, gentlemen are only gentlemen when properly introduced. We shall see that each girl is formally presented to each of our guests. No lining up for selection as in other houses. There shall be no cry, 'In the parlor girls,' when visitors arrive. Be patient is all I ask. Remember the Everleigh Club has no time for the rough element, the clerk on a holiday, or a man without a check-book."

"It is going to be difficult at first," she continued. "I know. It means, briefly, that your language will have to be lady-like and that you will forgo the entreaties you have used in the past. You have the whole night before you, and a $50 client is more desirable than five $10 ones. Less wear and tear. You will thank me for this advice in later years. Your youth and beauty are all you have. Preserve it. Stay respectable by all means. We know men better than you do. Do not rush them or roll them. We will permit no monkeyshines, no knockout drops, no robberies, and no crimes of any description. We will supply the clients; you amuse them in a way they have never been amused before. Give, but give interestingly and with mystery. I want you girls to be proud that you are a *butterfly* in the Everleigh Club. That is all. Now spruce up, and look your best."

"What do we do if a man wants to have intercourse?" Victoria's question was so innocent it made the sisters and the other girls smile.

"My dear... You simply use the phrase that has worked for thousands of years. 'I beg your pardon, sir, but I'm afraid I do not know you *well enough* quite yet,'" Minna answered with her sweet Southern accent.

Minna's comment put Victoria quickly at ease. The other girls thought it was hysterical. Maddie was laughing as she put her arms out and then hugged Victoria. "Do what Minna told you to do, Victoria. She is a wise woman. Remember we are dealing with gentlemen, and a man always loves the hunt."

Victoria Pearl had chosen her station to be close to the piano. She loved music. Her mother had taught her to play. Many times she would play the exquisite gold piano at the Everleigh Club late in the evening as everyone was getting ready to retire. The music created a peaceful ambience throughout the mansion, and it always took her to a magical world of her own where she fantasized about what the composers were feeling and attempting to communicate when creating each piece. It reminded her of her young teenage years when she played for her parents. Molly would crochet Irish lace, and Brian would read while they quietly enjoyed listening to their daughter play as her parents sat by a warm fire.

The temperature outside was 8 below zero. There had been no publicity, advertising, or press. There were two different groups of musicians playing and the chef had prepared various foods for elegant dining. The Everleigh Club was ready for business.

At 8'oclock, the doorbell rang. A group of men stood at the door wanting to come in. It was quite clear by their appearance they were not the clientele the sisters would allow inside. "I am sorry," Minna said with charm and grace. "I believe you have the wrong house."

A half-an-hour later, a group of men from the theatre showed up at the door. Minna was quite aware that although the theatre group could be very entertaining in their own right, they did not make the kind of money that could easily afford what the Everleighs had to offer. They were also told that they were mistaken and had the wrong house.

The experienced girls had never seen clients actually be turned away before and began expressing their concerns. One of the girls was pouting. "It's opening night. We have been waiting for this for weeks! I feel like a princess, all dressed up for the ball, but there's no ball."

"No one is going to want to pay these prices! It is all just a bluff!" another girl responded.

"We will be out of a job before we even get started!"

Victoria stayed quiet. Each time the doorbell to the Everleigh Club rang butterflies would flutter in her stomach. She was not sure if it was fear or excitement. It even slightly took her breath away.

Minna decided to pick up the paper. The headlines read, *Rites for Philip Danforth Armour Jr*. will be held at 3700 Michigan Ave. The Armours owned a meat packing company which was a huge enterprise in Chicago and Michigan Avenue was in the elite neighborhood. They were among one of the wealthiest families in Chicago. One of the young women who had been complaining walked over and slyly looked over Minna's shoulder to see what she was reading. She quickly ran back to the other girls. "We have her all wrong; Minna knows the all right. I caught her reading about Armour Jr.'s funeral, and she acted as if she had known him!"

Ten minutes later, Mozella came to Minna and reported the *backstairs conversation*. "The girls are talking as if you are friends with the Armour family! You are a clever one, Miss Minna!"

Minna laughed good-naturedly. "It worked, Mozella. I have never heard of Armour until today," she whispered. "Do not tell anyone I told you!" Both women laughed.

Finally there was another knock at the door. When Minna Everleigh opened it, to her delight, she saw several Texas cattlemen standing there with hats in hand. "Welcome to the Everleigh House, Gentlemen!" she said with a big smile. "The ladies are anxious to make your acquaintance!"

The Music Room

A Texas Gentleman

When Victoria saw those Texas cattlemen walk through the door, she was amazed. They were different from any of the men in Chicago she had ever known. They even walked differently. The Texas men certainly had a presence of strength and vitality. All of them were smiling, and they reminded her of children in a candy store. The men were wearing suits and ties and collectively they were exceptionally handsome. The Everleigh sisters were making introductions to the girls. As Victoria watched, she remembered the ladies always said, "Gentlemen are only gentlemen when properly introduced."

"My hands are cold," Victoria heard Ada say to a ranch king. With that the Texan quickly called over a waiter. "Two bottles of champagne for the lady!" Then he turned to Ada. "The champagne will warm those pretty patties," he said sympathetically. Victoria was impressed.

Music was playing, and the money started to flow. Victoria was not forthcoming whereas many of the more experienced ladies knew how to flirt with their eyes and get a man's attention. She decided to keep her eyes on the piano player and focus on the music. She didn't notice the tall handsome gentleman who had been standing back watching her from across the room. Sensing that someone was approaching her, Victoria looked up and saw Minna leading the gentleman who had been watching her by the arm. "Victoria dear, this is Robert McKnight. Robert, I would like to introduce you to our most gracious Victoria Pearl."

"Very pleased to make your acquaintance, my dear," he said as he kissed her hand. "Miss Minna, I believe I would love to have dinner and share a bottle of champagne with this lovely lady."

All of a sudden, the fluttering feeling in her stomach doubled, and for a few moments, Victoria could not speak. She was completely mesmerized with the bluest eyes and the kindest smile she had ever seen. Victoria was especially impressed by the way he spoke. She had never heard anyone pronounce words so musically and speak so slowly. Robert crooked his arm, and

Victoria smiled as she slowly reached through the opening he provided for her. Making contact, she could feel his strength and his warmth all at the same time. It was like holding on to a warm steel bar. Victoria was forgetting what her role was at the Everleigh Club and what function she played. This was a good thing. "Be polite and forget what you are here for" was a mantra the sisters ingrained into the girls. "Remember you are a butterfly, a beautiful fantasy."

Robert and Victoria sat at an elegantly set table with a linen tablecloth and napkins, fine silver and gold rimmed china dishes. A bottle of chilled Pol Roger 1892 was formally presented to the table. The waiter opened the champagne as if he were performing a sacred ritual. Victoria watched as Robert gallantly took a sip. She felt like she was in a fairytale, and she certainly looked the part.

"Magnifico! Thank you. This will be fine," Robert said. He motioned his hand to Victoria's glass, "For the beautiful lady." The waiter elegantly poured a glass of champagne for Victoria. After the waiter topped off Robert's glass, he lifted it and proclaimed, "To the good life, my dear!"

Victoria repeated, "To the good life!" She smiled as she felt the cool, tiny bubbles tingle and slide down her throat and then settle into her stomach.

"So, who is the very beautiful Victoria Pearl?" Robert asked with curiosity.

Victoria felt her cheeks flush, shyly looked down and grinned. She could feel her heart was racing. Upon gaining her composure, she charmingly asked, "Actually, Mr. McKnight, I would like to hear about you. What is Texas like? I have only read about it. Texas absolutely fascinates me."

"Texas is God's country, Victoria. She is wide open spaces with beautiful rolling hills in the center, grassy plains in the north, lush green forests in the east, and majestic mountains in the south. The West Texas deserts have the most colorful sunsets you have ever seen and there are white beaches with sugar fine sand that border the deep blue waters along the Gulf of Mexico. Texas has rivers and streams, cactus, wild flowers and old oak trees that could tell you quite a story if they could speak. At night the stars are so bright you feel like you can pluck them right out of the sky. Texas is where a man is only as good as his word, and a deal can be made on a handshake alone."

"It sounds like a wonderful place!"

"I raise cattle, and I have a ranch at the edge of the Hill Country. My great-grandparents came to America from Scotland and were able to acquire a land grant for settlers brave enough to take on the new Western Frontier. The McKnights have been ranching and farming ever since. Mother and Dad both passed a while ago, and my little brother, Neil, was killed last September falling off his horse at a round up. He was a real character. He loved to ride and whoop and holler, rounding up the herd. I remember it was a Tuesday morning, just another working day. His horse got spooked and bucked him off. His foot was caught in the stirrup, and he was dragged quite a ways. By the time I got to him, he was in a bad way. He looked at me and said, 'Love you, brother.' Then he died."

Robert paused as sadness fell over him like a room losing its light when the sun goes down. "I really miss him. My brother was my best friend," he sighed. "Wish I knew what spooked that horse. I guess it was just Neil's time to meet his Maker."

Then as quickly as the sadness came, it left, and Robert perked up. Victoria was fascinated. She loved hearing his stories about Texas, and she kept wishing the night could go on forever.

Robert was a handsome man, tall and lean with slightly weathered brown skin that crinkled when he smiled. His teeth were white, and when he laughed, it made Victoria's heart feel light. Victoria was enamored; Robert was intrigued. She listened to every word as he explained the cattle business and what his life was like in Texas.

Robert told her of the fresh water springs that flowed on his ranch and the way the wild flowers brought in the spring with a rainbow of colors. He was like a little child when he told her about his prize bull and how he had raised it from a calf. Robert smiled when he talked about watching it frolic with his mother. "We call him Big Jake."

"Do you live on the ranch alone?" Victoria asked.

"There are two families who work and live on the ranch. Jose's father worked for my dad. He and Maria Rosa live in one house, and John and Angela live with their children in the other. Maria Rosa is a great cook and keeps the ranch house clean. Angela tends to the garden and makes the best tortillas in the world. She is also quite a rider. The men take care of the livestock and work for a percentage of the profits."

Robert could not take his eyes off Victoria. He found himself lost in her eyes, and the warm glow from the candle enhanced her beauty even more. It was a perfect evening, and both Victoria and Robert laughed as he shared his ranching stories and how so many times animals seemed to make more sense than people. One time after telling a story about his brother, his eyes were full of tears when he had finished.

"I am so sorry." Victoria gently reached across the table and held his hand.

Robert put his hand over hers. "I know this sounds crazy, but somehow I feel like I have known you all my life," Robert whispered.

A warm smile arose from Victoria's heart. "I know what you mean. I feel the same."

"You are quite lovely, Victoria Pearl. You are unique in your beauty just like our Concho pearl in West Texas."

"Concho pearl?" Victoria asked.

Robert had already paid his bill. He rose from the table and reached out his hand to Victoria. With style and grace, she took his hand and stood up. He walked beside her and again crooked his arm. This time she snuggled into his warmth. She could feel his strong muscles, and again, it felt like butterflies were dancing in her stomach.

Victoria led Robert up the mahogany stairs to the Rose Room. He had made arrangements to have the room until morning. Victoria opened the door and walked inside. The room was beautiful. The golden light from the fireplace created a romantic ambience across the room. Against the wall was a brass canopy bed with white linens. In front of the bed were two beautiful red and gold brocade curtains tied on each side of the curtain rod. A table with a crystal pitcher and glasses stood between two elegant chairs with colorful ottomans. Exquisite oriental rugs woven with deep rich colors decorated the floor. The subtle fragrance of rose oil created a pleasant ambience as if those in the room were standing in the middle of a rose garden.

Victoria became extremely nervous. She had only done this one time before, and realized she had no idea what she was doing. Although she had read every book she could get her hands on about Venetian courtesans and Kama Sutra techniques, Victoria suddenly forgot all she had ever read on how to please a man. Maddie was the only person she had told about Ian. The other girls had assumed Victoria was as experienced as they were. She started to question herself, "What if I am a huge disappointment? I really do not know what to do!"

Victoria opened the door. "Make yourself comfortable, Robert. I will be back in a few minutes."

"Where are you going?" Robert asked.

"Oh, I will be right back! I am going down the hall to have the maid help me undo the buttons on my dress," she answered. Victoria had lost any sense of composure.

"Ma'am, I would like to undress you if you don't mind," Robert said with his smooth Texas drawl.

Robert reached over Victoria's shoulder and gently pushed the door behind her. With his hand still on the door, he reached down and softly kissed her mouth. Passionately his warm strong arms around her as he kissed her deeply. Robert put his hands on her shoulders and tenderly turned her around. One by one, he undid the hooks on her dress. Victoria's heart was racing. She felt her dress loosen around her shoulders and then fall to the floor. Victoria slowly stepped out of the dress and put on a champagne colored satin dressing gown the chamber maid had laid on the bed.

Robert took off his jacket, vest, and tie and neatly laid them on the back of the one of the chairs. Victoria playfully took off his boots just like she used to do for her father. Robert watched as she seemed to glide across the room. He could not speak; he could only stare. Robert had never seen a woman so lovely. She took the pins from her hair and picked up a hair brush. He walked over and took the brush from her hand and began slowly brushing the long, thick hair opening night her back. His touch was soft, and his voice was husky and low. "You are a real beauty, my dear."

"Thank you," she said. The champagne had completely worn off by now, and Victoria wondered if Robert could see how nervous she was.

Apparently he was reading her mind. "Would you like a glass of port?" he asked in an attempt to lighten the mood.

Victoria could see there was a bottle of Ferreira Vintage Port Wine on the small table. "That would be lovely." she smiled, slightly embarrassed.

Robert poured two glasses of port and gave one to Victoria. "Here's to good times and the great state of Texas!" he announced as he raised his glass.

"To good times and Texas!" she repeated. Both of them took a drink.

For a long moment, their eyes met with a sense of familiarity of two souls reuniting in a space of timeless understanding. Robert looked at her with desire, and Victoria completely surrendered herself to the moment at hand. It was as if they were bonded with a golden light. Robert slipped the robe down Victoria's shoulders and pushed her hair to the side. Victoria was watching him in the mirror. He bent down and kissed the back of her neck, and when he did, every nerve in her body began to tingle.

"You are quite exquisite, Victoria Pearl."

Robert took Victoria's hand and gently led her to the bed. She sat on the edge and looked up. He was so handsome, and his blue eyes seemed to know every thought or feeling she had ever had. Robert slowly laid Victoria down and untied her gown.

His speech was slow and deliberate. "Lay on the pillow, my dear. You are absolutely gorgeous, Victoria."

Victoria was feeling the depth of Robert's desire for her. Her body was trembling in a way she had never known before. Robert's breathing became deep and husky. Victoria unbuttoned his shirt and was in awe of his muscular chest. Robert's hair was soft, and as she ran her hand over it, Victoria thought of how it felt like new spring grass bending beneath her hand. Robert ran his fingertips ever so lightly across Victoria's entire body. She could feel an electric current shooting chill bumps up and down her spine. Victoria took Robert's hand and placed it over her heart. "Feel me, Robert. Feel me… feel my heart!"

"I want to savor this time with you, Victoria. It has been quite a long time since I have been with a woman."

Robert softly touched every part of Victoria with his hands and made soft gentle kisses all over her body. Victoria felt adored. She closed her eyes and responded to every move he made. It was like doing a dance, and she felt alive and free. Robert lightly stroked both sides of Victoria's waistline with the back of his hand and then across the middle of her stomach. "Your body is shaped like a violin, Victoria."

As Robert worked his way below Victoria's naval, Victoria's heart began beating so hard she thought it might burst from her chest. These were feelings she had never known before. Robert stood up from the bed and finished taking off his clothes. He looked like the pictures she had seen of Michelangelo's, *David*. "What do you want, Victoria. Tell me what you want me to do. What will make you tremble and want me, Victoria?"

Robert then gently put his hand on her womanhood and slowly massaged her with small gentle circles. "Do you like this? What do you want, Victoria?"

"You, Robert, I want you."

Victoria felt like she was in a completely different dimension as if she had walked through the looking glass. Robert explored unknown places waking up erotic senses she never before knew were there. As he continued to gently caress her body, Victoria moaned with pleasure and slowly moved her body back and forth with delight.

"Are you going to enter me?" she asked.

"Only when you invite me, Victoria, you let me know when you are ready."

Robert and Victoria spent the whole night together performing the lovers' dance several times that evening. When she awoke the next morning, he was still holding her. Never before had she felt like a complete woman. Her experience with Robert was beyond her dreams. Now she knew what it was to be made love to by a real man, a Texas gentleman.

Victoria's sexual encounter with Robert McKnight was like a beautifully, orchestrated dance. The next evening Robert returned to the Everleigh Club and requested Victoria Pearl again; in fact, they spent three consecutive nights together, and each time Robert reserved the Rose Room for the evening. Every evening of sexual playing and seduction left Victoria with Robert's essence lingering over her entire body.

When it was finally time to say goodbye Victoria felt both happy and a bit sad. Now she knew what it was like to feel like a complete woman. As she stood before him she could still feel the tingling of the places on her newly explored body.

"I will write to you, Victoria. I promise." It was the last thing Robert said to her before he left.

Maybe he would... perhaps not. One thing was true; Victoria had beautiful memories with Robert McKnight to carry with her the rest of her life.

Butterflies

"Oh no," Maddie said. She had seen that look on many a girl before. "You let him have his way with you, didn't you Victoria?"

"It was fantastic, Maddie." Victoria smiled at her friend, still basking in her ecstasy. She crossed her arms and put her hands on her shoulders then began twirling around in circles. "I have never felt so much like a woman!"

Maddie gravely shook her head. "Did you forget all that I told you, Victoria?"

"Please, Maddie. I know you are concerned, and I know I need to be realistic. However, just for right now, I am the heroine in a beautiful love story, and I am not just reading about it, I actually lived it, and it was divine."

For the last few nights, Minna Everleigh had seen the interaction with Robert and Victoria and decided it would be a good idea to have a talk with her. At the afternoon meal, Minna asked Victoria to meet her in the library when she was finished eating. Victoria happily agreed. It seemed like nothing could ruin this amazing feeling she had. It was like none she had ever known. Minna had seen this before. She liked Victoria, and she was concerned.

When Victoria walked into the room, Minna was waiting for her. "Shut the door, Victoria." Minna's tone was kind but stern.

"You look happy," Minna commented.

"I am, Minna. I am beyond happy! I just spent the three best nights of my life with a handsome, charming Texas gentleman, and I feel like a brand new woman."

Minna smiled. "I know we tell you to forget why you are here, and you did an excellent job at doing just that. Perhaps too good of a job in this case, Victoria. Mr. McKnight is a good-looking, charismatic man. I know the two of you had a wonderful time together. I guess I just want to know what your expectations are. Not all of our clients are like your Texas gentleman; in fact, he is one of the most handsome men I have ever seen. Did you happen to notice the other clients the girls were entertaining?"

"Not really. I mean, certainly I noticed them, but I have to admit I was not paying attention to anyone else other than Robert."

"Exactly! You did your job well, Victoria. The way you took care of Robert McKnight is precisely what we do here. Our objective is to make our clientele feel like kings, men who should be worshipped and adored. I am sure Mr. McKnight is feeling like the highest of royalty especially after spending three glorious nights with you," Minna expressed, raising her eyebrows. "You will learn soon enough not all clients will be like your Texas gentleman. Remember, they pick you; you do not pick them. We are here simply to provide a service, not to find Prince Charming to carry us away to his castle. Although it is not impossible, it is not our reality. Do you understand what I am telling you, Victoria?"

"Yes I do, Minna. I know I am not as experienced as the other ladies, but I am very aware of what it is we do here."

Minna relaxed. "Men with money like to have nice things, Victoria. They wear fine clothes, ride in fancy carriages, eat at elegant restaurants, and belong to exclusive clubs, many which they can join only with a formal invitation. These men are willing to pay generously to be with a beautiful woman whom they find interesting to talk to, and who will laugh at all of their jokes, feed their egos with charm and grace, and creatively satisfy their fantasies behind closed doors. They are not here shopping for wives; in fact, many of them already have one. They are here to experience the essence of a lovely, elegant woman with no strings attached. I just want to remind you that your Mr. McKnight came here specifically for that purpose. For you it was like one of the Chicago Cubs hitting a grand slam at the bottom of the ninth inning on their first time up to bat. For him it might be just a pleasant experience with a beautiful lady in Chicago."

"Yes, I know Minna. I like to think of it as a fairytale. This one is called, *The Lady and the Texas Gentleman*." It is a wonderful story. Even if it ends today, and I never see or hear from him again, it is still a beautiful story."

"This can be a heartbreaking business, Victoria. Protect yourself. Remember the men pay us well to be their fantasy dreams come true. They may even make promises and tell you wonderful things in the heat of the moment that can completely change at the break of dawn. We are exceptionally good at what we do here. Even though you are not experienced with men, you are intelligent and creative. You know there are several satisfying ways to please a man, Victoria."

"Yes, I am aware of that, Minna. Madeline has been teaching me some of her tricks."

"May I suggest you develop a method that is unique and exciting? You can apply different techniques to not only obtain your objective but also to stay in control of the fantasy game. Any woman can lie down on a bed. Those women are likely to pick up a disease, become pregnant, or both. That is not what we do here. We want our girls to use creative methods to sexually satisfy the clientele." Minna was speaking in her business tone. "You are a beautiful woman, Victoria. I am sure someone will want you tonight. It is your job. Remember they pick you; you do not pick them. Are you up for it?"

"Yes, Minna. I know." Victoria's happiness was slowly diminishing, and her memory of Robert McKnight was beginning to fade away. "Thank you."

"You will be fine, Victoria." Minna stood up, gave Victoria a little hug, and opened the library door. Victoria walked out and looked around the Everleigh Club. The sisters were masters at creating elegant ambience. Every room was exquisite and impeccably decorated. Victoria loved living in opulence and luxury. The staff waited on the girls as if they were ladies of the queen's court. After a parlor was used for entertaining, the maids were quick to go in with a fresh, clean set of sheets to put on the bed along with a sweeper and a duster to clean the room as if it had never been used. They would also clean and shine the $650 solid gold spittoons that were in every room.

"How did it go with Minna?" Madeline asked her friend.

"It went well," Victoria sighed. "Unfortunately, she brought me back to reality."

"Remember, Victoria, all men love pretty women. Our job is to entertain the wealthy ones. Tonight when you go to work, just think of yourself as an actress playing out a part. Then it will not be so personal."

Victoria decided to go to her room and read one of her favorite books, *The Arabian Nights*. The story is about a Persian king who learns that his wife has betrayed him. The king becomes extremely bitter and angry and has it in his mind that women cannot be trusted. Every night he marries a new virgin, and has her beheaded the next day. A thousand women have all perished until finally he meets one of his high official's daughters, Scheherazade. Scheherazade loves to read, and she especially likes poetry and has collected over a thousand stories of histories, kings, and departed rulers. She is beautiful, polite, wise, witty, charming, and extremely well-bred.

Against her father's wishes, Scheherazade volunteers to marry the king. She and her sister devise a clever plan. That evening she asks the king, "Please may I bid farewell to my sister, Dinazade?" Dinazade then asks Scheherazade to tell her a story. The king lays awake through the long night and listens in awe as Scheherazade masterfully tells her sister the first story. Finally at the break of dawn, the story reaches a climax, and Scheherazade stops talking. "What happened?" the king asks anxiously.

"Dear Master, it is dawn and time to stop. I will finish the story tonight." Scheherazade answered.

Scheherazade's life is spared. That evening she finishes the story and begins another one. Again Scheherazade's life is spared. And so it continues for one thousand and one nights. Because of her stories, the king has become a wiser and much kinder man. He marries Scheherazade and has three sons by her.

"Scheherazade," Victoria thought to herself. "I will be like Scheherazade."

That evening Victoria chose a coral colored gown to wear. She looked especially radiant, probably because Robert had awakened her long dormant womanhood the night before. Again she took her place by the piano, allowing the music to take her to another world. Unlike the other girls soliciting their charms, Victoria's eyes were closed, and she smiled with contentment as her head swayed to the rhythm of the music, all this actually making her even more intriguing.

Suddenly, she was awakened from her contentment to Minna's voice. "Victoria, this is Christopher Baker. Mr. Baker, may I present to you our beautiful, Victoria Pearl."

Victoria opened her eyes and gracefully stood up. "Very pleased to meet you, Mr. Christopher Baker." She reached out her hand, and Christopher Baker ceremoniously took it and kissed it without taking his eyes off her.

He was obviously pleased with his new companion. "The pleasure is mine indeed, Miss. Victoria," he responded.

"Do you play golf?" she asked. She could tell by his haircut and outdoor complexion he was an athletic type.

"As a matter of fact, I do," he answered.

"I have always wanted to learn. Such a fascinating game!" She looked at Minna, "The music is wonderful this evening." Victoria lightly put her fingers on her throat, "I believe I am a little thirsty."

"Miss Victoria Pearl, I would be deeply honored if you will allow me to buy you a drink," Christopher expressed in a most charmed, gentlemanly fashion. "In fact, I would appreciate your company this evening. Will you be so kind as to join me for dinner?"

"Thank you. That would be lovely."

Minna smiled with satisfaction. Victoria was going to be just fine.

Victoria and Christopher spent the next two hours chatting and dining. Although he was nothing like Robert McKnight, he was nice enough, and Victoria performed her job well. She laughed when he laughed, and she used her eyes to capture his attention. When he told her she was beautiful, Victoria smiled coyly. She was witty, charming, and interesting and, indeed her manners were impeccable.

Victoria had made a special request to use the Egyptian Room for the evening. After dinner she led Christopher up the mahogany stairway. The most profound quality of the Everleigh Club was the silence in the hallway that connected all of the parlors. The air was laden with the scent of flowers and sweet perfume as Victoria escorted the eager Christopher to their den of fantasy. The Egyptian Room had thick carpet to muffle any sound and was decorated with gold and white linens. As a special touch, there was a masterfully crafted effigy of Cleopatra herself.

Victoria had planned a fantasy game, and she would perform it skillfully this evening. Her tone was seductive as she gently closed the door. "Won't you sit down, Christopher. We are going to have an evening together you shall never forget."

Obediently, Christopher Baker sat on the fully stuffed golden sofa. He was like a school boy waking up on Christmas morning, anxious to open his presents. Christopher Baker was completely mesmerized with Victoria's seduction and responded to everything she said with genuine excitement. "Do you know the story of Cleopatra and Mark Anthony, Christopher?" Victoria whispered.

Victoria kept her promise and gave Christopher Baker a memorable evening he would take with him throughout his lifetime. She had found her niche. Victoria was Scheherazade and Christopher Baker would certainly be back for more. They would all come back for more. Victoria created stories to go with all of the different rooms, that is, all but the Rose Room. Everyone knew not to give that room to Victoria. Her time with Robert was sacred as far as she was concerned, and sharing the room with anyone else would only destroy the fantasy.

Victoria enjoyed her new life immensely. Although a part of her understood it was a short-lived lifestyle, she found wealthy men to be charming and especially interesting. For the most part, she also learned they were extremely polite and respectful. Wealthy men had impeccable manners and knew how to appreciate a beautiful, intelligent woman. Victoria had great respect for the self-made man. These were men who seemed to have the most stamina and character. She met high political officials, wealthy bankers and businessmen, celebrities, and then there were those Texas cattle barons.

It was May 4th 1900, Victoria's twenty-second birthday; Minna walked into her room, holding an envelope. "Looks like you have some mail from Texas, Victoria."

Robert had indeed kept his promise. She always felt in her heart she would get a letter one day. The first night they were together he had told her that Texas gentlemen were true to their words. Her heart was beating so hard she felt it might jump right out of her chest. "Thank you, Minna."

Minna remained standing at the doorway. She didn't want Victoria to be alone if it was some kind of disappointing news.

"He's coming to Chicago, Minna! He'll be here next week!" Victoria was elated.

"We will make sure the Rose Room is reserved for you, Victoria. Just remember what I said, "Protect yourself. Let him be your fantasy Texas cowboy for now."

Robert's letter said to expect him Thursday evening. Victoria was on pins and needles all day long. She hadn't been able to eat or sleep well for the last few days, anticipating his arrival. Finally, Thursday evening, Robert walked in with a group of Texas cattlemen. Minna welcomed him with open arms. "How's my boy?" she chimed with her standard greeting. She then took his arm and led him straight to the piano where Victoria was anxiously waiting for him.

"Mr. McKnight, you remember our Victoria Pearl," Minna announced in her most gracious tone.

Robert elegantly bowed and kissed Victoria's hand. He looked even more handsome than she remembered.

"Lovely to see you again, Mr. McKnight," she said with a song in her voice.

"Would you give me the honor to dine with me this evening, Miss Victoria?"

"I would be delighted, kind sir."

For the next three nights, Robert and Victoria celebrated their sacred time in the Rose Room. They performed the love dance eye-to-eye, heart-to-heart, and soul-to-soul. Robert was smitten, and Victoria knew he had her heart.

The morning Robert left Chicago, Victoria decided not to be sad. She realized that in any moment for the rest of her life she could bask in the memory of their precious time together. No one could ever take away the vision she played over and over in her mind every day. Now Victoria completely understood the memorable words of Alfred, Lord Tennyson: "*It is better to have loved and lost, than to never have loved at all.*" Victoria decided to write about Robert in her journal. She wanted to always remember even the tiniest details of their sacred moments of making love fresh and new.

Throughout the next few months, Victoria became more experienced and began making important friends. Men admired the fact that she was an avid reader and stayed current with the latest trends and politics. Because Victoria was a good listener, she learned about business and how men think. Although sex seemed to be the attraction of the Everleigh Club, Victoria learned that it was not necessarily always the ultimate goal. The wealthy gentlemen who came were buying companionship with a classy, intelligent, beautiful woman who made them feel important and admired. It was an elegant place where a rich man could enjoy himself with other men of the same social status. After all, if it were just sex they wanted, Chicago had plenty of other places for that.

Victoria thought about Robert often, and she wondered if he ever thought about her. She wrote about Robert in her journal as if they had an ongoing exciting love affair. Sometimes she would write fantasies about taking trips with him to Europe or exciting cities like New York, San Francisco, and New Orleans.

By now Victoria had made friends with most of the girls, but she was especially fond of Mozella. She had learned that

Mozella had worked as a "lady of the evening" in what was now referred to as Storyville, a red light district in the city of New Orleans. Mozella's grandmother had been a concubine to a sugar plantation owner in Louisiana. His name was John Bradford and was Mozella's grandfather. Mozella's mother grew up on the plantation and moved to New Orleans after the Civil War. When Mozella was 17 years old, her mother died, and she and her brother, Duke, went to work for Madame Louise on Basin Street in the red light district. Duke played the piano where Mozella worked.

Mozella told Victoria about her life in New Orleans. She also shared stories about living on the plantation with her grandmother. "Mammy was a character! Told me the only real free women were black women with their white lovers on account of white women havin' to go along with what their husbands want whether they likes it or not."

When she was 26 years old, Mozella moved to Omaha, Nebraska with a white man who left her after a few months of living there. Omaha is where she met Ada and Minna Everleigh and was hired to take care of the housekeeping staff at the bordello they ran during the Trans-Mississippi Exposition. When the sisters moved to Chicago, they asked Mozella to join them.

Victoria trusted Mozella and confided in her about her feelings for Robert. "Of all the men I have come to know, this one has my heart, Mozella."

Within the first year at the Everleigh Club, Victoria had two marriage proposals, both from wealthy men capable of giving her a life of luxury. Victoria politely declined. "I am your pleasure girl," she told them. "Making me your wife might change your fantasies about me." The truth was she would rather be independent than spend the rest of her life with a man she did not love.

Working as an "Everleigh butterfly" had been quite an adventure for Victoria. She had come to love the lifestyle and socializing with important men and pillars of society. Victoria made the effort to stay busy and continued her love of reading. On Sundays, when the sisters allowed visitation from the girls' special *beaus*, Victoria found her joy in reading a good book.

She only wanted Robert in that way. Although she attempted to keep her heart in a safe place, his memory sometimes came crashing through like a tidal wave on a beach of shifting sand.

The Christmas holiday season at the Everleigh Club was an extravaganza. Ada and Minna spared no expense in decorating the club; it was a festive time for all. One of their favorite clients, "Uncle Ned," as the Everleigh *butterflies* affectionately called him, was especially fond of Christmas. All through December he enjoyed sitting in a chair in the middle of the room with his feet planted in a bucket of ice. He then insisted the ladies circle around him and sing, "*Jingle Bells*." Uncle Ned joyfully played a tambourine and drank sarsaparilla while the girls danced around him and sang the familiar Christmas carol.

Regular clients showered the girls with gifts, and Ada and Minna received bonus checks from the gentlemen who appreciated their efforts in maintaining such a regal and exquisite establishment in the heart of the Levee. One man in particular gave the sisters each $5,000. The next year the same man married a woman he met at the Everleigh Club after being with her just one night. Her name was Suzy Poon Tang.

A week before Christmas, Minna Everleigh came to Victoria's room. "A package from Texas," she smiled as she handed it to Victoria.

The name on the return postage read, "Robert McKnight." Inside the brown parcel was a small box wrapped with golden paper and white ribbon with a card that read:

> *To my beautiful Pearl. Merry Christmas to the woman who has my heart. Love, Robert McKnight*

Mozella had come to stand next to Minna, and the two women watched as Victoria opened her gift. "Oh my!" she declared, holding up a stunning 3 carat diamond necklace. Also in the box were two iridescent pink Concho pearl earrings.

"Oh, Victoria, they are absolutely exquisite!" Minna exclaimed.

Mozella smiled. "Looks like your cowboy has been thinking about you too, Miss Victoria."

The next few years Robert came to see Victoria several times and each time brought her jewelry made from beautiful pink Concho pearls. He never talked about his personal life, and Victoria never asked. It was always an unsaid rule at the Everleigh Club. Minna often said, "What the men do outside these walls is none of our business."

In just a short time, the Everleigh Club's reputation had spread all over the world. In March 1902, Prince Henry of Prussia visited the famous club on a trip to America to pick up a ship built for his brother, German Kaiser Wilheim II. Although Chicago had planned many fine events in his honor, Heinrich's only real interest was to have the Everleigh experience. Ada and Minna planned a bacchanalia for the visiting prince. As one of the "Butterflies" performed a can-can, her shoe flew off, causing a bottle of champagne to spill into it. One of the prince's men gallantly picked up the shoe. "A beautiful woman must not get her dainty foot wet," he stated with a chivalrous flare before drinking the bubbly champagne from her shoe, thus initiating a new tradition at the Everleigh Club.

Although the Everleigh sisters appeared to be lovely, delicate ladies gushing with Southern charm, they were also brilliant business women who understood the concept of superior marketing tactics. Several times a week, Minna and Ada called for their fancy carriage to carry them to the bank to deposit large sums of money. Led by two magnificent dappled gray horses, the sisters always brought a "beautiful butterfly" to accompany them. Like the Venetian courtesans who floated on gondolas throughout the canals of Venice, the richly clothed coachman paraded the ladies through the great open spaces of Chicago. They did not need a band to attract attention. With great success, the dramatic scene flamboyantly advertised the quality of woman available at the now famous Everleigh Club. People went out of their way for the privilege of catching a glimpse of the elegant Everleigh sisters as they rode by with a "beautiful butterfly" in their fancy carriage. "There they go. Aren't they grand!" said the onlookers. "I am saving up for the day I can call on them."

The men who frequented 2131 Dearborn Street completely trusted the Everleigh sisters because their integrity was absolutely impeccable. Their privacy was always secured. It was an honor and privilege to be allowed into the exclusive Everleigh Club. Money was only one requirement. Minna and Ada did not tolerate rudeness, obesity, or anyone with an unpleasant stench that might take away from the lovely perfumed scent in the parlors. There were those who came just to drink and dine and saw the beautiful butterflies as a side attraction. One evening one of their wealthy clients spent $1400 dollars ($40,000 in today's money) on a lavish party with champagne, women and gourmet food. The next day he sent an agent to pay his bill. When the man came to the door, because the sisters did not know him, they politely informed the agent that the gentleman who sent the money had never set foot in their establishment before and turned the money away. Several days later, the patron happily paid the bill himself. Needless to say, he was incredibly impressed.

It was not easy keeping trouble away from the Everleigh Club. The sisters continually donated thousands of dollars to the First Ward Aldermen, "Bathhouse" John Coughlin and Michael "Hinky-Dink" Kenna, to ensure their freedom of enterprise. Ada and Minna allowed press and legislators in for free. They were all familiar with the phone number Calumet 412. This came in handy one year when evidence showed that one of the girls had shot Marshall Field Jr. The Chicago tribune reported he had died from an accidental shooting in his own home.

Victoria was always amazed at the variety of women who came to work at the Everleigh Club. One day a gorgeous, voluptuous woman named Phyllis showed up. "I hope you like me," she said to the sisters, adding simplicity and humility to her other virtues. "The man to whom I was engaged died suddenly of heart failure. I just had to get away from unpleasant surroundings. I have no parents, and here I am. It is a strange adventure for me, but I am sure I can learn. From what I overheard on the train, a life of shame in this adorable house must be the most glorious existence imaginable. May I stay?"

Understanding the stimulating excitement of mysterious anticipation, Phyllis liked to blindfold her clients before leading them up the mahogany stairs into one of the boudoirs she had personally prepared herself. When unmasked, the patron would feast his eyes on an impeccably decorated room with deep rich colors designed to visually take him into sensual fantasy. The parlors had subtle lighting on curtains made of royal blue, dark red, purples, or green silk that cast inviting, amorous hues. Several vases of fresh cut flowers filled the room with beauty and a natural, pleasant fragrance. Within a week, men were fighting over Phyllis.

Another girl named Valerie had a rich, beautiful voice and sang like a bird. Because she loved to attach herself to anything white, she called herself, "Little Miss Purity." The Everleigh sisters made arrangements for Valerie to join a vaudeville act, and the main performer instantly fell in love and married her. They made it big and became highly successful in the theatre world. Alas, her husband fell for another woman who had joined the theatre group, and when they divorced, she came back to the Everleigh Club. "I don't understand!" she sobbed. "I did everything you taught me. I was clean and attentive. Then she came along. What did I do wrong?" Again the sisters made connections for Valerie, and she went back to the theatre. This time she became more famous and an even bigger star than before.

Then there was Myrtle, a naturally born actress but a girl too lazy to follow that kind of career. She came from a farming town in Illinois, and although Minna and Ada clearly disapproved of it, Myrtle loved to chew tobacco. One night, when a party had become dull, Myrtle summoned Edmund, a black servant adorned in red and gold braid. "The tray, Edmund!" The servant disappeared, and when he returned, he was carrying a shiny, sterling silver tray on which was placed a huge plug of chewing tobacco. As previously rehearsed, Edmund presented the tray, and Myrtle eloquently accepted the tobacco with style and flare and then bit off a big chaw. When she returned the plug to the tray, Edmund dramatically bowed, and everyone in the room laughed hysterically. From then on,

Myrtle regularly honored requests to repeat the performance. The seriousness and eloquent display made it funny.

"We do not approve of anyone spitting on our Oriental rugs," Ada commented. Although the sisters thought it crass, they went along with it to please the customers. Eventually Myrtle married a nice, overweight young man in the oil business who built her a beautiful home and made her switch to cigars. They had 2 children and lived happily ever after.

From the first evening they were together, Robert McKnight possessed Victoria's heart and soul and was constantly in her thoughts. Robert had been her "fantasy cowboy." Through the years, Victoria read everything she could get her hands on about Texas. She read about the Alamo, the Battle of San Jacinto, and the Texas War for Independence. She knew the stories of men like Davey Crockett, Stephen F. Austin, Sam Houston, and Jim Bowie. Robert's family had been among the early settlers who had acquired land grants in the spring-fed land near the San Saba River, and on his visits to Chicago, he told her about the cattle business. Chicago played a huge role in selling and trading Texas cattle, and Victoria made a point to learn all she could about pricing and making deals.

Three and a half years had passed since the afternoon Victoria had first walked into 2131 Dearborn Street. Before that day, she had been a librarian from a small town 40 miles outside the Chicago city limits. All she had ever known about the world was what she had read about in her books. Now Victoria had entertained and dined with politicians, wealthy businessmen, and dignitaries. At 26 years old she was becoming more aware that her time at the Everleigh Club was only temporary. She had enjoyed being surrounded by elegance and luxury, but it was only where she lived; none of it belonged to her.

Victoria had great insights to the way men think and knew intimate secrets about powerful men the rest of the world would never know. Learning from Ada and Minna had served her well. She became knowledgeable about politics and basic human nature and had acquired a strong, sound business sense. Through the years, men had bought her expensive jewelry and had given her money. Some took delight in buying elegant gowns for her to wear "just for them." Victoria liked the feeling of both making money and saving money. One of her regular clients was an investor in the stock market. She had done well with her personal investments, listening to his knowledge and strategies over dinner and wine.

It was the spring of 1904. The World's Fair known as "The Louisiana Purchase Exposition," was being held in St. Louis, Missouri. A new invention called the "automobile" was introduced. The fair had a 340 foot Ferris wheel called the Observation Wheel that inspired a new song, "*Meet Me in St. Louis, Louis, Meet Me at the Fair.*" Robert McKnight did just that. He invited Victoria to meet him in St. Louis to attend the World's Fair.

Robert was waiting for her at the train station when Victoria arrived. They spent five days together in St. Louis where they ate a new popular food called the hamburger, drank iced tea, and enjoyed a new dessert invented at the fair called the ice cream cone. It was different making love away from the Everleigh Club, and Victoria felt she had truly gone to heaven.

Finally on their last evening, they rode the St. Louis Ferris wheel which had been built with parts from the same Ferris wheel Victoria had ridden with her parents eleven years before. When the wheel had circled around and reached the top, under a crescent moon, Robert McKnight, the handsome gentleman from Texas, asked Victoria Pearl to marry him.

"Miss Victoria Pearl, would you consider making me the happiest man on earth and do me the honor of becoming my wife?" Victoria's dream had come true!

"Yes, Robert! Yes!" she declared with no hesitation. As he placed the sparkling diamond on her finger, Victoria truly felt she could reach up and touch the stars.

Goodbye Chicago

Before Victoria went to St. Louis to meet Robert she had never been out of the state of Illinois, and now she was going to Texas. Somewhere she had read the word itself means "friend" in the language of its indigenous people. Minna and Ada were genuinely happy for her and gave Victoria a going away party. Most of the women in their line of work did not end up with stories that had fairytale endings. Many of the girls who worked on the Levee died in their thirties from a drug overdose or taking a fatal swim in the Chicago River or Lake Michigan. When their youth was gone, so was their value. The Everleigh Club, on the other hand, had a high rate of marriages. Minna liked to share her philosophy, "Gentlemen appreciate a woman who can be a lady in the parlor and a seductress in the bedroom,"

"They are going to pay for it either way," Ada would add with a grin.

Of all the people and friends Victoria had come to know, Mozella was the most difficult to say "Goodbye" to. "I shore am gonna' miss you, Miss Victoria," she said with a tearful hug. "You are smart and ever so kind. I know you will be happy with that handsome man. I've seen the way he looks at you. The way you look at each other. I do not believe in love at first sight, Miss Victoria; it's much deeper than that. You and Mr. McKnight were lovers before in other lifetimes. People don't meet their soul mates, Victoria; they just remember each other. That is what love at first sight truly is. The Bible says, '*The eyes are the mirror to the soul.*' From that first moment you looked into each other's eyes and your souls reconnected, he became a part of you once again. Soul mates are forever part of your heart and spiritual existence. I love you, Miss Victoria. You call me if you ever need a friend."

Victoria handed Mozella a box. Inside was a perfectly round, shiny iridescent pink Concho pearl on a golden chain. "I want you to have this, Mozella; in fact, we both want you to have it. Now turn around so I can put it on you." Mozella laughed with delight as she pivoted. "There now, it looks beautiful on you. Do not forget me, Mozella. I surely will never forget you!"

"Thank you, Miss Victoria. It's so pretty. My goodness… a real Concho pearl from Texas! Give Mr. Robert a big ol' kiss from Mozella." With tearful eyes, the two women embraced each other.

"I have never been so happy, Mozella!"

Minna and Ada had called their coachman to take Victoria to the train station.

"Your carriage is here, Cinderella!" Minna announced.

Ada gave Victoria a big hug. "Be good, honey. You were one of our best!"

As Minna hugged her, Victoria's eyes swelled up again with tears. "Thank you for everything, Minna," she whispered.

"Your Prince Charming awaits, my dear! Good bye Victoria, take care of your sweet self!"

Victoria Pearl McDougal had walked into the Everleigh Club a young librarian and was walking out a wealthy woman. As she walked down the hallway for the last time, she looked to her left and saw her reflection in the big mirror just as she had on that first day she had met Minna and Ada for tea. This time she saw a happy, wealthy, worldly woman excited about beginning her new life.

Minna, Ada and Mozella stood outside the Everleigh Club and waved until Victoria's carriage disappeared.

Mozella's eyes were full of tears. "I'm gonna' miss that one, Miss Minna. We have been friends from the start. Miss Victoria has been in love with Mr. McKnight for a long time now."

"Indeed, Mozella. We really do love our butterflies. After all, where would we be without them?" Minna commented.

"I have to agree with you, Mozella," Ada added. "Victoria was one of our best. I must say, I am quite happy for her. So nice to see our butterflies find a home."

Hello Texas

Love has a way of enhancing the world. Victoria had never seen the sky so blue or the trees and land so green. The air was warm, and as the train headed southwest, Victoria felt like the colorful wild flowers swaying in a soft breeze in the fields, were performing a dance exclusively for her.

It was the sixteenth of June when Victoria finally arrived at the Santa Fe Train Depot in San Angelo, Texas. Robert was waiting for her with flowers and a big smile on his face. Victoria looked especially elegant in her  mauve travelling suit and brand new hat. Her face was radiant, and anyone at the station could see Robert and Victoria were in love. A carriage took them to the elegant St. Angelus Hotel, where Robert had a room reserved. The hotel had just been rebuilt after having been destroyed by fire two years before and was the premier place in town for elegant dining and overnight comfort.

That evening Robert presented Victoria with a lovely golden ring. "I thought we could go to the Justice of the Peace tomorrow and get married, that is if you'll still have me. I know I might be rushing things, but I…"

"Of course, Robert. Yes! We will marry tomorrow. This means I will be a June bride. Tomorrow is perfect!"

The next day Robert married Victoria in a simple, quiet ceremony, witnessed by a man and woman they had never met. It all seemed so surreal. Victoria felt like a butterfly, free from her cocoon. Texas was her home now, and everything in her life was new, that is with the exception of the love she had for Sir Robert, her knight in shining armor. Perhaps Mozella was right. Perhaps they had been lovers in previous lifetimes. Whether or not that was true, it was a nice thought. All she knew for sure was for the first time since her father and mother had passed away, Victoria felt loved and safe. Her dreams had come true, and she was determined to make Robert a happy man. Victoria was now Victoria Pearl McKnight, the happiest woman in the world!

After the ceremony, Robert and Victoria walked outside as man and wife. Victoria looked around her and took a closer look at San Angelo. It was so different from Chicago, simple and uncomplicated. She loved that! To her it was paradise. As far as she was concerned, any place was paradise as long as she was with Robert. "Now for your wedding present," Robert said with a mischievous little smile. "We are going to the Concho River!" They climbed onto the padded seats of the carriage. Victoria sat beside her new husband with her arm snuggly hooked into his. With Robert, Victoria felt complete. She was amazed how they always fit together so well.

The Concho River looked peaceful and serene. Victoria could feel the warm dry West Texas wind blow gently on her face. "Here it is," Robert said proudly.

"Here is what?" Victoria asked. All she could see was the river and the land around it.

"It's your wedding gift, Victoria. This is where I am going to build you a house!" he gleamed with his arms stretched wide. "Here!"

"Oh, Robert, it is quite lovely. Peaceful, wonderful and lovely!" Victoria exclaimed with joy.

"I realize you're a city girl, Victoria, and for a long time you have lived in a pretty fancy place! I want to build a house for us in San Angelo, right here on the Concho River. The ranch is 50 miles southeast from here, way away from the life in the city like what you're used to. I have good help, and I don't have to be at the ranch all of the time." Suddenly his tone changed.

"Victoria, there is something I have not told you. I was married once many years ago but my wife died giving birth to our first child. It was a boy and the poor little guy never even took his first breath. Since then all I've been doing is working hard, and then I met you. Hell, I didn't even want to go with those guys that night in Chicago. We'd come up to do some cattle business, and one of the men heard about y'all. I think he said he heard about the new club opening from a lady friend he knew in the business. They had to talk me into coming! When I saw you in that pretty dress sitting by the piano, I was mighty glad I had gone with them. I felt like I already knew you, like you had something that belonged to me. There hasn't been one day since that first night, I haven't thought about you. I love you so much, Victoria Pearl. You are my heart."

Robert was so sincere. He had never talked to her that way before. "I love you, Victoria, but grandmother wouldn't have been nice to you at all. She just didn't like Yankees or Catholics, and God knows, what would have happened if she had ever found out about the Everleigh Club! She died last February. Since then, I have been getting things in order to bring you to Texas, hoping, of course, you might agree to come."

Victoria suddenly realized she had not known about Robert's grandmother or even that he had lost his wife and a baby. All this time he had been thinking of her the way she had been thinking about him. None of it mattered now. She was with her Robert McKnight, and she loved her new life.

That evening Robert and Victoria ate a lovely dinner and celebrated their marriage alone with a bottle of champagne. They made love as man and wife all night long. It felt different knowing he didn't have to leave. Now they were married; their union was sacred and magical. Her name was now Victoria Pearl McKnight, and somehow it seemed as if all time before this moment had been erased. June 17, 1904 was their bright new beginning, and they were full of joy and love for each other.

Victoria gasped as the buggy pulled into the Five Star Ranch. She had never seen anything so lovely in her life. A cascade of fresh spring water fell onto a brimming 3 acre pond full of colorful lily pads. As she listened to the sound of the falls flowing so peacefully, Victoria knew she was hearing a new kind of music. There were oak trees and vast grasslands where cattle were grazing peacefully.

"I love Texas, Robert!" she exclaimed. "I just love Texas, and I love you!"

As they neared the house, two friendly brown and white Brittany spaniels greeted them with wagging tails and happy barks. "Meet Polly and Barkly," Robert laughed.

Victoria's new home was a two story farm house with a porch that wrapped around it. Robert helped her from the carriage, and then to Victoria's surprise, he swept her up and carried her over the threshold.

A woman, perhaps in her mid-30's, was standing to the side of the great room, smiling at their happiness. "Buenos dias, Senor Robert. Bienvenido a casa!" she greeted Victoria warmly.

"This is Angela," Robert said. "Her family has been with our family for over 60 years. Wait until you taste her tortillas! You are going to love Angela's tortillas!"

That evening, wearing a lovely strand of pearls Robert had given her on one of his trips to Chicago, Victoria presented herself to her new husband. "Some women do look good in pearls," he breathed in a low sexy tone. He repeated his compliment several times that evening, every time they made love. Throughout their marriage, walking into a room wearing only her favorite pearls would become a tradition on special occasions or sometimes, just to set an amorous mood.

The next week Robert took Victoria to Menardville, a small town on the San Saba River about 15 miles from the ranch. At one time, it had served as an overnight stop and trading post on north and west cattle trails. "There has been a lot of bloodshed in the state of Texas," Robert told her. "One of the saddest stories happened right here on this river. Back in the 1700's, the Spanish saw this as an ideal place to build a mission and fort because it was on the route from San Antonio to El Paso. Unfortunately, the fort and the mission were a couple of miles apart. The Comanche saw the settlers as intruders. One day two thousand Comanche Indians and their allies attacked the mission and tortured and killed two of the padres who were here. A third padre managed to live and tell the story of what happened. The details are too awful to tell you, Victoria. It was the start of the war in this land between the settlers and the Comanche Indians."

"Her song is peaceful, Robert. It almost seems as if the river is singing the sad story of what happened here."

"Several years ago the Great Western Cattle Trail travelled through Menard County along the San Saba River between Stock Pen Crossing and Peg Leg crossing. Back in the day, over 7 million head of livestock came through this area. The cowboys would pen the herd in the abandoned Presidio Compound, then go into Menardville to do their banking and visit the friendly ladies and saloons."

Victoria looked at Robert and smiled.

The next few weeks Robert and Victoria were inseparable. She even liked to watch him work. Most days were spent riding horses around the ranch and their evenings making love. To Robert's delight, Victoria didn't miss anything about Chicago. The country air was fresh, and there was something about Texans that was refreshingly honest. "I know it might sound strange, but somehow it feels as if Texas has wrapped her arms around me and welcomed me home, Robert."

"Like any good mother," he grinned. "Texas will rock you like a baby, close to her heart."

Victoria wore simple dresses now, and for the most part, she wore her hair down or in a long braid when the days were hot. Robert loved just looking at Victoria: the way she moved, the way she played with Polly and Barkley, and especially her sly, seductive looks that said, "I want you, now." They laughed often, and made love every day, twice on Sundays. Robert was Victoria's happiness, and she was completely content being his wife.

Victoria had always wanted to go to her mother's village in Ireland. Robert's family was from Scotland. Connecting with the land of their ancestors was soulfully emotional for both of them, and their feelings ran deep. That fall, Robert took his bride to the Misty Isles. Every evening they found a pub where

Victoria recognized some of the limericks and songs her parents had sung. The Irish brogue especially warmed Victoria's heart. It was as if a part of her mother and father was still alive. They visited small churches and took long rides throughout the vast green countryside.

As she visited places her mother told her about and ate the same cooking her mother used to prepare, Victoria felt reconnected to both her parents. She remembered those Sunday afternoons her mother would smile and say, "Your father and I are going to rest a while Victoria," and then shut the bedroom door. Now she fully understood exactly what that smile meant. It was the look of a woman in love.

The voyage on the ship coming home to America was rough for Victoria. Not once did she get seasick on the trip over. Now she was sick at her stomach every day. Robert was patient and Victoria kept apologizing. "I do not understand. I was fine crossing the ocean."

When they finally reached America, Victoria continued to be ill on the train ride home to Texas. By the time they returned, it was quite evident that Victoria was pregnant. Robert was gravely concerned. It was painful enough when he lost his first wife and baby in childbirth. He would be devastated if he ever lost Victoria.

"Do not worry, me love," Victoria said in a strong Irish brogue. "I come from a line of strong Irish women, and in a few short months, I will present you with a strong young laddie to work the ranch and bring the cows home!"

Every day she was pregnant, Robert continued to tell Victoria how beautiful she was. One day as she was reading on the front porch, he marveled at the sunlight glistening in her long, flowing hair.

"You are the most gorgeous creature I have ever seen!"

Victoria laughed. "Robert, me love, I believe you need glasses. Look at me! I am swollen up like a hot air balloon, and my breasts are as big as a cow's tits! Mooooooooo!"

"To me, you are the most desirable woman on earth! Besides you only have two tits. Oh, my sweet sexy Lassie! Look at what you're doing to me!"

"Well, I say, Mr. McKnight! I do believe you are in the want of a woman!"

Robert reached for Victoria's hand and took her inside. He slowly undressed his bride and laid with her on the bed. After they made love, he kissed the roundness of her belly. Suddenly he felt a slight thump against his cheek. "Just saying hello to his daddy," she smiled.

"You are absolutely glowing with beauty!"

Victoria tenderly took his hand and laid it on her stomach under hers. "Feel your son moving around! There... I think he wants to play."

"That is amazing! Oh, Victoria, I love you so much. So very, very much!"

As it turned out, Victoria was wrong about having a son. On June 25th, one year and eight days after they had been married, Victoria gave birth to twin boys, Michael and David McKnight.

Plans for the house being built in San Angelo had been postponed. Victoria was happy and content living on the ranch with her family. She loved watching Robert play with his two young sons, and for the first time in her life, she felt like a complete woman. Now she was a lover, a lady, a mother, and a wife. Victoria enjoyed her life in Texas with all of her men. "I am quite content with my family here on the ranch," she told Robert one day. "I am not so sure we need to build a house in San Angelo." Robert sold the land on the river, and the McKnight family continued living happily on the Five Star Ranch in Menard County.

America was growing by the thousands. The automobile was revolutionizing the country. By the time the twins were 10 years old, they knew how to handle a horse and drive a truck. When the train station was built in Menardville in 1911, the railroad said the name was too long to fit onto the sign. Because of this the town was renamed "Menard."

The new train station was fewer than 15 miles from the ranch which made it easier for the McKnight family to travel. Victoria was in love with Texas and set out to visit all of the places she had read about. "I want the boys to know music and theatre and to be exposed to the outside world, Robert. There is so much for them to see and learn, and I want them to be educated. It is important!"

Robert and Victoria took David and Michael on trips to Austin. They visited the missions and the Alamo in San Antonio, played on the white beaches in the Gulf of Mexico, and explored the exciting Galveston shipping port. The family always travelled together when Robert went to San Angelo on business trips. Victoria wanted her sons to be exposed to as much as possible. "Knowledge is power," she told them.

From that first day when Victoria arrived at the Santa Fe Depot on North Chadbourne, the town had dramatically grown. To her, she found San Angelo to be a fascinating place. At one time the town was originally known as, "the place across the river," with brothels and saloons servicing cattle driving teams and soldiers stationed at Fort Concho. By the early 1900's, the town had become the largest trading city in West Texas. Word got out that San Angelo was an ideal place for people with tuberculosis because of the high altitude and dry, clean air. As a result, thousands of people settled there in an effort to cure their disease. In 1911 the Orient Railroad established a train that travelled as far south as Chihuahua, Mexico. What once was a small town with old wooden structures and streets built wide enough for wagons to turn around, was now a growing city full of big sophisticated buildings made of brick and stone.

With the agricultural boom, San Angelo was buzzing with commerce and supported a strong sense of civic pride. It had 6 clothing stores, 8 hat stores, 12 dry good stores, 6 men's clothiers, 11 tailors, 11 shoe stores, 6 boot stores, and 6 "fancy" stores. There were over 40 grocery stores, bakeries, dairies, meat markets, 6 cigar stores, 16 saloons and a successful ice cream company. People could enjoy a stage production at the Crystal and Yale Theatres and the San Angelo Opera House. The Landon, the Angelus, and the Nimitz were 3 first-class hotels, and although there were 14 boarding houses as well, many times it was hard to find a room in town. Whenever the McKnight family went to town, Robert managed to buy Victoria a gift from Holland's Jewelers. Although San Angelo was nothing like Chicago, the town had everything Victoria could ever need or want and more. Most of all, Victoria liked the fact that the people were so friendly.

A stately three story mansion had been built on the land Robert had bought Victoria for their wedding day. Sometimes she went by to look at it with a little regret in her heart, remembering how excited he was presenting it to her as the place he wanted to build her a home. It was a lovely mansion with several porches and balconies, all with a lovely view of the Concho River. By 1913, San Angelo was dramatically different from that first day Victoria and Robert spent those enchanting nights at the St. Angelus Hotel. For her it would always be the magical place where she married the love of her life and for this, San Angelo would always hold a special place deep within her heart. As far as Victoria was concerned, the Concho River would always sing their eternal love song.

As the war in Europe progressed, a grim cloud of depression settled over the nation. From Tom Green County alone, 842 young men were sent overseas to fight in World War I. Victoria and Robert were grateful that their sons were too young to go. In 1917, West Texas experienced a devastating drought. Only 9 inches of rain fell that year, and the economy in San Angelo began to suffer. People started moving away from the city, and the prosperity boom ceased to exist. World War I ravaged the nation, and the boys who returned found it difficult to resume a normal existence. It would be the first time in America's history that the term "Shell-Shocked" was used to describe the condition. The entire country was forced to heal from its wounds after losing so many American lives. Many of the soldiers had died because of illnesses, and in 1918 a worldwide epidemic of the flu claimed the lives of millions. In 1919 the Spanish flu would claim the life of Victoria's beloved Robert.

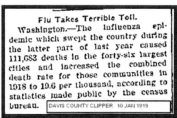

Goodbye My Beloved

Robert had just returned from a business trip in San Antonio. Victoria usually went with him, this particular time she had stayed home with her boys. "I'll only be gone 2 days, Victoria. I'll be home before you know it." As Victoria watched the train pull out of the station, a strange fear overcame her. The next 2 nights Victoria hardly slept. She tried not to let the boys see her worry, but Maria sensed her concern. "I do not know what is wrong with me, Maria. I know he will be home tomorrow."

When Victoria saw Robert at the train station, he could hardly walk. "Take me home, Victoria. I'm sick." He was barely able to speak. For three long days, Victoria never left his side. She read to him, put cold rags on his head, and held his hand, while singing and reminiscing of their times in Chicago. Victoria talked about the Rose Room and how Mozella used to tease her days before she knew Robert was coming for a visit. "Your cowboy is coming, Miss Victoria. The Texas cowboy is coming to see his favorite pearl!" Mozella had sung.

Robert went to heaven on a Sunday afternoon. Victoria could not understand how the beautiful spring waters were still singing their song, the West Texas breeze had not stopped gently blowing through the leaves, and the cattle were peacefully grazing in the pasture. For Victoria, life had completely stopped and had transformed into a strange dark silence. She had lost the love of her life and she felt like her heart was going to burst with pain. Robert was 55 years old when he passed, and Victoria was angry at God. How could this possibly be? A week ago they were making love, laughing, and making plans for the boys. What would she do now that her precious Robert was gone?

As Victoria prepared to bury her beloved Robert in the family plot beside the springs, she thought of the day she had arrived in San Angelo and how happy they had been. Today was the saddest day of her life. The ranch hands prepared a place in the family plot not too far from the springs. David and Michael, both 15 years old, were sullen and found comfort in each other's company the way they always had when they were upset.

Victoria refused to wear black. To her Robert was still alive in her heart. She put on a lovely lavender frock and pulled up her hair the way Robert liked it. "Put it up so I can watch you shake it down," he would say.

Victoria was sitting on her bed putting on her white gloves when Maria knocked on her bedroom door. "Excuse me Señora, but there is someone here to see you."

"Oh, Maria, I can't see anyone right now. Please send them away."

Victoria heard a familiar voice begin singing like a rescue ship in the night. It was the only voice that could ever penetrate her darkest moments. "What do you mean send them away? I've come all the way from New Orleans to see my girl, and I ain't goin' nowhere!"

"Mozella? Oh Mozella! He's gone! My cowboy is gone!"

Mozella ran by her side, sat beside her on the bed and put her arm around her. "I know baby girl. Mozella is here. I know." Victoria sobbed a comforting release while Mozella rocked her in her arms. "Mr. Robert will be watching you from heaven now, Missy. He was a good man, and you know he's dancin' with the angels."

"But I want him here with me, Mozella! I want him here with me!" Victoria screamed, pounding her fists on the bed and sobbing uncontrollably.

Victoria buried her head in Mozella's shoulder. "Let it go, honey, let it go." Mozella held her tight with loving tenderness, in an attempt to comfort the pain with love.

When she finally calmed down, Victoria sat up and looked at her friend with curiosity. "How did you find out, Mozella?"

Maria was standing at the door. "I called her, Señora."

"Thank you, Maria. Thank you so much."

Victoria had never known this kind of pain. Her heart was broken on the passing of her beloved Robert. Although she loved her boys, when she was at the ranch, everywhere she looked reminded her of her cowboy. With Robert the ranch was heaven on earth. Now it was a picturesque gigantic grave with all of her dreams buried beneath the land.

Victoria invited Mozella to stay on at the ranch. She had been her rock in Chicago, and her loving friendship brought both comfort and peace to Victoria's immense grief. For the next several months, Victoria spent several hours a day sitting by Robert's grave. The flow of the cascading fresh spring waters on the ranch brought her peace and cleansed the grief from her soul. Sometimes she burst into tears. Some days she barely said anything at all.

Finally one morning Victoria woke up with an attitude of renewal and strength. She washed up, dressed herself, looked in the mirror, and declared, "Enough!"

Victoria Pearl walked downstairs and into the kitchen where Mozella and Maria were drinking coffee and fixing breakfast. "Get yourself ready, and pack an overnight bag, Mozella! You and I are going to San Angelo!"

Maria prepared a lunch for Mozella and Victoria, and together they went to the Menard train station and embarked on the train to San Angelo. Although the last few years the city had experienced some hard financial times, recently, life had gotten better for the people of San Angelo. West Texas was overcoming the financial setbacks from the drought, and people throughout America were healing from the pains of war.

The train ride took them through Brady and Brownwood. When they pulled into the Santa Fe Station at 4th Street and Chadbourne in San Angelo, memories of her first day in Texas passed through her mind gently like old friends. She remembered the excitement of her new life with Robert as well as the anticipation of a world she had never known. As the train pulled into the station, she remembered Robert's smile as she waved to him from the train car. The vision was forever etched in her mind, and Victoria felt nostalgic, melancholy, and grateful all at the same time.

As they disembarked, Victoria began telling Mozella the story of her first days in Texas. "This is where Robert picked me up the day I moved here from Chicago. This is where he was standing when I first saw him…"

Mozella nodded her head and smiled with every detail Victoria shared. Finally she stopped and looked at her friend, then started to cry. "We were so happy, Mo, so very happy."

Victoria quickly pulled out a handkerchief and dried her tears. "I want you to know I have decided to focus on the love Mozella. I only want to think of the love and not the loss. I am so thankful for the time Robert and I had together. Not everyone has the opportunity to experience a love like we had in their entire lifetime."

Victoria hired a cab for a couple of hours and took Mozella on a personal tour of the city. From the train station, they drove by Fort Concho. "Mo, I know you have heard of the Buffalo Soldiers - you know, the black soldiers who enlisted in the army after the Civil War. This was one of their main posts. It was built to protect settlers and travelers from the Comanche," Victoria told her friend.

From there they went to the St. Angelus Hotel where they walked inside for a moment. Victoria looked at the reception desk where she and Robert checked in many a night when he had business in town. "This is where we spent our first night as man and wife," she sighed. "We were so in love."

"I remember the way that man looked at you, Miss Victoria. The way you looked at each other. Never seen anything like it before."

Next, Victoria told the cab driver to drive them to the Justice of the Peace. "And this is where we were married," she said as they stepped out of the car. "I do not remember who the witnesses were or even their names," she laughed.

Mozella patiently watched as her friend reminisced, the way good friends do.

"Let's go down by the Concho River. I want to show you one more place."

Upon Victoria's instructions, the driver took the two ladies to the place on the river where Robert first presented his new bride with her wedding gift. On the lot stood an imposing three story mansion with a stately view of the Concho River. "This is where Robert brought me on our wedding day. Then it was a big open space. He told me he was going to build me a house here because he was afraid I would be bored living as a rancher's wife," she said with a tearful laugh. "I could have lived in the middle of the Sahara Desert with that man, and it would have been the most glorious place on earth. He was my happiness, Mozella, and now he's gone." Pearl cried again softly.

Mozella looked at the impressive mansion. "It is truly a magnificent house, Miss Victoria!"

"Look, Mozella! The house is for sale," Victoria exclaimed pointing to a sign in the window. Apparently the family who had built the house had fallen on hard times and was anxious to sell. "What do you think, Mozella? Think we can make some money here?" Victoria asked her friend with a glimmer in her eye.

"It's as good a place as any! You always did like making money."

"The boys can take care of the ranch. They have plenty of help, and they learned from the best. That was Robert's plan all along. He was always telling the boys the ranch would be theirs one day. You are right, Mozella, I do like making money. I will do it with class, just like the Everleigh sisters."

"Here in San Angelo?" Mozella asked.

"Yes! San Angelo is close enough to the ranch where I can go home when I feel the urge. The economy has been picking up the last few years, and San Angelo is still the wool capital of the world. You know, San Angelo at one time was known as *The Naughty City*. As long as there are men with money who are willing to pay for a woman to be nice to them, I believe we can do well. It is all a matter of supply and demand."

"You learned from the best!"

"I do like San Angelo. It is an interesting place," Victoria said changing the subject. "The people are the friendliest I have ever known, much different from Chicago. Are you in, Mo?"

"It is a magnificent house, Miss Victoria," Mozella smiled. "You learned from the best!"

"The name is Pearl, Mozella. We shall call our new business Miss Pearl's Parlor! The prettiest girls in West Texas! As the great philosopher Plato once said, 'The God of Love lives in a state of need.' If they need it, we will have it!"

"Yes Ma'am," Mozella said with a hearty laugh. *"Ruth 4: He will bring you a new life and support you in your old age."*

That afternoon Victoria Pearl bought herself a mansion overlooking the Concho River in San Angelo, Texas, for a ridiculously low price. The FOR SALE sign that was in the window was gone, and once again in her life, Victoria Pearl was on the threshold of a new adventure

New Beginnings

Some people say that when we let go of the past we have the chance to be reborn again. Buying the house in San Angelo gave Victoria a sense of renewal. Although she was interested in getting on with her new venture, she was not in a real hurry to move away from her boys. Robert had taught the twins the ranch operation well, but both agreed they wanted the boys to have a college education. For now she decided to see the house in San Angelo as a project to keep her busy until Michael and David were ready for Austin. Operations on the ranch continued to run smoothly. Victoria had full confidence in the families who had been there for three generations and trusted them implicitly.

A couple of weeks after Victoria bought the mansion on the Concho River, she received a letter from her friend, Madeline. After working at the Everleigh House in Chicago, Madeline had moved to New York City to live with her sister. The two women had casually kept in touch over the years.

"Look Mozella. It's from Maddie! I remember when Robert would leave Chicago, she always tried to cheer me up. 'I do not know why you would ever want to be with a cattleman,' Pearl mimicked, imitating Maddie's English accent. 'They probably smell like cow most of the time! Oh and their boots! There is no telling what they have on those boots! Phew!'" Victoria laughed as she remembered her friend's jovial wit. "I wonder if she knows about Robert? I do not know how she could." Full of curiosity, Victoria opened the letter.

Dear Victoria,

I hope this letter finds you well. My sister belongs to a group of Catholic women who have partnered and formed an investment group. They are currently looking to invest in an oil drilling project in West Texas. The women seem to be excited, as the project was presented by a smooth talking Irishman who could sell ice to the Eskimos. I told my sister I know someone who lives in Texas whom I trusted. I would appreciate it if you can look into a small oil company called "Texon" in Fort Worth, Texas. I believe they call them "wildcats" or something like that. I appreciate you helping me in this matter. Please give my regards to Robert.

Sincerely,
Madeline Rose (Maddie)

"Look at this, Mozella."

"Well I'll be…Maddie!" Mozella replied.

"It seems strange how she talks about Robert as if he's alive. I guess I assumed because losing him has been so terribly hard everyone in the world knows he is gone." That afternoon Victoria sent a telegram to New York. WILL CONTACT YOU AS SOON AS I LEARN ANYTHING. VICTORIA PEARL

Victoria rode the train to Fort Worth and met with Frank Pickrell. He and his partner, Haymon Krupp, had formed the Texas Oil and Land Company together. Something about him reminded her of her father. His aggressive Irish spirit impressed her as well as the fact that he and Krupp had already taken great financial risks themselves to drill this well. Victoria knew all about taking risks. She thought of the risks her parents had taken coming to America with nothing but what they could carry to the boat leaving Ireland. She thought of that first day at the Everleigh Club and how choosing to work there changed her life forever.

"Well, Mrs. McKnight?" Pickrell started. "What would you like to know?"

"Tell me why you think this oil drilling project is a good investment," Victoria answered. Frank Pickrell was suddenly aware he was not dealing with an ordinary woman."

"I'll be honest with you, Ma'am. There is absolutely no doubt you first need to be a gambler and willing to take a risk on this venture. I'll tell you right up front. This is not a sure thing."

"I know all about taking risks, Mr. Pickrell. I appreciate your honesty," Victoria replied in a curt, business like tone.

"Do you believe in fate Mrs. McKnight" he asked.

"As a matter of fact, I do," Victoria answered.

"I was walking down the street with my business partner, Haymon Krupp, and I ran into Rupert Ricker, an old army buddy of mine. He had come to Fort Worth looking for investors for an oil drilling project in West Texas, but everyone in town had shot him down. Rupert told us he had done extensive research and was convinced that there is oil in West Texas near Big Lake. We went to his hotel where he spreads out maps and charts all over the room. Crazy enough, they seemed to make sense. He told us he got excited when a professor at the University in Austin says his findings were valid. My partner and I had just formed an oil company and we were looking for some kind of prospect. As it turned out, he needed $44,000 to rent the land or his permits were going to expire in just a few days. Unfortunately, it was a detail he had overlooked! Can you believe that? My partner bought the entire deal from him for $2500. It is our first venture in the oil business and we are excited!"

Victoria watched Frank's eyes as he talked. She had learned much about business from the men she knew at the Everleigh Club. For some reason the Club seemed like a safe place to tell all. She could see that the Irishman was full of passion, and he was not afraid to look straight into her eyes when he spoke. Victoria liked that. "I'd like to invest in your oil well, Mr. Pickrell," Victoria heard herself say out loud. There was something about Pickrell that made her feel confident. Perhaps it was the fact that he sounded just like her father when he talked.

After the meeting, Pearl sent another telegram to Madeline and told her what she had learned. THE OIL DEAL LOOKS GOOD. STOP. I AM INVESTING AS WELL. VICTORIA.

Madeline showed the telegram to her sister, and the Catholic women agreed to invest in what was named the "Group 1" stock. The women included a couple of nuns from affluent families. The thought of drilling oil in West Texas seemed romantically exciting, much different than anything they had ever known in New York. To them drilling for oil in the rugged lands of West Texas was comparable to the spirit of the gold rush in California. Upon signing the contracts, the women threw a big party and celebrated with champagne.

Victoria promised Madeline that she would maintain a firsthand account and notify her with updates concerning the well drilling efforts in West Texas.

January 12, 1921
Dear Madeline,

I have been doing some travelling and keeping myself busy decorating the house in San Angelo. I hope you can visit us someday. San Angelo has an interesting history and the economy has been picking up. Mozella is living in the house taking care of my affairs when I am not here. She has been such a good friend since Robert passed away. I thought I would give you a personal update on our oil venture. Enough money has finally been raised to begin the drilling. Apparently, we needed to start on or before midnight January 8, 1921. The geologist selected a site several miles from the Orient Railroad tracks near Big Lake, Texas, but they were not able to get the equipment there in time. Frank Pickrell asked the Texas State Land Office if the actual drilling had to start on January 8th or if land preparation was good enough. The commissioner told him it was the law and to get it done. It didn't matter if it was even a water well. Just some kind of drilling had to begin before midnight of January 8th. Pickrell spent all day of January 6th gathering water well equipment. Two days later, he convinced the Orient Railroad to delay the train 12 hours to allow the drilling equipment to be loaded onto a flatcar. The Orient train reached the location at dusk. The men worked hard, and the equipment was loaded onto horse-drawn wagons as quickly as they could. It was after dark before the crew was able to get it to the well site. With just a few lanterns, Pickrell's men started digging a water well just minutes before midnight.

At the last minute, someone remembered there needed to be eye witnesses to assure that drilling had indeed begun on time. Just then they saw a set of headlights coming down the road. The men jumped on their horses and flagged down the car. This in itself was a miracle, Madeline. The chances that a car would show up in the middle of nowhere at midnight in Big Lake, Texas, are slim-to-none because it is the most remote place I have ever seen in my life. Frank Pickrell was able to convince the people in the car to sign an affidavit in town that they had indeed witnessed the fact that the well drilling had begun on time. Consider it our first miracle! This will turn into an oil drilling operation as soon as the derrick is built. I have to hand it to Frank Pickrell. He is very persistent!

Sincerely yours,
Victoria Pearl

Late that summer, Victoria updated her friend with some good news.

August 20, 1921
Dear Madeline,

I hope these days find you well. Here is a brief update on our well. As you already know, the driller's name is Carl Cromwell, and they say he is one of the best! He commissioned R.S. McDonald of Big Spring, Texas, to build the oil derrick, and despite the July heat, they finally got it done. The man is amazing. He was able to purchase $50,000 worth of drilling equipment for only $5,000 in Ranger, Texas. Apparently the oil boom had died down there. They finally spudded the oil well 3 days ago. The location is just 175 feet from the Orient Railroad tracks. It would have been too expensive to haul the equipment to the first place they wanted to drill. I like this Cromwell fellow. Looks like we're on our way!

Sincerely yours,
Victoria Pearl

Victoria was impressed with Frank Pickrell's methods of getting things done. The following spring she wrote Madeline again:

> *March 27, 1922*
> *Dear Madeline,*
>
> *Good news! There has been a small oil show at 950 feet. There have been several setbacks with equipment breaking down. Mr. Cromwell and his assistant, Dee Locklin, have moved their families to the location. They have recruited some cowboys they call "roughnecks" to work on the rig, but it has been difficult to keep workers because the conditions are so hard and the location is in a barren country that is hot, lonely, and dry. Every time the Number One runs out of money, Frank Pickrell finds some creative ways to raise some more. I have visited the location a couple of times, and all I can say is I continue to admire their tenacity. The way I see it, as long as they keep drilling, the dream is still alive. In the meantime, I have been busy with my business in San Angelo, and I have a few girls working for me. Mozella is doing a great job taking care of my affairs when I am not here.*
>
> *Sincerely yours,*
> *Victoria Pearl*

A few months later Madeline received a letter to assure the Catholic women; Frank Pickrell was indeed a man of his word:

> *May 1, 1922*
> *Dear Madeline,*
>
> *It's been several months now since they first spudded the well. The crew is using a cable tool and is only able to drill just a little over 4 and a half feet a day. They just pick it up and drop it down over and over again. Frank Pickrell told me about his trip to New York. I loved the story of how the Catholic ladies shared how they were*

concerned about their investment and had gone to their priest to ask him to pray for the well to come in. Frank told me the priest suggested that if it did come in they should name it after Saint Rita because she is the patron saint of impossible things. He told me how the nuns brought an envelope containing rose petals blessed by their priest to the train station to him.

As you know, the Irish are famous for believing in blessings. Please tell the ladies that Frank did what the nuns told him to do. Upon their request and to the amazement of the drilling crew, Frank took the rose pedals in the envelope and climbed to the top of the rig. While everyone watched from below, he scattered the red pedals from the top of the derrick and proclaimed, "I hereby christen thee the Santa Rita." I like a man who does what he says he will do. I can certainly understand now why they call oil explorers "wildcatters."

Last week I invested more money into what is now known as the Santa Rita Number One. By the way Mozella has also invested in the well. Apparently the Everleigh sisters had been generous with her throughout her years, and she managed to save a sizeable amount of money. Believe in the miracle, Madeline. Frank is a man who won't give up!

*Sincerely yours,
Victoria Pearl*

Although the next letter showed failing glimmers of hope, the courage to pursue was still very much in play:

*February 9, 1923
Dear Madeline,*

The money has almost run out on the Santa Rita, and the permit will expire the end of May. Every day the "roughnecks" are still working hard. Tell the ladies to go double time on those prayers. After all, what is it that God cannot do? I cannot get over how much Frank reminds me of my father. He is so tenacious and strong willed. Last week I visited the site again. The land seems so dry; and there are hardly any trees. However, the men are still working every day, and Frank told me he will see it through to the end. My goodness, it has been almost a year and a half now since they put up the oil derrick.

The economy in San Angelo has picked up again, and business is good. I have ten lovely young women working with me and have maintained the standards we learned at the Everleigh House. My butterflies call me "Mother Pearl." Some of our clients talk about the Texon drilling efforts in Big Lake. I heard one man say, "They're just digging a big hole up there!" Another one said, "They are just a group of amateurs throwing their money away!" I said nothing although my Irish blood was boiling inside. It just seemed so flippant. I have to say that even though they do not agree there is oil in Big Lake, they are amazed that the "Texon wildcatters" have not yet quit.

Even though the circumstances look bleak, I refuse to be disheartened. It is not over until it is over, my friend. I wish you well. I would like to think you will be coming to San Angelo soon to celebrate the Santa Rita Number One coming in!

Sincerely yours,
Victoria Pearl

Finally Victoria Pearl wrote Madeline her last letter regarding the Santa Rita Number One:

May 12, 1923
Dear Madeline,

The Santa Rita Number One has reached 3,000 feet, and Frank is feeling completely discouraged. From the beginning, the rig has averaged 4.7 feet a day, and lately there seems to be new problems developing with every foot drilled. The permit will expire at the end of May, and they have just about run out of money. This is it. It is time for Santa Rita to start answering our prayers or all of our efforts will soon be over. I am trying my best to stay optimistic. Say hello to the ladies and your sister and tell them to keep praying! We need Santa Rita to step in and do the impossible. I will hold the vision of you and me celebrating with a bottle of champagne when the Santa Rita Number One finally comes in!

Sincerely yours,
Victoria Pearl

"Mozella," Pearl sighed as she sealed the envelope. "I think I will go down to the river to do a little fishing. I need to have a talk with Saint Rita."

PART TWO

The Lady Pearls

Texas Katie

San Angelo was a town that played by its own set of rules. It was not uncommon to hear about a fatal gunfight over some trivial disagreement; at least not serious enough to get shot over! Some people thought of San Angelo as a dangerous place to be, especially at night in the downtown saloons and bordellos.

On the other hand, Miss Pearl's Parlor was a different story. All the men in town knew they were not allowed to be disrespectful to any of the Lady Pearls. Miss Pearl did not tolerate the slightest bit of abuse and insisted the men treat her girls with kindness and appreciation. If a man acted less than a gentleman or started any trouble at all, he was asked to leave at once. If he protested, he had to deal with Texas Katie. She was a crack shot with either hand, and everybody knew it. Her first shot was always a warning shot, straight between the legs. Then she'd say, "I won't kill ya if I don't have to, but if ya don't get the hell outta' here right now, I might just shoot at somethin' yer quite fond of!"

Katie's Story

Katie was born an only child on a ranch just outside of Menard, Texas. Her mother died when she was born. It was clear by the way her daddy raised her that he had probably preferred she be a boy. He had four brothers himself and didn't know much about little girls. Growing up, she only had one dress at a time until she outgrew it. The only time she wore a dress was when they'd go to church, which was once a month, if that. The rest of the time Katie wore dungarees. Her daddy kept her hair short which made folks think she was a boy.

By the time Katie was five years old, she had learned to hunt and fish. When she was twelve, she could easily shoot a complete row of cans from 20 yards away. Her daddy could throw a can high into the air, and Katie would riddle it with holes before it landed on the ground. She could hit a bulls-eye with a bow and arrow, break a horse, start a fire by rubbing two sticks together, and dress a mess of fish for dinner. She was loyal and trustworthy, and she had a wealth of common sense. Katie had a great love for the state of Texas and was extremely proud of the fact that her Great, Great Uncle Ben had been part of the raid on Santa Anna's army at the Battle of San Jacinto when Texas won its independence.

Katie was a fighter, and all the boys knew to leave her alone, especially after she gave Froggy Bowman a black eye and sent him home crying after he had sneaked up behind her and tried to steal her minnow bucket. Katie was constantly guarded by her German-shepherd, Rusty, her most loyal friend and companion. They spent countless hours dove hunting. She'd shoot, and Rusty never missed retrieving the birds. Later, Katie dressed them and cooked them for supper. He was a good working dog, and Katie loved him dearly – the feeling was mutual.

One day Katie asked her father, "Pa, do you wish I were a boy?"

Her father looked at her and smiled. "Katie, I don't guess we'll ever know the answer to that. All I know is I love you, and it's just fine."

Her father was a hard working stubborn old man and had a high tolerance for pain. One day he came limping into the house. "What happened, Pa?" Katie asked.

"Fell off a ladder in the barn. Damnedest thing. Was nailing some loose boards, and a step on that old ladder just gave way. Next thing I know I was on my butt looking up at the ceiling of the barn. Got up and turned the ladder upside down so I could finish what I was doin'. Then I thought I better come back to the house."

"Good Lordy, Pa! Let's see what ya' did. Lay down here on the sofa, and let me have a look."

When Katie pulled off his boot, she saw that his ankle had blown up like a melon. "Looks like you broke your foot or your ankle, or both! I'll go to town and get the Doc. Rusty, you better stay here with Pa."

Katie saddled up her horse and rode into town to Doc Brown's place. About two miles from the house, while crossing the creek, a strange feeling came over her like some evil force was watching her. Katie had never known fear before. She had shot many a rattlesnake and was not afraid of anything that moved. One day she shot a bobcat while she and Rusty were fishing at the river. This felt different.

When she got to Doc Brown's, he was tending to a little boy who had taken a nasty fall off a hay wagon. "I'll be there soon as I can, Katie. Kind of busy today. Mrs. Lancaster is in labor. Don't worry, it's her fourth, and it shouldn't take too long."

Katie was anxious to get back to her father. She decided to go the General Store and pick up some pain medicine before she left. When she walked in, she saw two men she had never seen before looking at her. They were dirty, and their stench was so offensive she put her hand up to her nose to avoid the smell.

"Howdy Ma'am," the taller one leered. There was a knife scar along his right cheek. His yellow teeth were stained with tobacco and his friend was just as nasty.

Katie didn't respond.

"Hey pretty lady, I'm talkin' to you!" the scar-faced man shouted with contempt.

Katie still ignored him and turned to the clerk. "I need some headache powder and half a pound of hard candy, please."

"What's wrong? Too good to talk to us? Goddamn uppity bitch!"

The clerk pulled out a shotgun from behind the counter. "You won't be talkin' ugly like that in here! I think you boys best get out now and leave Miss Katie alone!"

"Miss Katie, eh? Yeah… we'll leave pretty little Katie alone," the shorter man sneered.

"Uppity bitch!" the scar faced man repeated.

Both men snickered as they sauntered outside. Their laugh was so sinister it sent a chill up Katie's spine. The shorter man smashed a bottle on the front porch.

CRASH!

"Hey! Looks like ya got a mess out here!" he laughed.

The clerk ran outside with the gun in his hand. "Y'all get the hell outta' here!" he yelled and shot the gun twice in the air. Both men laughed again and left in their truck.

"Damn, Joe! Who were those men?"

"Never saw them before, Miss Katie. Sorry bunch they were."

Katie picked up her items. "Thanks for coming to my rescue, Joe. You're a true gentleman and a scholar," she smiled.

As she rode out of town, Katie thought of those two disgusting men back at the store. She'd never seen men like that before, and the thought of them gave her a queasy feeling in the pit of her stomach.

As Katie rode home, the quiet was deafening. The men at the store had made her feel dirty, and all she wanted to do was to get home to her father. She pulled out her pocket watch to check the time. "If all goes well with that new baby, Doc shouldn't be more than a couple of hours," she thought to herself. Katie had keen instincts. Suddenly her heart started racing, and she wished Rusty was with her. Every nerve in her body was alert as if something evil was lurking around her. Although Katie was halfway home by now, it seemed as if she couldn't get home fast enough.

She had just put her pocket watch back into her saddle bag when suddenly one of the men from the store appeared from behind a clump of bushes and fired a shot. At the sound of the gun blast, Katie's horse reared up and pawed the air. She held on tightly and was able to stay on her horse. When the hooves finally hit the ground, the man grabbed the reins.

"Hey, Pretty Katie. Hey, Pretty Katie," the man with the scar chanted sarcastically.

By now the shorter man had come out and pulled Katie off her horse onto the ground while "scar-face" quickly tied the horse to a tree. Katie was strong, but the two men were stronger. She fought and kicked the men with all her strength. Their stink was putrid. Their laughter was diabolical. They looked at her like ravenous animals that hadn't eaten in days.

Katie managed to scratch the shorter man on the face, and when she did, she drew blood. The man screamed and hit her on the side of the head with his fist. Stunned for a moment, she stopped fighting. The two men took advantage of their weakened prey, tearing at her clothes.

The shorter man was strong and was holding her down. "Looks like we got us a virgin, TJ!"

"We're gonna' make sure you ain't no virgin no more, bitch. You're gonna be our whore," his partner sniggered unbuckling his belt.

No one was around. No one could hear her screams; at least that's what the men thought.

Katie had fought as hard as she could. At first the men seemed amused with Katie's struggle. The more she fought the more excited they became. She bit the scar-faced man on his arm. It made him angry and he slapped her. "Not so pretty now Miss Katie, you uppity bitch! You're just a nasty ugly whore!"

As the men invaded her precious body, Katie thought she was going to die. The pain was almost too much for her to bear, and at one time, she felt as if she were being torn in two. Katie instinctively decided to go limp like a possum who fakes his death. At least the hitting stopped. She kept coming in and out of consciousness and had lost all track of time. All she could do was wonder if the next breath she took, might be her last.

From outside her darkness, Katie heard one of the men bellow with agonizing pain. Rusty had heard her screams and was out for blood. Her loyal protector was gnawing on the scar-faced man's neck with a vengeance, showing no mercy to his victim. Both men, still wearing boots, were bound by their britches, limiting their ability to move freely. The shorter man was trying to scoot away from his partner's fate. Katie rolled over and grabbed a river rock lying beside her. With all the strength she could muster, she slammed it into his skull so hard the man stopped moving.

The taller man's pants were still wrapped around his ankles, and Rusty's muzzle was covered with his blood. The man was still screaming, while his partner was lying unconscious face down in the dirt. From some unknown place, Katie found a new source of strength that enabled her to run to her horse and pull her 30-30 from under the saddle blanket. She held it on the two men. Her face was bruised, and blood dripped down her leg. Her torn clothes hung loosely on her body. Both of the men were on the ground, bound by their own britches, preventing them from escaping.

Katie called Rusty off the screaming man; as he slowly regained consciousness, the shorter man began moaning and writhing in the dirt. Both men were bleeding. Her body was trembling with a burst of adrenaline that emerged from deep inside her soul. Now the look of fear was on their faces. The two men sensed that their doom was near.

"Bitch? Whore?" she repeated calmly, "Sorry fellas… 'fraid I'm gonna have to make sure you boys never do this again. Hell… you're both half dead anyway. Goodbye, boys. Can't say it's been nice knowin' ya."

BOOM!

BOOM!

Before either of them could say a word, Katie shot both of the men right between the eyes. For a moment, she stood and stared at their lifeless bodies. The evil was gone. Only the gentle sound of the West Texas wind blowing through trees remained.

"Good boy, Rusty. Good boy."

Katie dragged their corpses under a clump of bushes and covered both men with branches and brush. The men had hidden their truck in a patch of trees. Katie figured it was as good a place as any for it to be, at least for now. What Katie didn't notice was that the license plate on the truck buried in the trees read, "ARKANSAS."

Katie tottered into the creek and called Rusty to join her. She washed the blood off his fur and cleaned herself up. Katie put on an extra shirt and a pair of pants from her saddle bag. She couldn't think about the pain. Right now all she knew was that she had to get to the house as quickly as she could. Doc Brown was expected any time, and she wanted to be there when he arrived. She looked at her timepiece and was surprised that the whole ordeal had only taken less than half an hour. To her, it seemed like an endless visit to hell.

Katie mounted her horse, her body sore and shaky from her horrible ordeal. Riding home she felt emotionally numb. Katie decided to ignore her pain but rather to focus on taking care of business. When she entered the house, she found her father peacefully asleep with his foot elevated on a pillow, totally unaware of his daughter's nightmare. She went into the washroom, washed her face, and fixed her hair. There was a huge bruise on her left cheek, and her lip was cut and swollen.

Katie took Rusty outside to the barn and finished cleaning him up. "You saved my life, boy. You saved my life." As Katie wrapped her arms around her loyal friend, feeling her pain, he whimpered and licked her face.

An hour or so later, Doc Brown finally showed up in his motor car. Katie met him at the gate. "What in the world happened to you, girl?" he exclaimed when he saw Katie.

"I guess it just ain't our day, Doc! Went out to the barn to get a pail, and when I reached up the shelf fell, and a box full of tools fell on my face. I'll be all right. Just feeling kind of silly about it. Believe me, it looks worse than it really is. Did Mrs. Lancaster have her baby?" Katie asked, trying to change the subject.

"An 8-pound baby girl. Pretty little thing. Kind of reminded me of you when I brought you into the world. Your mother was a brave woman, Katie, God rest her soul. Such a nice lady."

Doctor Brown took care of Katie's father. "Don't think you broke it, Jim, but looks like a pretty nasty sprain. Just keep it wrapped up and try to stay off it a couple of weeks so it can heal. You're going to be fine real soon."

"Thank you, Doctor Brown. Sure appreciate you coming out here." Katie was doing her best to seem normal.

That night the moon was almost full. Katie waited for her father to fall asleep. She went to the barn and found a lantern and a shovel, saddled her horse, and rode out where she had left the two men's bodies. Rusty went with her. That evening Katie dug a deep hole and rolled her assailants' corpses into it. Katie felt satisfied.

"You'll never hurt anyone else again, you monsters, you filthy monsters!"

Katie worked all night and covered the grave, moving bushes and rocks. She made sure no one could ever find them. When Katie returned to the house, there was a bright line of orange and gold on the horizon welcoming a new day. Her father was in the kitchen drinking coffee. "Where ya been, Katie?"

"Rusty woke me up like he heard something. Went outside to check it out. Just an old coon messin' with the chickens. I took care of it, Pa." The story seemed to satisfy Katie's father. "How 'bout some breakfast?"

That night after Katie had done the dishes, she fell into her bed exhausted. All afternoon she hadn't shed a tear. Even now she was too tired to cry. She had just been too busy doing what she had to do.

For the next few weeks, Katie took care of the chores while her father's ankle healed. She couldn't get him to stay down. He was on his crutches soon, trying to resume his chores. "Now Pa, you know what Doc Brown told you; get off that ankle! I need you to get better!"

Three weeks later Sheriff Tusky drove up to the ranch. Katie and her father met him on the porch.

"How y'all doin'? Just came by to ask you folks if you know anything about a truck some kids found down at the creek bottom."

Katie's heart started racing. She realized this day had been inevitable.

"No sir, I don't," her father replied. "Been laid up with a bad foot the last couple of weeks."

Katie was trying to keep her cool. Her heart was thumping and her right knee began to shake. Luckily, no one noticed.

"It's from Arkansas. Found out it's stolen."

"Arkansas? That's strange," Katie commented in a matter-of-fact tone.

Katie's father thought of the night Katie had come in at dawn. He knew then that something wasn't right, and now he knew it had something to do with that truck.

"You're right, Katie. It's kinda strange. Way out of the ordinary for anything around here. Store clerk said there were two men who…" The sheriff looked at Katie hard for a long minute. He had known her since she was a little girl. Katie watched as both revulsion and sadness fell over him like a storm cloud darkening the day.

"Guess we'll never know," Sheriff Tusky surrendered. "Sorry to have bothered you folks. Good day, Miss Katie," he offered, tipping his hat.

Katie and her father watched Sheriff Tusky drive away. Both of them stood silently for a moment. Her father thought of Katie's bruised cheek and cut up face and her story about the coon in the chicken house. He knew then she was lying because she had never lied to him before. Now he understood she had been protecting him from the truth. "You know anything 'bout that truck, Katie?"

"I've been taking care of business since you hurt your foot, Pa. All is well," she answered.

"Good enough," her father encouraged. He opened up his arms and Katie saw the saddest eyes she had ever seen. "Come here little girl."

"Oh, Daddy…DADDY!"

It was the first time she was able to cry since that horrible day her precious virtue had been destroyed. Katie's father gently wrapped his big strong arms around her as she fell into his chest, sobbing. Her tears released three long weeks of anguish, worry, and pain.

"I love you, little Katie. I love you. We'll never speak of it again."

That evening Katie snuggled up close to her father like she had done so many times when she was a little girl. The warm light danced on Rusty's back as he lay contently on his blanket in front of the fire.

"Rusty saved my life, Pa. He saved my life."

"I know Katie. I know." He remembered how Rusty had burst through the screen door that afternoon he hurt his foot. "I love you, little girl."

"I love you too, Pa." For the first time since that horrible day at the creek bottom, Katie felt a sense of peace.

It was all that needed to be said, and although her father was gravely concerned, it was never mentioned again. Katie had two more wonderful years with her father on their West Texas ranch. Then one morning, Katie walked inside with some fresh eggs and found her father lying on the floor next to the kitchen table. His face was blue. She tried to revive him, but it was too late. Katie's father was gone.

Although Katie did her best to bury the memory of that terrible day, her life was never the same again. Now that her father had died, there was no reason to stay. She decided to sell the ranch and leave Menard County; however, she did manage to retain the mineral rights. The day before she left what Katie had come to know as home, she took Rusty to the creek bottom to visit the unmarked grave of the men who had so brutally violated her. It was the first time she revisited the area since that fateful day when two strangers had completely changed her world as she knew it.

The land seemed so peaceful that it was difficult to think it had once been hell on earth. She reached up, took a deep breath and, as she slowly lowered her arms, felt the warmth of a soft breeze blowing on her skin. As she looked at the trees surrounding her, she heard nature's music singing to her soul. "All is well. All is well."

Katie listened to the sound of the breeze blowing through the leaves and imagined what they would say if the trees could tell her story. "Once upon a time there was a little girl who liked to go fishing with her father. She came to the river often with her faithful dog, Rusty. One day the most horrible thing happened…"

Katie looked at the ground and remembered. The vision was too ugly to bear and in her mind saw the fear in the two men's faces. In that moment, she knew she didn't want *their* violation to be a part of her reality any longer. "I forgive you," she proclaimed aloud. "I forgive you." Suddenly the warm Texas breeze gently blew across her face and through her hair. Her heart felt free.

Katie found some small rocks and formed two crosses over the unmarked graves. "Father, please forgive me, as I forgive them."

Just then a small monarch butterfly fluttered out of the brush, dancing with delight. To Katie's surprise, it landed on her arm.

For a long time, the butterfly didn't leave. It even climbed on her finger. Smiling, she put her finger up to her nose. The butterfly lifted its delicate wings up and down slowly as if to say, "You are free now. Remember you are never alone."

"Thank you my little messenger." Katie looked up into the sky. "Thank you, God."

Katie and Rusty moved the 70 miles to San Angelo, Texas. One day while Katie was fishing on the Concho River, two women arrived with a bucket of minnows and began fishing on the bank a few yards down. One was a happy black woman and the other, an attractive middle-aged lady wearing a large brimmed sun hat. She looked over at Rusty and Katie.

"I like your dog," the woman smiled. "Beautiful day, isn't it! My name is Pearl."

Annabelle

Annabelle was quiet. Although her physical presence was lovely, sometimes it almost seemed as if she were an apparition who had crossed the veil of mystery into a world in which she did not belong. Her whimsical smile was intriguing to the men, but all the girls knew it only masked the emptiness that lingered deep within her heart. The look in Annabelle's eyes told a story of love-lost and a soul wandering in the darkness of loneliness and grief. The love of her life was gone, and she had learned how to be a superb actress in order to survive.

Annabelle's Story

Annabelle's father left when she was only three years old, and when he did, her mother became a housekeeper for the Williamson family in Kansas City. Annabelle's mother, Clarissa, had long wavy brown hair and crystal blue eyes. For many years, she was a beautiful woman hidden behind an apron and a broom. They lived in a small bungalow behind the Williamson's mansion where sometimes Mr. Williamson, usually with a strong smell of liquor on his breath, visited Annabelle's mother in the middle of the night. He stumbled and laughed and made stupid remarks as if he were the funniest man in the world. Annabelle remembered her mother looking at her with sad eyes as she moved her daughter from their bedroom to a small sofa in the front room. There she would sleep while her mother entertained Mr. Williamson behind a locked door.

When Annabelle turned sixteen, Mr. Williamson commented on how pretty she was. "She's a real beauty, Clarissa. I'll bet you looked like that when you were her age."

One afternoon, he came into the kitchen where Annabelle was alone, cutting vegetables while her mother was in the dining room polishing silver. He gave her a package wrapped in white paper and a frilly red bow. Annabelle opened it to find a dainty ornate silver music box and smiled as the tune "Daisy Daisy" played in her hand.

"Thank you, Mr. Williamson," Annabelle replied politely.

He picked up a strand of Annabelle's long wavy golden hair, "I like giving you presents, Annabelle. I want to buy you lots of presents. Anything you want if you are nice to me."

Clarissa overheard him from the dining room. She panicked and ran quickly into the kitchen. Mr. Williamson glared at her with a twisted smile, and she stared back for a long silent moment.

Breaking the spell, Mrs. Williamson sauntered into the kitchen from the main hallway. "Hello, everyone," she chirped. "Hello, dear," she sang to her husband. "What a lovely music box, Annabelle. Clarissa, remember the Turners are coming for dinner tonight, and Mrs. Turner is allergic to chocolate so make a lemony dessert. Also the cat made a mess upstairs in the blue bedroom."

Mr. Williamson mumbled, shook his head, and left the house. Although she was aware of the matter at hand, Mrs. Williamson acted as if nothing was going on. She knew everything that went on in her house, including the fact that the gift to Annabelle was from her husband. She had a small collection of music boxes she had received when they were first married; Clarissa had collected a half dozen, herself. Although nothing was said between the two women, they had a mutual understanding.

Clarissa gave into Mr. Williamson's desires to keep her job and never complained. As long as Clarissa was taking care of her husband, Mrs. Williamson didn't have to. Both women knew they were better off pretending nothing was really going on. For years, Clarissa quietly had done her work, going through the motions day-to-day, trying to manage and raise her daughter as best she could. She didn't have many options for work and was grateful to have a job at all.

Clarissa had run away with Annabelle's father when she was only seventeen; her own father was abusive to Clarissa, and although her mother knew her father was molesting their daughter, she never challenged him. Clarissa had an Aunt Beverly whom she adored. Her aunt's husband was a professor at Northwest Missouri State University in Maryville. When Clarissa was a young girl her mother sent her to visit Aunt Beverly to get some relief from the situation at home.

Panic washed over Clarissa with the events of the morning. Mr. Williamson, master of the house, always got what he wanted, no questions asked. Clearly, Annabelle was the new object of his affections, and Clarissa was worried. She felt like she was in an uncompromising situation and was afraid Annabelle would be trapped like she had been. She wanted more for her daughter, and sending her away was the best solution, at least for now.

That evening, Clarissa packed up Annabelle's belongings. The next day she would put her on a train to stay with her Aunt Beverly in Maryville, Missouri.

"Annabelle, dear, I called your Aunt Beverly. I've made arrangements for you to stay with her for a while. I think it will be the best thing for now. I'm not sure how much longer I'll be working here. Mr. Williamson will be angry when he sees you are gone, but I'll think of something. You deserve better, Annabelle, you just deserve better."

"But Mama, I don't want to leave you," Annabelle cried.

"You will only be 20 miles away, honey. We'll be together again, I promise. Aunt Beverly is a wonderful lady and will take good care of you. I'll figure it out," Clarissa promised and hugged her daughter. As she watched, Annabelle waving from the window of the train, she realized what a lovely young woman she had become.

Aunt Beverly was a 74 year old spunky woman, full of life, and although she missed her mother terribly, Annabelle quickly fell in love with Aunt Beverly and adapted well to her new home. In Maryville, a quaint town with friendly people, Aunt Beverly belonged to a quilting circle. Even though she was a bit feeble, her spirit was strong. Annabelle picked up extra money watching children during the day.

The first time Annabelle saw Billy sweeping off the porch of the grocery store in the downtown square of Maryville, he had just graduated from high school. Since Billy was an orphan, his Uncle Charlie, who owned the grocery store, had taken him in and hired Billy to stock, clean, and deliver groceries.

When Annabelle saw him, she could not stop staring. "Who is he?" she asked herself. As if he was reading her mind, Billy glanced up, tipped his hat, and smiled. Startled, Annabelle managed to return the smile.

"Hello, pretty lady!" Billy grinned.

"Hello," Annabelle responded with a smile.

It was love at first sight. "Hey, I get off in an hour. Why don't you come back, and I'll buy you a soda."

After that first day, Annabelle went to the store every day at 5:45 and waited for Billy to get off at 6. They spent every evening together; people smiled when they saw them together. Billy made Annabelle laugh, and Annabelle made Billy feel more like a man.

One evening in September, Billy presented Annabelle with a ring. "Marry me, Annabelle. You make me want to be a better man. Uncle Charlie is helping me get into the university. I'll work and go to school at night. I can do it as long as I have you. I love you so much!"

"Of course I'll marry you, Billy!" It was decided they would marry in June.

World War I had turned into a major blood bath, especially for the British. As the number of casualties grew overseas, it was becoming more and more apparent that Billy might be drafted and called to serve. The young couple decided not to wait. Therefore on March 7, 1918, Annabelle and Billy recited their wedding vows with the Justice of the Peace in Maryville, surrounded by Clarissa, Aunt Beverly and Uncle Charlie.

It was both a happy occasion and a very solemn one as well. Clarissa was both excited and worried for her daughter. Billy moved into Aunt Beverly's with Annabelle. Sometimes Beverly went to a friend's to give the couple some privacy for a few hours. Whenever the newlyweds had the house themselves, as far as they were concerned, it was the happiest place on earth.

By June of 1918, Billy had been drafted. Billy and Annabelle did their best to cheer each other up, but the darkness of the war took the young couple from joy to despair. A few days before Billy left, they spent the weekend in a small cabin on Mozingo Lake. It rained all day Saturday, so they spent all day in bed, the happiest and saddest day for them both.

The day Billy left, Annabelle had a horrible feeling she might never see him again. "I'll write you every day!" she promised. "Come home to me, Billy!"

As soon as she returned home from the train station, she ran inside, went directly to the desk, pulled out a piece of paper, and started to write.

My Dearest Billy,

It has been less than an hour since I have seen you, and my heart aches so much I feel it will burst! I am thinking about our time at the lake, and if I close my eyes, I can relive every precious moment of our time together on that rainy Saturday. I see the light in your eyes when you looked at me when we made love and the way you held me in your arms after our sacred union was complete. You made me laugh so hard when you danced around the room. It was the best day of my life. I think of the first day we met and all of our happy times together. I choose to think of these memories when I am missing you, my darling. Our tears at the train are still washing over my broken heart. I love you so much, Billy. You are my life and my soul. I can't write anymore right now. The tears have clouded my eyes, and I can no longer see. I will write you tomorrow my love.

Your loving wife,
Annabelle

Aunt Beverly invited Clarissa to move in; she gladly accepted. She had had enough of Mr. Williamson and more than that, she needed to be close to her daughter. Clarissa found work as a clerk in downtown Maryville. Annabelle wrote Billy every day, sometimes two or three pages, sometimes just a paragraph. Either way, she kept her promise. Getting mail to the soldiers was difficult, but when letters finally arrived, nothing was more precious. Billy kept a photo of Annabelle with him. He was not emotionally prepared for the hell of war; none of the boys were. His company had to shave the hair on their bodies because they had been infected with lice. Rotting corpses of boys and young men in shallow graves were so common he became immune to the reality of what he smelled. Fear consumed Billy as random bullets blew by, sometimes killing a young man he had been talking to just minutes before.

The day he opened Annabelle's letter with the happy news, Billy cried out loud with joy, "I'm going to be a dad everyone! My wife's going to have a baby!" Billy was filled with excitement. He was going to be a father and that changed everything. He managed to find some paper and wrote:

My Dearest Annabelle,

I just received the news that you are carrying our child! Right now, I am the happiest man on earth because the most beautiful woman in the world is having my baby. I think we can both agree it was that rainy day on the lake. I remember the exact moment we conceived. It was in a perfect timeless moment where love is all there is. Because I love you so much, I want to tell you what is on my heart.

I am scared, my dear Annabelle. I am not afraid of dying, only of the possibility of never seeing you again. My life is under constant threat. We never know when bullets will be fired at us and shells are exploding every minute of the day. Men all around me are dying; if not from a stray bullet, they are falling with fever and disease. I can hardly sleep because of the booming and banging of the shells from both sides. I sleep on a bunk which has been placed in a dug out section of the trench. The floor and the roof are both made of mud, and the constant threat of the random bullets keeps me awake.

The smell is unbearable with body odor, death, and sewage. The mustard gas lingers for days after an attack. Rain constantly fills the trenches, and the men have sores on their feet that are so painful they can hardly walk. Four friends in my squad have already died and my best friend JT shot himself in the foot because he couldn't take this crazy war anymore. He's in an army hospital and will be going home soon.

Last night most of the A and B squads were killed before they were even 10 yards out of the trench. My squad will be climbing out of the trench tonight to attack the enemy. It all seems so barbaric and a futile waste of human life, but the powers seem to think we need to move forward even though they keep sending these poor souls to their deaths.

If I die tomorrow, I know I have experienced both heaven and hell in this lifetime. You are my heaven, my joy, and my happiness. I love you beyond words, and I love our little baby. Love is the greatest power of all, and I know we will somehow be together again.

Please take care of yourself and know it is the thought of you that feeds my soul and fills my heart every moment I am in this hell-on-earth. I pray this letter finds you and that this will be one of many more letters to come. However, if I never see you again in this lifetime, know that I am with you always.

I love you with all of my heart, my sweet Annabelle. Your loving husband, Billy

Billy's letter arrived several weeks after the telegram came. Both broke Annabelle's heart. Clarissa answered the door and took it to Annabelle who was sitting on the sofa.

IT IS MY PAINFUL DUTY TO INFORM YOU THAT A REPORT THIS DAY HAS BEEN RECEIVED FROM THE WAR OFFICE THE DEATH OF WILLIAM ELLIS KING WHICH OCCURRED ON OCTOBER 14, 1918 AND I AM TO EXPRESS TO YOU THE SYMPATHY AND REGRET OF THE

ARMY COUNCIL AT YOUR LOSS. THE CAUSE OF DEATH WAS KILLED IN ACTION.

Annabelle wailed at the news. "No! No! No!" she screamed. She rocked back and forth as she held her middle, feeling the tender life moving inside her womb. Then she fainted.

Annabelle was heartbroken, beyond grief. Many days Annabelle did not get out of bed, and when she did she wandered around the house singing, *"Over there, over there, the Yanks are coming, the Yanks are coming,"* in a daze. Clarissa was fearful that Annabelle was losing her mind. She was in her third trimester, and Clarissa and Aunt Beverly had to force her to eat.

Sometimes Annabelle said crazy things, like "Mama, I'm going to the store to see Billy. He gets off at six you know. We'll be home for dinner."

One day out of the blue, Annabelle, with tears rolling down her eyes, whispered "He's gone, Mama." Clarissa was on the sofa knitting a blanket for the baby. It was the first time her daughter had made any sense or even cried since that horrible day she had fainted when she learned the news that Billy had died in action.

Laying her knitting down, she gently put her arms around Annabelle. "I know, baby." Clarissa led Annabelle to the sofa and helped her sit down. Then from the depths of her soul Annabelle screamed, "My Billy's gone, Mama! He's gone forever!"

Clarissa reached for a pillow and put it on her lap. With tears streaming down her face, she held her daughter and stroked her hair as she felt Annabelle's body shake with long painful sobs. "My Billy is gone, Mama. He's never coming back!" Weeks of anguish purged from Annabelle as her mother struggled to sooth her despair. Nothing she could say or try to do could make it better. Her heart was breaking for her daughter.

Finally the blessed day came, and Annabelle gave birth to a healthy baby girl. "I will call her Julie Marie," Annabelle declared. Billy's mother's name was "Julie."

Little Julie became Annabelle's whole world. She was a beautiful child with blonde curly hair and her father's big blue green eyes. Annabelle loved on her, danced and played with her, taught her songs, and read to her every night. Although the small family was destitute, they were happy, and little Julie was the light of their lives.

When Julie Marie was two years old, Clarissa was making less than $9 a week as a clerk, and Aunt Beverly had become feeble and never left the house. Annabelle stayed home and took care of little Julie and her Aunt. Money had become so scarce that Clarissa became desperate. There was no money and debts had to be paid. There was no way out. Clarissa went to Kansas City to ask her former employers if they could please help out, but when Mr. Williamson saw her he was hateful and rude. All those years she had satisfied his needs meant nothing to him. Mrs. Williamson managed to give Clarissa money when he left the room. "Here's $400, Clarissa. It's the least I can do, you putting up with that old son-of-a-bitch all those years."

"I am so sorry. I didn't know what to do, and I was afraid he would fire me if I told him no. I knew you had to know," Clarissa exclaimed. She had always suspected his wife knew. After all this time, the two women were finally able to acknowledge it.

"Of course I did. In fact, I feel a little guilty, Clarissa. All those nights I told him no when he was drunk, I knew where he went. The way I saw it, every time you were doing my wifely duty, I didn't have to, so I never fussed about it."

With that, both women hugged each other knowing that neither of them really had a choice to do what they had done.

"Take care of that little grandbaby of yours. I will be praying for you," Mrs. Williamson demurred. "I wish I could have had children. You are blessed."

"Thank you again for the money, Mrs. Williamson!"

"Call me Edith," she smiled.

On a Sunday morning, a few days after Clarissa returned from Kansas, Aunt Beverly drew her last breath. Now that she was gone, it changed everything.

"I don't want to stay here, Mama. Let's go start over somewhere," Annabelle pleaded.

Annabelle went to Uncle Charlie, who had kept them in groceries the last year since Billy had died in the war. "Mama and I need to go, Uncle Charlie. Everywhere I look I see Billy. Can you help us?"

With Uncle Charlie holding an estate sale and buying the house and furniture, there was enough money to pay off all their debts. So with the money Mrs. Williamson had given her and the little money left over from selling the household goods, Annabelle, Clarissa, and little Julie Marie went to the train station. All they had were their suitcases and a couple of Aunt Beverly's trunks filled with some essentials and some precious keepsakes like the family Bible.

"Where should we go?" Clarissa asked her daughter, as they stood in line to buy their tickets.

"Let's go to Texas. Billy often said he wanted to go to Texas."

"Why not? Let's go to Texas!" Clarissa declared.

The women were both excited and fearful. The future was a mystery, and they felt they were walking into an abyss. They took their seats on the train and began a new adventure to God-knows-where. Looking out the window, little Julie Marie slapped on the glass and squealed with glee, waving to people as the train pulled out of the station. People smiled and waved back.

Clarissa patted Annabelle's hand. "God will provide, sweetheart. We need a little faith. Remember the story of the mustard seed."

Julie Marie played with her doll as Annabelle stared out the window. She looked at the countryside passing by, putting distance away from the only life she had ever known. After a few minutes, she noticed that Julie Marie was playing peek-a-boo with an attractive middle aged woman, sitting in the seat across from them. The woman had a kind smile and was elegantly dressed. Annabelle watched as the woman put her hands over her face and then spread them out playfully, saying, "Peek-a-boo!" Every time she did, Julie Marie giggled with delight and did the same.

"She likes you," Annabelle smiled.

"She's a beautiful child," the woman beamed. "I can't wait to get back to Texas. My husband died over a year ago and I've been in Chicago visiting some old friends. I have a new friend with me but she's resting right now."

For a few minutes, the women rode in silence, Annabelle staring out the window and thinking about her Billy and their weekend on the lake. Tears filled her eyes as she replayed that magical day like the thousands of times before.

"I lost my Billy in the war. This is our little girl. She looks just like him," Annabelle told the woman.

"He must have been handsome. She's a beautiful child. Where are you going, if I may ask?" the woman inquired.

"We're going to Texas!" Clarissa chimed in.

"Where in Texas?" the woman asked.

"It might sound crazy but we're not really sure," Clarissa replied. "We're starting a new life. My name is Clarissa. This is my daughter Annabelle and this little lady is Julie Marie."

"Very pleased to meet all of you. Such a lovely family." The woman looked at Clarissa. "I can see where Annabelle gets her good looks."

Clarissa hadn't heard a compliment like that in years; it made her feel good. "Thank you," she blushed.

"Wass-ure name?" Julie Marie asked in her sweet little voice.

"My name is Victoria little princess, but you can call me Miss Pearl. Very pleased to meet you," she smiled.

Ginger

Hard as nails, difficult to impress, cold and beautiful, Ginger gave the illusion that she had a heart of stone. However, people who knew her were well aware that she was as loyal as a ropin' horse, smart as a whip, and sexy as hell. At 24, Ginger was the oldest, most experienced girl at Miss Pearl's Parlor. She knew what to do and how to do it with style. Ginger had learned all she knew about being a first class courtesan in New Orleans and was a star student in the School of Hard Knocks. It was rare to see Ginger smile, but when she did, it was like a ray of sunlight in a forest thick with trees. There were men who saw her as a challenge and loved her bitchy ways. Ginger always had the same phrase for each client every time she shut the door. "Let's see whatcha got, Lover Boy."

Ginger's Story

Ginger Lee was born in the heart of the bayou amongst still cool water, cascading cypress trees and Spanish moss. Only crickets and small choruses of bullfrogs broke the silence of the darkness of the swampland. The bayou was eerie and full of mystery to those unfamiliar with its musty air, but to Ginger it was home. Ginger grew up in a small wood framed house with no plumbing or electricity, and the only time she wore shoes was in the winter and to church on Sunday. Her father hunted alligators throughout south Louisiana and sold their hides. Ginger's mother worked in a place called Storyville, a red-light district in New Orleans. As Ginger grew older, often her mother was gone for weeks at a time. This always seemed to be all right with Ginger's father because the way he saw it, the longer his wife stayed away, the more money she would bring back home.

Daisy Parks was a black girl whose family lived on the bayou and Ginger's best friend. In those days white children went to different schools from the "colored." Besides school, Daisy and Ginger shared their lives. Daisy's people spoke Creole, a language created from English and from French and Native Americans of the region. Some of the young men from the area, including two of Daisy's cousins, had been recruited to serve as French interpreters in the war overseas. Ginger's parents spoke English, so Ginger knew how to converse in both worlds.

Ginger stayed with Daisy's people most of the time. Daisy's family were sharecroppers and opened their hearts and their home to little Ginger. The girls were inseparable and spent most of their days at Daisy's grandmother Mamie's house. Living on the bayou was a happy time with Daisy's family, full of singing and laughter. They treated Ginger like part of the family, and because of this she never knew she was poor, or that she was white, or that she was trash. When her mother was home, she and her daddy were drunk and treated Ginger like she was invisible.

Every Sunday morning Ginger and Daisy went to church together. Although everyone in the church was black, they never treated Ginger differently. The first Sunday of every month was the best because all the women took "soul" food, turnip greens, cornbread, mashed potatoes, black-eyed peas, fried chicken, cobblers, and banana pudding. It was in this little country "black church" on the bayou where Ginger learned how to sing. When Mayasha Jones opened her mouth, her heart and soul rose and spread like sunshine across the room. Her delivery was so powerful that people swore heaven would open the gates to let Mayasha's voice ring throughout the celestial realm. Everyday Ginger practiced singing, doing her best to imitate her idol, Mayasha Jones.

When Preacher Joplin spoke about Jesus and his great promise of love, the Holy Spirit moved through the congregation. At first it started slowly like a soft breeze. People shouted "Amen," affirming the preacher's words as he told stories from the Bible. Ginger especially liked to hear about Moses in the desert. Like a powerful tidal wave, the spirit washed over the entire congregation. The black folks sang and waved their hands in the air. Many of them had their eyes closed. There was nothing like it in the world! When Preacher Joplin spoke, the power of the Holy Spirit and a great appreciation for the love of Jesus and his sacrifice were flowing like a raging river through the souls of these good people. This was Ginger's real family, and when she was at church, her heart was full.

One night sitting on the front porch of her grandmother's house, Ginger and Daisy saw an iridescent light rising up from the ground like smoke.

Daisy was curious. "What is that Mamie? It looks like a ghost!"

"Oh, honey, that be foxfire," Mamie told the girls. "It don't happen too much, just when the night is still on the bayou and the air is cold and some animal or tree has died. Gasses rise up from the dead and make a stream of light that look like colored smoke. It's a little creepy, but it can be pretty."

Life on the bayou was good for Ginger when she was at Mamie's house. Mamie took care of her when her mother was gone, which was most of the time. Ginger loved Mamie and especially loved to hear her stories about the slaves who worked on the big Southern plantations. "Mother said singin' was the only real thing that got them through the day. They'd sing songs about Jesus, the River Jordan, and how good it was going to be when they reached heaven. Sometimes they'd make up their own words and used the singin' fo' communication. The white folks didn't allow the black folks in the field to talk with each other 'cuz they was afraid they'd be makin' plans to run," Mamie smiled. "My grandmother told me white folks took their drums away after losin' some of their slaves. That drummin' can stir up the soul and make a body run faster than the wind. Singin' was how the slaves learned about the Underground Railroad. Seemed there was always a black snitch gettin' special treatment for reportin' anything suspicious back to the mastah. When he'd show up they'd start singin' *Jimmy Crow.* Ya know a crow is a blackbird that yaks too much. That was the signal to go back to singin' the spirituals. Sometimes white folks paid a lots of money for slaves. Some of them folks was so mean. They did things to slaves I won't evah' tell you children. Mother's people were treated all right. That's why they stayed loyal even after the war."

Sometimes Ginger's Uncle Ed hung around the house. He chewed tobacco and his smell was nasty and foul. When Ginger was 10 years old, she learned it was not a good idea to be with Uncle Ed alone. One afternoon when her folks were gone, he suggested she do things to him that made her feel sick in her stomach.

"No Uncle Ed!" she screamed. "I don't want to!"

"I'll give you a dime," he grinned with the few teeth that were left in his mouth. "And some candy too."

Ginger pushed herself away, kicked him in the shins and ran away to Daisy's house. She told Mamie what happened.

"Some men are like that honey. They're just like that. You stay away from your Uncle Ed." From then on, Ginger's stomach turned every time Uncle Ed came over to her house. When he did, she'd go to Mamie's and stay. Ginger couldn't bear to even look at him. Ginger's mama didn't care where her daughter stayed. One day, Ginger told her Mama about Uncle Ed, and when she did, her mother didn't say a word. She just lit up a cigarette and sauntered outside.

Daisy and Ginger were like sisters. Ginger never understood why the white folks always thought they were better than black folks and why she had to go to a different school. When Ginger was 12 years old, the state of Louisiana started punishing children in schools for speaking French. This was another rule she didn't understand - punishing someone for talking the way they always talked?

Ginger turned 16 years old in May of 1915. Her mother was home more these days, so Ginger tried to stay away from her house as much as possible. Her mother was either passed out or at least half drunk and said hateful things to Ginger. Ginger had always made good grades in school, but her mother could not have cared less. She had never gone to school past the fourth grade and had never so much as looked at any of Ginger's report cards.

"You think you're so high and mighty. I bet you think you're better than me!" her mother slurred. "Well ya ain't. You're white trash, girl, and don't you forget it!"

At 34 years old, Ginger's mother had lived a hard life. The years were catching up to her. As Ginger made her transition into an attractive young lady, the woman was becoming more and more jealous of her daughter.

"You still got your cherry?" she asked Ginger one day.

"What's that?"

"You still a virgin, girl? I mean you ever had a man stick his thing in you?"

Her mother had never looked at her that way before. She had a nasty smile on her face, and Ginger felt like she had the day Uncle Ed wanted her to do those horrible things to him.

"I gotta go, Mama!" The sound of her mother's laughter sent a cold chill up Ginger's spine as she ran out the door. Like so many times before, Ginger ran to Daisy's house to find refuge from her mother's drunkenness.

"Mamie!" she cried. "Mama asked me if I'm a virgin! She asked me if I still had my cherry. What does all that mean?"

Mamie was gravely concerned. "Oh child, dear child," she answered, shaking her head. Like everyone else in these parts, she knew about Ginger's mother. Mamie was fearful for Ginger, but she knew there was nothing she could do about it. Hiding her could only bring danger to her family. All she could do was pray for the Lord to take care of her adopted granddaughter. When Ginger came home the next evening, her mother was gone. Summer vacation had begun, and Ginger and Daisy had decided to make a kind of summer camp for the younger children at the church. They had been making plans for weeks, and the children were excited.

Daisy was enthusiastic. "We can teach them stories from the Bible. We can make it fun."

"I want to sing with them," Ginger piped in. She loved to sing and had become very good at imitating Mayasha's style. Sometimes Ginger went to Mayasha's house and the two of them sang together.

"You can do it, Ginger! You've got the gift. Just close your eyes, and let the Spirit move through you," Mayasha told her. "Singing for folks is about making people feel what you feel. When you sing with your soul, their soul hears it; so let it go, girl!"

Two weeks after Ginger's mother had left, she showed up again one afternoon with a brand new attitude. She even looked different than Ginger was used to seeing her. Her mother was dressed in a clean white cotton dress, and her hair was brushed and neatly pulled up.

"Ginger, honey, I'm sorry I've been so ugly to you. Looky here. I have a new pretty dress I bought for you in New Orleans. I'm taking you there, Baby! I'm taking you to New Orleans!" Ginger had never been to town or the city before.

"Oh Mama! Thank you, Mama! I need to go tell Daisy I'm going to New Orleans! We're supposed to start summer camp for the kids at church on Sunday. I need to tell her I'm leaving. How long will we be gone?"

"There's no time for that now, Ginger. We'll be back by Saturday. You can buy Daisy a present when we're there. Now get your dress on, and let's go. We're going to have so much fun!"

Ginger had not seen her father in weeks, and although she didn't know it at the time, she would never saw him again.

Ginger had never been more than two miles from the little shack in the bayou and had never called it home. Mamie's house was Ginger's home, as far as she was concerned. On the train making its way to New Orleans, Ginger was in awe of all of the new sights. There were different kinds of trees, and the land had countless different shades of green. Ginger saw big houses, little houses, small towns, wild flowers, farms, and grazing cattle. Ginger spent the entire trip at the window and barely spoke to her mother. She wanted to take it all in!

"Thank you for bringing me to town with you, Mama."

Ginger's mother neglected to respond at all. She just lit up a cigarette

When the train arrived in New Orleans, Ginger's stomach was filled with butterflies. In the train station, she saw a black man playing a saxophone with a few coins in his saxophone case. As they headed into Storyville, her mother barely spoke to her. The three story mansions stacked together

closely on Basin Street were like nothing else Ginger had ever seen. If the walls could have talked, what colorful stories they would tell. Storyville was the home of painted ladies, the birthplace of jazz, and a place where laughter and lonely hearts came together as one.

Ginger's mother stopped in front of one of the big mansions, took a deep breath, and then looked at the daughter she barely knew. "We're going in to meet Miss Georgia Louise Allison, Ginger. I want you to smile and be on your best behavior."

When Ginger's mother knocked on the door, a black man dressed in a dark suit and white gloves answered. Ginger's mother was anxious. "I have an appointment with Madame Georgia."

"Yes Ma'am." He wouldn't look at Ginger. "Won't you come in, and have a seat? Can I get you some iced tea?"

"That would be nice," Ginger's mother answered.

A few minutes later, a middle-aged woman wearing strands of pearls and a diamond ring on every finger appeared.

"Is this her?" The woman asked. "You were right. She is a pretty girl. What's your name, honey," the woman asked.

"Ginger."

"Well, Ginger, we're going to get you all prettied up. Tonight is the big night, you know. We've got some men coming just to see you."

Madam Georgia looked at Ginger's mother. "You sure she's a virgin?"

"Yes, yes," she answered. "Can I have my money now? I gotta go."

Madame Georgia handed Ginger's mother a bulging envelope containing $1000. She opened the envelope and looked inside. "It's all there like we agreed," Madame Georgia assured her.

Ginger's mother headed toward the door.

"Mama, where are you going?" Ginger asked.

"You be a good girl, Ginger. Just do what Miss Georgia tells you, and you'll be fine."

"Mama?"

Her mother did not even say "goodbye." Ginger never saw her mother again.

"You look like a good investment. I'll get at least 3 times what I paid for you tonight alone," Madame Georgia told her.

A woman in her early twenties entered the room. Georgia's tone was stern. "This is Carla. You will spend the afternoon with her. She'll get you ready and tell you what you need to do. Don't let me down, Ginger. You belong to me now, and I'll take care of you. Just don't let me down!"

As Ginger followed Carla up a massive circular staircase, her heart was fearfully thumping. Her mother was gone, and Ginger had no idea how to get home. Carla led her into a big room full of women sitting on single beds. She sensed Ginger's fear and tried to be helpful. "You don't know do you, honey?"

"Know what?"

"Your mama sold you, Child. You belong to Madame Georgia now."

Ginger felt confused and alone. She thought about Uncle Ed, but this was ten times worse. At least then she had Mamie to run to. This is why she was so concerned. She wanted her Mamie; she wanted Daisy; she wanted to run!

Sensing Ginger's fear, Carla took her hand and gave it a squeeze. "It'll be okay, honey. We'll help you through it. You ain't the first girl whose Mama sold them to Miss Georgia."

Ginger was unable to speak. All she could do was stare.

Carla was kind to Ginger and introduced her to the other girls. Most of them looked her up and down. Some attempted to be helpful and give her advice. Joanie, a big busted girl, tried to make light of it. "What we do here, Ginger, is a noble thing. We're just trying to prevent men from going blind!" With that, all the women in the dormitory laughed.

Another girl with long red hair spoke next. "If you don't like it, just close your eyes and pretend you're somewhere else. It works for me!"

Carla was more sympathetic. "All you need to know is that it will be over soon enough. Most of the time, it don't even take 5 minutes!"

"Yeah, we call that 'wham, bam thank ya Ma'am,'" Joanie mimicked sarcastically.

"Try to relax, and whatever you do, don't let anyone see you cry, especially Madame Georgia!" Carla advised.

The word had spread quickly that Madame Georgia had a new virgin she was going to sell to the highest bidder. Carla told Ginger what she needed to do. By the time the festivities for the evening were on their way, Ginger was as ready as she could ever be. For the first time in her life, Ginger took a bath in a real bathtub. Madame Georgia gave her a new lovely white dress to wear, and Carla helped her fix her hair and painted her face with rouge and lipstick. The redheaded girl gave Ginger a shot of whiskey. "Drink this, honey. It'll relax you."

That evening, Madame Georgia sat Ginger in a chair that looked like a throne, sitting on a small stage. Ginger had a strange sense that she was not in her body, to everyone there she looked like a porcelain doll. Was she having a bad dream? It was as if she were deep inside of a well listening to strange echoes bouncing off the walls. "Two-thousand! Twenty-five-hundred!" As she heard the men call out the numbers, Ginger thought of the stories Mamie would tell about slave auctions. The whiskey had made her emotionally numb, and the faces in the room were swirling around making the whole event seem surreal.

Finally the bidding stopped at $3500, the highest bid at the brothel to date. Everyone applauded as Madam Georgia ceremoniously led Ginger and a small framed, middle-aged gentleman up the stairs.

An hour later, he came down and when he did, everyone applauded again. Madame Georgia took Carla to the side. "Go upstairs, and check on Ginger," she directed. Carla knocked, but when she heard nothing, she opened the door. Ginger looked at Carla with her brown eyes as big as saucers.

"Are you all right, honey?" Carla asked with concern

"I thought you said it would only take 5 minutes," Ginger quizzed.

"Oh, honey, I'm so sorry. Everyone is different. Remember I said most of the time."

"I don't even think it took 2," Ginger commented looking confused.

Carla laughed. "Oh my, Ginger honey! What did you do for an hour?"

"We just visited. He was a real nice man. He told me he needed to stay up here a while to impress his friends. He gave me a $100 tip! Kept telling me I remind him of his daughters."

Carla laughed again. "It's either that or their nieces. Men can be so predictable sometimes."

That night, for the first time in her life, Ginger slept on a real mattress with real sheets that smelled like fresh soap. The next morning she had eggs, bacon, roasted potatoes with onions and bell peppers, coffee, and orange juice. She loved living in a big fine house, and she quickly adapted to her new lifestyle.

Ginger's mother had signed the proper documents; Madame Georgia was now Ginger's new legal guardian. The next week Georgia bought her 5 new dresses, shoes, and stockings. All of the girls at Madame Georgia's were friendly enough, and Ginger quickly learned the trade. Three weeks after Ginger had arrived at Madame Georgia's, she was homesick. She missed Daisy, Mamie, and all of her friends on the bayou. Wondering if Daisy had done the church camp without her, Ginger realized she had fallen in love, with jazz, good food, new clothes, clean sheets, and having money to spend. Some called it a *den of sin*, some called it a *good time.* Whatever it was, Ginger had fallen in love with New Orleans.

One night a Creole man named Ferdinand LaMothe, went to Madame Georgia's to play the piano and entertain for a special party. Basin Street knew him as Jelly Roll Morton. His grandmother had kicked him out of the house when she learned he had been playing music in Storyville. Although his grandmother called it "devil music," it was said that Jelly Roll invented jazz piano. He had recently had success with his composition, "Jelly Roll Blues," the first real jazz sheet music ever published. As Ginger listened to Jelly Roll play, she felt like she was in music heaven because his style and rhythms reminded her of going to church on the bayou. Ginger had been humming along while Jelly Roll played a slow, bluesy tune. He picked up on her style and called her over to the piano. "Girl, you got that soul. You is a black singer in a white body. I can feel it in you. Sing me a song."

"'*Wade in the Water*' is my favorite," Ginger smiled. "Mamie said it was a song slaves sang to each other to remind black folks who were planning an escape to stay in the water to throw bloodhounds off their trail."

As Jelly Roll broke into a slow slide with a walking base, Ginger closed her eyes, humming and moving with the music. All eyes were on Ginger. As she sang, the men lusted and the girls smiled. Ginger remembered what Mayasha had told her, "Close your eyes, and feel it from your soul. If you do, anyone listening will hear it in their soul at the same time."

At first her voice was soft and deliberate. "*Wade in the water, wade in the water, children, wade in the water, God's gonna trouble the water.*" Ginger closed her eyes and forgot anyone else was in the room. She let the Spirit move through her and everyone felt it. With each verse, Ginger's voice became louder, "*Wade in the water, wade in the water, children, wade in the water, God's gonna trouble the water.*"

It was as if she and the piano were one, like dancing a perfect dance or making love with a good lover. Ginger, singing from her soul, saw Daisy and Mamie. In her mind she could see Mayasha, and then she saw everyone at the church on the bayou. "*Who's that young girl dressed in red, must be the children that Moses led.* Ginger thought about her first time with a man. *Who's that young girl dressed in white, must be the children of the Israelite.*" Ginger thought about how her mother betrayed her, and her heart felt a bolt of pain. "*Who's that young girl dressed in blue, must be the children coming through. God's gonna trouble the water."* Ginger thought about how Jesus was betrayed and forgave. In that moment, she forgave her mother. The Spirit was moving through her, and she felt free. For the first time ever, Ginger felt free. *"Wade in the water, wade in the water, children, wade in the water, God's gonna trouble the water."*

When the piano stopped, the room had ceased to breathe. Jelly Roll stood up from the piano and kissed Ginger on the cheek. The Spirit had moved through this white girl with the black soul. Both men and women had tears in their eyes. Jelly Roll Morton sat back down and played his "Jelly Roll Blues," and Ginger's spell was broken, at least for now.

From then on, Madame Georgia featured Ginger as a singer in her parlor. She became popular and business picked up as Ginger's reputation spread throughout the city. Piano players in Storyville were known as "professors." The regular piano player at Madame Georgia's was an older black man named Duke, a master at playing slide piano blues and jazz. Ginger loved singing with Duke, and Duke loved playing for Ginger. When Ginger turned 18, Madame Georgia gave her a huge birthday party. Jazz musicians from all over the city showed up, including Jelly Roll. Ginger had become accustomed to her life in Storyville. Jazz was in her soul, and Ginger became as much a part of New Orleans as the French Quarter.

America had entered the War in 1917. Because of the huge outbreak of syphilis, the American Social Hygiene Organization had organized a campaign to shut down places like Storyville. In the early days of conflict, 4 American soldiers had been murdered within only a few weeks of each other in Storyville. The Secretary of the Navy cited Storyville and forced the popular district to close down under strong protest from the New Orleans government. Now that Storyville was officially shut down, the "sporting" business was forced to go underground. There was segregation between white and black brothels, and "the business" changed. Ginger found work singing with different jazz bands and kept a few favorite clients on the side. The money wasn't as good. Ginger had saved a little, and the clients she had kept got her by.

In 1918, when World War I was finally over, America began repairing itself. Women who had taken jobs were out-of-work when the men returned, and unemployment for women skyrocketed. Now jobs for women were limited. Other than being a department store clerk, a maid, or a factory worker, women found it difficult to be employed. It was the prostitutes that made the most money.

Prohibition had taken over, and underground bars called "Speakeasies" opened throughout big cities everywhere including New Orleans. Ginger landed a job, singing with a jazz band at a speakeasy in the French Quarter. Duke was still her piano player.

"I think I'm ready for a change, Duke," she told him one day. "Think maybe I'd like to move to Texas. I like Texas gentlemen. They were always so nice to be with."

"I've got a sister in Texas," Duke told her. "Her name is Mozella; she is working for a woman she knew from her days in Chicago. I believe she is opening a business in San Angelo. Her name is Victoria Pearl."

Ginger wrote Mozella, and they exchanged a couple of letters before Ginger decided to go to San Angelo, Texas. Before she left for Texas, she decided she wanted to find her friend Daisy.

It didn't take too long for Ginger to figure out how to make her way back to her roots. Somehow the bayou looked different now or was it she who had changed? The house where she had grown up was deserted and covered in vines. There was no sign that anyone had been there for years and she wondered about her parents. She never did learn that her mother had overdosed six months after she had taken Ginger to Basin Street.

Ginger went to the church where she had learned to sing. It had seemed so much bigger when she was a little girl. When she arrived at Mamie's house, it was empty, so she made her way to Mayasha's house. At first Mayasha didn't recognize her. It had been 5 years since they had last seen each other. When Mayasha realized who it was, she spread her arms wide, and in her big bellowing voice, she screamed, "Lord have mercy! It's Miss Ginger!"

The two women hugged and hugged. Ginger's heart was full, and she cried happy tears, the first tears she had cried since she was a little girl.

"My, you have turned into quite a lady, Miss Ginger! C'mon in and I'll fix us some tea!"

"I'm a singer, Mayasha! I've been singing in New Orleans. I remember when I was a little girl, I wanted to sing just like you. You taught me how to sing. Where's Daisy?"

"Daisy married Tom Jackson, and they moved to Baton Rouge 2 years ago right after her Mamie died."

Ginger burst into tears again. "Mamie died? My sweet, sweet Mamie! She was so good to me!"

"Mamie and Daisy cried for weeks after you disappeared. She was so worried about you. She knew what your mama had done and it broke her heart."

Mayasha and Ginger spent the next two hours visiting and catching up, a final closure to Ginger's past. A few days later, Ginger arrived in San Angelo. She went to the address Mozella had sent her and knocked at the door. Mozella came to the door with opened arms, just like Mayasha had done the week before and gave Ginger a big hug.

"You look like Duke," Ginger smiled.

Mozella's laugh was just like Mamie's. "Of course I do, honey! He's my brother. Welcome to San Angelo!"

An attractive lady strolled out onto the porch. "Hello dear. You must be Ginger. My name is Pearl, Victoria Pearl." With that, she also opened her arms and welcomed Ginger with a quick warm squeeze. "Welcome, Ginger. Let me show you to your room," she smiled.

And for the first time in her life, Ginger felt like she had come home.

Betsy

Betsy, with her rosy red cheeks that blushed easily, was the friendliest of all the girls at Miss Pearl's Parlor. She "ooed" and "cooed" at every little thing a man said to her. With her warm smile and Southern charm, Betsy went out of her way to make the men feel welcome. The way Betsy would throw back her head and lay her hand on her chest when she laughed naturally made people smile. Only those who knew her well knew that the more Betsy was laughing, the more pain she was trying to hide.

Betsy's Story

Elizabeth Ann Smith, named after her grandmother, was born in Beckton, Kentucky, a small farming community outside of Bowling Green. Everyone called her Betsy. The only girl in her family, Betsy had 5 brothers, 3 older and 2 younger. Her family raised their own food and farmed wheat, tobacco, and corn. Every morning Betsy woke up at 4 o'clock to help her mother fix a big, hearty breakfast while her father and her brothers did their early morning chores. There were cows to milk and pigs to feed. Betsy was in charge of feeding chickens and gathering eggs in the hen house.

Living in the country was the only life Betsy had known. She attended church every Sunday and sang in the church choir. Betsy loved to cook and had a wall of blue ribbons for baking the best pies and cakes at the local county fairs. Her mother had taught her to raise a vegetable garden as well as how to be a talented seamstress. Sometimes she sketched pictures of the rolling hills of Kentucky; she especially liked drawing old barns. Betsy attended a one-room schoolhouse and was fond of history and reading novels about faraway places that she dreamed about visiting someday.

Good farmers have a genuine understanding of nature because their survival is so connected to the land. Growing up in a farming community, Betsy understood the importance of sharing and helping neighbors in times of need. When a new baby arrived or somebody's loved one died, people brought food to the family's home. When a barn burned down or a home was damaged by a tornado or a bad storm, the men arrived with tools and supplies for a "barn building party." The women made sure everyone who participated was fed and had plenty to drink. Everyone in the community knew each other, and because of country store gossip, most people knew everybody's business as well.

Summer was Betsy's favorite time of year. Behind the farmhouse the family had a 5 acre pond that was loaded with catfish, bream and crappie that made a great place for fishing and swimming. On the bank of the pond was a giant oak tree with a swinging rope hanging from a huge branch that reached over the water. Betsy looked forward to that first refreshing splash the day school let out. The coolness of the water marked the beginning of those hot summer days of playing on the swing and the good times the neighborhood kids shared, laughing and teasing each other. Sometimes the boys challenged other local neighborhoods in the county to baseball games. Although they were unaware of it at the time, the kids in Kentucky were creating happy memories that stayed with them all their lives.

Johnny Wayne Harper, who was two years older than Betsy, lived on a farm close by. His mother had grown up with Betsy's mother and they were best friends. Johnny Wayne was friends with Betsy's brothers and they attended the same school and church together.

Johnny Wayne knew in the second grade, without a doubt, he was in love with Betsy. He loved the way she giggled, and every day he tried to think of ways to make her laugh. Seeing Betsy smile was Johnny Wayne's greatest joy. Sometimes he brought her presents like a flower or a pretty stone he found on the way to school. Betsy always gave him the sweetest smile when he gave her a gift. "Thank you, Johnny Wayne. You are so nice," was music to his ears. One day in the second grade he gave her a pink rose, and Betsy kissed Johnny Wayne on the cheek. He didn't wash his face for over a week.

When Betsy was ten years old and he was twelve, Johnny Wayne proclaimed his never ending love for Betsy by carving "*Johnny Wayne loves Betsy*" inside a giant heart on the trunk of the huge oak tree they had come to know as a friend. After carving his masterpiece, Johnny Wayne took her hand, kissed it and then gently held it to his heart. "I love you, Betsy. Someday we'll get married, and I'll take good care of you, I promise." Johnny's voice was sincere. He presented her with a ring that he had woven out of grass. "One day I will give you a ring made out of real gold, Betsy. You are my sweetheart forever."

"Thank you, Johnny Wayne," she beamed as he put it on her finger. Then Betsy looked at him and smiled that sweet *Betsy smile* he had come to love so much. "It's beautiful," she gasped.

Thelma Jane was Betsy's best friend. She lived with her grandmother, but spent so much time at Betsy's house, it was almost like having a sister. Sometimes they shared secrets. "One day I'm going to travel the world, Thelma Jane!"

"What are you talkin' 'bout, Betsy? Everybody knows you're gonna marry Johnny Wayne and probably have a messa kids."

"You'll see. I will visit castles and beaches and…"

Thelma Jane rolled her eyes. "Yeah right… and I'm an Egyptian princess."

Betsy continued reading books about faraway places. She had never been more than 25 miles from the family farm until one day when she was 17 years old and begged her father to go with him on a trip to Louisville. He sometimes worked three months at a time for a-dollar-a-day as a blacksmith, building flatcars for the railroad. The boys took care of the farm while he was away. Betsy's father had a brother in Louisville who built flatcars for the railroad there; her father stayed at his house when he went to the city to work.

Union Station
Louisville, KY

"Please, Daddy! I won't get in the way! I promise! I'll help Aunt Jane with chores and…"

"All right, Betsy. I'm sure your Mama can manage without you for a few weeks. Besides, now that you've graduated, it might be time you have a glimpse of the big city."

Betsy was always a daddy's girl and her father had a hard time telling her, "No."

Betsy was never more excited in her life! She gasped when they pulled into Union Station. As they drove to her uncle's home, Betsy was amazed at how close the buildings were. She saw grand Victorian homes with stained glass windows and buildings 15 to 20 stories high. The Ohio River was nearly a half-a-mile wide, which was so different from the small creeks and the Little Barren River back home.

"Oh, Daddy, thank you so much! Louisville is beautiful!" That first night in Louisville, Betsy hardly slept. Images of the train station, the river, and the beautiful mansions floated around in her mind. One day Betsy's aunt took her into the city where she marveled at the restaurants and the stores for shopping. They drove by the magnificent mansions on Alta Vista, a street that ran along the Ohio River. Betsy had acquired a glimpse of city life, and her fantasies of living as a grand lady found a niche in her dreams. "I'll live in a grand home one day," she thought to herself.

Johnny Wayne saw the change in Betsy when she returned to Beckton. She was restless, and raved about Louisville and how wonderful it had been to be in the big city. What used to make Betsy happy bored her now. She yearned for more than Beckton had to offer. Johnny Wayne was concerned.

Betsy's brother, Bobby, had proposed to Judy Haney and had set an August 11th wedding date. When Betsy woke up that morning, she had no idea this day would change her life forever. Everyone in the community was invited, and Betsy was Judy's maid of honor. Betsy wore a flowing pink chiffon dress and a simple white hat. Although the dress was not fancy, with her natural beauty and simplicity, Betsy looked stunning. Her dark hair glistened in the sun, and her bright blue eyes sparkled like the water on the back pond at mid-day.

As the church filled, Betsy noticed a distinguished, well-dressed woman sitting on the bride's side of the church. Visiting relatives always stood out at weddings in Beckton, Kentucky. It was Judy's eccentric Aunt Beverly who had a thoroughbred breeding farm just outside of Louisville. At the reception, Betsy asked Judy to introduce her to her aunt. "So pleased to meet you, Ma'am. I love Louisville!" Betsy exclaimed. "I spent three weeks there in June. The city is so beautiful, and the Ohio River is absolutely majestic!"

Aunt Beverly was impressed with Betsy's bright personality and found her naiveté and appreciation for the big city charming. She especially liked the way she laughed. "How would you like to visit Europe, Betsy? I am looking for a travelling companion this fall, and I believe you would be a delight."

"That sounds wonderful!" Betsy exclaimed.

Johnny Wayne overheard the conversation and intervened. "Betsy, you can't leave! What about us?"

"Whatever do you mean, Johnny Wayne? What about us?" Betsy was irritated with Johnny Wayne's interruption.

"I want to marry you, Betsy. Now that you have finished high school, I figured… My gosh, Betsy we've been talkin' about it for years."

"Miss Beverly, I would love to be your companion." Betsy turned to Johnny Wayne and smiled. "It's just for a little while Johnny Wayne. We have the rest of our lives!"

"I don't like it, Betsy. I don't like it one bit." Johnny Wayne put his punch down on the table and solemnly walked outside. He was too sad to speak and he didn't want to spoil Betsy's happiness or make her mad. In the same instance Betsy's dreams were coming true; Johnny Wayne's dreams had shattered like broken glass.

Betsy continued her conversation with Judy's aunt, and before the bride and groom left for their honeymoon, Betsy had agreed to accompany eccentric Aunt Beverly as her travelling companion on a cruise ship to Europe. Within a few days, arrangements had been made.

Although Europe sounded like a fabulous opportunity, Betsy's family was not happy at all about her leaving. It would be the first time she had ever been away from home. Europe seemed so far away, and her mother was sick with worry, imagining all kinds of bad possibilities that might happen to her daughter. "It could be dangerous, Betsy! Remember those poor souls on the Titanic?"

"Oh, Mama, don't be silly. I'll be home before you know it!"

Three weeks later, Betsy was on a train to New York City. Aunt Beverly had bought her a new wardrobe, and Betsy felt like she had to keep pinching herself to make sure she was not dreaming. Tears filled her eyes when she saw the Statue of Liberty, thinking of all the immigrants who came through Ellis Island with only what they could carry and a dream of a better life. Now her dream was coming true.

Beverly was demanding, and it didn't take long for Betsy to know her place. Although she wore fine clothes and ate well, Aunt Beverly made it clear she was her servant, a lady's maid. Betsy made sure that Beverly's clothes were put away, having been laundered and pressed, and Betsy laid out Beverly's wardrobe after her bath. She spent long afternoons playing cards with Miss Beverly and fetching her every whim.

Their European trip consisted of visits to England, Spain, France, and finally Italy. Betsy's favorite part of the trip was traveling on the train. She was amazed at how much of the English countryside reminded her of her home in Kentucky. When they visited Spain, she thought of conquistadors on their quest for gold in the New World. France made her think of Roman legions, and she loved visiting the castles and the beautiful French Riviera. When she was in Italy, she was in awe of the David in Florence and the breathtaking countryside in Tuscany. Rome made her feel like she was in a time warp as she imagined gladiators coming to life in the Roman Coliseum.

Betsy's favorite time of day was during Miss Beverly's afternoon nap. This gave her some time to explore the sights on her own. The Italian men she found to be extremely attractive. Betsy saw looks of approval, and heard admiring whistles when she bounced down the streets. "Americana? Bella! Amore!" She had never had attention like this, and it felt good to be considered attractive and even sexy.

After several glorious weeks in Europe it was time to go home. The morning the ship pulled out of the seaport in Rome, Betsy couldn't help but think there was so much more to see and was feeling frustrated about returning to the farm in Kentucky.

That afternoon, while Miss Beverly was snoring away in her cabin, Betsy found a chair to enjoy her last view of the Mediterranean Sea. A man who looked to be in his mid-twenties approached her. "Rome is a beautiful place." The man had a strong Italian accent. He swept off his cap and took a bow. "Permit me to introduce myself. I am Lorenzo."

"Nice to meet you Lorenzo," Betsy cooed with her friendly Southern style. "My name is Betsy."

Like everyone who met her, Lorenzo was instantly charmed by Betsy's smile and bubbling personality. The fact that she seemed so fresh with a passion for life added to his attraction for her.

"Who are you travelling with?" Lorenzo asked.

"I am with my Aunt Beverly," Betsy answered. She had decided quickly it was better to give the illusion that she was Beverly's niece and not her lady-in-waiting. Betsy was certainly dressed for the part. Beverly had been polishing her companion's social skills so that anyone might believe she had been born into a family of high standing. Betsy told Lorenzo that she was taking care of Aunt Beverly and meeting her might not be such a good idea because she was sometimes delusional.

Lorenzo had jet black hair, olive skin and a pearly white smile. His eyes were hypnotic; he could make a woman feel like she was the only woman in the world worth spending time with. Betsy found it difficult to disagree with anything he said. Lorenzo told Betsy his father was a wealthy textile merchant and that he worked in the family business. Every afternoon at 1:30, while Miss Beverly was taking her nap, Betsy met Lorenzo on the deck of the ship where they had first spoken. She became lost in his charm and the fantasy of a secretive, exciting romance.

Two nights before the ship reached port, Betsy slipped out. She and Lorenzo spent the whole evening bundled up under a blanket, looking at the stars, the moonlight shining on the deep Atlantic. His kiss was deep and passionate, and at the same time soft and sweet. Her body tingled with desire but her strong moral upbringing made her stop him when he attempted to make love to her. "I'm sorry Lorenzo. I just can't."

By the time the ship reached New York, Betsy was in love or at least she thought so.

"I love you, Elizabeth." No one had ever called her that before. "Come with me to California. I am going to San Francisco, and I want you to go with me."

Aunt Beverly was unaware of the romance going on between Betsy and Lorenzo. Betsy was in love with a handsome, romantic, rich, Italian man and had forgotten all about Beckton, Kentucky or Johnny Wayne. She arranged to meet Lorenzo at the train station in Louisville on the day she was scheduled to return home. When they returned to Louisville, Miss Beverly paid Betsy the money she promised for services rendered. "Thank you, Betsy. It was a pleasure getting to know you."

"Oh, Miss Beverly, thank you so much for all you did for me! I loved every minute and I so appreciate having the opportunity!"

"You are welcome Betsy dear. Do stay in touch. Perhaps we can do this again!"

After they exchanged their goodbyes, a taxi took Betsy to the train station. Her heart raced as she thought of her rich, handsome Lorenzo, sweeping her off to San Francisco. Betsy knew she was breaking all the rules; her desire for adventure had completely taken over her senses. Lorenzo was waiting for her on the train.

By the time they reached Kansas City, Betsy and Lorenzo were lovers. No longer was she Betsy, a farm girl from Kentucky. She was now Elizabeth in love with a handsome, wealthy Italian man named Lorenzo who was sweeping her off to San Francisco on a romantic adventure full of mystery and intrigue. She was experiencing her own fairytale, and this time she was the princess.

Betsy and Lorenzo stayed a few nights in Chicago and then Kansas City. Lorenzo took her to fine restaurants and Betsy reveled in the attention. The night before they reached Dallas, Betsy woke up to find Lorenzo gone. She put on her coat and found him in the club car playing poker. Betsy walked in just as Lorenzo showed a losing hand. A fat bearded man with a smelly cigar laughed as he collected all of his chips from the table. Lorenzo lost his temper and was invited to leave the room. "This is a gentleman's game," the man with the cigar declared. "And you, sir, are no gentleman!" Lorenzo was furious when he stood up and huffed away.

He looked at Betsy with surprise. "What are you doing here?" he snapped.

His attitude startled her. "I was looking for you." Betsy suddenly realized she didn't know this man.

"Let me have some money," he demanded anxiously. His breath reeked of liquor and his hair was disheveled. There was a frightening darkness in his eyes Betsy had never seen before. "I need to get back in the game."

Betsy wasn't the only one who had created an illusion. Lorenzo was a gigolo who made his living charming wealthy women and gambling in high stake games. In only a moment, Betsy's dream had turned into a nightmare.

"No, Lorenzo. No!" Betsy cried. "I don't have money to give you."

"I know I can get what I lost right back. I was so close! I can get it back, I know I can. If you love me, you'll give me some money." The look on his face was both desperate and frightening.

"I'm not rich, Lorenzo! Miss Beverly isn't even my real aunt. I was her travelling companion!! What about your family? Call your father!"

Lorenzo started laughing. "You stupid girl! Stupid, stupid girl!" Lorenzo yelled. "Go back to bed!"

Betsy didn't know what to do. All night long she waited for Lorenzo to come back and tell her it was all a big misunderstanding and they were still in love. The next morning when the train pulled into Dallas, Betsy realized Lorenzo was gone.

Sitting in a train station, somewhere in Texas, Betsy felt alone and afraid. She couldn't go home. What would she tell her family? They would be so ashamed. And what about poor Johnny Wayne? How could she ever look at him again? She felt like God was punishing her. The only place Betsy wanted to be was Beckton, Kentucky with the people who loved her. She sat at the train station; all she could do was cry.

"Here honey," a voice said. "Drink this. It will make you feel better."

Betsy looked up and saw a tall, blonde attractive woman holding out a bottle of Coca Cola.

"Thank you," Betsy sobbed.

The woman sat down beside her. "It's gotta be a man. It's always a man that makes women cry like that. I'm Ginger. What's your name?"

"Betsy. My name is Betsy."

"Where ya goin' Betsy?"

"I don't know. I don't know!"

"You like cowboys?" Ginger asked.

"I don't know. I don't know." Betsy cried.

"You like Texas?"

"I don't know. I don't know." Betsy couldn't think.

"I live in San Angelo. Maybe I can help you work this out. You hungry?"

"I don't know. I don't know." Betsy sobbed.

"C'mon, kid. I'll buy you a sandwich." Ginger stood up and extended her hand.

It was a new day. Little did Betsy know she was about to embark on an exciting adventure.

Next stop, San Angelo, Texas.

Maggie

Everybody loved Maggie! Cute, funny, adorable Maggie was a shining light to all. If anyone needed a friend, Maggie was a good listener. She had a heart of gold and was generous with her things and with her time. Spending time with Maggie was always fun. She told every man he was the best lover she had ever had, and he always believed her. Sex should be playful and enjoyable as far as she was concerned. Every man who experienced Maggie walked out the door grinning, with his head held high.

Maggie's Story

Growing up, Maggie was a feisty little girl, getting into mischief and trouble. She had two brothers and did everything with them. While other little girls were playing with their dolls, Maggie climbed trees or fished. She lived in her own world, catching fireflies and ladybugs. For her, it was just more fun getting dirty. Maggie was a joy and she had a knack for finding the bright side of every situation.

Maggie loved animals, and they loved her. Butterflies landed on her and she could convince a bird onto her finger. One time she found a baby bird that had fallen out of its nest and nursed it back to health. She'd wake up twice each night to check on it. Two dogs named Honey and Speckles, a cat named Moses, Hazel the cow, and Barney her pet mouse were Maggie's best friends.

When Maggie was ten years old, her mother died while giving birth to a stillborn baby girl. Shortly afterwards, when her father, who was in the army reserves, went overseas, she and her two brothers, Jacob, 11 and Jesse, 8, went to live with their grandmother. "Granny," a big woman with a heart of gold who loved to laugh, loved her grandchildren and smothered them with hugs and kisses every day. Granny worked hard and had a roadside stand where she sold eggs and vegetables from her garden. Throughout the county she was known for her homemade jams, preserves, and pickles. People who knew about

Granny's canning came from miles, and she knew them all by name.

Granny's house was full of love and was a happy place to be. Every Sunday she took her grandchildren to church. "We need to pray for your Daddy, children. We need to pray that my son comes home from that nasty war, alive and well."

Maggie loved going to church. It wasn't the sermons or the stained glass windows she loved, and it wasn't because of the music although she did love to sing. It was Bobby Ray, the preacher's son. He was two years older than Maggie, who looked forward to going to Sunday school just so she could look at Bobby Ray. Her heart fluttered like a butterfly when she saw him with his sandy blonde hair, shiny brown eyes, and a deep dimple in his left cheek. When he looked at Maggie, he smiled in a way that made her want to jump up and put her finger right into that dimple. One time she actually did!

"What are you doing, Maggie?" Bobby asked.

"Putting my finger in your dimple, Bobby Ray!" Maggie answered giggling.

"Why are you doing that?" Bobby Ray asked with a grin.

"Now Bobby Ray, you absolutely have to know by now I've always wanted to put my finger in your dimple!" Maggie exclaimed with her contagious laugh. Then she quickly kissed him on the cheek and ran away.

As the years went by, Maggie became more and more beautiful. She was petite, curvy and adorable, and had dark curly hair. Every time she smiled at Bobby Ray, her green eyes twinkled like bright stars. During the summer of 1919, Maggie was 15 years old. In her room, she heard Granny scream and then the front door slam. When she ran out of her room and through the front screen door, she saw her Granny in their front yard, hugging a man in a military uniform.

"Daddy! Daddy!" she cried. Maggie ran to her father, "Daddy!"

"Hello, Angel. I hardly recognize you. You look just like your pretty Mama."

Maggie threw her arms around him, but when she did, he flinched. "Sorry, Baby. I have a bad place there on my arm. Golly, it's good to see the both of you!"

Jacob and Jesse had been outside by the barn and had run to the knot of three. "Jacob? Jesse?" their father admired in disbelief.

They had seen their father flinch and waited anxiously for him to approach them. "My God, I can't believe how big you are!"

"What happened to your arm, Dad?" Jacob asked.

"Wrong place at the wrong time," their father answered.

Captain Jonathan Buchanan hugged his two sons one at a time with his good arm. They learned later that he would not discuss the war with them.

"Look at all of you," he exclaimed. "I have dreamed of this moment for years. I can hardly believe I'm actually here."

"I'll get you a glass of tea," Granny offered.

Her son seemed like only the shell of the man who had left them five years before. She remembered how he had mourned for his sweet Louise after she had died. When he was called to go overseas and serve as a medic, he had welcomed the opportunity to get away. At that point, Jonathan didn't care whether he lived or not; that had frightened his mother.

Jonathan had no idea of the hell he would experience in the ensuing years. A medic in the war, he tended the wounded and tried to save the life of anyone still breathing. He saw boys barely old enough to shave screaming, disfigured for life, and scared. Trench warfare took 1 out of every 10 soldiers. The carnage was horrific. He could still smell that unforgettable stench of death as he and other medics picked up what was left of young American soldiers on the battlefields between the trenches.

That first night that her father was home, Maggie was awakened by his screaming in his sleep. Although he was safe inside his mother's house, his mind was still in hell. Many nights he sat in a chair until dawn, staring out the window. Memories of the war were vivid. Granny was beside herself with worry. Her strong son was gone, and in his place was a broken man, needing love and compassion. To his good fortune, Granny had plenty of both. His eyes, however, had lost their shine, and, although he attempted to participate in chores, most of the time, he sat on the front porch, lost in his dark memories.

The farm was different now. Maggie's father had brought home a dark cloud. Every day Maggie tried different ways to cheer up her father.

"I wish I could see my Daddy smile," Maggie told her Granny one day.

"We need to love him through it, honey. We can't imagine what he's been through. I guess he'll have to come to terms with his demons on his own."

Jonathan was not alone. When the war was over, 35 million people, including soldiers and civilians, had been killed in World War I. Those who experienced trench warfare returned "Shell Shocked" and emotionally damaged. The fear on the battlefield was agonizing as the soldiers moved from their trenches toward enemy lines. Every day the men lived in fear of being poisoned with mustard gas. At the end of the day, anyone still standing considered themselves lucky.

Several of the war veterans from the area were having trouble adapting to a normal life. Bobby Ray's father started a support group at the church, attempting to help the men release their nightmares, lodged deeply within their souls. Maggie's father went twice a week, and after a while, it seemed the program was helping him.

Granny reminded the children, "We need to love your daddy through this. That's all we can do. Lord knows what my boy's been through!"

When Maggie walked into a room where her father was, she made it a point to say, "I love you, Daddy."

It didn't matter to her if he said it back or not; Maggie felt like it was important for his healing and wellbeing.

Although circumstances had changed at Maggie's house since her father's return, Granny never stopped working.

"Time is a healer. Your Daddy is in God's hands. There is no better place to be."

Life at the farm gradually became better, and by the time school started, Maggie's family had adjusted to being together. By the third week in September when Maggie had just turned 16, the church held its annual Fall Fest to raise money for the local orphanage. Granny had baked pies and a jam cake for the cakewalk, and the veterans had a ring toss booth. There was good food, music, and dancing. Everyone was in good spirits.

Bobby Ray found Maggie. "Let's go for a walk, Maggie."

"OK."

The full moon was so bright they could see their shadows lit on the ground. They walked down to the lake and watched as a turtle jumped off a rock and swam to the bank. Moonlight danced on the water, and they felt the coolness of the fall in the breeze on their skin.

"We're moving, Maggie." Bobby's voice was quiet.

"What? You're moving! Where?"

"We're going to Austin. My dad got a bishop's position in the Methodist Church. We're leaving in a couple of weeks. No one knows yet, so don't tell anyone, not even your Granny."

"This makes me sad, Bobby Ray. This makes me really sad."

"I want to kiss you, Maggie. I've wanted to kiss you for a long time."

"Ok, Bobby Ray. I've wanted you to kiss me for a long time, too."

Bobby Ray bent down and gave Maggie her first kiss. Then he kissed her again. "Come with me, Maggie. I want to show you something."

Bobby took Maggie to his "secret place." There was a blanket and a pillow stuffed in a pillowcase sitting on a big rock.

"Lay down with me, Maggie. Please. I think I'll burst if you don't lay down with me."

"OK, Bobby Ray." Maggie couldn't bear to tell him no. He was so anxious. She went along with all that he said and did everything he asked her to do.

"I love you, Maggie. I've always loved you!"

Bobby Ray and Maggie made love that night. Neither of them knew what they were doing, but it didn't matter. They let nature take its course. All Maggie really knew was that she liked it. As a matter of fact, she liked it a lot. When they were finished, Maggie didn't feel bad or even dirty. After all, he was the preacher's son, and he wouldn't make her do anything that was wrong!

For the next few weeks, Maggie and Bobby Ray saw each other as much as they could. They made love several more times and then once more the night before Bobby Ray and his family left. That evening Bobby Ray and Maggie promised each other that one day they'd be together again.

Maggie' voice was firm and deliberate. "You write to me now, Bobby Ray! I'll be waitin'!" Then she smiled, reached up and put her finger in his dimple. "I love you, Bobby Ray."

"I'll write you, Maggie. I promise." She believed him, but it was the last thing Bobby Ray ever said to her.

Maggie ran to the mailbox every day, and every day there was no word from Bobby Ray. Finally, after several weeks had passed, she went into the house weeping.

"Granny! He told me he'd write to me. I've written him three times, and I haven't heard a word!"

Granny had spent most of her time worrying about Maggie's father and trying to keep her family from falling apart. She was a strong woman, but even she had her limits. She held Maggie and let her cry. "Sometimes life doesn't give us what we want, baby girl. Don't worry. I promise it will turn out just fine. It always does if you wait long enough."

Finally, 6 months after Bobby Ray left for Austin, a letter came in the mail addressed to Maggie Buchanan. The top left hand corner read: Bobby Ray Jones, 5467 Willowbrook Ln. Austin, TX.

She opened it as fast as she could, her heart thumping in her chest. With every sentence, her heart just sank deeper.

Dear Maggie,

I hope this letter finds you well. I have received your letters and enjoyed every one of them It pains me to write you like this. You certainly deserve better. When I first moved to Austin, I missed you so much, it hurt my heart. I know I should have written but honestly, I just didn't want to think about you. I met a girl who goes to our church who looks a lot like you. She seemed nice enough, so we went on a couple of dates. I kept telling her how much she reminded me of you. At first, she seemed OK with it. Then she told me, I couldn't talk about you anymore. We had sex Maggie. It was her idea. She told me she was going to make me forget you. It was only one time, I swear! I was missing you so much. It was nothing like what you and I have shared. I thought she'd be like you. Nobody is like you, Maggie! Now she is going to have a baby. I had to do the right thing and marry her. We have to keep the baby a secret with Dad being the bishop and all. I really messed up, Maggie. I'd give anything to see you again, but now I know that can't happen. She isn't as nice as you, as pretty as you, and, for sure, she isn't as funny as you. In fact, nowadays, she's cranky most of the time. She gets sick in the mornings, and heck, Maggie, she's just not you. I tried to make her you but she is certainly not you. I'm so sorry, Maggie. I really messed up. God is punishing me now for not keeping my word with you. I still think about you every day. There's nothing I can say except, I'm sorry, and I wish she was you. I guess I need to say goodbye now.

Yours truly,

Bobby Ray

Maggie was too sad to cry. She read the letter three times just to see if she could make sense of it.

"Not me? Of course she's not me! Bobby Ray, you stupid, stupid. Stupid… AUGHH!!" she screamed.

Maggie walked into the kitchen where her Granny was peeling potatoes for dinner that night.

"Granny! Tell me about sex," Maggie asked.

"Why in the world are you asking me that, Maggie?"

"Bobby Ray just wrote me and told me he had sex with a girl, and now they're going to have a baby. He had to marry her."

"Oh, Lordy sakes, child! Let me think about this a minute." Granny laid down her peeling knife.

"OK. Sex is when a man and a woman, uhm, it's when a woman and a man, uhm. OK. Remember when Honey and Speckles were hooked together, and you asked me what they were doing? That was sex. Then remember Honey had those three little puppies. That's what happens when men and women have sex. They make babies." Caught completely off guard, Granny was obviously uncomfortable with the question.

Maggie's father, listening to the conversation through the back screen door, walked in grinning from ear-to-ear, the first time anyone had seen him smile since he had returned from the war.

"Come outside, and sit with me on the front porch, Maggie. I'll tell you what you need to know."

"Sex is when a man and a woman experience oneness, Maggie. It can be a beautiful experience if it is done in the spirit of love like your mother and I. You know how Speckles has a penis and Honey just has an opening, the same goes for men and women. Your brothers each have a penis. Sex happens when the penis becomes stiff and it is inserted into the woman's opening to plant the seed for a baby to grow."

In an enlightening moment Maggie put it all together. "Ohhhhh! I guess then I had sex with Bobby Ray, Daddy. I just didn't know what it was. I just know it was nice." Maggie's father deeply looked into his daughter's innocent face and couldn't help but smile. How could he be upset with her? No one had ever told her about sex before. She didn't even know if it was wrong or not. Maggie's father loved her openness and honesty; her naiveté made her even more sweet and innocent. He thought of the different women he had found comfort with during the war and of his beloved Louise and the way she smiled at him after they had made love. Soon afterwards, she asked him to make love to her again.

"Maggie, I believe you and Bobby Ray made love. Even though technically it's the same action, sex and making love are really two different things. Sex is just the act itself. Even Honey and Speckles didn't make love; they just followed their instincts. Humans are different because sex can be an expression of love for a man and woman to share in the most intimate way."

"OK, Daddy. I think I understand it better now. But Bobby Ray and I didn't make a baby. How come?"

"It doesn't happen every time, Maggie. If I were you, I'd consider myself lucky."

"Daddy, do you think Bobby Ray made love or just had sex with that girl. He told me she reminded him of me."

"Men are made different from women, Maggie. They have basic physical urges to have sex, and love is not as important to them as it is to women. Unfortunately for Bobby Ray, I think he just had an itch that needed to be scratched. Now he has to pay the consequences. I feel kind of bad for him."

"Thanks, Daddy! You must miss Mama terrible. I miss Mama too." She kissed him on the cheek.

Maggie went back into the house to her room. Granny walked out onto the porch to talk to her son. "Good job, Jonathan. Aren't you angry about Maggie and Bobby Ray?"

"Mama after what I've seen in the last five years, two young people making love is not on my list of terrible things. On the battlefield I saw boys die whose only sexual experience had been with a prostitute. A lot of them had syphilis. No, Mama, love is always a good thing and I believe Bobby Ray loved Maggie in a puppy-love kind of way."

"I guess you're right, son. Boy! Did she ever throw me for a loop! I honestly didn't know what to say to her. No one told me about sex before I married your Pa. In fact, the night before my wedding, your grandmother told me that *it* hurt and *it* was a shameful thing to do but you had to do *it* to have children. She said *it* was a wifely duty. The problem was she never explained what "*it*" was! She just kept calling it, "IT!'"

"Poor kids." Jonathan shook his head. "Too bad the way it worked out. I actually feel worse for poor Bobby Ray than Maggie. At least Maggie is free."

Maggie decided to put Bobby Ray in the past. He would always be her first love, but he had a family now. Bobby Ray was a memory of a sweet time of her youth and innocence.

One July morning in 1921, Maggie woke up as usual, and went into the kitchen to pour herself a glass of orange juice. For seven years, Granny had been at the stove cooking every morning when Maggie woke up, but this was the first time Granny wasn't there. She wandered down the hallway and knocked on her bedroom door.

"Granny... Where are you, Granny?"

Seeing Granny still in her bed, Maggie walked over and saw that she looked like she was sleeping peacefully. Then Maggie realized, she wasn't breathing. The angels had come and taken her Granny away during the night. Hundreds of people from all over the county came to pay their respects and say good-bye to "Granny." At her funeral, everyone talked about the way she threw her head back and laughed at things most people didn't even think were funny. Jonathan hardly spoke for weeks after his mother had died. He remembered something Granny used to say when someone she knew had died.

"When it's your time, it's your time."

He thought about the soldiers who had died. He thought about the soldiers who had survived.

"Who chooses that?" he asked himself. "Why am I still here? Why did God take Louise and our baby girl? Why? Why? Why?"

Two months later, Maggie's brother Jacob married his long-time girlfriend, Patsy, and they took over the business on the farm. Patsy sometimes helped Granny and had all her recipes. The house was again filled with the smell of Granny's cooking. Jonathan moved Maggie and her little brother Jessie to town where he got a job at a hardware store in Henderson,

Texas. Although the last year had gotten better, sometimes he still had night terrors, nightmares of boys crying from fear, boys losing their limbs, dead boys with their eyes still opened, and dead boys on the battlefield. Six months after moving to town, Maggie's father married Angie, a sweet lady and a widow whose husband had died in the war. Angie had two children, a girl 10 and a boy 8, and for the last few years, she had been living with her parents.

Maggie and the girl had to share a room which was something Maggie wasn't used to but she knew she only had one more year before finishing high school. Angie and her father seemed happy enough, so she decided that after she graduated, she would move away someplace more interesting. Because Maggie was the new girl in school, she didn't really fit in too well with the other girls who had grown up together. Besides, she had gotten along better with boys anyway. Girls were just a little too frilly for her taste. When a new girl named Sarah showed up at school, Maggie and Sarah simply exchanged hellos at first. One day Maggie saw Sarah eating lunch alone and sat on a seat across the table from her. "Hi, I'm Maggie. You're new here, aren't you? Tell me about yourself."

"My name is Sarah," the girl responded, barely loudly enough for Maggie to hear. "I live with my grandparents, and I have a cat I call Kitty," she responded.

Sarah's quiet gave her an element of mystery that intrigued Maggie. Unlike the other girls, Sarah appeared to harbor a sinister secret. In fact, in many ways, Sarah reminded Maggie of her father when he returned from the war. Had Sarah been through her own war? Maggie was never at a loss for words, and as they ate their lunch together, she even managed to make Sarah smile a couple of times. Finally, getting ready to go back to class, Maggie felt like she had made a friend. "Let's have lunch again tomorrow, Sarah. Somehow I feel we are going to be friends for a long time."

Maggie was right when she guessed Sarah was troubled with sinister secrets. Her new friend had been through hell on earth.

Sarah

People saw Sarah as a stunning, charming, smart, sweet young woman. What they didn't know was that she was a frightened, insecure girl with no self-confidence at all. Several men came to Miss Pearl's Parlor just to see Sarah, and some told her they loved her. In just 6 months she had had three marriage proposals. Something about her sad, aloofness made men want to rescue her. Although she was friendly enough, Sarah was a prisoner in the darkness of her mind.

Sarah's Story

Sarah had never known her father, and her mother, a sweet kind woman named Beth, hardly spoke of him. She only knew that she was conceived one night under a blanket of bright Texas stars in the most magical evening of her mother's life. When Beth's father learned she was pregnant, at 16, he disowned her and threw her out of the house. Beth knew a girl who had become pregnant and moved to Oklahoma. There she joined her friend and took refuge in a home for unwed mothers. When Beth first saw her baby girl, she fell instantly in love. "How do you do, little one. My name is Beth, and I am your mother. I am going to call you Sarah because it means "princess." You are my little princess, sweet Sarah."

Beth could not bear the thought of giving up her new baby girl for adoption and prayed for a miracle. In a church, where Beth went asking for help, an elderly couple named Anderson took in both mother and child. Because the Andersons had lost a daughter to scarlet fever when she was only two years old, Sarah brought joy back to the Anderson household. In addition, Beth cooked and cleaned for them for several years. One morning, as Mr. Anderson was coming back into the house after picking up the morning paper, Beth saw him grab his chest and fall. By the time she got to him, Mr. Anderson had passed away. One of the policemen who arrived on the scene was a man named Stanley Beben. Everyone on the force called him "Stan the man."

Stan attended Mr. Anderson's funeral mainly to see Beth again. That afternoon when they returned to the house and all of the friends paid their respects, Mrs. Anderson went to Beth with a heavy heart. "I'm going to go live with my sister in San Antonio, Beth."

Beth

During the next several weeks, Beth and Sarah helped Mrs. Anderson put her life in order and packed what she wanted to keep. Everything else was sold, including the house. During that time, Stan stopped by when patrolling the neighborhood and took Beth on a couple of dates. One night Stan took Beth to dinner and presented her with a simple golden ring. "Marry me, Beth. I've been so lonely since my wife died. Please marry me." With Mr. Anderson's death, life as they knew it had changed; Beth realized that she and Sarah had nowhere to go. Although Stan, with his round potbelly stomach, was not what anyone would consider an attractive man, he seemed nice enough. Beth had no job, and she had to think about what was best for Sarah. The next week Beth married Stan at the courthouse, and she and Sarah moved into his two bedroom apartment.

At first their new life seemed good enough. Beth got a job as a waitress, and Stan worked the night shift so Sarah didn't see him too much. One night she heard him screaming at her mother and slapping her around. Sarah ran out of her room and found her mother on the floor in a fetal position, Stan flaying and kicking at her. Stan looked at Sarah with crazy yellow eyes. She hardly recognized him. "Go to bed!" he shouted. The screaming had stopped, but Sarah never forgot the look on her mother's face as she was pleading with Stan to stop kicking her.

Stan was a binge drinker. The drinking always set him off, making the abuse unpredictable. Beth and Sarah never knew why or when Stan might start drinking, but when he did, he transformed into a monster like Doctor Jekyll and Mister Hyde. The worst part was the next day he had no memory of the horrible things he had done the night before. When he saw the damage he had done to the house or to Beth's face, he'd break down and bawl like a baby, "I'm so sorry, Beth. Please forgive me! Don't leave me, Beth. It will never happen again, I swear!"

Over the next few years Sarah became frightened and confused as she witnessed the sporadic episodes of abuse. One night when Sarah was spending the night with a friend, Beth was hurt so badly she had to be admitted to the emergency room. Stan had kicked her in the stomach, broken her nose, and had put his gun to her head, telling her he was going to kill her and then kill himself. The next day he brought her flowers and cried again. "Don't leave me! I love you so much, Beth. I'll get help; I promise!" Stan told everyone Beth had fallen down a flight of steps and she went along with his story.

"He's a cop, Sarah. They won't believe me over him. It's just better this way. Anyway, he says this time, he's really going to get help."

"But, Mama, he hurt you," Sarah pleaded.

Sometimes months went by without an incident, and life for Beth and Sarah were at the very least, bearable. Some of his buddies on the force kept some confiscated cases of bootlegged whiskey for their own pleasure. When this happened, Stan usually went on his drinking binges and all hell broke loose. When Sarah was 16, she went home from school one afternoon and found Stan sitting in his chair. Her mother was at work.

"Hey, pretty Sarah." Stan had been drinking, and he now had a new victim, the booze transforming him into a monster. "If you don't do what I say, I'll kill your Kitty." Sarah had never been so frightened. She did every horrible thing he told her, all making her sick to her stomach. "Good girl. Don't tell anyone or you'll find Kitty hanging from the shower rod one day when you go to take your bath." Sarah ran to the bathroom and threw up.

After that, Sarah did all she could to avoid being alone with Stan. Finally, Sarah went home one morning after a sleep over and found her mother at the kitchen table, holding a towel over her face, her eye reddish purple and swollen shut. Holding ice on it to ease the pain and reduce the swelling, she also had an ugly cut on her mouth. Beth was gently petting Kitty on her lap with her other hand. There was an eerie darkness in the quiet, as if a cloud of evil lingered over the apartment.

"I'm sorry, Baby. I'm so sorry," her mother whimpered in a defeated tone. Warm salty tears were rolling down her cheeks.

"What's happened, Mama?" Sarah asked, suddenly afraid. "Where's Stan?"

"I think I killed him, Sarah. He came home drunk and started calling me horrible names and saying awful things about you. I knew what was coming and tried to reason with him. Then he came after me and pushed me down. I decided to fight back, honey. When I did, he laughed, pushed me down again, and kicked me again and again. He kept kicking me, Sarah. I think I have some broken ribs."

Beth's mother was wearing a yellow robe. She opened it up and showed Sarah a yellowish patch of skin on her side with splotches of green and dark purple.

"Finally, he put his hands around my throat. I couldn't breathe. I quit fighting and went limp. That probably saved my life because when I did, he stopped." Sarah's mother's voice stayed unusually calm. "He said nasty things about you, Baby. Nasty horrible things! I'm so sorry Sarah, I'm so sorry, I had no idea. My poor baby!" she wailed, her shoulders shaking. She began to cry softly, clutching her heart as she did.

Quietly, Sarah's mother continued, "When he passed out in the bed, I hit him with my big iron skillet from the stove! I couldn't stop! I wanted the ugly to go away. I don't know how many times I hit him, Sarah. When I finally quit, blood was all over the pillow, and he wasn't breathing. He wasn't moving and he wasn't breathing."

"Oh, Mama!" Sarah cried. "What are we going to do?"

"I don't know, Sarah. I don't know. He's a cop, for God sakes! I don't know! They're going to hang me, for sure."

Sarah washed the blood from the frying pan with bleach and put it in the cupboard. "Mama, I'm going to call the police and tell them you need an ambulance. We'll tell them that Stan hurt you. It'll be all right. Don't worry Mama. It'll be all right!"

"That's a good girl, Sarah. Call the police. That's a good girl." Sarah's mother was acting peculiar and unusually calm, as if she had a magical solution to fix the problem. She wrote a name and address on a piece of paper and handed it to Sarah. "This is the address and phone number of your grandparents in Texas. There's money in a red box on the top of the bookshelf in the living room. Everything is going to be okay, Baby." Beth smiled but at the same time, with sorrowful pain in her eyes. "Now, come give your mama a kiss."

Sarah kissed her mother's cheek. "I love you, Mama."

"I love you too, Baby. Now go on and call the police." Sarah's mother got up slowly from the table and shuffled to the bedroom where Stan was laying on the bed and shut the door."

"Operator, I need the police, please. There's been an accident, and my Mama's hurt bad. Our address is 522 Grapevine Aven…"

BOOM!

The shot came from the bedroom, sending a chill running down Sarah's spine. She dropped the phone, screaming, "Mama! Mama! Mama!"

Sarah found her mother slumped in a chair with a wound to her head, Stan's gun lying on the floor beside her. Sarah screamed hysterically. "Mama! Mama! No, Mama!"

The police found Sarah with her head on her mother's lap, sobbing profusely, and with Kitty lying beside her. Sarah heard the police. "O shit! What a mess. Yeah, it's Stan the man all right… what's left of him. Damn! He surely pissed somebody off!"

Next, Sarah found herself sitting on the sofa in the living room with Kitty on her lap. A neighbor lady had come over to console her. "You'll stay with me tonight, Sarah. The police have located your grandparents in Henderson, Texas."

Sarah's grandmother, a timid woman, was waiting at the train station when she arrived. Sarah thought she looked like an older version of her mother. When she saw Sarah, she exclaimed, "Such a pretty girl! You look just like Beth did…when she left home…" Crying and pulling a handkerchief from her purse, she continued, "Oh, my poor little Beth. My poor, poor little Bethy Anne. How I wish I could tell her how much I loved her. I loved her so much! I cried for months when her father sent her away. I begged him not to, but he was so angry! Such a stubborn man! Oh, my poor Bethy!"

Sarah called her grandparents, "Grandmother" and "Grandfather." Although her grandfather barely spoke to her, her grandmother tried her best to make up for the indifference her husband showed. The next week, Sarah started her senior year of school in Texas, yet no one knew her story. She kept to herself most of the time and avoided talking to boys at all because her grandfather didn't let her date. "You're going to turn out just like your mother if you start seeing boys." he huffed. "Everyone's gone crazy with that new jazz music and dancin' all around. Women making themselves up like clowns. Heathens, all heathens!"

Sarah, the gorgeous new girl in town that everyone talked about, had all the boys' attention, which certainly made it hard for her to make friends with the girls. Sarah had never felt so alone. She missed her mother, and most nights she cried herself to sleep. One girl, Maggie, was nice to Sarah. Maggie wasn't popular with the girls either, however; the boys loved her because she was cute, friendly, and funny. The girls called her a tramp.

Life at school became better the day Maggie saw Sarah eating lunch alone and sat across the table from her. "Hi, I'm Maggie. You're new here, aren't you? Tell me about yourself ."

Sarah was startled. It was the first friendly conversation she had since the day she started school. The last thing she wanted to do was to tell anyone about herself. "I live with my grandparents, and I have a cat I call Kitty."

"Is that it?" Maggie asked.

"That's it," Sarah replied making it clear she wanted to remain private.

"Well, all righty then," Maggie grinned. Sarah smiled back, and they spent the rest of their lunch talking about how their history teacher needed to learn to not talk through his nose and how great it would be if women could wear trousers like men.

Maggie put her head down and whispered. "Hey, look over there! Michael Collins is looking at you!"

Michael Collins, a handsome athlete, was the absolute bee's knees according to all the other girls. They all wanted to date Michael Collins, and he knew it. He carried a supply of condoms with him because his mission was to experience as many girls as he could before he graduated from high school.

"You've got to be careful of that one. He's only after one thing!" Maggie warned.

"Aren't they all?" Sarah commented. From that day on, Maggie and Sarah ate lunch together despite unpleasant looks from the other girls.

Sarah had a difficult time warming up to boys. The emotional damage from her stepfather's abuse had resulted in horrible nightmares that would wake her up in the middle of the night. Although she liked Maggie, she didn't want anyone to know her story, but she didn't realize that Maggie had a story of her own. Sarah's grandfather was exceedingly strict with the times she left and came home. As far as she was concerned, she wanted to get through the school year and graduate. Her grandmother was a sweetheart and was quietly apologetic, but it was clear her grandfather ruled the household. Living with him was like walking on thin ice. He was aloof and hardly spoke to Sarah. "You were spawned from the devil himself!" he growled.

Michael Collins had his eye on Sarah. Despite Maggie's warnings Sarah felt special, to know he was interested. He thought himself quite the stud. The girls he slept with never admitted to anyone that they had been with him for fear of ruining their reputations. Michael Collins, always the charmer, said and did whatever it took for a girl to say "Yes" to his advances. The girls who had sex with him were not aware that Michael *did* in fact, kiss and tell his close buddies. He had a collection of undergarments and showed off every one of them. Sometimes his friends presented him challenges; Sarah was the new challenge.

Michael decided early on that Sarah was going to be difficult though he tried all his tricks. He used his best lines, but none worked. He began to doubt himself. Sarah barely spoke to him and avoided any eye contact, frustrating him because Michael knew his strongest assets were his clear blue, puppy dog, bedroom eyes outlined by his long dark eyelashes. Dang! What was up with her?

Sarah enjoyed Michael's advances but she knew that, if she broke her grandfather's rules, she would be out on the streets. Maggie found it all amusing. She had never been enough of a challenge for the great Michael Collins to be interested in her. He knew Maggie was a sure thing and often teased her about it.

"You haven't lived until you've been with the great Michael Collins, Miss Maggie," he boasted.

"I guess I'll go to my grave pining my loss and wondering," she retorted with her hand over her brow in a dramatic gesture.

The truth be known, Michael was too conceited for Maggie to want to be with him. She preferred the boys who appreciated her for herself. However, she did enjoy the teasing, which ultimately made them friends. Michael was persistent, and Sarah let down her guard. "Be careful, Sarah. He can be a heartbreaker," Maggie told her. Sarah enjoyed the attention and the fact that the girls who didn't like her liked him. Finally, Sarah agreed to meet him for ice cream after school one day. He put on his best game, and she found herself swept away with Michael's charms. Those bedroom eyes were so alluring that she realized she enjoyed the attention.

For weeks they met after school for ice cream and walks in the park. Sarah made her grandfather's restrictions clear. For example Sarah had to be home by 5 every afternoon. Their relationship was perfect: Sarah, a good listener, was quiet and he liked to talk, especially about himself. Michael found himself looking forward to their time together. He even stopped talking about himself so much and became more interested in learning more about her. Michael could make Sarah laugh and she loved gazing into his beautiful blue eyes.

Their relationship became a soulful connection neither of them had ever known. He had not even held her hand, yet she felt a deep mysterious connection with him. His friends continued to ask him if he had scored with Sarah. Michael was after all their "woman-getter hero," the one who *always* got the girl! As Michael had become more and more enchanted with Sarah, his original intentions completely disappeared. He wanted to be with her, but no longer saw Sarah as a challenge. She had his heart, and he was not ashamed to let his friends know.

"Sarah's different. I really think I love her. No more asking or I'll have to hurt you," he announced with a grin, and his friends understood.

With graduation two weeks away, Sarah and Michael sat on a bench by the football field and he asked, "Sarah, will you go steady with me?"

"Yes, yes I will!" she replied hugging his neck. They touched, and both of them felt a powerful surge.

Michael gave Sarah a golden locket. "Read the inscription on the back," he exclaimed.

"Michael loves Sarah forever. Oh, Michael it's beautiful!"

Sarah, happier than she had ever been, thought about her mother, wishing she were able to show her the locket and tell her about Michael Collins.

Even though her grandfather stayed home, her grandmother attended her graduation. Sarah was so happy. Michael and Sarah attended the big party at the community center together to celebrate their graduation. Michael, the most handsome boy in school, and Sarah, officially his girlfriend, danced and held hands all night long. That night on a blanket beneath the Texas stars, Michael and Sarah made love.

"I love you Sarah. I really love you."

"I love you too, Michael. With all my heart."

When Michael took Sarah home, it was almost midnight. As they approached the house, holding hands, they spied Sarah's grandfather sitting on a chair waiting for her on the porch. "Don't worry, I've got you," Michael whispered.

"Where have you been? Who is this man?" her grandfather screamed.

"I have been at my graduation party, Grandfather. This is Michael. He brought me home."

The young couple walked up on the porch. Michael reached out his hand. "How do you do, sir, my name is Michael Collins," he replied politely, though he had never met anyone so dark and sinister.

Sarah's grandfather's pupils were like dark beads darting back and forth in his yellowing eyes. His voice, low and gravelly like a demon speaking from the pits of hell, "You're just like your mother, you heathen child! You were spawned from bad seed!"

Sarah's grandfather, taking a pistol from under the blanket on his lap, aimed at Sarah's chest. Insanely, he spat, "You are bad seed! It's time you burn in the fires of hell where you belong!"

Michael jumped forward. "No!" he screamed.

BOOM!

The gun went off. Sarah had heard that sound before, the second time she heard a fatal blast that had sent a cold chill down her spine. Her beloved Michael, who just an hour before had made love to her, was lying on his stomach on the ground. The sound of the shot that killed Michael was even more devastating than the one that had taken her mother. Both would forever be permanent memories.

It was one o'clock in the morning when the sheriff took Sarah's grandfather away. She couldn't speak for weeks. She just sat in her room, stroking Kitty, looking out the window. Sarah never took off her locket. It lay over her broken heart like a medal of valor.

Maggie, her wonderful friend, visited Sarah every day. Sometimes they cried together, and Maggie hugged her friend, rocking her like a baby. When she did, she felt the pain deep inside Sarah's heart. Many days she had to her force her to eat.

"I don't want to eat. I don't even want to live, Maggie. I want to be with Mama and Michael," Sarah cried out one day. This worried Maggie and from that moment on, she never left Sarah's side.

A few months after he had been arrested, Sarah's grandfather had a heart attack and died in prison. Her grandmother wandered around in a daze most of the time. Beth's older sister Katherine, Sarah's aunt, came to the house to take care of her grandmother. Katherine had run away when she was 16 and had not seen her mother since.

Sarah's grandfather, who had been horribly abusive to both of his girls, locked them in dark closets and made them do things too evil to speak about. When Katherine had left home, she hooked up with a man who had taken her to San Angelo, Texas, but after a few weeks, he got on a train and hasn't been seen since. In San Angelo, Katherine known as "Miss Kitty," learned how to survive by working in a house full of women who made a living being nice to men. "After the hell we had as children, every day away from that old bastard was just like heaven!" she claimed.

Katherine spent that summer in Henderson, looking after her mother and Sarah. Everyone including the doctors knew Grandmother wasn't going to live long. Sarah fell in love with her Aunt Katherine. Katherine's upbeat attitude and smile brought them close. "Sarah, you remind me so much of Bethy Anne. You even laugh like her."

In September, Sarah's grandmother passed away. Katherine was somber. "Mama's finally at peace. Only the good Lord knows the hell that man put her through."

The day after the funeral, Katherine, Maggie and Sarah went up into the attic and found a trunk full of memories that her grandmother had saved over the years. It was like finding a hidden treasure, clothes, old toys, a couple of dolls and some old photographs.

"I thought my doll was gone forever when that old bastard took it away. Mama must have hidden it. Look, this one was your mother's." Katherine handed the doll to Sarah.

"Look here Sarah! This is me before I ran away."

"May I see?" Maggie asked. "What a funny hat!"

"Here's Bethy when she was a baby."

Sarah looked at the photograph for a long time. Tears rolled down her face. "She's so cute. Why would anyone want to hurt her, Aunt Katherine? Hurt both of you? I don't understand."

"I don't know, Sarah. I guess we'll never know. Why don't you come back with me to San Angelo? I have a house close to the river that one of my gentlemen friends bought for me. You can bring Kitty. Yeah, bring Kitty to Miss Kitty's," she laughed. "I'm going to sell everything here. There are hundreds of reasons I never want to see this place again."

A few weeks later Katherine and Sarah were on their way to San Angelo. "Don't forget to write me, Sarah! You are my best friend. I will miss you!"

"Come visit me, Maggie. Come visit me soon!"

Sarah moved to San Angelo, Texas, with her Aunt Katherine in the fall of 1922. Katherine had maintained a select few clients over the years, including the man who had bought the house for her. Sarah took walks along the Concho River when her aunt was entertaining.

Maggie was worried about Sarah. That November she decided to visit her in San Angelo. When Sarah saw her at the train station, she realized how much she had missed her and was grateful to have such a loyal friend.

"How long can you stay, Maggie?"

"As long as it takes, Sarah."

It was a crisp cool afternoon, the Wednesday before Thanksgiving. "Get yourself ready, Maggie, we're going out," Sarah told her friend.

"Where are we going?"

"We're going to visit the orphanage. Aunt Katherine visits the children every week. She takes them money and plays games with them. I like to go with her. Aunt Katherine is so much fun, and the children love her."

Katherine heard the girls talking and stood at the doorway of Sarah's room. She shared a secret with them not many people knew. "When I was very young, I had a baby. I wasn't able to take care of him. One evening I left him on the doorstep of some nice people I knew that were not able to have children. I threw a rock at the door and watched from behind a bush as they brought him into the house. Soon afterwards I began working at Miss Hattie's. He doesn't know me but I know him. I've secretly watched him grow up. He's so handsome, and has a little boy of his own. I'm a grandmother!"

"That's so sad," Sarah sympathized.

"His name is Joshua," Katherine smiled tearfully. "That's what the note in the basket read when I gave him away. I like to visit the orphanage. It helps fill the hole in my heart. Some of the children who live there were born in the local bordellos." Katherine wiped her eyes. "Be careful now. The little dickens will steal your heart away. Right, Sarah?"

"That's true. I always look forward to visiting the children," Sarah agreed.

"Sometimes I wish I could bring them all home with me," Katherine sighed.

As Maggie, Sarah and Aunt Katherine approached the orphanage, they met a woman carrying a basket of different colored balls of yarn.

"Good Morning, my friend!" Katherine greeted the woman. "What do you have in the basket?"

The woman picked up a red ball of yarn, "I thought today I would teach the girls how to make yarn dolls today. My mother taught me how to make them when I was a little girl, and I remember playing with them for hours. Usually I bring storybooks and read to the children. I thought I would do something different. And who do we have here?" the woman asked in a friendly tone.

"This is my niece, Sarah and her friend Maggie. Girls, I'd like you to meet my good friend, Miss Victoria Pearl."

Heather

Heather, best known for being the most playful girl at Miss Pearl's Parlor, was always a memorable experience. Everyone knew her for the many creative ways she used feathers to entertain her clients. Heather had a way of fantasizing and caressing a man with her long fluffy plumes that made her famous throughout West Texas. Whenever she was working, she began with a short poem she wrote:

> *"Hello handsome,*
> *I'm Heather with my feather!*
> *I can tickle your ears; I can tickle your nose*
> *I can tickle your fancy and I can tickle your toes."*

Heather's Story

Heather, number five of ten children, grew up as a farmer's daughter in Lisbon, Illinois, where, in those days, people in rural areas saw having children as creating a work force. Her two older sisters took care of Heather when she was young, and then as they married and moved away, Heather took care of the younger ones. The family home had only four small bedrooms. For the longest time, her mother had one baby after another. Just about the time one began to walk, Heather's mother announced that there was another one on the way. With ten children in the family, Heather never felt important. In fact, half the time, her mother called her by another name.

Heather's creative imagination began when she was in the first grade and played an angel in the Christmas pageant at school. From then on, the front porch was her stage. She sang, danced, and even made up stories with herself as a princess in a magic castle. It didn't matter if her audience was a dog, a cat, a doll, or her little brothers and sister, Heather loved acting. She blossomed early into an enticing young lady. Everyone in the county noticed. By the time she was sixteen, Heather had made up her mind that she was going to be on the stage. She learned countless songs. Because she had a powerful voice and enthusiasm, the local musicians invited her to sing with them at barn dances. Performing became Heather's favorite pastime because she loved helping people have fun. She was good at it!

On the evening of the Big Harvest Dance, Heather first met Tony Marino, a handsome, dark haired man who stood out as different. Tony, in town attending his great aunt's funeral, went to the barn dance with his cousin Vinnie. "There's a girl you gotta see," Vinnie had told him earlier. "She's really good!" During her first song, Tony realized that Heather had talent but even more, he was impressed with how the crowd responded to her. Heather had learned early that if she enjoyed herself, then her audience had a good time as well.

Tony sought her out after her second performance. "You've got talent, kid! How old are you?"

"I'm eighteen." Heather smiled.

"How'd you like to make some money singing for me? I own a place in Chicago. You could do well. I'll pay you $35 a week, and you can keep your tips. I want you to sing jazz. Here's my card. I need to know now." Heather knew she had to think fast. She considered her mother, dad, brothers, and sisters. Times had been hard; they could certainly use the extra money. Two of her sisters and a brother had married and moved away, and one of her sisters already had two children. Marriage didn't interest Heather, but she always dreamed of singing in the big city.

"Mama probably won't like it much," she thought to herself. "Aw, she'll get over it, especially if I send some money home to help out. Anyway, if I don't like it, I can always come back home."

"I'll do it, Mr. Marino!" she replied quickly. Heather realized this might be a once-in-a-lifetime opportunity. "In fact, I'd love to. I'd like to have an advance if you don't mind. I'll need train fare." With ten children in the family, Heather had learned to ask when she wanted something. Most of the time the answer was "No" but she knew the answer was always "No" if she didn't ask.

Tony reached into his pocket and pulled out a hundred dollars. "I like a woman who is not afraid to ask for what she wants. Here's money for your trip, and here's the address. You can start next Saturday. See you then, honey."

All the girls knew that Heather's father saw the boys as more valuable because they could work the farm: Within hours, Heather was packed and on a train headed for Chicago. She gave her parents $20 from the money Tony had given her. "I was paid in advance, Mama. I'll send more when I start working." Although her mother was concerned she was grateful for the extra money. Heather was more excited than afraid of her new life. Actually her brothers and sisters seemed more upset at her leaving than her mother and father, probably because they had one less mouth to feed.

The big city excited her even though she knew no one in Chicago. When Heather stepped off the train, this country girl marveled at the unfamiliar sights and sounds of her new adventure: big buildings, fancy cars, restaurants, and parks. Heather checked into a modest boarding house not too far from Mr. Marino's restaurant. After unpacking, she went downtown to a secondhand store and bought two dresses and two pairs of shoes. She wanted to be thrifty just in case her job didn't work out. Heather went to Woolworth's and bought a red lipstick, powder, mascara and some dark grey eye shadow and liner to create the new trendy smoky eye look. Her sister, Janet, had given her a bobbed haircut a few days before she left the farm.

"This will do for now," she thought, as she put away the purchases of the day. "I'll get some nicer dresses soon enough." That afternoon Heather spent over an hour putting on her new make-up and fixing her new hair style, creating the new singer in Chicago. She put a band around her forehead and clipped it with a big shiny earring that was missing its mate that she had bought at the thrift store. Heather picked up a feather and stuck it in her band, the perfect finishing touch. After carefully applying her lipstick, she kissed herself in the mirror. "Hello, Heather with your feather! Glad to meet you." She stared at herself for a long time, her eyes filling with tears as she thought about her family, especially the faces of the younger ones when she had bid them farewell.

"Stop it, Heather! It's time to grow up!" she scolded aloud.

Even though Heather had been modest with her spending that day, her perfectly rounded hips mixed with her sultry attitude made her breathtaking. When Heather walked out onto the street, men smiled in appreciation. When she saw them look, she held her head higher and pretended not to notice, making her even more alluring. Like an actress walking across the stage, Heather walked slowly and deliberately as she made her way to Mr. Marino's restaurant.

Tony Marino had told her to come early to rehearse with the band. At 6:00, as she peered through the window and saw several people eating at tables with linen tablecloths, gleaming silverware and glistening glasses. Each table had a fresh red rose in a tall slender crystal vase. The rich aroma of garlic, cheese, and cooking tomatoes met her when she pushed open the door. These were new smells to Heather, and were quite different from the cornbread, potatoes, greens, and pinto beans from home.

Tony was sitting at a table near the kitchen door when he saw Heather walk in. First he whistled, and then he smiled. "Look at our new singer, Harry," he motioned to a man sitting next to him.

"How ya' doin', Sweetheart?" Harry called to Heather, tipping a dark grey cap. He was the bandleader for Tony's speakeasy downstairs. Both men were clearly impressed with Heather's sensational womanly curves that swayed suggestively as she walked toward them. She had rehearsed this moment for years.

"I am wonderful, Mr. Marino!" Heather cooed, breaking her stride. She posed, "I'm Heather with my feather!" she announced with a flare.

"Well, Miss Heather with her feather, Harry here is the band leader. Harry, meet your new singer, Heather Brooks," Tony boasted.

Tony, looking his new girl up and down with approval, suggested "Let's go downstairs. The boys are waiting for you." He escorted Heather through an ordinary door. Instead of opening to a back alley, the door led down a staircase to another door with no doorknob on it but rather a small sliding window in the center. When Tony tapped a rhythm on the door, it opened to reveal an elegant room with a decorative gold plated mirror hanging behind a long highly-polished mahogany bar. The musicians were setting up their instruments on a round stage surrounded by tables. In front of the stage was a dance floor.

"Pinch me; I think I'm dreaming," Heather thought to herself.

"Let's find your song keys, Kid," Harry suggested in a friendly tone. "Tony told us you can sing, and Tony ain't too easy to impress." Harry sat down at the piano. "Whatcha know, girlie girl?" he grinned. Heather pulled out her song list with the keys she sang them in and handed it to Harry. "I'm impressed! Most dames don't have a clue what key they sing a song in."

"One of my friends back home helped me put my song list together before I left. How 'bout "Cuddle Up a Little Closer? Not too fast." Heather liked to slow songs down just enough to flirt a little with her audience. "Key of A." When Heather started singing, one-by-one the musicians joined her on stage. She had never heard music played like that before. The band sounded heavenly together; she knew it was going to be a great night.

That evening, Heather was a sensation, smiling and cooing at her audience. Her slower tempo and tenor range gave her a unique style that wowed the audience. The band loved her, and people danced long into the morning. Heather was having the time of her life. Tony, sitting at one of the tables watching the way the room reacted to Heather, knew his instincts had been right. He found himself even more impressed with her than he had been when she had sung at the barn dance.

"Beautiful, honey! You were great! I have a car to take you home. Tomorrow I'll have a cab waiting for you at your boarding house at 8:30 sharp. Don't be late!" From then on, Tony made sure Heather was picked up and brought home from the club every night.

The next evening at 8:30 sharp, a cab waited for Heather outside the boarding house to take her to the club. Heather did not see Tony when she walked into the speakeasy that night. She was wearing the other dress she had bought at the thrift shop two days before and again had put herself together well. When Heather walked into her dressing room, she was elated and surprised to find five of the loveliest gowns she had ever seen hanging on the wall. On the dressing table were headbands, and feathers of all colors, as well as a tall vase filled with a dozen fragrant red roses with a card that read, *"Beautiful gowns for a beautiful girl, Tony."*

Heather was overjoyed with her new wardrobe. Now her dream really was more like a fairytale. She chose a royal blue silk gown that fell loose around the neckline. It flowed beautifully along the shape of her body, making her feel elegant for the first time in her life. Admiring herself in the mirror, she heard a soft knock at the door. It was Tony Marino wearing a white suit and looking especially handsome. "May I come in?" he asked.

"Oh, Mr. Marino! I feel like a princess! Thank you so much for the lovely gowns," she gushed, hugging his neck. Tony took advantage of the moment and wrapped his arms firmly around the small of her back and pulled her close. Heather had never had anyone hold her like that before. Overwhelmed, she felt a chill down her back and saw a lustful glare from his dark eyes.

Tony smiled. "You are welcome, my dear," he responded as he pulled away. "Turn around. Let me look at you."

Heather was anxious, confused, and excited all at the same time. She turned around and when she did, Tony reached into his pocket and adorned her neck with a set of lovely pearls, lustrous and cool. Heather saw her reflection in the mirror next to the red roses. "They are beautiful!" she whispered.

Tony kissed the back of her neck, "You're beautiful," he breathed passionately. His breath ignited a burning desire throughout Heather's body and she was unable to speak. Was she dreaming? Whatever it was, she liked it!

After the show, Tony went into Heather's dressing room. "You were irresistible tonight, Heather. You are irresistible now." His finger lifted her chin, and he gently kissed her on the lips. At first his kisses were soft and Heather responded. Heather had never been kissed before and it felt nice. As the soft changed to passionate, Heather answered his every move. Both breathing hard, Tony kissed her, tracing every curve of her body. Suddenly Tony stopped, his eyes bright with wanting, "I want to make love to you, Heather. I want to make love to you now."

Heather was unprepared for this moment. What she knew about sex was what she had learned from the animals on the farm. Speechless, she knew that he was making her feel good. Her body was trembling all over. Heather was caught in the confusion of right and wrong. At the same time her mind was saying, "No," her body was saying, "Yes." The only thing that was real was the wonderful tingling she felt when Tony touched her.

Tony kissed her ever so gently, turned her around, and slowly unzipped her dress. Heather did not resist. He slipped the shoulders down, and the royal blue fabric fell to the floor. Heather stepped out of it and slipped off her shoes. With an expert flair, Tony carefully removed her undergarments, never taking his eyes off her face. Heather stood before him wearing only her pearls. "Exquisite," he murmured with a low deep sigh.

Tony slipped off his jacket and tie, and picked up a long white plume from the dressing table. Tony was staring at her. "I want to drink you with my eyes." He slowly ran the plume down her back and over her shoulders. "Lay on the sofa," he instructed.

"I've never done this," she admitted, as she lay down and looked up at Tony with her innocent eyes. What was she doing? This had already gone way too far. The more she tried to resist, the more she was submissive to his desires.

"You are a goddess," he nibbled into her ear. That comment made Heather smile and she began to relax.

Tony was an expert at pleasing a woman. He took his time stroking Heather, first with the feather and then gently with the tips of his fingers. He knew the erotic nerves and crevices. Heather completely surrendered to Tony's every move as he awoke the sensuous places on her body. He knew what to do to light a fire in her womanhood. "I want you Heather. I want you all the way."

Again Heather could not speak. She watched as Tony took off his clothes. The hair on his chest was soft and smooth, and his manhood was erect and firm. As he climbed on top of her, he kissed her deeply, and when he did, Heather felt her body rise in response. She felt Tony enter her. Only a minute later, she felt a warm rush of fluid release from her. This seemed to excite Tony even more. They spent the next hour making love.

When they had finished, Tony put on his pants, shoes, and shirt. Heather, however, could hardly move, her body was tingling with ecstasy and erotic pain. She could feel Tony's essence all over her. She wanted him to hold her. Tony on the other hand, was ready to leave and flung his jacket over his shoulder. "I have arranged another place for you to stay, Heather. I will have a driver pick you up at 1 o'clock tomorrow to take you there. Have all your things ready to take with you. Get dressed now. I have a cab waiting for you outside."

"OK, Tony. Whatever you say," Heather mumbled, a little confused.

With his pants back on, Tony's demeanor changed from passionate lover to businessman. Suddenly Heather became self-conscious of her nudity. He sensed her concern. "Don't worry, Baby. Now, be a good girl and get dressed. Leave the new gowns here. You can get them tomorrow."

"OK, Tony."

The next day at one o'clock sharp, Heather found a driver waiting for her with the new gowns. They drove several long city blocks before the driver stopped in front of a fancy building. A doorman opened the car door for Heather, "We've been expecting you, Miss Heather," he greeted. "Mr. Burns has your keys at the front desk in the lobby."

With a spectacular view of Chicago, Heather's new apartment took her breath away. Once again Heather thought she must be dreaming. Another dozen red roses, a bottle of expensive perfume and a card that read:

"*Welcome to your new home, Tony*," waited on a table in the dining area.

Until now Heather had asked no questions. Two months ago she was living on a farm pretending she was a star. Now she sang on stage, wore fine clothes and jewelry, and lived in a fancy apartment on the ritzy side of Chicago. Tony continued giving Heather nice presents, and she continued accepting them. She had never experienced this kind of attention, and she had certainly never received expensive gifts.

Heather had fallen in love with Tony Marino. An amazing lover, he spoiled her with jewelry, clothes and expensive perfume. Like a golden trophy adorned with fine jewels, Tony Marino took Heather to fancy places where he could show her off, always introducing her as the singer at his club.

Heather loved singing for him and learned songs she knew he liked. She had become popular, and business had doubled in the few weeks she had been there. Tony kept Heather isolated and forbade her from talking to customers. "You can't be easy to get to, Kid. They won't think you're special if you do."

During Heather's first month in Chicago, Tony went to see her every afternoon. She took a bath in lavender soap and waited for him. Tony always brought lunch, and they spent hours making love. When Tony started skipping days, Heather felt lonely and thought of her family. Tony had given her a raise, and most weeks Heather sent as much as $20 home. Her mother and dad never asked questions about the money. All they knew was Heather was singing somewhere in Chicago.

One afternoon, Tony called to tell her he had some business at the club and would see her later that evening. Although Tony wanted Heather at the apartment waiting for him, Heather decided to go shopping on this beautiful day. While she was out, she decided to buy Tony a gift. In one of the department store windows, she spied a blue striped silk tie that she bought and had gift wrapped. Heather was so excited that she wanted to give it to Tony right away. She decided to surprise him by dropping it off at the club even though Tony had specifically told her never to come to the restaurant before 8 o'clock in the evening. Heather was too excited to wait.

Through the window of the restaurant, Heather saw Tony sitting at a large table full of people, older people, men, women, and children, all talking, laughing, and eating. Harry was the only person she recognized. Heather walked through the door with the gift in her hand and stood at the front of the restaurant for a moment, watching for an opportunity to signal for Tony's attention. When he did finally look up, she smiled and waved his gift in the air. Tony quickly spoke to Harry, who instantly got up from the table and hurried over to Heather, "Hug me, Heather! Quick! Hug me like a long lost friend you haven't seen in years. Quick, Heather! Do it now!"

Heather put her arms around Harry's neck and convinced everyone in the room she was there to see him. She really was, after all, an excellent actress. "When did you get in town?" Harry exclaimed. "You're looking wonderful! Let's go outside."

Harry took Heather by the arm and pushed her outside. "What in the hell do you think you're doing, Heather?"

"I bought Tony a present, Harry. I just dropped by to give it to him. What's the matter?"

"Are you crazy? That's his wife and kids in there! It's his son's birthday party for God sakes!"

"Wife? Kids? What are you talking about?" Heather cried.

"Tony's married, Heather. Has been for 13 years. His whole family is in there, and so is hers."

"Married? Tony's married? Dear God!" Heather wept.

"C'mon, Kid. I'll take you home." Harry offered, putting his arm around her.

The whole affair *was* a dream. It really had been too good to be true! Too damn good to be true! Heather was devastated. It made sense. A few hours here, a few hours there, not wanting her to talk to customers, the gifts, the apartment, the isolation, the waiting for him to show up. "How could you be so stupid??" Heather demanded of herself.

Heather cried all afternoon. She was so in love with Tony. Now her life had changed. He had her heart, and although he had never told her he loved her, she had been sure he had. After all, he had bought her expensive gifts and just the way he looked at her...wasn't that love? Life was all about Tony. This can't be happening! Could she be more naïve??

Heather suddenly felt insecure. That night when Heather went to work, she made sure she looked as seductive as possible. With the exception of her red rimmed eyes, Heather was alluring and acted like an enchantress to everyone in the room. For the first part of the evening, Tony was not there, and Heather took the opportunity to mingle with the men who had become her fans. She was charming and witty and flitted from man-to-man, enjoying lustful stares like a social butterfly.

Since she had learned Tony was married, she had a deep desire to have her beauty validated. A part of her felt like she was competing with another woman. If Tony saw that other men found her attractive, he would surely see her as a keeper. As she was singing "I Ain't Got Nobody," Heather saw Tony walk into the room. He looked angry and did not even glance her way. She had never seen him look so dark. That made her nervous.

After the song, Heather smiled broadly and quickly dashed to her dressing room. What was going on? This morning she had woken up in love with a handsome man who made love to her with undying passion and who showered her with gifts. Now she was feeling lost, used, and even afraid. When she looked in the mirror, she saw a young, sexy, seductive woman, but inside she was a frightened little girl. Just because she wanted to surprise the man she loved with a gift? What had she done wrong?

Thirty minutes passed, and it was time for Heather to sing again. Someone knocked at the door. When Heather opened it, she found Harry deeply concerned. "You're on, Kid; are you up to it?"

"Sure I am, Harry. What's wrong with Tony? He looked so angry when he came in."

"You broke his rules, Heather. Tony don't like it when his rules are broken. In fact, real bad things have happened to people who break his rules. Why do you think he has a driver pick you up and take you home every night? He don't like his dames talking to anyone but him. You broke two rules today, Heather, and it ain't good. Tony is a hot tempered, jealous man, and when he gets angry, he's dangerous!"

Coming from the door, a woman's voice announced, "I think Heather is finished for the night."

"Hello, Miss Victoria," Harry uttered respectfully.

"Get your things, honey; you are coming with me," the woman demanded.

"Who are you? Where's Tony?" Heather asked hurriedly.

"Tony is busy," the woman replied. "Come with me now, Heather, or there is a good chance you might end up in the Chicago River tonight."

"What?" Heather gasped.

"Do what she says, Heather. You won't be the first dame Tony put in the river," Harry remarked. "I've seen Tony do real bad things to girls who break his rules. I'm outta' here!"

Fear completely consumed Heather. Trembling, she understood that she had never seen Tony that angry before. In fact, she had hardly recognized him.

The woman insisted, "Listen to me, Honey! Tony is insanely jealous! I have known him for years and he is dangerous. He likes to cut up women. One of the customers made a lewd comment about you that sent him into a fury. I came here tonight with an old friend who knows Tony, and he told me what's going down. My friend admires you and he does not want to see you get hurt. He's keeping Tony busy for now, but there's no time. We have to go, honey. NOW! There's a car waiting in back. I am taking you to Texas!"

Lucy

Talented, cute, sassy and amusing, Lucy loved men! She especially loved cowboys, and the cowboys loved Lucy. She didn't see her profession as work; she saw it as fun. Lucy was the life of the party. She loved to sing and dance. In her spare time, Lucy loved to be outside with her watercolors, painting landscapes of the Concho River, a West Texas sunset, or a group of prickly pear with colorful blossoms. Smiling and bubbly, Lucy was a joy to be around. Her heart burst with love, yet she spoke exactly what was on her mind. A friend to all, Lucy enjoyed a good time.

Lucy's Story

Lucy Armstrong had grown up in "the Houston Heights," a streetcar suburb close to Houston, Texas. Her family lived in a Victorian home on Nicholson Street. Lucy had four older sisters. Before she was born, Lucy's mother had lost a baby boy who had died in his sleep when he was only three months old. The baby's death put Mrs. Armstrong and her husband into a deep depression. Her husband, who had wished for sons, considered Lucy a huge disappointment, and even Mrs. Armstrong felt as though she had failed him. She resented baby Lucy. Except for nursing her, she gave her hardly any attention.

Mary, the family housekeeper, was a big woman who had come to America from Scotland with her husband, but when he had died, she had begun working for the Armstrong family. Mrs. Armstrong, pregnant with Lucy at the time, had been adamant about wanting a boy. It had saddened Mary to see how Mrs. Armstrong had resented her new baby girl. One night, awakened by Lucy's crying, Mary had gone into the nursery to find her mother completely ignoring her. Lucy then had become "her baby." She had sung to her and rocked her to sleep as if she were her own. Since Lucy had only brought Mrs. Armstrong distress, she had been fine with Mary taking over Lucy's needs. Her mother preferred spending time with the older girls, and paid virtually no attention to little Lucy.

On the outside, the Armstrongs had appeared to be the perfect family. Lucy's parents had raised their children right, at least as far as they were concerned. Every Sunday the family had attended church, scrubbed and clean. The girls had worn matching hats and the same colored dresses, tights and shoes. They had been taught good manners, and their mother had made sure all of her girls behaved like ladies. Each girl had her own porcelain doll, and the nursery was filled with toys. Lucy's sisters weren't mean to her; they had learned to ignore her from their mother. Lucy hadn't minded and had learned to be content, playing in her own little world.

Lucy didn't really know her father. He didn't interact with his girls and showed them no affection. Mary continued to love little Lucy and gave her the attention her mother withheld from her. When Lucy was 4 years old, she caused a commotion in her Sunday school when she proudly displayed her new bloomers to the class. Embarrassed, her mother began labeling Lucy the "trouble child." If there were mud tracks on the floor or something was broken in the Armstrong household, Lucy was probably the culprit.

When Lucy was 5, Mrs. Armstrong gave birth to a healthy baby boy. Little Matthew became the center of attention for the entire household. The older girls played with him and fought over who could hold him. Lucy became lost in the excitement of the new baby. If it hadn't been for Mary, Lucy would have had no attention at all.

Lucy was obviously different from her sisters, and sometimes even lived up to being "the trouble child." Mary only saw her as having a strong spirit and willing to take risks. "People who don't make mistakes aren't trying very hard," she used to say. She didn't want to break Lucy down and considered her a free spirited young horse running free across grassy plains. As Lucy matured, Mary did her best to hide any evidence when Lucy had messed up and made every attempt to protect her from trouble.

One day when Lucy was in the second grade she brought a note home:

Dear Mrs. Armstrong,
We find it best to inform you that we gave Lucy three swats at school today for talking in class.

It would be the first of many. "*Lucy was running in the hall.*" "*Lucy hid Josephine's notebook.*" "*Lucy tore up Monica's picture.*" Although Lucy had a perfectly good explanation, her mother seldom took her side and often sent her to bed without supper. Mary would sneak Lucy food, her heart breaking when her favorite little girl got into trouble. "They don't know that child," she remarked to herself. Mary was the only person who listened to Lucy when she tried to explain why she did what she did. For example, she told Mary that the reason she had been running in the hall was to tell the teacher that her friend had fallen and hurt herself. She had hidden Josephine's notebook because she had taken her crayons and wouldn't give them back. She had torn up Monica's picture because Monica had used a black crayon to scribble all over hers. By then even the teachers labeled Lucy the "trouble child." She was always the one who got the swats.

"Don't let them break your spirit, Lucy," Mary advised. "You are a precious child of God. Never forget that!"

When Lucy was 10, Mary noticed Lucy walking slowly and carefully when she came home from school one day. She could hardly sit down. "What's the matter with you, Lucy?" she asked.

"My teacher hurt me, Mary," Lucy whimpered, with tears in her eyes. "Please don't tell Mother!"

"Let's go up to your room and let me take a look at that," Mary soothed.

To her horror she saw 6 huge welts on Lucy's backside. Two of them were oozing blood.

"My Lord, child! What did those monsters do to my sweet baby?"

Mary brought out ointment and bandages from the first aid cabinet. "Lucy, I believe I need to tell your mother about this."

"No, Mary, please don't! You know how angry she gets! Mother will send me to bed without supper if you do!"

"What in the world happened to make them do this to you?" Mary asked. Her heart was breaking.

"Agnes Foster was being mean to my friend Linda. She told her she couldn't be in her stupid club because Agnes's mother said Linda's mother is nothing but a whore. I don't know what a whore is, but it must be something bad because it made Linda cry. I grabbed both her pigtails and threw her on the ground. Her dress got real dirty. Then she started crying like a big baby and ran and told the teacher."

Mary grinned her "*that's my Lucy*" grin. "Lucy Girl, I love you!"

"What's a whore, Mary?" Lucy asked.

"You're right, honey. It's not a nice word, and you should never say it again. It's a bad name for a woman who is nice to men." Mary helped her put on a clean dress. Just then the doorbell rang.

"I'll be back in a minute, baby."

Mary saw a scowling woman and a girl about Lucy's age with long brown pigtails, standing on the front porch. The girl had the same kind of pinched up look on her face.

"I am here to see Mrs. Armstrong. My name is Mrs. Eloise Foster, and this is my daughter Agnes," the woman announced before Mary had even opened the door.

"Yes Ma'am," Mary replied calmly, although she felt herself boiling. "You can wait in the parlor."

When Mrs. Armstrong came into the parlor, she instantly knew the root of this visit had to be Lucy. It was always Lucy. "Yes, may I help you?" she asked.

"Lucy assaulted my poor little Agnes today and your daughter needs to apologize and be punished!"

"Just a minute please," she replied. "Mary, please go upstairs and bring Lucy in here to me."

Mary found Lucy. "Agnes Foster and her ugly Mama are downstairs, honey. Now keep your temper. Be nice, and just listen. Don't talk unless you are spoken to and whatever you do, just say you're sorry."

"But I'm not sorry, Mary! I'm not sorry! She's a mean girl!"

"Just do what I say, Lucy. Just do what I say."

When Lucy and Mary entered the room, the two mothers were talking. Agnes had a nasty smirk on her face, and Mary saw her stick her tongue out at Lucy.

"Her dress was filthy when she came home! Lucy owes my daughter an apology," Mrs. Foster demanded.

Mrs. Armstrong was not happy. "Lucy, apologize to Agnes."

"No!" Lucy answered.

"See, Mama, I told you she was mean and rude."

"Lucy, apologize now, young lady!" Mrs. Armstrong insisted.

Mary nodded at Lucy. "I'm sorry, Agnes," she sighed with her fingers crossed behind her back.

"I assure you she will be punished. This will not happen again," Mrs. Armstrong promised.

Agnes threw Lucy one last smirk as she and her mother left the Armstrong home.

"Lucy! What in the world were you thinking?" her mother asked.

"Pardon me, Miss Armstrong, but Miss Lucy has already been punished."

"What do you mean?"

"The teacher hit me with a cane, Mother."

"I don't believe you. Let me see."

"I've already dressed the wounds, Ma'am," Mary offered.

"What?? Why wasn't I told! Let me see!"

Mrs. Armstrong unbuttoned the back of Lucy's dress and saw the huge welts on her back. "O my!" she winced, but then she straightened up and raised her nose. "You deserved it, Lucy. You certainly deserved it. Mary, do not set a place for Lucy this evening! I can't bear to even look at her." Lucy's mother left the room.

With warm salty tears running down Mary's face, she buttoned her dress. "I'm so sorry Lucy. Try to stay out of trouble. It hurts my heart to see you hurt, baby girl."

Lucy hugged her favorite person in the world. "I love you, Mary. I know you love me too. I don't like to see you cry, Mary. I will try to be better, I promise," she assured her.

After the incident at school, Lucy and Linda became best friends. Although Lucy remained feisty, being friends with Linda helped her to stay out of trouble. Linda had long dark auburn hair. One day, while sitting on a bench at the park, they saw a beautiful red cardinal land on a bush close to where they were. "What a pretty red bird," Linda commented.

"You're pretty too, Linda," Lucy remarked. "I'm going to call you 'Redbird' from now on!" Lucy and Linda spent many days together, and for once in her life, Lucy didn't feel like an outcast. She came home and told Mary all about her friend Redbird and that made Mary happy.

At their all-girls school, Agnes and a group of friends enjoyed thinking that they were better than anyone else. Thinking themselves as the elite of the school, they made life miserable for the other girls. Lucy and Linda were friendly to everyone, and made it their personal mission to rescue girls who had been mistreated by Agnes Foster and her group.

On Linda's twelfth birthday, Lucy had painted her a beautiful watercolor of a red cardinal on a branch. On the bottom right corner in calligraphy, she had written, *To Redbird, my very best friend. Love Lucy.*

She had spent all week working on it, making it just right. To her great disappointment, Linda was absent from school that day. She was absent the following week as well. When she did return, Linda acted tired and looked sad.

"What happened?" Lucy asked when she saw her friend. "Are you OK?"

"My mother left us, Lucy. She moved to New York with some man. My brothers cry themselves to sleep every night, and my father is so sad. I'm worried about him, Lucy."

Agnes Foster and her pack of she-wolves sauntered over to where Lucy and Linda were standing. "Heard your whore mother moved to New York with a handsome rich stud," she smirked.

Feeling her friend boiling, Linda grabbed Lucy's arm. She didn't want Lucy to get into trouble. It was all Lucy could do not to pull Agnes down on the ground again.

"You're going to be just like her. Everyone knows girls like you end up just like their mothers," Agnes snorted in a snobby, ugly tone. She laughed and her friends joined in.

"Then I guess you're going to be an ugly, gossipy, nasty old hen," Lucy blurted out. "Cluck, cluck, cluck, cluck, cluck, cluck, cluck!"

Linda held Lucy's arm even more tightly. She knew Lucy could whip Agnes and she was afraid of the consequences.

Agnes was livid. "Cluck cluck, cluck, cluck, cluck, cluck, cluck!" Lucy repeated over and over, delighted she had made Agnes angry.

"I'll get you, Lucy Armstrong! One day I'll get you good!"

As Lucy got older, she became more rebellious. The opposite of her mother's vision for her, people referred to her as the "black sheep of the family." Lucy made some effort to conform to the rules of charm school where Mrs. Armstrong sent all her daughters, but the "la dee da" attitude of being ladylike, however, she found boring and trite.

Lucy found a new world in painting, working with water colors. She proudly showed each finished work to Mary. "Oh yes, Lucy girl. You are an artist and a good one! I can see your spirit in these paintings. The colors are bright and cheerful, and your lines are strong and bold just like you are." Lucy gave most of her paintings to Mary. She was the one who appreciated them because she knew Lucy's spirit and soul.

Every year Lucy's sisters attended the cotillion ball, and Mrs. Armstrong always had a coming out party for each of her daughters. Lucy's junior year in high school should have been her year. Although Mrs. Armstrong allowed Lucy to attend the cotillion, she had decided not to host a coming out party for her. "She'll just embarrass us," she told her husband.

Although Mary was upset, Lucy was all right with it. She thought the whole thing was silly and over rated anyway. "You are a beautiful young lady," Mary told her. "If I were your mother…"

"You are my Mama, Mary. You always have been. I don't need a stupid party to prove I'm worthy to date some snobby man from a rich family!"

On the night of the cotillion, the girls were dressed in their white gowns. Lucy wore a hand-me-down dress from her older sister. As Mary helped her get ready, she gushed, "You are gorgeous, Lucy! So pretty. You will be the belle of the ball!"

Linda and Lucy were by far among the prettiest girls at the dance. Agnes Foster and her pack of she-wolves were also there. Although the girls had managed to avoid each other through the years, they remained mortal enemies. This night, Agnes aimed to wreak her revenge on Lucy; Agnes's friends were in on it. The revenge had been planned for weeks. They were going to ensure that Lucy be thrown out of the cotillion.

Having slipped sleeping powder into a glass of punch, Agnes brazenly marched over to Douglas Brown, a skinny kid with big teeth and glasses. "Lucy Armstrong has a big crush on you!" she announced with excitement. "She talks about you all the time. Take this over to her and talk to her. She's over there with that redheaded girl."

Poor unsuspecting Douglas Brown eagerly walked over to where the girls were standing and presented Lucy with the glass. "Hello, Lucy. Would you like some punch?"

"Sure, Douglas," Lucy replied sweetly. Agnes and her pack of she-wolves watched as Lucy took a sip and then another.

"Would you like to dance?" Douglas asked.

"I'd love to, Douglas."

Lucy put the drink down, and Douglas Brown escorted her onto the dance floor. In the meantime, Agnes quickly disposed of the glass of punch. In the middle of the dance, Lucy told Douglas that she was feeling dizzy and needed to sit down. The room started spinning, and Lucy could hardly breathe. From across the room, Linda saw her friend stagger and quickly ran over and sat down beside her.

"Lucy, Lucy, what's wrong?"

"I don't know Linda... I feel so dizzy." Lucy had had just enough of the drug to make her dopey. Agnes's plan worked perfectly.

Two of the chaperones approached Lucy. "We hear you've been drinking, young lady, and you are intoxicated. You'll have to leave. We've called you a cab."

"What!" Linda exclaimed. "She hasn't been drink... Oh no."

Linda looked up and saw Agnes and her friends laughing hysterically and suddenly knew what had happened. "I'll go with her," Linda told the chaperones. Linda and the cab driver stood at the door propping Lucy up when they rang the doorbell at the Armstrongs' home.

Mary helped her onto the sofa where Lucy's mother found her. Mortified, she demanded, "What in the world happened?"

"Agnes Foster put something in her drink. I know she did," Linda offered. "Agnes told the chaperones that Lucy was drunk."

Mary brought a cold wash rag and laid it on Lucy's forehead.

"This girl is trouble; she's always been trouble. I'm done with her!" Lucy's mother stormed and stomped out of the room.

The next day Lucy's mother called her sister in San Angelo, Texas and made plans for Lucy to stay with her. Linda and Mary were both heart broken.

Before Lucy left, she saw Agnes one more time. She knew Agnes had a big crush on Mark Donahue, the captain of the football team, and wrote her a note that read:

Dearest Agnes,
I just have to see you. Meet me at the lake by the big rock tonight at 7.
I'll be waiting.
All my love, Mark Donahue

Agnes showed up like Lucy knew she would. When Lucy surprised Agnes at the rendezvous site, Agnes looked at her fearfully. "You're not so brave without your she-pack, are you, Agnes? I want you to know, not today, and maybe not tomorrow, but someday I assure you, you're going to pay for the mean things you've done to me, Linda, and everyone else you've hurt. Keep looking over your shoulder, Agnes, 'cause I swear one day, I'll be there!"

That night she went to Linda's house to say goodbye. "I wish you could have been there, Linda! You should have seen her face! It was fantastic! She ran away screaming. I think I really scared her!" she boasted.

"What am I going to do without my best friend?" Linda cried.

"We'll figure it out," Lucy assured her. "I'll see you again, Redbird! I promise!"

The next day, after a tearful goodbye with Mary, Lucy boarded a train to start her new life in San Angelo, Texas.

Redbird

The girls who lived at Miss Pearl's Parlor were the prettiest girls in San Angelo. Just like the Concho Pearl, each one was unique and beautiful. Redbird was known as being especially kind-hearted. Everybody loved her. A friend to all, she had a sixth sense and knew when someone was off her game. Whenever Redbird felt a friend was troubled, she often asked, "Are you OK?" Her friends were her treasures, and Redbird, in addition to being incredibly intelligent and loyal, was an excellent listener. Redbird laughed when they laughed and cried when they cried.

Redbird who had shiny, thick, auburn hair, also had, as one man put it, "Legs up to there." Charming and appealing, she knew how to make a man feel like he was the most important, smartest, sexiest man she had ever met. Sexually, Redbird was extremely talented. A man always felt like he could take on the world after spending time with Redbird.

Redbird's Story

Redbird, whose real name was Linda Donovan, had grown up in what some in Texas referred to as "high cotton" and was the epitome of a well-bred lady. Her father, Michael Donovan, was a tall, robust, self-made millionaire who had started his working career as a lowly dock worker. He and his brother Donald owned an international importing company in Houston, Texas. Both brothers had vibrant red hair and were respected for their integrity and vigorous work ethics. Offspring of Irish immigrants, their father had also worked on the docks. They began their business in Galveston  but then relocated to Houston in 1900 after the deadliest hurricane in American history took the lives of over 8,000 people and destroyed most of the buildings on Galveston Island.

Tragically their own dear mother had been killed in the storm, and her body was never found.

When Linda's father was 37 years old, he had married Alice Gallagher, whom he had fallen in love with the first time he had ever laid eyes on her at a business lunch between her father and the brothers. When Alice's mother died, she travelled throughout Europe with her father on business trips. Although she was only 17 years old, her maturity, poise, and elegance captivated him as much as her dark curly hair, ivory skin, and sparkling emerald green eyes. Michael was twenty years her senior, but from the first time he had seen her, he was smitten.

Alice, a beauty, and Michael, strikingly handsome, travelled extensively during the first five years of their marriage. He took her back to Europe on his business trips. They spent at least a week in New York before and after they crossed the Atlantic. When Linda was born, Alice hired a Nanny so the baby could travel with her parents. Several years later, when Linda's brothers were born, although they still travelled to Europe once a year, her parents stayed in Texas most of the time. To make up for the lack of European travel, Michael found creative ways to entertain his bride.

Michael Donovan was a romantic. Every Saturday night, he hired a string quartet and he and Alice dined and danced on the terrace, always decorated with candles and flowers. Michael had a custom wooden dance floor installed because he knew how much Alice loved to dance. Alice also loved to entertain. Linda remembered her mother's long elegant gowns, gracefully flowing as her father glided his bride across the ballroom in their home. Michael loved Alice so much that, whenever she was present, it was as if she was the only other person in the room. Linda stayed in the nursery with her younger brothers and kept them entertained while her parents carried on their fairytale romance.

Many times children are wiser than they are given credit for. When Linda was ten years old she became aware that her mother had a wandering eye. Men looked at Alice and often took an extra moment to gaze deeply into her eyes for a covert response. Linda watched her mother respond with a coy smile. No wonder she was the envy of so many women; she flirted with their husbands. Although Linda's father was aware of his wife's wandering eye, he tried to pretend that nothing was going on. Linda noticed her father watching her mother with sadness in his eyes. Then she watched as he would intervene with whomever she was flirting with as if nothing were going on.

Linda loved her father so much that it hurt her heart when she saw his sorrow. Her mother gradually left the house more and more frequently and was coming home later and later. When Alice was at home, she drank heavily and started trivial arguments to give her an excuse for sleeping in another room. Finally, Linda's parents were sleeping in separate bedrooms. Linda felt her father's sadness and frustration. The once beautiful music and romantic evenings on the terrace turned into hateful arguments, ending with Alice's stomping into her bedroom and slamming the door. Linda's little brothers cried. Linda tried her best to console them.

On October 9th, Linda's 12th birthday, she awoke to the sound of her father's crying, a strange sound. It was the first time she had ever heard him cry. Linda ran into his room to see what was wrong. "She's gone, Linda. Your mother is gone."

"Oh, Daddy, surely you're mistaken," Linda cried, although she knew it was true.

"She left this note," he sobbed.

Dear Michael,

I know now I never loved you. I was so young when we married, and I confused admiration with love. Take care of the children; I know they will be fine without me. You are a responsible man, and I am confident that you will see to their welfare. Nathan Carter is relocating and has invited me to live with him in New York City. You know how I love it there. I believe he is the true love of my life. Tell the children, "Good-bye."
Alice

"Oh, Daddy!" Linda cried. She fell on the bed and wept.

From that day forward, Linda tried to keep up the spirits in the household, yet no matter how she tried, she never saw her father smile again. Often she heard her younger brothers, Alex 7 and Anthony 4, cry themselves to sleep. Sometimes they would find her in the night and crawl into bed with her. Their family had been destroyed and she knew she needed to be the glue to hold things together.

Linda's father went into a deep depression, most days coming home early from work and isolating himself in his room. Some days, he didn't go to work at all. Linda tried, but nothing she did helped to cheer him up. His spirit was shattered and his will to live faded away. A little over eight months after her mother had left, Linda found her father in bed not moving, his heart so broken it finally just stopped beating. He was fifty two years old.

Donald Donovan, Michael's brother and business partner, was the appointed guardian of Linda and her two younger brothers. Three years older than Linda's father, he was an aloof man, focused entirely on business. His wife, Gertrude, was a matronly, cold woman incapable of showing affection to anyone. Their sons had both married long ago, and it was clear Gertrude was not happy about taking on new wards.

Linda's aunt and uncle moved into the grand, elegant house where Alice and Michael Donovan once carried on a fairytale romance on the terrace, entertained with beautiful parties, and held garden teas. Every room held a memory of Linda's parents. She chose to forget the fighting and only remember the laughter and the happiness she saw in her father's eyes as he danced with his beloved Alice on those magical Saturday nights.

Linda's Uncle Donald worked long hours and Aunt Gertrude lived by the code "Children should be seen and not heard," which left Linda and her brothers emotionally lost. Linda tried to warm her brothers' hearts in an environment that was cold and conversation was formal and hostile. She knew that she was the only light in her brothers' lives and that she had to be strong. She created games and codes and formed a secret club that made Aunt Gertrude the mortal enemy. The children rarely left the nursery where Linda masterfully created a fantasy world for them. She told her brothers stories of faraway lands and castles, called them names like King Alexander and Sir Anthony, and commended them for slaying fierce dragons. They even made up "Gerty," an evil witch named after their aunt. Her creativity worked well in masking their reality. The boys adored their big sister.

As the years went by, Linda became a stunning young woman with beautiful long auburn hair, emerald eyes and ivory skin just like her mother. Tall and slender she glided across the room with grace and style. Aunt Gertrude was not happy about the men's attention to her niece. The prettier Linda became, the more hateful her aunt was to her. "She's going to turn out just like her mother," Linda heard her aunt tell her husband. "I see trouble on the way."

The harder Linda tried to get along with her aunt, the more distant she became. When nothing was ever good enough for Aunt Gertrude, Linda stopped trying. Because Alex and Anthony were so important to her, she kept them busy and made sure their homework was finished every night. Thank goodness, for Linda's best friend, Lucy, the only female in her life that she ever trusted. Lucy patiently listened to Redbird's secrets and frustrations.

In the 5 years she had been gone, Alice Donovan had made no contact with her children. The boys were silent in their grief and pain. Being abandoned by their mother made them dependent on Linda, and although she was also in emotional pain, she rose to the occasion with strength and valor. Linda made sure her brothers had decent birthdays with money she got from her Uncle Donald. She learned that her uncle would give her money when she asked, as long as Aunt Gertrude wasn't around. Although the boys rarely climbed into bed with her anymore, Linda kept her bedroom door unlocked, just in case.

One Christmas their mother sent a huge box full of gifts addressed to Linda, Alex, and Anthony. Linda had mixed emotions. She didn't know if she should be glad, sad, angry or indifferent and her brothers were completely lost. It was as if a stranger had sent them Christmas gifts. They did not know how to respond. Alex barely remembered his mother, and Anthony's only memory of her was the day she left and kissed him goodbye. Linda decided not to open the gifts for fear that their hurt and grief might surface. She suggested that they give the presents to the church and her brothers agreed.

Aunt Gertrude's jealousy of Linda and her Uncle Donald's apathy pulled the siblings closer. Every evening he'd shut himself in the library with a bottle of whiskey. He chose to distance himself from his family, putting his energy into his work. Linda didn't really blame him. Everyone in the house had different ways of coping with Aunt Gertrude. Linda didn't date because she was dedicated to her brothers. The older they got the more she felt they needed her.

At school, Lucy had been her best friend and confidant, had been her sunshine. After Lucy had been drugged and accused of being drunk at a dance, her mother had sent her to live with an aunt in San Angelo, Texas. Devastated, Linda had never felt so alone. She railed at her mother for leaving them and making her father ill. The pain of abandonment was almost too much to bear. Living with Aunt Gertrude built up resentment. For therapy, Linda began writing short stories that helped with her pain. "Gerty" was always the villain. Sometimes Linda referred to her as "Dirty Gerty." She created characters that expressed her emotions, and sometimes she even wrote poetry. Writing helped her unleash the deep pain that dwelled inside her heart.

When Linda graduated from high school at the top of her class, Uncle Donald and the boys attended the ceremony, but Aunt Gertrude stayed home. A few weeks later, Linda's cousin, Kyle and a business partner, Conner Murphy came to visit. Conner's family was extremely wealthy and he was investigating a business venture with her uncle's company. The negotiations and business conversations had been going well until Conner met Linda at dinner one evening, when his focus shifted. During the meal, Conner could not stop staring at Linda. She was wearing an emerald green dress that beautifully complemented her shapely curves and long red hair. The way he looked at Linda made her uncomfortable. This was a man who was used to getting his way.

After dinner, Conner and Kyle shared brandy and cigars on the front porch. "Why don't you come outside with us, my dear?" Conner slurred. He had already had too much wine at dinner.

"No thank you," Linda answered. "I will be retiring upstairs early this evening."

"She's not very friendly," Conner commented as he stumbled outside. "Kind of snooty."

Upstairs with her brothers playing Parcheesi, Alex observed, "That guy was creepy, I didn't like him at all."

Anthony concurred.

"He'll be gone soon enough," Linda consoled. "Let's just play and forget about him."

That night Conner slipped into Linda's bedroom and locked the door. He climbed on top of her and clamped his hand over her mouth. "Don't scream. I know people who will hurt your brothers in ways you can't even imagine! Just do what I tell you to do."

Linda had never been so frightened in her life. She wanted her father! She wanted her mother! The night was horrible. After he had finished, he stood up and stumbled onto the night stand, knocking a large porcelain lamp onto the floor. It made a loud CRASH and broke into hundreds of pieces.

Aunt Gertrude heard the noise and shook her husband to wake him up. Together they ran to Linda's side of the house and encountered Conner stumbling out of her room. "What is going on here?" Aunt Gertrude screamed as she entered Linda's room. Although it was completely clear what had happened, Gertrude ignored the fact that Conner was drunk and that Linda was hysterical. Instead she took full advantage of the situation. "You nasty girl! You nasty, nasty girl! I want you out of my house immediately!"

Her house! It was Linda's house. Her brothers' house! Aunt Gertrude was an intruder. It wasn't HER house, it was theirs!

Anthony and Alex chimed in. "No, No, Aunt Gertrude. Please No! Don't send Linda away!" they pleaded.

"I want all of you out of my house! I'm through with the lot of you. I've had enough, and I will tolerate no more," she taunted with a dramatic flair. Gertrude now had a sordid story, all she needed to justify her diabolical plans.

Uncle Donald didn't argue and chose not to pick this battle. He had learned long ago that it was far better for him in the long run to let Gertrude have her way. Besides, whiskey and work were all he cared about. He figured in light of the evening's events, it was probably better that Linda leave to protect his business interests with Conner's family.

Kyle, sympathetic and even remorseful to his cousin, quickly took the drunken Conner out of the house and checked him into a local hotel. The next day Kyle, as weak as his father, pretended nothing had happened. Fewer than 20 minutes with Conner had ruined Linda's life and separated her from Anthony and Alex. Her family had been destroyed and she was powerless.

The next day was a nightmare. Aunt Gertrude instructed the maid to pack Linda's bags. "I am leaving for the day. I can't stand to be in the same house as you. You are trouble and a nasty, nasty girl!" Although it was obvious to everyone what really happened, Aunt Gertrude would not back down. "I can't even look at you and I hope I never have to again!" were the last words Linda heard from her Aunt Gertrude.

Linda was heartbroken and worried about her brothers, who wept as she bid them goodbye. "Don't worry. We'll be together again soon. I'll find a way. I promise we will be together again."

Uncle Donald gave Linda $500 and sent her on her way. "Take care of yourself, Linda, and keep in touch. You can reach me at the office," was all he had to say. He was strictly business with no time for emotional concerns. The next week the boys were enrolled into a summer camp and then boarding school. Aunt Gertrude finally had her way. The big house was finally completely hers.

Linda thought of her friend Lucy who had moved to San Angelo to live with her aunt after her mother had kicked her out of the house. Lucy had written Linda to tell her that she was working at the Landon Hotel. In the letter she had told her she missed her and invited her to visit anytime. Linda thought that was as good an option as any, so she bought a train ticket on the Orient Railroad to San Angelo, Texas.

When Linda arrived at the train station, she realized that this new world was quite different from Houston. It was a dust bowl compared to the greenery and tall pine trees that she had always known, yet she was impressed with how quiet and peaceful it seemed. A warm dry breeze felt good on her skin. Linda had only known the humidity of Houston. This new arid climate seemed like a nice change.

Linda had decided to check into the Landon Hotel, a first class hotel. Linda was impressed with the interior design. She checked into a room and unpacked her bags. Tired and hungry, she called room service and ordered lunch. She thought of the days when she was a little girl and the family went to Corpus Christi and enjoyed holidays on the beach. Although she hadn't been in a hotel since she was a little girl, she remembered that her mother ordered room service for lunch and saved the dining experience for the evening meal.

Still sore from her horrible ordeal only two nights before with Conner, Linda decided to take a bath after lunch. In the peace of her room, Linda realized she was alone. Sitting in the warm tub, she sobbed.

For the last 48 hours she had suppressed her feelings. Ever since her mother left, Linda had been taking care of first her father and then her two little brothers. She had been taking care of someone else and had seldom considered her own sadness and abandonment. Instead, she had opted to fill the void by tending to her family. Today it had all come to a climax. She cried herself to sleep and didn't wake up until dawn.

When Linda did wake up, she realized her nightmare was real. Ever resilient, however, she rolled out of bed, washed her face, and put on a lovely yellow dress, one of several nice dresses she owned. Her uncle had never been stingy with her father's money and allowed Linda to shop regularly even though Aunt Gertrude protested strongly.

In the Landon's lobby, Linda watched the bell clerks tending to luggage in the hustle and bustle of the new day. She walked outside and headed in the direction of the Concho River. The sun felt warm on her skin, and the river sparkled as if it knew she needed cheering up. Linda focused on her new life.

Although she was missing her brothers, at the same time, she was ecstatic to get away from Dirty Gerty and she was looking forward to seeing Lucy

After a long stroll by the Concho River, Linda headed back to the Landon Hotel. In the lobby she asked the front desk, "Excuse me. Can you please tell me where I might find Lucy Armstrong? I believe she is one of your employees."

The two clerks behind the desk looked at each other, both rolling their eyes. The taller one finally spoke up, "Lucy doesn't work here anymore. You can find her at Miss Pearl's Parlor. It's the big three story mansion on the Concho River on the northwest side of town. You can't miss it. Here's the address."

"Thank you kindly," Linda chirped. The clerks stared at her for a moment and watched her walk away. Then looked at each other with smirky grins.

After breakfast Linda took a cab to Miss Pearl's Parlor, a glorious mansion with a lovely view of the Concho River. After thanking the cab driver, Linda curiously walked up the steps and knocked at the door. A black woman greeted her with a friendly smile.

"Yes, Ma'am. Can I help you?" The woman looked Linda up and down with approval, "My! What a lovely yellow dress."

"Thank you. Yes Ma'am my name is…"

Suddenly a familiar voice screamed her name.

"Redbird!!"

Harmony

Just before breakfast every morning, beautiful piano music played throughout Miss Pearl's Parlor, gentle and soothing, creating a harmonious ambience in the house. Harmony, who played both piano and guitar, believed her purpose in life was to provide music for people to enjoy. She loved playing the 10-foot-Steinway in the Parlor's Main Room. Her rich sounds created a pleasant way for the girls to wake up or to even sustain a bit more much-needed sleep. By the time Harmony started playing, Mozella and her staff had already begun their chores for the day. Somehow cleaning the speakeasy, changing linens in the "entertaining parlors," and making the Main Room look as if no one had been there the night before was easier when music filled the house. Often when Mozella entered the room, Harmony started playing a "negro spiritual" like "Amazing Grace" or "All My Trials" for her to sing. Mozella had a beautiful, rich singing voice, and Harmony was thrilled to accompany her on the piano.

Harmony's Story

Harmony's mother named her, "Harriett Jane," and when she introduced their baby girl to her husband, his face lit up and he played with her tiny hands. "These little fingers will play the piano one day." Her father, a musician who played for the Methodist Church in town, had learned music from his mother at an early age. Sadly, Harmony's parents both perished in a house fire in Sonora, Texas when she was only a year old. Even though her father managed to rescue the baby from the blazing house, he died trying to save her mother. After losing her mother and father, little Harriet lived with her paternal grandmother, Opal O'Howell, in Austin, Texas.

Opal was a generous woman who loved to laugh. When she was just a toddler, little Harriett sat next to her grandmother, "Nana" and listened to her play the brown, square grand piano made of satinwood that faced the window in one of the small parlors. Sometimes the little girl stood on the floor and reached up to bang the high keys while her grandmother played. Little Harriet felt her contribution made a big difference and that she was actually helping her grandmother out. One day, her grandmother showed little Harriett how to use just her index finger. "Just play with one finger, dear. That's how you make music. If you bang the notes, it's just noise." As little Harriet carefully played one note at a time on the treble keys, her grandmother accompanied her with a bass line. "Very good, honey! You made harmony! It sounds wonderful."

"I am Harmony?" little Harriett exclaimed.

"You certainly are," her grandmother smiled. From that day forward she became, "Harmony."

When Opal's husband had died in a farming accident, Opal had moved in with her sister, Ruth Ann, who taught several grades in a one-room schoolhouse. Female school teachers in Texas were not allowed to marry, and although some ladies left the teaching profession to have families, "Aunt Ruth" never really got around to it. She was devoted to her students and felt great satisfaction in mentoring and teaching young minds. Opal made her living teaching piano and playing and singing for churches and socialite parties.

By the time she was 3 years old, Harmony could pick out melodies on the piano, and by the time she was 10, Opal began teaching her how to read music and understand music theory. After a while she began creating melodies of her own. One day her grandmother listened as Harmony played a hauntingly simple, beautiful melody. "I've never heard that piece before, sweetheart. Who is the composer?"

"I wrote it, Nana. I like making my own music. It makes me feel free!"

"You are just like Clara Schumann! She was a composer and quite an accomplished concert pianist. She was actually married to Robert Schumann."

"The composer who wrote 'Träumerei'?" Harmony asked.

"Exactly! She was a child prodigy herself and a strong woman. In the later years of their marriage, when her husband became mentally ill, she played concerts to support the family.

She survived countless tragedies with her children and was good friends with the composer Johannes Brahms."

"As in 'Brahms Lullaby'?"

"Yes, Ma'am!"

"Why have I never seen her compositions, Nana?"

"Probably because she was a woman. Think about it. How many women composers do you know?"

"Up until now, I guess just me," Harmony smiled.

"Do you think you are the only woman who ever composed music?"

"I never thought about it, Nana."

Harmony attended the one room schoolhouse where her Aunt Ruth taught school. Although she was a bright girl and always made good grades, her first love was music. For her twelfth birthday, Opal bought Harmony a guitar. "This is so you can take your music with you." Opal taught Harmony how to play chords and sing and play folk songs. In addition to singing in the church choir where her grandmother played, sometimes she tagged along to play a couple of pieces at social events where her grandmother had been hired to play. When Harmony played, she would lose the sense of anyone else in the room, and pulled her audience in with her passion and dynamics.

Progressing through her teens, Harmony changed into a charming young lady. Some nights she tied rags in her hair to form long, golden ringlets that bounced when she walked. Although Opal and Ruth were not wealthy they knew how to make it look as if they were. Aunt Ruth taught Harmony the etiquette and grace to be a lady and the epitome of class as if she had attended the finest of charm schools in Texas.

As Harmony grew into her beauty, Opal noticed that she attracted the attention of more and more men. Harmony's focus however, remained on the music and she was not aware that men were noticing her and although she was polite she remained shy. Her sole interest was playing the piano to make people feel the music. Her "music trance" actually drew people into her performance. Her body swayed back and forth as her fingers glided across the piano keys like a bird in flight. Harmony's music was hypnotic and at times so moving, her playing brought tears to both men and women in her audiences.

As more and more people experienced her music, Harmony's reputation spread and the demand for her performing began to increase. Opal was extremely proud of her granddaughter and would beam when she received rave reviews. Harmony played music in some of the finest homes in Austin. She especially loved the stately homes with enormous columns and wrap-around porches.

A few weeks after Harmony's 16th birthday, she had been asked to play for an anniversary party for one of the members at the country club. Among local affluent families that had been invited were the Jacksons. Entering the hallway, after her performance, Harmony overheard some girls discussing Judith Jackson's debutante ball. Apparently one of the girls had suggested Harmony be invited to Judith's coming out party.

"What do you mean invite Harmony to my debutante ball? Are you kidding? She's not one of us!" Judith screeched. Judith, dressed in ribbons and white, spied Harmony and snarled, "What do you want? If you are looking for a powder room the one for the help is in the kitchen. Now go away!"

Harmony had certainly never been talked to like that before. All she had known was applause and compliments on how well she played. She ducked into the kitchen and found the small bathroom. When her grandmother picked her up, she broke down in tears in the car.

"Nana, Judith was so mean! She said I wasn't one of them! What does that mean?" she sobbed.

Opal was livid. Harmony was not only talented, she had beauty and grace, and Judith was obviously jealous. Now her granddaughter was finding it difficult to understand why she had been so hateful to her. The two sisters had kept her protected from the world, treating her like a musical princess.

Nana was disgusted. "I know the Lord loves everyone equally and sees no person as better or less than another. I've seen Judith and her parents at church. Her mother never says, 'Hello' to me. It's obvious she clearly sees me as the help. I have never understood why some people call themselves Christians but think they are better than anyone else!"

Harmony took her refuge with her Nana and Aunt Ruth. Performing music was a different experience now. Before her encounter with Judith, Harmony had felt special and saw her talent as a gift to be shared. The experience with Judith changed her and she couldn't get over it. Judith's words, "You're not one of us!" rang in her ears every time she walked into a beautiful mansion, fancy country club or hotel. Although she played the piano beautifully, she knew she would always fall short of ever being a lady of society.

Music became her survival. Harmony had used music when she wanted to lose herself in another world, but with the pain of Judith's ugly words, her playing became emotionally more intense. She played Chopin and Beethoven to express her heavy heart, Bach to bring order to her chaos, and Debussy to bring beauty into her tormented world. She never noticed that she became even more interesting to those who loved her and ignited more contempt with those who were jealous. As long as Harmony was able to pretend to be alone in a room the music enabled her to detach herself from reality.

On a Saturday afternoon, the Country Club was hosting a garden party to raise money for the orphanage and had hired Harmony to play the piano. David Prescott, tall and slender with light hair and soft brown eyes, had been enchanted with Harmony for years. Today he mustered enough courage to speak to her. "Hello, Miss Harmony. May I get you something to drink?"

"That would be lovely, David," she responded.

Green with envy, Judith Jackson decided to remind Harmony that she was unqualified to mingle with any of the young gentlemen there. Although Judith was relatively attractive, her attitude repelled the pure of heart. Judith gathered up some of her friends and approached Harmony like a pack of wolves. "Poor little Harmony, can't be what she wants to be," Judith sung in a nasty tone as she sauntered up to where Harmony was standing. The other girls laughed.

Nana, however, had prepared her for this moment. "Don't let anyone steal your power, Harmony! Remember what they did to Jesus. People are only mean when they are afraid, and the biggest cowards surround themselves with other cowardly people. Individually, they are weak. Next time Judith Jackson or anyone for that matter is ugly to you, look straight into their eyes, and smile. It will confuse them. Consider the source. Ugly people say ugly things. Don't take it personally, in fact, you can even feel sorry for them because they are usually insecure, unhappy people. Their words belong to them until you decide to own them. You might even tell them you feel sorry for them. That will really confuse them and disarm their power."

"Hello Judith," Harmony smiled. Some of the girls appeared uncomfortable with Harmony's direct approach. She locked herself into her antagonist's hateful gaze. At that moment, David handed a drink to Harmony. "Thank you, David," she said sweetly not taking her eyes off Judith. "I'm sorry for you, Judith," Harmony offered calmly. "You must be having a bad day." Judith's face turned crimson with fury.

This time Judith yelled at her, "DID YOU NOT HEAR ME? I SAID, 'POOR LITTLE HARMONY, CAN'T BE WHAT SHE WANTS TO BE!!'" Obviously, Judith had created the phrase and practiced it many times. Her face was all scrunched up like she had just sucked a lemon.

"Nana was right. She does look ugly!" Harmony thought. Judith's bellowing created a scene so that everyone in the room stopped talking. All eyes were on the two girls.

Harmony still smiled benevolently.

"YOU DON'T BELONG HERE!! I SAID, 'POOR LITTLE HARMONY, CAN'T BE WHAT SHE WANTS TO BE,' AND YOU NEVER WILL!!"

"What do I want to be?" Harmony asked calmly.

"YOU WANT TO BE LIKE ME!! YOU WANT TO BE LIKE ME!!" Judith screamed.

Seeing everyone staring, the other girls scattered. The ladies were horrified at such a display. The men thought it amusing. Poor David Prescott had no idea what to do. If Judith had been a man, it would be easy. However, this was a woman challenging the object of his affection.

"Oh no, no, dear Judith. To be like you is the last thing I ever want to be," Harmony answered, shaking her head back and forth, still smiling.

The room started laughing, everyone except Judith's mother. Judith threw her glass of red fruit punch at Harmony. Everyone gasped. The laughter died.

Harmony looked down at her dress and then back into Judith's hateful stare. "I can always clean my dress, Judith, but you're always going to be mean. I really do feel sorry for you."

Screaming, Judith ran out of the room, her mother running after her.

With her head held high, Harmony turned to David, "I believe it is time for me to leave. David Prescott, would you be so kind as to escort me."

"It would be an honor, Harmony," David replied with a dramatic bow. He smiled and crooked his arm like gentlemen do.

Taking David's arm, "If you don't mind, kind sir, I need to pick up my music books. Please excuse me, everyone. Forgive me, but I will not be able to play for you today."

Mrs. Jackson reentered the room, wearing her daughter's same ugly scrunched-up face. She glared at Harmony with contempt. "You'll never work in Austin again! I'll see to that! Same goes for your grandmother. I'll have her fired from the church!"

"Yes, Ma'am," Harmony retorted politely. "After all, you are a good Christian lady. I've heard you say it many times."

Harmony shook as David escorted her outside. "That was amazing! I have heard people say, 'Kill them with kindness' and now I know what they mean. May I have the privilege to take you home?"

"Oh yes, please, David. That would be lovely."

"I am leaving for the army in a few weeks," he told her as they drove along. "I was wondering if I might write you, Miss Harmony. Our government is recruiting heavily since we have joined the war. I want to follow in my grandfather's footsteps and become a Colonel."

"You are very brave, David. Of course I will write you."

When Harmony entered the house and burst into tears, Nana was waiting for her with a big hug. Mrs. Jackson had called and repeated the ugly threats over the phone. David stood at the door watching, "Harmony was amazing tonight, Mrs. O'Howell, a perfect lady. She didn't back down. You would have been so proud. She brought those Jackson women to their knees!"

"I did what you told me, Nana. Judith said something hateful to me, and when she did, I smiled at her. It was strange how calm I felt at the time." Harmony sniveled through her tears. "She said I want to be like her. She's mean, Nana. I don't want to be like her!" she sobbed.

David wanted to put his arms around her and console her. He didn't know what to do. All he knew was that his heart was aching for Harmony. "I think I'll be going now."

"Why don't you stay, David. We have fried chicken, biscuits, greens and mashed potatoes," Nana offered.

"Yes Ma'am, I'd love to." David agreed eagerly.

That night sitting on the front porch, David gave Harmony her first kiss. It was sweet. For the next few weeks, David and Harmony were inseparable. David loved to listen to her sing and play. "Play Yellow Rose of Texas," he asked every day. "It's my favorite song." She played it every day for him on both the guitar and the piano. Their favorite outing was to picnic at Barton Springs, where Harmony took her guitar and sang for David. Sometimes he sang along. David took her to dinner several nights, and sometimes they strolled along the river. Although Nana was happy for her granddaughter, she felt a strong concern. War was ugly business, and she was worried for David's safety.

David's parents loved Harmony. Although on holiday in Mexico when the incident at the Country Club happened, they heard about it when they returned. "I never liked the Jackson's much anyway," his mother admitted to Harmony. "Their name should be the Jackassons!" she chuckled shaking her head. Her comment made Harmony smile in surprise.

The night before David left for active duty, the Prescotts invited Ruth and Nana to their house for dinner, along with a few close friends and family. Everyone was concerned for David. There was grave concern throughout America for all of the young men called to war since the United States had joined the alliance. "I will wait for you. Come home safely. I love you, David!" Harmony cried. She presented him with a picture of herself playing the piano. "Every time you look at this, know I am thinking of you."

The next morning, friends, family, and Harmony went to see David off at the train station. He looked so handsome and brave as he waved goodbye. "I love you, Harmony! I love you, Mama! Goodbye! Write me!"

It was the last time they saw him alive.

When the news came, the scream pierced the air around the Prescott house. There is no cry like a mother who has lost her child. When the phone rang to the O'Howell house, Nana took the call. Harmony knew when she saw her face. "Is it David, Nana? Is it? Is it, David? O no, is it David? No, Nana! No!!"

"Come here child." Opal reached out her arms and held her until Harmony fell, exhausted from crying.

When David's remains arrived, the full reality of his passing finally set in. Before that, Harmony had lived in the illusion of hope that his death might be a horrible mistake. At the front of the funeral procession, David's uncle led a saddled horse with boots in the stirrups facing backwards, symbolizing the loss of a fallen comrade. He had done the same for his grandfather during his funeral.

For weeks after the funeral, Harmony never left the house. Music was her refuge from the real world and was the only way she could find comfort. Hauntingly and slowly she sang, *Yellow Rose of Texas*. "It makes me feel closer to him, Nana. Sometimes I feel like he's here with me, singing along like he did before."

Opal did not lose her job playing the piano at church or anywhere else. Mrs. Jackson was not as powerful as she believed she was. However, Harmony did stop playing at social events. The thought of running into Judith was too painful to imagine, especially after losing her beloved David. Opal tried to help her granddaughter through her grieving, but there was only so much she could do, although Harmony's depression deeply concerned her. She played the piano, read David's letters and cried. "Everything reminds me of David, Nana."

One morning several weeks after she had received the news about David's death, Harmony found her Aunt Ruth on the porch holding her Nana's hand. Opal had her eyes closed, sitting in her rocking chair as if in a peaceful sleep. "She's gone, Harmony," Ruth whispered as she continued holding her sister's hand. "My Sissy is gone," she wept, with tears streaming down her face.

They buried Opal the next Saturday. Hundreds of people attended her funeral. Flowers were everywhere. At the graveyard, Harmony was completely numb through the whole ordeal. She felt isolated, as if she were in a dark chamber with voices echoing from the outside. At the house, when people brought food and paused for a brief word with her, she couldn't understand what anyone was saying; it all seemed so blurred. Later in the evening, Harmony sat at the piano and played. The piano was like an old friend to comfort her sadness. She played heavenly music for her Nana and her beloved David as if they were in the room with her, silent partners to her grief.

A week after she lost her Nana, David's mother knocked at the door. Harmony hadn't seen her since David's funeral. "Oh, Mrs. Prescott!" she cried.

"Harmony, I have a friend in San Angelo who runs the St. Angelus Hotel. It has an elegant dining room and the owners are looking for entertainment. I suggested you. I know there are too many memories for you here, and I believe a change will do you good."

Aunt Ruth agreed fully. Within a matter of days, Harmony was on a train to San Angelo, Texas. Mrs. Prescott was right. The St. Angelus Hotel dining room was exquisite and Harmony enjoyed playing the glossy black grand piano.

Harmony met Miss Victoria Pearl her first night on the job. Although she was an elegant lady, she seemed different than the socialites she had known in Austin. Miss Pearl came to the St. Angelus often, usually accompanied by different men. One evening Pearl handed Harmony her card. "I can see there is sadness about you, my dear. I'd like to invite you to tea this Saturday. You are so attractive and you are obviously a talented young lady."

Harmony took the card and looked straight into Miss Pearl's blue-green eyes. "Thank you, Miss Pearl. I will see you Saturday."

PART THREE

1923

Miss Pearl walked through the door of the huge mansion on the Concho River she had come to call home. Emma Grace, quickly gathering up her suitcase and overcoat, followed her into the parlor. Never before had she ever been surrounded with such elegance. As they walked from the Spanish tiled foyer into the "Grand Room," she could smell the soft scent of roses coming from a fountain by the west wall. The fourteen foot ceilings and crystal chandelier made her feel like a princess walking into a palace. "It was so kind of you, Miss Pearl, to give me a job. I really am a good cook!"

"You are welcome, Emma Grace. As long as you are useful, you may stay until you know what you want to do," Pearl assured her.

Emma Grace had never seen a house so grand. Fresh spring air gently blew through the open windows, making the lacy white curtains hanging throughout the house look as if they were dancing. The "Great Room" was decorated with Oriental rugs, mahogany tables, plush velvet couches and damask chairs. A ten-foot Steinway stood silently in the corner of the room poised for someone to sit on the bench and bring her to life.

Mozella, wearing a powder blue cotton dress, a white duster hat, and a clean white apron frock, entered the room with a stack of fresh towels in her arms. "This is Emma Grace, Mozella. I have hired her to help you in the kitchen. She says she can cook," Pearl told her friend.

Mozella looked approvingly at Emma Grace. "I can see why you invited her in, Miss Pearl. There's no doubt she's a pretty one! Come on, honey, I'll show you the kitchen and the room where you'll stay." Emma Grace followed Mozella through the kitchen to a small room with three beds. "This is where you'll sleep. There are some clean aprons in the closet. You can hang your things in there and put your suitcase under the bed. Get your pretty-self ready now, girl. There's work to be done! The cowboys are coming tonight, and they will surely be hungry when they get here."

Mozella was friendly but firm. As she walked back into the kitchen, Emma Grace heard her say, *"Proverbs 22, He who is generous will be blessed,* and Miss Pearl is truly generous."

Emma Grace laid her suitcase down and sat on the bed for a moment, crying grateful tears. "Thank you, God," she whispered. "I know I am here for a reason, and I also know you will help me figure out what that reason is." She wiped her face, changed her clothes, and walked into a new life. Emma Grace's prayers had been answered.

Meanwhile, prayers were also being answered in Big Lake, Texas. Earlier that day at the depth of 3050 feet, the Santa Rita Number One clearly showed the presence of gas and oil in the Permian sands. After years of dreams and a year-and-a-half of drilling for oil, the Santa Rita Number One was finally hitting the pay! The whooping and shouting resounded so loudly in Big Lake, Texas, the man in the moon could hear it. The men stopped the drilling and within 18 hours had secured over 30,000 acres of oil leases from surrounding land owners. San Angelo was on its way to becoming an oil boom town!

The Cowboys

It was just before dusk when the last golden glow of light casts itself across the land and the sun prepares to adorn the sky with brilliant colors before it sinks into the west. Lucy was pointing out of the window from the second floor of Miss Pearl's Parlor. "I can see them! Look, Heather…they're coming! The cowboys are coming!" Lucy shouted excitedly.

"Let me see!" Heather ran over to the window to stand beside Lucy. She gently pushed the light white curtain to the side for a better view.

"You're right!" Heather squealed with delight. "There's a dust cloud heading this way, and it's getting bigger and bigger! Let's go tell everyone!"

Both girls sprinted to the hallway, and Heather started knocking on doors. "The cowboys are coming! The cowboys are coming!"

Betsy ran out of her room, fastening a button on her dress. "Are they almost here?" she asked excitedly. "I can't wait to see Danny again!"

Lucy went to the back of the house to find Miss Pearl and Mozella outside enjoying the view of a brilliant West Texas sunset. In a matter of minutes, it looked as if God had taken a giant paintbrush and, with a few vast strokes of indigo, magenta, and bright, yellow-orange, had created an impressive masterpiece to bid farewell to another beautiful day. "Miss Pearl, the cowboys are coming!"

"Thank you, Lucy. We will be there in just a minute," Miss Pearl responded.

Upstairs the girls dashed around spraying mists of perfume in provocative places and took one last look in the mirror to check their make-up and primp their hair. Heather grabbed a large white plume from her room. It was important to her that men remembered their experiences with the now famous Heather and her feather. She liked to recite a little rhyme she created when she met a potential client. Playfully, she stroked her plume and recited, "I'm Heather with my feather. I can tickle your ears. I can tickle your nose. I can tickle your fancy and I can tickle your toes."

By now the girls had gathered on the porch to greet the cowboys. Miss Pearl stood stately and elegantly at the doorway of the house. "Be friendly, but do not act too eager, girls. The night is young, and we are all going to need our energy."

The women could see the dust cloud growing bigger and bigger as the horses galloped closer and closer to the house. The cowboys looked like men on a mission. Coming to town was the one adventure the cowboys looked forward to. The ladies were ready to show them a good time. Miss Pearl made an exception with the cowboys, who weren't the wealthiest clients who patronized the Parlor. As far as she was concerned, cowboys were sexy and good for morale.

Their muscular bodies were strong, and their skin was bronzed from working outside in the West Texas sun. The Texas cowboys' smooth western drawl had always impressed Miss Pearl. As long as the men were clean, respectful, and treated her girls like ladies, they were welcomed. Pearl especially liked the way they tipped their hats and said, "Yes, Ma'am or No, Ma'am."

The colorful West Texas sky served as a backdrop to the spectacular display of manhood riding toward them. When the cowboys reached Miss Pearl's Parlor, they lined up like a Fourth of July parade, tipping their hats to the ladies on the porch as they rode by. The cowboys had begun this little ceremony months ago, and the girls loved it.

Betsy waved her hand, yelling, "Hey, Danny! Hey, Danny!"

Cleanliness was mandatory at Miss Pearl's Parlor! After their promenade, the men headed to Miss Pearl's stables where there was fresh water and hay for the horses. Pearl had built a small building next to the stables with two showers and sinks with mirrors where the boys washed up, put on clean shirts, and dusted off their boots. Miss Pearl knew most of them by name. She was particular in choosing her clientele and tolerated no disrespect to her ladies. One time someone asked, "Why don't you have men hired to protect your girls?"

"Because I do not need them," she replied. "We have Texas Katie! If anyone gives us any trouble, she will not kill them, but she might shoot at something they don't want shot at. Our Katie doesn't miss, and everyone knows it."

Tonight there was a new face among the young men who gallantly rode up to Miss Pearl's. Flirting and laughing, most of the cowboys had already gone inside with the girls; it was going to be a fun evening. Still standing on the porch, Miss Pearl saw Dusty Miller talking to a new young man. "C'mon, Tommy Lee!" Dusty coaxed. "For crying out loud, it's your twenty-first birthday!"

Tommy Lee, a tall muscular young man with dark brown hair and long lashes that framed his crystal blue eyes, had a boyish shyness. Pearl noticed immediately that the young handsome stranger was treading on unfamiliar territory. However, Miss Pearl's Parlor was noted for assisting many a young man in achieving his manhood.

"Dusty, honey, who is your friend?" Pearl asked.

"Miss Pearl, this is Tommy Lee Kingston. It's his birthday, and the boys have all put their money together to treat him to his first time with a woman," Dusty grinned.

"How do you do, Tommy Lee? I am delighted to know you," Miss Pearl replied in her kindest and most gracious tone. "Happy birthday and welcome, we are glad to have you."

Tommy Lee blushed, obviously uncomfortable. "Much obliged, Ma'am," he responded, "Happy to know you too." Tommy Lee tipped his hat, and Miss Pearl looked straight into a set of blue bedroom eyes. When Tommy Lee looked back at her, she was startled by a light that glimmered so brightly, she could have sworn he was looking through her soul.

Another young man, Jesse Keaton, had joined his friends on the porch. "He's a bit shy, Miss Pearl. We could hardly get him to town," Jesse winked. "We all work on his daddy's ranch. He's a good friend, and we think it's time he learned about the many fine pleasures a good woman can bring."

"Jesse and Dusty, any friend of yours is most welcome," Miss Pearl assured them as she slipped her arm into Tommy

Lee's and gave his hand a secure pat. "Come on in, Tommy Lee. Let's get this birthday celebration started!"

In the corner of the Great Room, Harmony was playing the grand piano, creating a soothing background for those who wanted to relax or engage in conversation. The real party was happening downstairs. Prohibition made the public sale of alcoholic beverages illegal. However, for a nominal fee, Miss Pearl's speakeasy, located in the basement of the house, provided a place to dance, eat, and purchase spirits. In the corner of the speakeasy, a piano player Miss Pearl called "The Professor," played ragtime and blues on an upright piano. Heather, Lucy, Maggie, and Ginger were also regular entertainers. Texas Kate, in charge of policing the speakeasy, also occasionally checked on the Great Room upstairs. Pearl completely trusted her competence and her abilities to keep the peace. "Katie," as the girls called her, had great instincts and usually kept her station in front of the basement door that led outside. She made it her business to know what went on in Miss Pearl's Parlor.

Between her experiences living in Chicago and on the Five Star Ranch, Pearl had established a keen radar to keep tabs on what happened in the Parlor. Though she mainly stayed upstairs, she occasionally went downstairs to check on the speakeasy. This night, she saw that the cowboys and her girls were getting along remarkably well. Maggie and Lucy were singing a duet, the girls were flirting, and the cowboys were having a great time. They knew Miss Pearl had the best girls in town, and all of them were aware of her strict rules on behaving like gentlemen. Pearl's policy was clear, and everyone knew there were no second chances. "If you want to get drunk, rowdy, be disrespectful or act like fools, there are plenty of other places in town where you can do that," she lectured.

Fried chicken, okra, potatoes, beans, rice, and cornbread, Mozella had spent the entire day cooking *soul food* as she called it, especially for the cowboys. Pearl watched as Emma Grace tended to the table of food laid out in the speakeasy. She also collected money and kept a silent eye on all the activity happening in the Parlor. At the bar, Pearl saw Betsy hanging all over Danny, and by his body language, she could tell he was slightly annoyed. "Uh oh," she thought to herself. "Betsy is headed toward heartbreak city."

Right she was. When Danny saw the girl with the long plume, he excused himself from Betsy's grasp and struck up a conversation with Heather. He was clearly interested in exploring new territory. Betsy tried to enter the conversation, but Danny turned and politely said, "Betsy, I had a great time with you last time we were here. I think tonight I'd like to get to know Heather and her feather."

Although Betsy made an attempt to hide her hurt, Pearl saw that the smile on her face barely disguised her disappointment. "Sure, Danny. Heather's a really nice girl. Y'all have fun," Betsy managed with a stiff upper lip. Heather winked at Betsy. Both girls knew that this was the nature of the business. The men who came to Miss Pearl's Parlor were not there looking for a relationship. Like a stallion in a herd of mares, the cowboys were there to have a good time. Most of them wanted to experience a variety of women.

Miss Pearl watched as Betsy blinked back her tears and quickly wiped her cheeks. She shook her hurt feelings off and put a smile on her face when another cowboy flirted, "Hello, Little Darlin.'"

"She is becoming a pro," Miss Pearl thought to herself. "These are the lessons learned. It is just the way it is."

Within an hour, Miss Pearl began looking for Tommy Lee to see how he was faring. She had seen him earlier that evening having conversations with Lucy and Sarah. By the look on his face, she saw he was obviously impressed with Maggie when she sang, "A Good Man Is Hard to Find." What she didn't see was Tommy Lee's equally obvious enchantment with Emma Grace as she went about her chores.

"Are you having a good time Tommy Lee?" Pearl asked.

Still only halfway finished with his first beer, "Oh, yes Ma'am," he responded politely.

Just then Emma Grace hurried into the room, wearing a crisp starched white apron over a simple blue cotton dress Mozella had given her to wear. She was carrying a towel to mop up a drink that Jesse had spilled on the floor while trying to impress Ginger. Tommy Lee stared innocently. Emma Grace sensed his eyes on her and glanced up from her wet towel. When their eyes met, they locked onto each other's gaze in a timeless moment. Tommy Lee was spellbound. After a pause and sweet smile, Emma Grace anxiously looked back down and continued her work.

Noticing the exchange between the two, Pearl attempted to divert Tommy Lee's attention. "Which one of my girls do you find most interesting this evening, Tommy Lee? Tommy Lee? Tommy Lee!"

Emma Grace finished wiping the floor and continued her other duties. She began rearranging the "soul food" that had been laid out for the hungry appetites. Tommy Lee could not take his eyes off her. "Sorry, Ma'am, what did you say?"

Miss Pearl recognized that the chemistry between the two young people, at least on Tommy Lee's part, was overwhelming. "I said…which of my girls do you find most interesting?"

Emma Grace felt his eyes on her again. Again she smiled and quickly looked away. Slowly, she turned her head back again and found his soulful blue eyes staring at her. Tommy Lee returned the smile, and Emma Grace smiled back. She picked up a few plates from the table and quickly left the room.

Miss Pearl tried to divert his attention, "Tommy Lee… what do you think of our Lucy? I also saw you talking to Maggie. You know she can be fun, too!"

Emma Grace slipped back into the room with a tray of fresh cornbread, and again Tommy Lee's eyes followed her. "Miss Pearl, who is that?" he asked, looking toward the food table. "I feel like I already know her from somewhere."

"Oh, Tommy Lee, that is our Emma Grace. She just started working here this afternoon and has no experience with men at all. I really think it would be better if you consider one of the other girls for your birthday present."

Dusty, standing next to Tommy Lee, watching him and listening to the conversation, thought it best to bring him back to reality. "She's not what we came here for! She's pretty, but she ain't what we came here for, Tommy Lee! Remember why we came here!"

Tommy Lee was completely enchanted. "Miss Pearl, I have $25 I will give you if you would please just introduce me to Miss Emma Grace," Tommy Lee pleaded.

Miss Pearl took Tommy Lee's money and tapped Emma Grace on the shoulder, "Emma Grace, honey, come over here for a minute."

"Yes, Ma'am," Emma Grace responded obediently.

"This nice young man wants to make your acquaintance," Pearl smiled. "Tommy Lee, this is Emma Grace."

Tommy Lee his eyes off Emma Grace, and although she was shy, she couldn't help but smile at Tommy Lee. Simultaneously a surge of warmth flowed over their hearts. "It's a real pleasure to make your acquaintance, Ma'am!" Tommy Lee blurted out. "Miss Emma Grace, I would consider it a great honor if you would take a walk with me. The moon is so bright and shining so pretty on the Concho River tonight. Miss Pearl, I promise I will be a gentleman!"

Dusty was frustrated. He took his friend's arm and hustled him to the side. "No, Tommy Lee!!" he whispered. "You ain't gonna have no fun doing that! Holy Cow! It's your birthday!! Tonight's the night!"

"Sorry boys, but I can't think of a better way to celebrate my birthday than to take a walk with pretty Miss Emma Grace."

For Pearl the scenario brought back memories of the Everleigh Club's opening night in Chicago when a group of Texas cattlemen came to call, and she met her cowboy. The memory of that night lived vividly in her heart. "I feel like this will be all right, Emma Grace, if you are comfortable with it."

"What about my chores?" Emma Grace asked.

Pearl, a hopeless romantic at heart, surrendered. "I have already hired some extra help for Mozella. They will be here later tonight. She will be all right. It is Tommy Lee's birthday, Emma Grace, and he seems like a fine young man. Come with me, honey. Pardon us for a few minutes, Tommy Lee."

Miss Pearl guided Emma Grace to her room by the kitchen and shut the door. "Now, Emma Grace, I took you in today because you are a charming and pretty young lady, but I want you to listen to me now. You are a lady and a virgin at that. This makes you special. Remember a man might say the prettiest words in the world, and I believe that in the moment, he might even believe they are true. Do not give it away, honey, because after that, everything changes. Tommy Lee came to the Parlor to be with a woman, or at least that is what his friends wanted. Do not wander off too far, and whatever you do, remember you are a lady with virtue. You are not for sale, and he knows it. Listen to me, honey. I know what I am talking about. I have been in this business a long time. If you ever want to see him again, Emma Grace, you will have a better chance if you hold on to your precious chastity. You are not ready, and your heart can be broken."

Emma Grace didn't know what to say. No one had ever talked to her about such things before. However, she knew that she missed not having a mother, and it felt good to know Miss Pearl was concerned about her wellbeing. "Yes, Ma'am, I promise."

"You are a good girl, honey. Make me proud."

Pearl left the room and found Tommy Lee. "Emma Grace will be with you in just a few minutes, Tommy Lee. May I suggest you take her to the gazebo within the lights of the house? There are some rough people in San Angelo, and you do not want to find yourself in a compromising situation." She stopped for a moment and shook her head feeling like an oxymoron. "Lord! Forgive me if I sound like a mother, Tommy Lee. Emma Grace is a sweet girl, and I know you will do right by her. Do not let me down." Pearl surprised herself in how protective she felt.

"Don't worry, Miss Pearl. I won't let anything happen to Emma Grace. I saw the gazebo when we rode in. I believe we can go down and sit a spell. She's so beautiful, Miss Pearl. Of all the girls I've talked to tonight, she is by far the one I want to spend some time with. It's almost like I already know her. Her eyes spoke to me like we've known each other all our lives."

"I know that feeling, Tommy Lee. In fact, the same thing happened to me one night in Chicago. It is a strange phenomenon, and people tend not to believe it unless, of course, it happens to them," Pearl smiled.

"Tommy Lee, I must tell you that Emma Grace came here because she had no other place to go. Her daddy died from the lung disease, so she came here looking for work. I gave her a job to help out in the kitchen because she has no experience in doing what my girls do. You seem like a fine young man, Tommy Lee. I just think you should…"

Tommy Lee shook his head adamantly and touched Pearl's arm. "Don't worry, Miss Pearl. My intentions with Emma Grace are most honorable. No offense, but I really wasn't too thrilled about coming here tonight. But it's my birthday, and the boys…well, you know."

Emma Grace changed into a simple yellow cotton dress and walked back into the Main Room where Tommy Lee was waiting, standing next to Pearl. "You look so pretty, Emma Grace. Don't worry, Miss Pearl. I'll take good care of her and deliver her back to you safely," Tommy promised as he crooked his arm. Emma Grace slipped her arm into his, and together they headed down to the river.

Dusty and Jesse found Pearl outside. "Doggone it all!" Dusty steamed. "Tonight was supposed to be Tommy Lee's big night. Me and the boys' been planning it for weeks!"

"He ain't gonna get no lovin' from her!" Jesse exclaimed.

"That depends on what kind of lovin' you boys are talking about," Pearl sighed. "I have seen that kind of chemistry a few times in my life. I think your friend Tommy Lee is going to have a wonderful birthday."

Redbird approached the trio outside and took Dusty and Jesse both by the arm. "I'm thirsty, boys! Why don't you buy me a drink?"

"Yes Ma'am!" Jesse and Dusty chimed in unison.

Pearl watched the young couple from the porch until their silhouettes reached the gazebo. Smiling to herself, she remembered a night in Chicago when a Texas gentleman had escorted her down an elegant corridor into an exquisitely decorated room filled with the scent of roses. Butterflies fluttered in Victoria Pearl's stomach that night, and she imagined in that moment under the West Texas stars Emma Grace might be feeling the same. Pearl sighed and, smiling, moseyed back into the Parlor.

Emma Grace's heart was pounding as they sat in the gazebo by the river. She had never been alone with a man before, yet somehow she felt safe with Tommy Lee. He was so handsome and strong. Every time he looked at her with his kind smiling eyes, her heart lit up. She was anxious to know all about him.

Tommy Lee took her hand. "Emma Grace, I want you to know my intentions were not the same as what my friends had in mind for me tonight. I've never been with a woman in 'that way', so they decided it was time for me to as Dusty would say, 'achieve manhood'! I think I'm just a little different that way. I already know I'm a man. I don't need to prove it to anyone. They took up a collection to bring me to San Angelo for my birthday, so I just kind of went along with it. Wasn't sure what I would do when I got here."

Emma Grace felt a sense of relief. She had not anticipated any kind of uncomfortable situation until Miss Pearl spoke to her about it in her room. She only knew how she felt when Tommy Lee smiled at her. His gaze gave her a feeling deep in the pit of her stomach she had never known before.

"Thank you for telling me that, Tommy Lee. Somehow I already knew it, but I appreciate you telling me just as well. So who are you, Tommy Lee?"

"My family has a ranch near Dove Creek west of San Angelo where we raise sheep, goats, and cattle. My great-grandfather came here from Germany, and we've been ranching ever since. The boys have been working hard, so Dad gave everyone the weekend to go to town. Miss Pearl sure has a nice place. She's a real nice lady, too."

"Yes, Tommy Lee, I don't know what I would have done if Miss Pearl hadn't taken me in. I sat with my daddy every day for weeks until he passed last week with the lung disease. He suffered so much at the end. It really was for the best," Emma Grace whispered, tears falling down her sweet face. Tommy Lee produced a handkerchief from his back pocket and gently blotted her eyes.

"Thank you, Tommy Lee."

"Where's your Mama?" Tommy Lee inquired.

"Mother died a couple of days after I was born. Daddy told me she got to hold me and even feed me a few times before she passed. He said that his favorite memory was her singing lullabies to me even though she was so weak. Daddy really loved her. That's the part that makes Daddy's passing OK. I know he's with Mother Rose again. That was her name, Rose. I'll bet right now he's singing, "My Wild Irish Rose," in his beautiful tenor voice and they're dancing in heaven somewhere on a cloud. He told me it was her favorite song. She loved to hear him sing it to her. The thought of them together brings me peace."

Tommy was touched by Emma Grace's story. "Both of my parents live on the ranch. I have three younger sisters. All of us have a name that begins with a "T." Their names are Theresa Michelle, Tilly Christine and Tara Lyne. I'm the only boy. I can't imagine what it must be like for you, Emma Grace," he whispered.

"It's strange, but I know God will show me the way," Emma Grace stated, changing to a more positive tone. "Daddy used to tell me Mother Rose is still with me like an angel. He dreamed about her all the time. Daddy always said that when the good Lord called him home, I should get quiet and listen for his voice in my heart. You should have heard him sing, "Danny Boy." He told me his mother used to sing it to him. Maybe that's why she named him Daniel. Daddy said that remembering songs people sing to us in this lifetime can be comforting after they've passed through the veil."

"The veil?" Tommy Lee asked.

"Yes, Tommy Lee. Daddy told me that our loved ones who have passed are right here with us whenever we feel them in our hearts. He told me they hide behind an invisible veil where we can't see them, but they can see us. He says it's where the angels and the fairies live. Thinking about it makes me feel better. Even though I miss him, I'd like to think that Mother Rose and he can see me from the other side."

Tommy Lee smiled at Emma Grace. "Sounds kind of like a fairytale... I like it." Looking at her eyes twinkling in the night, he felt the urge to be closer. "May I put my arm around you, Emma Grace?"

Emma Grace nodded. The night was warm with a soft breeze blowing by the river. For a long time, they stared at the bright moonlight dancing on the Concho River. Emma Grace felt safe and secure with Tommy Lee. Every few minutes Tommy Lee patted Emma Grace on the arm and asked if she was okay, and every time he did, she responded with, "Yes, thank you. Everything is perfectly fine."

"Do you believe in love at first sight, Emma Grace?"

For a moment Emma Grace tensed, remembering Miss Pearl's words of warning. *"Remember a man might say the prettiest words in the world, and in the moment, he might even believe they are true."* Tommy Lee sensed her concern. "I'm sorry. Maybe I should have kept that thought to myself. I just spoke what was on my heart."

"It's all right, Tommy Lee," Emma assured him. "The question just kind of took me off guard. Let me think a minute," Emma Grace smiled and looked deeply into Tommy Lee's beautiful blue eyes. "I think I do believe in love at first sight, Tommy Lee. Poets write about it, and Daddy said it happened to him. He told me that the first time he saw Mother Rose, his heart stopped. *I felt like she had something that belonged to me*, he reminisced.

Tommy Lee tried to make sense of his feelings. "That's how I'm feeling right now, Emma Grace. It's just that I feel like I already know you somehow. But that's impossible!"

"I feel the same way, Tommy Lee. I believe it happened tonight. Maybe we ought not to think about it too much," Emma Grace responded.

"You're right, Emma Grace. Let's just enjoy the moon on the river."

"I'm kind of tired, Tommy Lee. Do you mind if I close my eyes for a minute?"

"Do you want to go back to the house?" he asked

"They're going to be up for a while, and it's noisy. Sarah told me that sometimes they go on all night until the sun comes up. I think I'd like to just stay here for now if you don't mind."

Tommy Lee smiled. "Sounds good to me. Think I'd like to rest my eyes too."

Pearl and Mozella meandered out onto the porch, looking toward the river, able to see the young couple's silhouettes in the gazebo by the light of the moon. Emma Grace had her head on Tommy Lee's shoulder

Pearl thought about how innocence is so fragile, so easily broken. "Why do I feel so protective of that child, Mo?" she asked her friend.

"It's because you are who you are," Mozella answered. "*Romans 8: All things work together for good!*"

Turning back into the house to take care of her guests, Pearl could hear that the party needed her inside to do her magic. Though everyone seemed to be having a good time, she suggested the *Professor* slow down the tempo of the music, which always worked in relaxing the atmosphere. The girls saw the change in tempo as a clue. Being with the cowboys was different; it didn't seem like work. There was something about those cowboys that appealed to the girls like candy to children.

Miss Pearl was successful in getting things back on track. The men had found their partners, and even though they were working, with cowboys it seemed more like play. The Professor kept the music slow and bluesy for a while and then finally called it a night. Miss Pearl and Mozella had their nightly cup of chamomile tea on the back porch before they went to bed.

"This was a good night, Mozella. Everyone seemed to be having a good time. That is what we are all about; everyone having a good time."

Tommy Lee, as he did every morning, awakened before dawn, but this morning he watched Emma Grace in peaceful sleep. The sound of her breathing satisfied his heart, knowing that she was content in his arms. He watched as the glowing reddish orange light cracked the horizon and listened as the quiet of the dark morning broke with birds chirping like miniature minstrels welcoming the sun to a new day.

Emma Grace stirred and opened her eyes. "Hello, handsome," she purred with a sleepy smile.

She watched as Tommy Lee stood and stretched. He looked out at the river then up to the sky. "Looks like it's going to be another beautiful day," he announced.

Emma watched him. "You make beautiful love."

"Ma'am?" he asked with surprise.

"With your eyes, Tommy Lee. You make beautiful love with your eyes!" Emma Grace smiled. "It's like you can speak to my soul with your eyes."

"That's a good explanation of how I feel, Emma Grace. You make beautiful love with your eyes too," he echoed as he kissed her on the forehead.

Tommy Lee and Emma Grace sat together in silence watching the West Texas sky fill with bright warm colors that changed into a bright blue. After a little while Emma Grace stood up. "I think I should be getting back. Mozella is probably awake getting biscuits ready to bake. I need to go help her."

"I'm going into town this morning and run some errands for my dad. May I see you again this afternoon?" Tommy Lee asked.

"I'll talk to Miss Pearl. I assume the girls won't be getting up for some time, and Mozella will need some help cleaning. I think it will be OK if you come by later on though."

Tommy Lee looked down into the sweetest green eyes he had ever seen. He put his arms around her and hugged her. "I've never met anyone like you, Emma Grace. May I kiss you?"

Emma Grace nodded and grinned. Tommy Lee gently gave Emma Grace her first kiss. It made her head spin and she felt a little dizzy. Tommy Lee took her back to the house and, as they got closer, they saw, through the kitchen window, Mozella was rolling out biscuits.

"Thank you for a wonderful evening, Tommy Lee."

"Thank you!" he replied.

Tommy Lee went to the stables. A few minutes later, Dusty joined him, a big smile on his face. "Spent the whole night with that little filly, Tommy Lee? Did you get some lovin'?"

"Not the kind you're talkin' about, Dusty," Tommy Lee snapped, obviously irritated with his friend's comments.

"Aw c'mon, Tommy Lee. You can tell me. Was she any good?"

"Shut up, Dusty!" Tommy Lee was clearly peeved.

"Did she give you a Happy Birthday present, Tommy Lee?" he teased.

"I told you to shut up, Dusty! She's not like that!"

"I saw the way she looked at you, Lover Boy!"

Tommy Lee hit Dusty with a punch that laid his best friend on the ground.

"I told you to shut up, Dusty! I love you like my brother, but, DOGGONE IT, I told you to SHUT UP about Emma Grace."

"Dang!" Dusty snorted. "Sorry Tommy Lee! I didn't know you were serious! It's just that we came here on a mission, and I thought…"

Just as Tommy Lee reached to help Dusty up, Miss Pearl appeared. "Everything all right boys?"

"Yes, Ma'am," Dusty answered, dusting himself off. He was well aware of Miss Pearl's rules about fighting. "Everything is just fine!"

Tommy Lee spoke next. "I apologize for getting Miss Emma Grace in so late, Miss Pearl. We fell asleep and the next thing we knew the sun was coming up!"

"Yes, I know, Tommy Lee. I saw you in the gazebo. I run a high class operation here and not much gets past me. Why don't you boys come into the house. Mozella has made some fresh biscuits and coffee." Pearl looked at Dusty who was covered with dirt from his fall. "Wash up before you come to the house, Dusty."

"Yes Ma'am!" Tommy Lee replied with excitement. Happy with the opportunity to be able to see Emma Grace again, he quickly forgave his friend.

"My head hurts," Dusty moaned.

"Head like that oughta hurt," Tommy Lee laughed as they went to the washroom to clean up.

"We'll go to town and run those errands for Dad after breakfast," Tommy Lee told his friend.

"Sure, Tommy Lee." They had been best friends for so long they felt like brothers. This wasn't their first altercation, but it was the first one over a woman.

"I think I love her," Tommy Lee told his friend.

Dusty gasped. "What? Love?"

Tommy Lee smiled. "Yes sir, she's got something that belongs to me. I just got to figure out what that is."

That weekend the cowboys had a big time with the girls. They spent their money, and the women were accommodating. They loved their cowboys! For two days there was flirting, singing, dancing and drinking. Pearl kept fishing poles in the stables, so some of the boys went down to the river and caught crappie. Mozella fried their fish and served them with some okra, pinto beans, fried potatoes, and peach cobbler for dessert.

Because Pearl had a special place in her heart for the cowboys, it was important to her they have a good time. Emma Grace and Tommy Lee were able to spend some more time together. Everyone could see they were enamored with each other.

Finally, late Sunday afternoon the boys headed back to the ranch after much kissing and goodbye-ing. The girls stood on the porch as the cowboys paraded by on their horses once more. With their hats in hands, they hollered a few cowboy whoops and headed west. The ladies waved, watching the dust cloud get smaller and smaller. Nobody went back into the house until the boys had completely disappeared.

That evening as Tommy Lee was brushing his horse, his father joined him in the stalls and asked him, "Did you have a good birthday, son?"

"Oh yes, sir! I met a girl in San Angelo, and I think I'm in love!" Tommy Lee grinned. "How did you know Mother was the one?"

"Well, son, the first time I saw your Ma, I felt like she had something that belonged to me."

"That's exactly how I felt when I saw Emma Grace," Tommy Lee eagerly added. "How do you know a good woman, Dad?"

"When you fall in love with a good woman, Tommy Lee, it's like falling in love with Texas herself. You know that wherever you are, she loves you, and no matter what age she is, you will see her beauty. Her loving eyes sparkle like diamonds just like the Texas stars on a moonless light. Son, when you're in love with a woman, her heart reaches deep and grabs ahold of your soul. Where did you meet this little gal, Tommy Lee?"

"I met her at Miss Pearl's Parlor. She's the one, Dad! Emma Grace is the woman I'm going to marry!"

Jed, Tommy Lee's father, continued brushing the horse, not looking at his son, fearing his eyes might say too much. After a pause, he said, "That's good, son." As they moseyed to the house, Jed patted Tommy Lee on the back, and suggested, "Let's wait a while before we tell your Ma."

Later that same Sunday night, the workers in Big Lake, Texas, were preparing for the final drilling and casing of the Santa Rita Number One as a producing oil well. At 6 am the next morning, May 28th, 1923, as Carl Cromwell and Dee Locklin, his "toolie," were eating their breakfast before resuming the drilling operation, they heard a hissing sound and thought there was a rattlesnake outside the shack. Suddenly the ground trembled like an earthquake, followed by a deafening hissing noise, and then a rumbling roar that thundered across the West Texas land! Drops of oil fell like rain on the drillers' shacks.

The two men raced outside to behold the most glorious vision an oilman can ever hope for! Without any help, the Santa Rita Number One had brought herself in. The first head of oil was spewing black Texas gold high above the ground like a gigantic fountain, a magnificent sight to see with a bright blue sky serving as its background. Their prayers had been answered. The Santa Rita dream had come true!

The Women

Late Monday morning the 28th day of May, 1923, was going to be another West Texas blue sky day. Throughout Pearl's Parlor, the sweetness of piano music filled the morning air. Harmony especially liked to play the shiny black Steinway when everyone was having coffee. "Harmony's music is as sweet as a nightingale," Annabelle sighed.

The girls had entertained the cowboys all weekend, and their manly presence still lingered with an overall feeling of contentment and satisfaction. The girls had shown the boys a good time, and as usual, the young women had enjoyed themselves as well. The cowboys' visit was the topic for girl talk as they reminisced over the events of the weekend.

"I like the way they walk," Lucy cooed.

"I like the way they talk," Heather added.

"I like the way they say, 'BABY' in the heat of passion," Maggie announced.

"Yeah, like Baby! Baby! BABY!!" Ginger laughed as she imitated her weekend lover.

"I got to spend some time with Johnny Ray! Shwooo! That man is an athlete!" Redbird commented. "He lifted me up and… Shwoo!"

"I wonder if they talk about us like we talk about them," Maggie giggled.

For the most part, the weekend had gone well. Betsy had fallen for another cowboy, and Katie only had one small incident with Jesse having had a little too much to drink. Maggie, confronting him, had taken charge of the situation, and Jesse had awakened a happy man. "Jesse's not a bad guy," Maggie offered defensively. "He just gets a little worked up. Believe me, we put all that healthy energy to good use. All he needed was a little TLC and me," she laughed.

This morning, Harmony's composer of choice was Bach. After playing his "Prelude in C," Harmony changed the mood with an A chord and broke out in song. *"There's a yellow rose in*

Texas that I am going to see; nobody else could miss her, not half as much as me!" A patriot of the great state of Texas, Katie immediately perked up and sang along. *"She's the sweetest little rosebud that Texas ever knew. Her eyes are bright as diamonds that sparkle like the dew."* Maggie and Lucy began doing the dosey doe in the middle of the room and joined in the singing as well. *"The yellow rose of Texas is the only gal for me!"*

Truly a "feel good moment," Katie took it upon herself to educate the girls with some Texas trivia. "Hey, everyone, did you know that it was a woman who was responsible for saving the great state of Texas?" she announced placing her hand over her heart. "Some call it a legend, but I believe that it's true," she exclaimed.

"Are you talking about Emily Morgan?" Lucy asked.

"Yes, Ma'am! *The Yellow Rose of Texas* was written in 1836 after the battle in San Jacinto during the days of the Texas War of Independence. Several weeks before, Santa Anna had gone on a rampage and attacked the Alamo. 185 Texans gallantly held down the fort for almost two weeks fighting off over 3,000 Mexican soldiers. Davey Crockett was there. The Texans didn't have a chance, but before they all died, they sure gave Santa Anna a good fight! A few weeks later, the son of a bitch killed over 300 unarmed prisoners in Goliad. Then he took his men to Galveston to loot the city. That's where he met Miss Emily Morgan, a sexy young mulatto slave. Santa Anna was enchanted by her beauty, and after some negotiation, he took Miss Emily with him."

"How did she save Texas?" Heather wondered.

"She had talents… womanly talents," Katie continued. "She knew the art of seduction! Several weeks after the Alamo, Santa Anna's army was camped in San Jacinto. Somehow, Miss Emily was able to get word to Sam Houston about an appropriate time to attack the camp. She told him she would make sure *El Presidente* was busy. On April 21st, 1836, General Santa Anna retired to his tent with some opium and the very sexy Emily, while the rest of the soldiers in his camp took a siesta."

"Sounds like Santa Anna wasn't thinking with his brain," Lucy giggled.

"Miss Emily must have been quite a woman! Although Santa Anna was usually a stickler for details, she obviously distracted him with her charms. While she was keeping him busy in the tent, the Texans attacked the camp yelling, '*Remember the Alamo! Remember Goliad*!' Eighteen minutes later, the battle was over, and the Mexican army surrendered."

"Wow! That's amazing!" Heather exclaimed.

Katie smiled. "Here's the best part!" she squealed with excitement. "Santa Anna was captured the next day in his underwear, pretty fancy silky underwear at that. He was really embarrassed."

"So why is the song about a yellow rose?" Lucy asked.

"Sometimes when the Negroes and white people make babies, their children's skin has a yellowish tint. They are called '*mulatto*'," Katie answered.

"Lots of mulattos in New Orleans," Ginger added.

"Ok, I get it," Heather commented. "I guess it was Miss Emily's self-appointed mission to make sure the General was caught with his pants down. That took some kind of courage! I would have liked to have known her."

"I'll bet she was a helluva woman!" Ginger smiled. "What happened to her?"

"No one really knows. Saved the great state of Texas, she did," Katie offered with pride.

"The Texans at San Jacinto sang 'Come to the Bower' as their marching song," Harmony added. "It was the only song all of them knew."

"I like your story, Katie," Pearl commented. "Many times throughout history, a woman has been responsible for a great event that has turned things around. Unfortunately, most of those stories we will never know. Let's go for a ride, girls! I want to go to Christoval and sit in the mineral springs at the Bath House. Mozella and Emma Grace can fix us a picnic."

That's a great idea!" Annabelle chimed. "I'll call Mama to bring my little Julie Marie over to the picnic."

"I will bring some yarn and teach her how to make yarn dolls," Pearl offered. "Such a sweet little girl."

"I always feel so good after soaking in the springs," Sarah commented.

"It's a great day for it," Maggie exclaimed. "It's Monday, and there probably won't be a lot of people we have to deal with. Sometimes I forget that I'm not supposed to know people I see when we're out in public. Even the slightest look can sometimes get me in trouble."

Miss Pearl agreed. "You are right, Maggie. Keeping secrets is part of what we do. Everyone who wants to go be ready in half-an-hour. This will give us a few hours at the springs. We can be home before dark."

Mondays were good days for the girls to take excursions. The rest and relaxation rejuvenated the girls after the weekend, and Miss Pearl understood the importance of shifting focus and letting the ladies have some down time. Miss Pearl's taking her girls in public was always quite a show. When her girls piled into the touring cars and rode around town, it was like a parade. Ginger and Maggie and Katie, the designated drivers, all kept guns under their seats except for Katie who usually brought her rifle. Pearl insisted that the girls stay together like a family. "There is always safety in numbers, girls," she liked to say. "I prefer that you do not wander off anywhere alone," was actually one of her rules.

The girls piled into the three cars, and Emma Grace brought blankets to sit on and a big basket of Mozella's ham sandwiches and a container of tea. Because Miss Pearl had the reputation for having the prettiest girls in San Angelo, people stopped on the streets to watch them go by. Sometimes, the girls waved, especially at the men. Miss Pearl considered showing off her girls as a form of advertisement. Today, driving the southern route out of town, they would not be so conspicuous.

Like children going to a circus, they made their way to the springs. Pearl's heart felt light to see the girls laughing and having a good time. Protective of them like a lioness with her cubs, she knew all of their stories and had grown to love each of the young women like her own. By the time the girls had reached Christoval, they were all singing, *There's a yellow rose in Texas* and talking about Miss Emily as if she were the greatest hero Texas had ever had. Christoval, relatively small, was quaint and scenic. The emerald green South Concho River flowed serenely through the center of town.

Water makes the body weightless, and the soul feel clean. Because the mineral springs in Christoval were believed to have special healing powers, people from all over, even from outside of Texas, went to the Bath House in Christoval. Many claimed that the sulfur waters had cured them from their ailments. The sun was warm on this day, and the water felt cool and fresh.  The girls took their turns soaking in the water, enjoying their time together. All had stunning figures and looked very attractive in their new bathing suits that Miss Pearl had special ordered for the summer. As she watched her girls, she felt a sense of pride and reflected on the women she had worked with in Chicago. From Minna and Ada Everleigh, Pearl had learned to be selective with her special young women.

After each of the girls had finished her time in the sulfur baths, one by one they put on their sandals to walk to the low water crossing on the south side of town. "Mommy! Mommy!" Julie Marie squealed when she saw Annabelle. The little girl had been waiting with her grandmother to share a picnic with her Mommy and her friends.

Pearl had waited for all the girls to finish soaking in the baths and was the last one to arrive at the crossing. The shade of the lush pecan trees protected the lily pads from the heat of the West Texas sun as they rested languidly on top of the South Concho water. When she saw Julie Marie she handed the little girl various colors of yarn dolls she had already made.

"Thank you kindly, Ma'am," she said in a voice that warmed Pearl's heart.

"We'll make some more dolls later if you like."

Betsy had brought a sketch pad and pencils and Lucy brought a canvas and pastels. It was a perfect day to paint the picturesque landscape vibrant with the vivid colors of spring. "Did you know there is an art camp here in Christoval?" Pearl asked. "The camp is becoming quite well known. One art teacher came all the way from Spain. Many of the art students that attend the camp are women. I believe both of you have a natural talent, and I think you could benefit from what the camp has to offer. I heard about it from Mr. Green. His ranch is not far from here and he is quite a character. He once told me that his father used to say, 'If you were to put a roof over the city of San Angelo, it would be one giant bordello!'"

Emma Grace found a place to lay down their blankets for their picnic. Mozella had packed big green dill pickles from the general store, fruit, fresh carrots, and ham sandwiches made with love. "Anyone hungry?" Pearl asked.

"Famished!" Katie answered.

"I'm ready to eat!" Maggie echoed.

"Count me in," Redbird shouted, coming out of the river after a swim. "The water feels great!"

Redbird freed her red hair from her bathing cap and shook it loose. Watching her fluff up her curls, Pearl couldn't help but think how stunning "Red" was. With her long slender legs, she swayed a graceful, slow rhythm when she walked, like poetry in motion.

Annabelle sat on a blanket with her mother and daughter several yards away, playing with the yarn dolls Pearl had made for little Julie Marie.

The girls were enjoying the peacefulness of the South Concho River, the sunshine making the air warm on their skin as they watched the orb's reflection sparkling like diamonds on the water. "Girls, have you ever heard about Suzy Poon Tang?" Pearl asked out of the blue, grinning mischievously.

Ginger nearly choked on her sandwich. "That's a word I would never have expected you to say, Miss Pearl! I've heard of *Poontang,* but I didn't realize there really was a person named Suzy Poon Tang!" she laughed.

"What's Poontang, Ginger?" Maggie asked. "I want to know!"

"I know what it is," Lucy giggled. "I heard Dusty tell Jesse, '*Tommy Lee ain't gonna get no Poontang tonight.*' I think he was talking about you, Emma Grace."

Emma Grace blushed and smiled. "Tommy Lee was a perfect gentleman."

"I knew a man back home in Kentucky who used to tell my dad, 'Think I'll go down to Miss Pauline's and get my pole polished,'" Betsy laughed. "Didn't know what it meant at the time, but now I do. Sometimes men are funny that way and have some funny sayings especially about sex."

"OK, I think I figured out what *Poontang* is," Maggie giggled, suddenly enlightened. "Tell us about Suzy Poon Tang, Miss Pearl. I'm sure this has got to be good!"

"I remember the day Suzy Poon Tang came to the Everleigh House. One of Miss Ada's multimillionaire clients had been telling the sisters about an Asian girl working for Madam Julie at the *Shanghai.* He was quite adamant. 'You absolutely have to have her here. The rumor is she is comparable to a fine work of art.' This particular client spent a lot of money at the Everleigh Club and had given the sisters, each, a $5,000 bonus at Christmas. Therefore, upon his request, Ada and Minna decided to check out Miss Suzy Poon Tang. They learned she had begun her career soliciting clients from doorways in Shanghai, China."

"She was a long way from home!" Lucy exclaimed.

"When Suzy learned that a group of girls were going to Chicago in America to work in a bordello called the *Shanghai* that specialized in Asian women, she decided to join them; but before she left, she had a cluster of roses tattooed several inches below her navel. When Suzy arrived in America, she came up with a brilliant idea. 'Hey, Lover boy!' she would say, 'How would you like to see a work of art more beautiful than the *Mona Lisa at the Louvre in Paris*?' Then for a $5 fee, she gave her clients a magnifying glass to gaze upon her rose tattoo. Some say she was an expert at doing erotic gestures with a piece of raw meat and could put on quite a show."

"I have never even seen a tattoo," Sarah commented.

"Neither have I," Harmony added.

"Because the Shanghai brothel was a little too sleezy for the millionaire client, he begged for the Everleigh sisters to hire Suzy Poon Tang. The man, certainly anxious to experience her many talents, was not willing to lower himself to visit the *Shanghai*. Because he was so generous and the sisters were good business ladies, Ada insisted her sister comply with their client's request. The afternoon that Minna visited Madam Julie, she learned that Suzy was one of her best girls and brought in a healthy revenue. The men paid ten dollars to spend time with her. After agreeing to make compensation to cover her losses, Minna hired Miss Suzy Poon Tang."

"But I thought the Everleigh Club was first class. Sounds like she might have been a bit rough around the edges," Lucy commented.

Miss Pearl agreed. "You are exactly right, Lucy. Minna put her with my friend Doll for a crash course on the rules of the Everleigh House. I remember the sisters had to sneak her up the back stairs to avoid any of the girls seeing her and becoming upset. Some of them knew about Suzy and might not have liked the competition. She and Doll spent that first night together."

"Did you know her very well?" Sarah asked.

"I knew nothing about her before she came to the Everleigh Club. Later, Doll told us she could never forget her night with Suzy Poon Tang. Although she gave Suzy an education in Everleigh etiquette, apparently Suzy taught Doll some new tricks as well. Doll always did like women more than men. Both women got an education that night!"

"Sounds like fun!" Maggie giggled with glee.

"I must say, I did not have the opportunity to know her well. You see... Suzy Poon Tang only lasted one night!"

"One night?" several of the girls chimed in unison.

"Yes! Just one night!" Pearl repeated with her eyebrows arched and a big crooked grin. "The millionaire client was so impressed with her talents that he whisked her to his North Side mansion and married her within the week! As my friend Doll put it, 'It was a done deal when he found those roses blooming at the gateway to ecstasy.'" Miss Pearl smiled as she recalled cute, feisty, little Suzy Poon Tang. "I remember all the girls showering Minna and Ada with kisses when Suzy left. Her new husband compensated them greatly for his new bride."

"So that's where 'Poontang' came from," Ginger chimed.

"You are correct, Miss Ginger," Pearl commented. "I guess you can say hers ended like a Cinderella story. Suzy Poon Tang became legendary."

"Hey, I just thought of something," Heather queried in an "aha" moment. "Do you think the term 'getting laid' came from the Everleigh house?"

"Some people say so," Miss Pearl grinned. "Wealthy men used to say things like 'I'm going to get *Everleighed* tonight' when they bragged to their friends about spending money with the butterflies there."

The rest of the day was spent relaxing after an enjoyable weekend with the cowboys. Some of the girls went swimming, and some basked in the sunshine. Ever since Coco Chanel had gone to the French Riviera and returned home with a tan, the latest fashion in high society was to have a little sunglow on the skin.

Harmony picked up her guitar and began singing some old Celtic folk songs. *"Was in the merry month of May when flowers all were bloomin' Sweet William on his death-bed lay for the love of Barbara Allan..."*

"I love songs that tell a story," Betsy sighed. "Poor William."

"He should have treated her better," Maggie commented. "He slighted her in front of his friends. Not a good thing to do!"

At four o'clock Miss Pearl was ready to leave. Mozella would have dinner ready at seven sharp, and Pearl was expecting some out-of-town businessmen later that evening. "Time to gather up your things, girls," Miss Pearl instructed. "This has been a good day."

Annabelle decided to stay with her mother a few days and ride the stagecoach back to San Angelo on Thursday. Within fifteen minutes, the caravan of beautiful women headed back to town.

The Santa Rita No. 1
June 10, 1923

As Pearl and the girls neared the house that evening, they saw Mozella on the porch frantically waving a newspaper in the air. She was so excited she didn't wait for Pearl to get out of her car; she ran to the first car of the caravan. "The Santa Rita! We're rich! WE'RE RICH!"

Pearl grabbed the paper and squealed! "Mozella! Are you saying what I think you're saying?"

On May 28th, 1923, the headline story of *The San Angelo Daily Standard* afternoon paper read: "BIG LAKE REPORTS GOOD OIL SHOWING."

"Yes, Ma'am! Mr. Frank called while you were gone." Mozella, waving her hands high in the air, feeling like she could touch the stars, began singing. "Alleluia! Amen and ALL THAT JAZZ!!"

"I knew it, I knew it, I knew it!" Pearl shouted with delight. She threw her arms around Mozella, "It's amazing what a little bit of faith can bring, Mozella!"

"Yes Ma'am! *Matthew 17: If you have faith as small as a mustard seed, you can say to this mountain, 'Move from here to there,' and it will move. Nothing will be impossible for you*," Mozella quoted in her most powerful preaching voice.

The two friends danced arm-in-arm and sang their way into the house. "*Santa Rita Boogie, Santa Rita Boogie, we'll do the Santa Rita Boogie, and we'll boogie woogie all night long*!"

The next day the Santa Rita Number 1 gushed twice, and by Wednesday, the well settled into a routine of flowing once-a-day with each head of oil gushing greater than the previous one. Saint Rita, the patron saint of impossible things, had come through. God had heard their prayers, and their dreams had come true!

A few days later, *The San Angelo Daily Standard* announced: "FIVE HEADS OF OIL SHOWING." The buzz was spreading everywhere, and West Texas was on fire with excitement. On the next Sunday, the Orient Railroad ran a special 85 mile ride from San Angelo to the Santa Rita well site.

Miss Pearl bought all her girls a ticket for the train's special run to Big Lake, and on June 10, 1923, they joined the thousand other people who journeyed to see that black, Texas gold spewing out of the ground.

It is amazing how an event like this can bring an entire community together. Prosperity was coming to West Texas, and everyone at the train station celebrated. The Lady Pearls looked lovely as always, wearing soft colored pastels, sunhats and like always, their favorite pearls. Mozella wore her best hat and Sunday dress. The girls found seats together toward the back of one of the cars. When they were in public, they were sure to recognize men they weren't supposed to know. For this reason, they always kept to themselves and avoided eye contact with anyone but each other. The passengers were buzzing with excitement as the train made its way to Big Lake, Texas, blowing smoke from the great steam engine stack. Throughout the train ride, every time the engineer blew the whistle, people cheered, and Pearl and Mozella experienced chill bumps all over their bodies.

Eighty-five miles later, the Orient train finally arrived at the Santa Rita No. 1. The air was filled with the smell of sulfur, much like the smell of rotten eggs. There were horses, wagons, and cars everywhere. Professors from the Texas University in Austin, ranchers, farmers, and oilmen from miles around had come to witness the Santa Rita displaying her riches buried deep below the earth. Around the base of the derrick, the rich thick blackness had spilled onto what once was referred to as "useless barren ground." The West Texas land in Big Lake was painting quite a different picture now and didn't look so worthless to anyone anymore.

"When is it supposed to blow?" Lucy asked.

"Somebody said it usually spews oil between 2 and 3'oclock," Harmony answered.

"It's almost 3 now!" Maggie exclaimed.

The hour of 3 o'clock came and went, and 4 o'clock the same. Over a thousand people had come to see the show, yet some showed doubt about seeing anything at all. Since the 60 foot oil derrick was only 175 feet from the track, some of the people decided to go back into the comfort of the train to look out the window.

The anticipation of an elegant woman making her entrance is always a thrill; the Santa Rita was fashionably late. When she finally decided to show herself to the crowd, she was spectacular! At 4:40 pm on June 10th, 1923, the earth trembled and hissed, shaking so hard in Big Lake, Texas that some feared it was the end of world. Most of the people gasped; a few even screamed. Then from the depths of the earth, a deafening roar sounded, followed by a burst of black crude oil that blew like a massive champagne bottle that had just popped its cork.

Spellbound, the crowd watched as the oil sprayed above the derrick and then drift hundreds of yards across the prairie. With the exception of a few oilmen, no one there had ever heard or witnessed a spectacle like this before. The display lasted nearly 45 minutes, punctuated with hundreds of *"oohs"* and *"aahs,"* cheers, and applause. People had to shout to be heard, but most were silent. West Texas history that would affect generations to come was being made. One man commented, "There is no question but that this is an oil well. All speculation counter to this is now wiped out." In Austin and College Station, the institutions were looking at West Texas with different eyes. In 1876 an endowment of millions of acres in the West Texas region had been granted by the State of Texas to The University of Texas in Austin and the Texas Agricultural and Mechanical College in College Station some call "Texas A&M." Any proceeds as a result from oil, gas, sulfur, and water royalties discovered on the endowment would go to these institutes of higher learning. Until now the barren land in West Texas had been considered insignificant, but the Santa Rita was telling a different story. Representatives from Austin and College Station had also come to the site that day with a new attitude. Everyone who witnessed the Santa Rita blowing high in the sky sensed prosperity and new beginnings, like the day someone yelled, "Eureka!" after finding gold in California. The word itself means, "I found it!" and in Big Lake, Texas, they surely had.

Witnesses to the Santa Rita Number 1 that day went away with an exciting tale to tell for the rest of their lives. No doubt none of them ever forgot it. By 5:30 the passengers had returned to their seats on the Orient Railroad. On the train heading east to San Angelo, the Lady Pearls sat together talking excitedly about the events of the day.

"That was absolutely the bees' knees!" Maggie exclaimed. Everyone agreed.

Mozella and her longtime friend smiled at each other with silent appreciation. Although no words were spoken, both women understood each other. Mozella wondered what the people on the train might think if they knew she would soon be reaping benefits as an investor in the Santa Rita No. 1. Victoria Pearl saw by the warm glow of the land that the sun was preparing to say farewell to a perfectly memorable day. Contemplating events from the last two years, she remembered the telegram from Madeline, the meeting with Frank Pickrell in Fort Worth, and the deadlines for drilling on time. She recalled the challenges of the equipment breaking down, the skeptics, the tenacity, and now finally - the reward. Pearl smiled, imagining what it must have been like to watch Frank Pickrell climb to the top of the derrick and sprinkle the blessed rose petals from the top as he christened her *The Santa Rita,* after the patron saint of impossible things. Suddenly Pearl thought of an unusual analogy.

"Mozella," she turned to her friend sitting next to her, "After what we saw today, it occurs to me that the Santa Rita experience is like a good lover. Think about it. Think about how the drilling tool penetrates the earth patiently and deliberately, until it reaches the magic spot that oilmen call *'the pay.'* When the tool finally reaches that perfectly glorious spot, Mother Earth trembles and shakes and lets out a roar of ecstasy as she brings forth hidden treasures deep inside. Just like any good woman, she is always willing to give if you have the patience it takes to explore her sacred mysteries."

"Miss Pearl, only you could think of something like that," Mozella chuckled, shaking her head.

"This is just the beginning, Mozella! West Texas is about to become the land of milk and honey, and we are going to be ready to entertain the gentlemen callers when it does! Today is a good day for Miss Pearl's Parlor!"

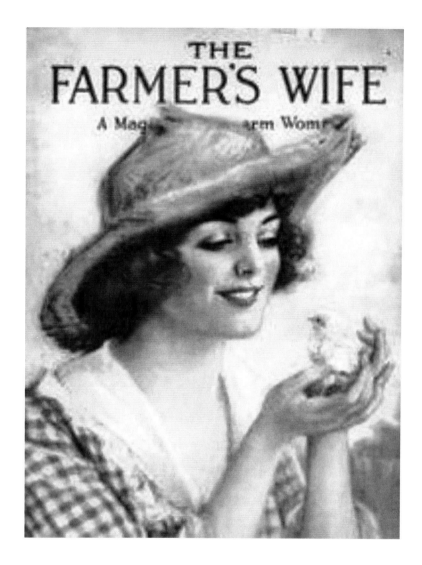

The Comstocks

In 1923 the Santa Rita No. 1 discovery began a new oil boom, bringing excitement that would change lives throughout Texas and beyond. Because of its location and size, San Angelo became the center of the West Texas oil business. Just like the rest of the town, Miss Pearl's Parlor also bathed in prosperity. The Angelus Hotel where Robert and Victoria McKnight had spent their first days as man and wife was constantly flooded with oil operators. Big oil deals were being made at The Petroleum Club located on the mezzanine floor of the hotel, and *The San Angelo Daily Standard* became the voice of the oil industry in West Texas. Many conversations and transactions were done at Miss Pearl's as well since confidentiality was a main ingredient in her business.

Everyone has a story, and now the Santa Rita No. 1 was part of Pearl's. The girls who lived at Miss Pearl's Parlor had stories similar to the ones she had heard from the young women she had worked with at the Everleigh Club in Chicago. Although the characters had different names and the girls had come from different places and walks of life, the stories of drama and emotions were all basic in nature.

Although not all madams took personal interests in their girls, Miss Pearl cared deeply about her "pearls" and their wellbeing, just as Minna and Ada had cared about hers. Sharing stories within the parlors created a bond with the girls as well as a profound sense of support. This understanding created unity and trust that formed a kind of sisterhood among the women. There were those who had been orphaned or escaped some kind of abuse. Others were pretty women who had families who were destitute and saw no better option to make some decent money. Some of the girls had a "love-gone-wrong-story" similar to Betsy's or to Victoria Pearl's experience with Ian. When a woman lost her virginity before marriage, she was considered *soiled*. Now that she was a *fallen woman* many women believed their chances for a decent marriage were ruined. Unfortunately, many times the circumstances made them feel they could never trust a man again.

Throughout her career, Pearl had entertained wealthy and notable men including dignitaries, politicians, and celebrities. One night at the Everleigh Club, she watched a man from the King of Prussia's staff gallantly drink champagne from a woman's shoe after it had spilled during the festivities of the evening. So noble a gesture, it became a regular occurrence and tradition at the Everleigh Club in times of celebration. The tradition had been passed on to Miss Pearl's Parlor. As Ginger put it, "If the tradition suits royalty, it suits me just fine!"

In 1923 Pearl, at 45 years of age, had the strong opinion that, at this point in her life, she had seen just about everything and nothing could surprise her. That is until that fateful afternoon when Ella May Comstock from a farm near Sherwood, Texas, knocked on her door.

Mozella answered the door to a woman wearing a short brimmed straw hat with a neatly tied pink ribbon and a row of pink paper rosebuds in front. She wore short white gloves and a modest low-waisted dusty pink dress with pleats in the front, topped by a crisp white collar. The woman, barely four feet eleven inches tall, was holding onto a small cinched bag in her dainty-white gloved hands clutched in front of her. Her short brown curls framed a freckled face, and her pursed lips showed a *no nonsense* expression.

"Good day, Ma'am. My name is Ella May Comstock, and I have an order of business to discuss with Miss Pearl, if you please?"

Mozella realized that the woman was probably not seeking employment. No telling what she had in her bag. Maybe she was somebody's wife? The woman certainly looked harmless enough, but caution never hurt just in case. After a few seconds and a closer look, Mozella concluded that the woman was harmless. She invited her to come inside the Parlor. "I will let Miss Pearl know you are here," Mozella stated formally. "You can wait for her here in the library."

Ella May walked over to the small, dark brown mahogany writing table and picked up a journal made of Italian leather. She closed her eyes, held it close to her nose, and took a deep inhale to relish its musty odor.

"Mmm, I love the smell of good leather," she proclaimed.

Ella May did not notice that Miss Pearl had walked into the room. For a moment, Mozella and Pearl watched as this funny little woman, who was obviously enjoying herself, sniff the leather on her book. "Hello, dear. I am Miss Pearl. Won't you sit down?" she offered with some hesitation and a curious little smile.

"Thank you, Ma'am," Ella May replied as she replaced the book in its rightful place on the table, running her hand over its soft texture. She sat straight as a board on the edge of one of the red velvet chairs; Miss Pearl sat at the writing table. For a few moments, the women looked at each other with equal curiosity.

Finally, Ella May broke the silence. "Miss Pearl, I want you to know, I am a good Christian woman. I go to church every Sunday, and I read my Bible every day. My husband, Henry, and I are farmers in Sherwood. We come to San Angelo for supplies. In fact, we will be staying at the One Stop Boarding House this evening."

"That is very nice, dear. What can I do for you?" Miss Pearl asked as Mozella brought in glasses of mint tea for the two ladies.

Ella May whispered, "Can we have a private conversation, please? This is top secret!"

"We can do that," Pearl promised with even more curiosity. "Kindly leave us Mozella, and please shut the doors."

"*Psalm 146, The Lord takes care of those who are in a strange land*," Mozella mumbled as she closed the big doors.

Ella May took a deep breath and began talking rapidly, fearing she might lose her nerve. "I think I will get straight to the point if you don't mind, Ma'am. I have a sister, Dora May, who lives in Big Spring, Texas." Ella May whispered loudly. "She told me about the *Magic Button*!"

"The what?" Pearl inquired. "I do not believe I clearly understand."

Ella May whispered more loudly and looked at the doors. "*The Magic Button*!! Dora May said it's a significant component of our womanly parts! She says it is designed with the sole purpose of bringing sexual pleasure to a woman."

Miss Pearl smiled with the thought, "Is she talking about what I think she is talking about?"

"Miss Pearl, I love my husband, Henry, with all my heart! But I don't think my Henry knows anything about the *Magic Button*. It's like it's some kind of big secret. My sister, Dora May, says that her husband Jimmy, before they were married, of course, got an education from a lady in your profession about the *Magic Button!* Dora May says that when her Jimmy finds that *Magic Button,* she starts to shakin'! Then a quiverin'! Goose bumps all over her body! Then she told me her breathing changes like this!"

Miss Pearl watched with amazement as Ella May started breathing long breaths, moaning "ahhs" that gradually grew in intensity. She had never seen anything quite like it before, at least without a man in the room. Fascinated, she watched as Ella May's breaths got shorter and shorter, while the "ahhs" got louder and louder.

Suddenly, Ella May stopped, looked at Miss Pearl, and exclaimed, "Then Dora May told me that from the depths of her being, she makes a big ol' loud sound just like a coyote on the Texas plains howlin' at the full moon above just like this!"

Ella May started howling like a wild animal. "Ahhhhhhhhhhhhh OOOOOOOOOOO!"

Pearl's eyes grew huge and round. She could hardly believe that such a big voice could come out of such a little woman. Ella May's howling brought Mozella barging through the double doors. "Ahhhhhhhhhhhhh OOOOOOOOOOO!!" she repeated over and over, not noticing Mozella standing in the room.

Pearl and Mozella watched as Ella May dropped her purse and threw her arms wide up into the air. "Miss Pearl, THAT HAS NEVER EVER HAPPENED TO ME WITH MY

HENRY!" she yelped while looking at the ceiling. The other two women could only gape at her in bewilderment.

"Everything all right, Miss Pearl?" Mozella asked with a *what-in-the-hell-was-that* look on her face.

"All is well, Mozella," Pearl reassured her friend, blinking her eyes. "And I thought there was nothing in this world that could ever surprise me. I was so wrong."

"Psalm 144, Deliver me out of great waters, from the hand of strange children," Mozella quipped, shaking her head as she exited the library, shutting the doors behind her.

Pearl had never had a meeting quite like this before, but admired Ella May and was impressed with her desire to explore new territories.

"Now Miss Pearl, I told you I love my Henry with all my heart! I AM a good Christian woman! However, my Henry used to ride broncs, and you know sometimes those cowboys can get confused in thinkin' eight seconds is a long time!"

"A fact we are certainly aware of here at our parlor, Ella May. Sometimes the young men get so excited they even forget to take off their boots!"

"Yes, Ma'am. No offense, but I wouldn't know about that," Ella May grimaced through pursed lips. "I saw you and your lady friends riding in your cars one Sunday in front of the church where Henry and I go when we come to town. I overheard some of the church women making unkind comments about you and your girls. I, however, thought you seemed like a nice lady and someone I might could confide in."

"I appreciate your saying that," Pearl kindly responded. "What do you want me to do for you, honey?"

Excitedly, Ella May exclaimed, "I got to thinkin' that maybe YOU could give my Henry an education!"

"Why, Miss Ella May! What do you have in mind?" Pearl asked with some concern.

"Well, again I mean no disrespect, but I don't believe my Henry would ever step foot into your place of business. He just wouldn't. So I came up with a plan. I have saved two dollars!" Ella May reached into her bag and pulled out two carefully folded one dollar bills and placed them on the writing table.

"I would be much obliged if you were to take this money and give my Henry an EDUCATION. Henry's down at the river fishing not too far from here. He's wearing a red shirt and a straw hat, and he's real cute. You can't miss him. I told him to expect a woman teacher to pay him a visit. That would be you, Miss Pearl. I told him you were an expert on science and had some new information that could help us out on the farm. I know lyin' is a sin, but if you think about it, I didn't really lie."

Miss Pearl picked up the money and handed one of the dollar bills back to Ella May in a one-woman-to-another gesture. "One dollar will be just fine, Ella May." I will go to the river and have a little talk with your Henry." Pearl was impressed with this woman's sincerity.

"Oh, Miss Pearl, thank you so much. You have been so very kind. Now if you'll excuse me, I have some errands to do. Good day, Miss Pearl. You really are a nice lady."

"I don't believe I have ever met anyone quite like you, Ella May Comstock. I certainly want to help you, and I will do my best to educate your Henry."

As Miss Pearl stood up from the table, the doors to the library opened up and Mozella, who had been listening at the door, walked in. She also had never heard or seen anything like she had just heard coming from the library. Whether it was from fear of the unknown or just plain curiosity, she wanted to stay close by just to make sure this woman wasn't crazy.

"Mozella, please show Mrs. Ella May Comstock to the door," Pearl instructed with a twinkle in her eye.

"Yes, Ma'am!" Mozella responded with relief. "This way, if you please."

"Thank you, Mozella," Ella May sang politely, picking up her bag. At the big doors, she turned back to look at Pearl, and with the sweetest smile, she gave Pearl a little wave. "Bye for now, and thank you, Miss Pearl. You *really are* a nice lady."

To ready herself for her lesson to Henry, Miss Pearl went upstairs and changed into a simple dress. Henry was expecting a school teacher so a modest dress was obviously the best choice.

"Mozella, I am going out for a short time. I need to find a man named Henry down at the river and have a little talk with him. I will return within the hour," Pearl announced, abiding by the house rule that Mozella was to be told if anyone was going out.

Mozella regarded her friend with love and admiration. Twenty-three years had passed since that first day Mozella welcomed Miss Victoria Pearl into the Everleigh House. "Heard the whole thing, Pearl. She's right; you are quite a lady."

"So many good things happen when women learn how to work together, Mozella. With any luck at all, I am about to provide some information that will change Mrs. Ella May Comstock's world! It really is not poor Henry's fault. He just needs a little education, and he's certainly about to get one."

Pearl left her mansion and walked along the river to find Henry. Not far from the house, she saw a nice looking man, wearing a red shirt, peacefully fishing on the grassy banks of the Concho. He turned around when he sensed Pearl approaching him. Probably because of the fact that she looked like a harmless school teacher, he smiled and waved a friendly wave. Pearl waved back.

"Are you the school teacher Ella May told me about?" he inquired.

"You must be Henry. Very pleased to meet you, sir," Pearl responded with grace and style.

"Yes, Ma'am, I am." Henry laid his pole on a Y-shaped stick stuck in the ground beside him. "Would you like to sit down?" Henry pointed to a small wooden bench he had obviously built probably for Ella May. "Elly says you're a biology teacher."

"Yes, Henry, I am a teacher. I teach about the birds and the bees and Mother Nature herself. I guess you could say my specialty is biology."

"Pardon me, Ma'am, but I am a little confused. Why, in the world would Ella May think I need a lesson in biology? I've been breeding cattle, sheep, and goats all my life. I know a lot about animals. I learned biology from my daddy. Why people from miles around would bring their animals to my daddy. He could always tell what was wrong with them. He was a natural veterinarian. Learned everything he knew from his daddy."

Pearl decided to take another approach. "Henry, would you mind if we might talk about farming."

"I know a lot about farming too! My daddy…"

Pearl asked a question to take control of the conversation. "Hold on, Henry. When you want to plant a crop, do you just go out and throw a bunch of seeds on the ground?"

"Oh, no, Ma'am!" Henry exclaimed. "We till the ground and get it wet so the seeds will germinate, and then we put it in rows so as to…"

"That is correct, Henry. You do not just throw seeds on the ground now, do you?" Pearl used metaphors when she wanted to make a point.

"No, Ma'am, I guess something could grow if you just throw seeds down, but it wouldn't be worth a dang."

"Not worth a dang? Now we are getting somewhere. How about a garden? Have you ever planted a flower garden?"

"Yes Ma'am. Elly has a real pretty flower garden. She also takes care of the vegetables we grow closer to the house. I helped dig the dirt for both gardens, and I got the soil ready to plant the seeds," Henry puffed with pride.

"That is just fine, Henry." Miss Pearl smiled and asked another question. "How did you get the soil ready?"

"Well, Ma'am, I loosen the earth up a bit…" Henry explained.

"Yesssss… Henry… then what do you do?" Pearl was pleased with the direction the conversation was heading.

"Well, Ma'am, I put my hands in the dirt and added some water and nutrients."

"You caressed the ground with your hands, Henry?"

"I guess you could say that. Yes, Ma'am, I worked with that soil," Henry continued eagerly.

"Like this Henry?" Pearl raised her hands and started massaging the air.

"Yes, Ma'am! Just like that." Henry raised his hands and joined Pearl in massaging the air.

"Do you get your hands in there real good, Henry?" Pearl asked as she continued to knead the air.

"Yes, Ma'am… real good!" Henry said slowly.

"Does it take some time, Henry, or do you just get it done as quickly as you can?" Both continued massaging the air as they spoke.

"Oh no, Ma'am, it takes some time. The more you put yourself into the land the more she gives you!" Henry declared respectfully.

"Then do you water it, Henry, and get it wet?"

"Yes, Ma'am, I do!"

"Nice and wet, Henry?"

"Oh yes, Ma'am! Nice and wet!"

"Henry! A woman is the same way!" Pearl exclaimed throwing her arms up in the air.

"Excuse me, School Teacher? What in the world are you talking about?" Henry asked as he slapped his hands on both sides of his waist.

Pearl resumed massaging the air. "Henry, if you prepare the soil, you harvest plentiful gifts from Mother Earth. Am I correct?" Pearl asked the confused young man.

"Yes, Ma'am. When we prepare the soil and God blesses us with sunshine and rain, the garden produces colorful flowers and delicious food," Henry replied eloquently.

Miss Pearl thought, "How fortunate Ella May is to have such a good man." She gently put her hands together as if she were holding a delicate secret between her palms. "Exactly! Henry… you are a lucky man. Your wife, Ella May, absolutely adores you. My dear man, your Ella May has another kind of garden that bears delicious fruit as well." Then Pearl whispered in confidence, "It is in the bedroom, Henry."

Henry gazed at Pearl with a puzzled look on his face. "What kind of school teacher are you anyway?"

"Henry. You are obviously a kind, generous man. How much do you love Ella May?"

"All there is Ma'am, Ella May is my life!" Henry exclaimed.

"Then listen carefully to what I am about to tell you, Henry. Women are complex creatures. Ella May has an exciting hidden treasure for you that you have never experienced before. It is not your fault, Henry. Parents do not teach their children about how to enjoy sex, and most people are uncomfortable talking about it at all. In fact, sadly enough many folks are not even aware of what I am about to tell you because it is perceived as dirty or bad, a very unhappy perception. You see Henry, a woman's body is much like a violin. Just like the violin it has lovely curves and the potential to stimulate the depths of the soul with beautiful music. If you keep it in tune and play it with love in your heart, a woman can take you to magical places you have never been before."

Henry hung on to Pearl's every word.

"A woman has erotic spots that when stimulated are like getting the soil ready for the seed. Every woman is different. Some love to be kissed on the back of the neck or the small of their backs. Others like to have their feet massaged. Some enjoy soft kisses on their breasts and their tummies. Some women like it all. The best approach is to simply ask. A woman will let you know if what you are doing is pleasing her. She might even make suggestions to you. Remember to be gentle and to move slowly. This will prepare her to give you a memorable experience."

Henry was fascinated; he had never heard anything like this before.

Pearl continued. "All women love to be told they are beautiful. All women love to be told they are desired, and all women love to be told they are loved. All women can deliver the most delicious sexual experiences if the man addresses her needs. All you have to do is ask what pleases her and let her know she is appreciated and adored."

Pearl kindly smiled at Henry. Her voice was gentle and almost musical as she continued.

"The deepest mystery of a woman is located in her womanhood. It is the place where life is created and new life enters the world. It can be the gateway to ecstasy if you know where the key is located. I believe your wife referred to it as the *Magic Button*. This is a good analogy because when we push a button, for instance on a car, when we ignite it, the car moves."

"Yes, Ma'am," Henry whispered.

"I like to think of the *Magic Button* as a beautiful pink pearl. It is located at the top of a woman's gateway to heaven, Henry, embedded like a Concho Pearl in a special chamber. The *Magic Pearl* holds the secret to a woman's complete pleasure. Although it is tiny, it is even more sensitive than your manhood, so be gentle with it and try to avoid direct contact. It must stay protected and can be massaged gently from the outside with small circles. When you find the *Magic Pearl*, dear Henry, your sweet Ella May will produce bountiful sweet honey from her secret chamber. Then right before your eyes, she will transform into a sensuous goddess of love. Just allow her to direct you to what feels right."

"Yes, Ma'am," Henry whispered.

"Henry, I am very good at judging character, and you seem like a kind and generous man. This next bit of information is probably the most important thing I am going to tell you today. Are you ready? It takes seventeen tender expressive minutes to awaken the goddess."

Henry shook his head. "I think you've lost me there, School Teacher."

"Inside every woman there is a sensuous goddess of love. This is how God created us. Sadly enough, many women have spent their entire lives with the goddess dormant inside of her. Only a tender, caring, sensual lover can awaken her magical essence. This takes seventeen complete minutes. Enjoy her, talk to her, and stimulate her for no fewer than seventeen minutes. If you do this, making love to a woman can be absolutely divine."

"Yes, Ma'am. Seventeen minutes to awaken the goddess, eh? Hmmm, I will remember that."

"Remember a woman can be delicious, Henry. Ella May will make it obvious if she is enjoying herself. Remind her that she is appreciated, respected, and desired. Then wait for the invitation. She will let you know when she is ready for you to join her as one in the greatest most beautiful union a man and a woman can ever know. If you wait for her invitation, you will experience the most exciting gift a woman's body can give to the man she loves. As you prepare to release, tell her you love her."

"Yes, Ma'am," Henry whispered. He looked out to the beauty of the green gentle flow of the Concho River. "You have given me much to ponder, School Teacher."

"Your sweet wife loves you. Trust me on this. I guarantee you will not be disappointed! Good day, Henry. Give my regards to your sweet Ella May."

"Good day, School Teacher," Henry whispered as he took off his hat.

Pearl smiled and pointed to Henry's fishing line. "Looks like you have a bite!" Henry reeled in a small white bass as Miss Pearl turned away. He never did learn Pearl's name. It was better that way.

The Landon Hotel

That evening Henry decided to take Ella May to the Landon Hotel instead of the One Stop Boarding House. After a lovely dinner, they retired to their room. Henry obviously had been a good student because twice that evening, Mrs. Ella May Comstock's joyful songs of ecstasy rang throughout the Concho Valley night.

An Engagement

It had been two weeks since Tommy Lee and his friends had gone to San Angelo and life as he knew it had completely changed. All day every day, Tommy Lee thought about his night with Emma Grace and how she had captivated his soul. Thinking about her bright smile and her delicate laughter made his heart flutter. Since the last time he had seen her, Tommy Lee had come to the conclusion that she was the woman he wanted to spend the rest of his life with. He had never met anyone so sweet. He loved the way she made him feel, and for the first time in his life, he was walking on air.

One bright morning he decided that this was the day when he would tell his mother, Marybelle, about his newfound love. Entering into the kitchen, he smelled the warm familiar aroma of fresh hot biscuits. He paused for a moment to watch his mother pull her flaky pastries from the oven and put them into a bowl like she had done every morning she didn't make pancakes. His father, Jed, sat at the kitchen table with his coffee.

"We need to move the sheep to the north pasture today, Tommy," his father instructed. "I need to go to San Angelo this week, and I'd like you to go with me. Time for you to get more involved in the selling part of our ranching business."

"You bet! Mother, can you come too? There is someone I'd like you to meet."

Before his father could stop him, it was out of his mouth. "Mother, I have met the girl I want to marry," Tommy Lee announced. Tommy Lee's father, not prepared for this moment, had, in fact, thought the romance had probably faded since that night when his son had told him he had met his future bride at Miss Pearl's Parlor.

Marybelle turned to her husband in surprise then looked lovingly at her son. "Someone we know?" his mother asked sweetly. "Is it Debbie Adams? I know she's been sweet on you since both of you were in school together."

"No, Mama. She lives in San Angelo. Her name is Emma... Emma Grace," Tommy answered.

"Emma Grace? What a lovely name. I don't believe I know anyone by that name, Tommy Lee," his mother commented. "When did you meet Emma Grace?"

"I met her on my birthday when the boys and I went to San Angelo," Tommy answered. "She is the most beautiful girl in the world, Mother."

"Jed, do you know anything about this?" Marybelle quizzed her husband.

Jed decided it was safer to keep his eyes on his breakfast and not make eye contact with his wife. "Seems like maybe Tommy Lee might have mentioned something 'bout it the other night when the boys got back."

"Where exactly did you meet Emma Grace, Tommy Lee?" she pleasantly inquired.

"I met her in San Angelo at Miss Pearl's," he answered, grinning widely. Tommy Lee, always honest, never had a problem telling the truth. In fact, lying was completely against his nature.

"Land sakes! Tommy Lee!" his mother gasped, holding her hand over her heart and collapsing into her chair at the table. "Miss Pearl's Parlor?" Tommy Lee didn't seem to notice his mother's reaction. "Jed!" Jed knew better than to get involved in this conversation.

"The first time I saw Emma Grace I felt like I'd already known her from somewhere before. It was kind of strange and magical all at the same time."

Tommy Lee's mother, trying to remain calm, furrowed her brow with grave concern. "Miss Pearl's Parlor?" she repeated softly.

"Yes, Ma'am!" Tommy Lee declared proudly. "Emma Grace is sweet as an angel and pretty like the wild flowers when they bloom in the spring. I'm telling you she is the most beautiful girl in the whole world!"

"Jed?" she asked in a *please-tell-me-I-didn't-hear-what-I-think-I-just-heard* tone.

Her husband was scratching his head the way some men do when trying to figure out the right thing to say, "Of course, Marybelle. It would be a fine time for us all to go to San Angelo, I reckon," her husband answered.

Tommy Lee's mother, a good Christian woman, liked to think she lived by a passage from the Sermon on the Mount: "*Judge not that ye should be judged,*" a quotation that sometimes challenged her the most. For a moment, she thought about her friend, Bonnie Wilcox, who had made it clear to her son that she did not like the woman he wanted to marry. As a result, he married her anyway and moved to East Texas to honor his new bride's request to get away from his mother. To this day, Bonnie still had not seen her 2 grandchildren.

Tommy Lee was his mother's pride and joy, but this was a grave matter. She decided to postpone any judgment or confrontation until after she had met her son's new-found love. "I would love to meet Miss Emma Grace, Tommy Lee," she managed to say in the most level tone she could muster. Tommy Lee had been raised to have strong character and high morals; his mother was absolutely confident in her son's integrity. It was his lack of experience that most concerned her, but she decided not to burst his bubble without first meeting Emma Grace.

Tommy's little sisters, Theresa, Tilly, and Tara came into the kitchen for breakfast. "What's going on?" Theresa asked.

"Seems like your brother has a new lady friend girls," Marybelle told her daughters. "I will be going to San Angelo with your father and brother at the end of the week. You can stay with Aunt Dora overnight."

"Tommy has a girlfriend. Tommy has a girlfriend!" the girls chanted.

"Now, girls, leave your brother alone. Time to get on to school," Marybelle warned her daughters.

Meanwhile, life wasn't much different for Emma Grace in San Angelo. At the same time that Tommy Lee was thinking about her, she was thinking about him. When she remembered those crystal blue eyes, Emma Grace felt a love flash that would first squeeze on her heart, then burn like fire throughout her body, and send chills up her spine.

That morning Emma Grace felt eager to share her feelings as well. "Miss Pearl," she asked at breakfast. "Have you ever been in love?"

"Yes, Emma Grace. My husband Robert and I were very much in love."

"How do you know when you're in love?"

"I knew the first night I met him."

"That's just like Tommy Lee and me! We both felt like we were hit by a bolt of lightning at the same time. I can't stop thinking about him, Miss Pearl."

"What does it feel like when you think about Tommy Lee, Emma Grace?"

"It's like a warm strong current that goes from my heart, to my tummy and then back up into my heart that explodes like a burst of fireworks. Sometimes it's so strong it almost hurts… in a good way. Kind of hard to explain," Emma Grace expressed as she crossed her arms over her chest. "Then a warm tingly feeling goes all over me like a shimmering rainbow."

"Sounds like love to me," Pearl agreed. "For years when I lived in Chicago, I felt exactly like that every time I thought about my Robert."

"Even after the first night?" Emma Grace asked.

"Every day of my life since that first night we were together. Time ceases to exist when it comes to love, Emma Grace. Even now, when I am alone, I can replay the entire first night I was with Robert in my mind just as if it had happened yesterday. I wrote about it in my journal. The way he looked and smiled at me when Minna Everleigh made the introduction. How he gazed at me as if I were a princess when we dined at supper that evening, and then the way he made love to me when we went into the Rose Room."

"Made love?" Emma Grace asked. "But you always say…"

"Yes, Robert made love to me the first night we were together. I remember my friend Maddie was concerned because I was acting just as you are now. When love is real, it really does not matter what the circumstances are. I know I met him at the Everleigh House as a working girl, but it never seemed to matter to him. It was almost like fate had taken it out of our control. I knew the first moment I saw him that I loved him. You cannot put logic to matters of the heart, Emma Grace, although I think for a long time we both tried to do exactly that."

"Then it can happen in one night?" Emma Grace asked.

"Yes, Ma'am, it surely can. After all these years and all the things I have witnessed, I believe Robert and I knew each other in a past life. The moment we first looked into each other's eyes, our souls recognized each other. I will never forget it. We spoke of it many times," Pearl remembered with a radiant glow that Emma Grace had never seen before.

"After spending time with my cowboy, I wrote in my journal about every detail. Things we said to each other. The way we laughed... the way he loved me," Pearl sighed. "I had no expectations and treated every time he came to see me in Chicago as if it might be the last. Writing details about our time together is how I kept the fantasy alive. Now I have all of those tender, exciting, loving memories to read again and again. It helps me on the days I am especially lonely for him. Sometimes I feel like he is still here with me. When I talk to him now, the deepest part of me knows that he can hear me. When it comes to love, the soul connects in ways only the heart can understand. It is forever. After I became his wife and moved to the ranch, I experienced a sense of completeness. Now that he is gone, I appreciate the fact that I experienced a love like that in my lifetime."

"When I was with Tommy Lee that night we met, it was like nothing else in the world existed. He and I, the moon and the bright Texas stars were all that was real. It was like heaven, Miss Pearl, just like heaven on earth!"

"When love is real, Emma Grace, we experience '*on earth as it is in heaven.*' Here at the Parlor, we create the fantasy of love. Of course, the fantasy is not real. I learned well from the

Everleigh sisters. Our work is to temporarily satisfy the deep hunger of every human being's desire to be loved. The men who come here pay for kindness and companionship with a pretty lady. It is an honest business really because no one has any expectations past the fantasy. Like I have told you before, men will say some of the nicest things you would ever want to hear when they want to have sex. However, unless they love you, most men change their demeanor with a woman as soon as their physical needs are met. Our business is simple. The girls at Pearl's Parlor receive money for their beauty and kindness. After the men are satisfied, the illusion of love is over."

"I think it's interesting how Maggie tells every man who comes to see her that he is the best she's ever known," Emma Grace giggled.

"And they keep coming back," Pearl commented. "Maggie is a sweet girl and likes men to feel good about themselves. Ginger, on the other hand, is always a challenge. Different men need different turn-ons. I learned a long time ago most men like a challenge."

"You're right. When men try to impress Ginger, she acts bored. Then they try harder."

"Exactly. At times I played a little hard to get with Robert. It was just a game, really. Have you ever heard, 'The harder the hunt the sweeter the meat'?"

"I don't believe I have," Emma Grace answered.

"Men do not like needy women. I try to tell that to Betsy. She is so afraid she is never going to marry," Pearl sighed. "Men who come to Pearl's are not usually looking for a wife. However, some of the girls who worked at the Everleigh House did marry some of the wealthy clients because their actions were impeccable - refined in public and exciting in the bedroom, like the famous Suzy Poon Tang. I remember the man she married was mesmerized with her talents. Within a week, she was betrothed and rich!"

"No disrespect, Miss Pearl, but I don't know that I can ever do what the girls do here."

"This line of work is not easy, Emma Grace. Most of the girls who are here have heartbreaking stories and came to work here because they had no better options. The girls have found temporary solace and refuge; plus the money is good at the Parlor. Most 'sporting women', as some like to call us, have tragic stories of abuse or abandonment. Poor little Annabelle is a widow with a mother and baby to take care of. Heather sends money home to her family every week. The girls are here because options are slim for single women to make any kind of decent money, yet I left Chicago a wealthy woman. Our business is really the only profession in which a woman of little means can actually become a millionaire. In fact, it was a black madame in Chicago who originally built the two mansions on the Levee we called *The Everleigh Club* and she paid cash!"

"My goodness!" Emma Grace exclaimed.

"If things work out for you and Tommy Lee, you will have what I call the most ultimate sacred experience between a man and a woman because neither of you have had the sexual experience yet," Pearl smiled. Robert and I talked about it many times. 'If I could do it all over, I would have brought you back to Texas that first time I met you,' he used to say.

"'Life gives us the lessons we must learn'," I told him. "'We are together now, and that is all that matters.'"

West Texas sported another blue sky day on the morning when Tommy Lee had told his mother about the love of his life and Emma Grace had confided in Miss Pearl. That afternoon, the phone rang at Miss Pearl's Parlor. "Is Emma Grace there, please?"

Mozella recognized it was Tommy Lee. "Just a moment," she handed the phone to Emma Grace. "It's for you, Honey," nodding her head up and down with excitement.

"Hello… Tommy Lee… You are? That's wonderful! They are? Okay then! Yes, I will meet you at the Angelus Hotel at noon tomorrow. I can't wait to see you!" Emma Grace slowly handed the phone back to Mozella.

"Honey child… You look like you just swallowed a bug! Are you all right?" Mozella asked.

"I think so. Tommy Lee is coming to San Angelo with his parents tomorrow. He wants me to meet them! Mozella! What if they don't like me? I can't go alone!"

"What is going on here?" Pearl asked, entering the room.

"Tommy Lee is bringing his parents to meet Emma Grace," Mozella answered.

"What am I going to do, Miss Pearl?" Emma Grace asked frantically.

"What any self-respecting woman must do, Emma Grace. We are going shopping! You will need a new dress to make you feel pretty," Pearl answered.

Later that afternoon, Pearl bought Emma Grace a lovely violet dress with a lacy white collar, new shoes, stockings and a simple cloche hat with a modest band of small purple flowers.

Driving home, Emma Grace suddenly panicked, thinking about meeting Tommy Lee's parents. "Would you please come with me tomorrow, Miss Pearl? I don't think I can do this by myself."

"Are you sure, Emma Grace?" Pearl asked.

"Yes, please, Ma'am!"

"Very well, dear. I will."

Emma Grace could hardly sleep that night. Excitement and fear ran together, and she tossed and turned in her small bedroom. The next morning after her chores, she took a bubble bath and put on her new clothes. "Pearl was right," she thought to herself. "Feeling clean and pretty does make a girl feel more confident."

Pearl picked a classy light blue simple frock and wore a cream colored cloche hat with a band to match her dress. Emma Grace knocked at her door. "I'm ready," she chirped in a happy yet nervous tone. "What do you think?" she asked when Pearl opened the door.

"They are going to love you!" Pearl reassured her. "By the way, my name is Victoria at lunch today, Emma Grace. I think it will make the conversation easier."

When the two ladies entered the dining area of the Angelus, they saw Tommy Lee sitting with his mother and father at a table by the window. As soon as he saw Emma Grace, he jumped up and smiled. Pearl had forgotten how gorgeous his eyes were. When she saw his mother, she noticed that he had gotten them from her.

"Mother, Pa, this is Emma Grace," Tommy Lee announced, not taking his eyes off her. Emma Grace stood beside him.

"Very pleased to meet you both. This is my friend, Victoria," Emma Grace said graciously.

"It's nice to see you again, Ma'am," Tommy Lee said politely.

Marybelle and Jed were both instantly impressed with Emma Grace's natural beauty and charm. For the first few minutes, the conversation was light and casual. They talked about the weather, and as usual, Pearl was a master at maintaining an interesting conversation. After the meal was served, Marybelle asked some questions that had been burning on her mind since she first had heard that her son was head-over-heels in love. "Are you from San Angelo, Emma Grace?" she asked sweetly.

"No, Ma'am. My family is from East Texas," Emma Grace answered. "Around Longview."

"I see. Do you live with your parents?"

"Mother died when I was born, and Daddy and I came here when he got the coughing disease. We had learned from his doctor that San Angelo was a good place to go because of the altitude and its warm dry climate. When Daddy died a few weeks ago, I really had nowhere to go, Ma'am. A very nice man gave me an address and told me I should go there to find work. Miss Pearl, I mean, Victoria was kind enough to take me in."

Marybelle looked at Jed, and with hidden frustration kicked him under the table. He started scratching his head. "I'm sorry about your father, Emma Grace," she managed to say with kindness. "It must be hard for you." Marybelle cleared her throat, and with all the graciousness she could muster, finally asked, "Emma Grace…why…that is… I guess what I'm trying to… *what kind of work do you do* at Miss Pearl's, Emma Grace?" Until she finally asked the question, Marybelle had been forcing herself to smile. She could see that her son was completely enamored with Emma Grace, and she did not want to spoil his happiness with her grave concern.

"I help Mozella in the kitchen, Ma'am. I mostly clean and cook… that sort of thing," Emma Grace replied with tender wide eyed innocence.

"Emma Grace came to me looking for work," Pearl interjected. "The child had nowhere to go. She sleeps in a room off the kitchen and is a marvelous cook." Pearl offered, patting Emma's hand to help put her at ease.

"She cooks for you?" Marybelle asked in surprise. "And cleans?"

"Yes, she does. Emma Grace is an amazing cook," Pearl commented. "I am very pleased with her work."

"Been cooking all my life for my daddy, Ma'am. I've been learning a lot from Mozella as well."

"That is **ALL** Emma Grace does at the Parlor. We are lucky to have her!" Pearl smiled, communicating exactly what poor Marybelle so desperately needed to hear.

Marybelle was giddy with relief! "Did you hear that, Pa? Emma Grace cooks, and she cleans! She cooks, and she cleans! And she's good at it! How wonderful, Emma Grace! Let me say again how so sorry I am about your daddy, my dear. She cooks, and she cleans, Pa! That's wonderful dear! And she's good at it, Jed! She's good at it!" Marybelle was now a very happy mother with a big smile on her face. Her attitude had been transformed.

Although Tommy Lee and Emma Grace had been too entranced to notice, Pearl and Jed watched Marybelle relax. The rest of the luncheon went well. The young couple spoke only to each other. Marybelle and Pearl graciously continued their small talk. Jed remained quiet and paid the bill.

"Thank you for a lovely luncheon; you are most kind," Victoria expressed gracefully. "This hotel is dear to my heart."

"You are welcome, Miss Victoria," he grinned.

"May I call on Emma Grace this evening, Miss Pearl?" Tommy Lee asked. "I have some business with my father this afternoon."

"Certainly, Tommy Lee," Pearl answered. "She can be finished with her chores by 7 tonight."

"Yes, yes, yes! We need to let Emma Grace do her job cooking and cleaning!" Marybelle laughed nervously. "She's very good at it, you know. Now I have some shopping to do."

"I will see you tonight, Emma Grace," Tommy Lee exclaimed.

That afternoon Tommy Lee went to Holland's Jewelers and bought Emma Grace a gold ring with a sparkling diamond.

At 7:00 sharp, Tommy Lee rang the bell and then knocked on the door at Miss Pearl's Parlor where Emma Grace, wearing her new pretty dress, was waiting for him. The crescent moon was glowing, and the West Texas stars were shining brightly, reflecting a shimmering sheen on the Concho River. Tommy Lee crooked his arm that Emma Grace graciously accepted, and together they strolled toward the gazebo.

Emma Grace seated herself on the bench and smiled up at Tommy Lee who stood before her. He slowly genuflected onto one knee. She could feel the butterflies in her stomach and a flush on her cheeks, her heart beating like never before. "Emma Grace, would you do me the honor of marrying me and being my wife forever?" Tommy Lee asked, his sparkling blue eyes full of sincerity and love.

Tears of happiness filled her eyes. "Yes, Tommy Lee! Oh, yes!"

Tommy Lee stood up and pulled her to him. They held each other tightly for a long time. When they sat down, Emma Grace snuggled up to Tommy Lee, and together they sat for hours watching the starlight on the Concho glimmering in the night, whispering to each other.

Emma Grace was not the only one with tears. From her window, Pearl had been watching the two young lovers in the gazebo below. When she saw Emma Grace throw her arms around Tommy Lee, she smiled, turned away, and picked up the photograph on the table beside her bed. "I miss you," she sighed as she remembered a Ferris wheel ride at the St. Louis Fair.

Happy Harvey

The next morning Pearl's Parlor buzzed with excitement. "Let me see the ring!" Lucy squealed. Emma Grace held up her hand for everyone to inspect.

One-by-one, the girls congratulated her and kissed her on the cheek. "Emma Grace, we are so very happy for you," Pearl exclaimed with pride. "Because of you and Tommy Lee, we now have a Cinderella story to tell at Pearl's Parlor!"

That afternoon Maggie and Heather were sitting on the front porch enjoying the warmth of the West Texas sun when they heard a familiar 'aoogha, aoogha' resonating through the peaceful afternoon. Rusty ran out wagging his tail; he knew that honk meant yummy treats. Harvey presented himself with warmth and love. "Hey, everyone! Happy Harvey's here!" From upstairs and downstairs, the girls ran into the main room. The young, fun-loving millionaire made his visits in the early afternoons. The ladies were crazy about Happy Harvey!

Harvey James Rochester was an attractive, wealthy, charming, witty man who cherished his *Lady Pearls* as he affectionately called them. Each of the girls kept a wish list active at Holland's Jewelers for clients who wanted to show their extra appreciation. Harvey was one of the famous store's best customers. He never missed a birthday and loved to buy the girls gifts. With the exception of Katie who wanted a Harley Davidson for her birthday, Harvey made sure that the girls were adorned with golden trinkets, favorite gemstones, diamonds, and Concho pearls.

On his afternoon visits to Pearl's Parlor, he first went to his bank for a stack of $5.00 bills. For a great big "snuggy huggy from Happy Harvey," Harvey gave each of the girls one of the bills. However, this particular afternoon, Harvey entered into the Parlor carrying a large box containing several smaller boxes.

"How is my boy?" Pearl asked Harvey. For years Pearl had heard Minna say those same words to every regular customer who entered the Everleigh Mansion.

"Wonderful, dear lady," Harvey exclaimed, kissing Pearl on both cheeks. "I bring gifts and treasures from travels abroad!"

Harvey had recently been to Europe, and everyone was excited to see what he had brought. Handing each of the girls one of the boxes, he gave a peck on the mouth as well as a, "This is for you, Sugar-lips!"

Heather was the first to open her box. "It's French perfume!" she declared. Harvey had carefully selected a different fragrance for each of the girls. They smothered him with smooches and hugs.

"This is for Julie Marie," he declared as he presented Annabelle with a Dream Baby Doll. "I picked it up in New York and I have a little baby bed for it in the car."

"She will love it! Thank you, Harvey. Look everybody!" Annabelle beamed as she held the baby doll up.

"These are for Rusty," he declared, handing Katie a bag of Derby dog biscuits.

"Thank you, Harvey," Katie replied. "Come over here, Emma Grace. You need to show Harvey your ring!"

Harvey took Emma Grace's hand. "Oh my! It is simply exquisite! This is so exciting. We must throw you a bridal shower!"

Harvey usually brought catalogs and newspaper clippings with current fashions and trends. "He's just like having an awesome girlfriend in a man's body," Lucy liked to say.

Sometimes he'd take the girls on shopping sprees and buy them new outfits. Though complimentary, at the same time, Harvey never hesitated to speak out when he felt that one of the "Pearls" needed a slight adjustment or change. Harvey kept up with all the latest beauty secrets, like soaking cotton balls in chamomile tea and putting them on eyes to get rid of dark circles or making sure their lip-liner made a perfect "Cupid's bow" before applying some bright red lipstick. He was quick to notice and comment when one of the girls had a new hair style or when anyone had changed her make-up.

"Guess what everybody! I met Coco Chanel when I was in France," he proudly announced.

"You did? Tell us all about it!" Redbird chirped excitedly. "What is she like?"

"Well! Coco came to a cocktail party I was invited to when I was in Paris. Oh, my goodness! I just love Coco! Ginger, you would look absolutely fabulous in the outfit she was wearing! It caused quite a ruckus when she brazenly strolled in wearing gold lamé sparkling trousers and a matching gold lamé man's necktie on a flowing white chiffon shirt. People are still not used to women wearing trousers. Personally, I see nothing wrong with it. Of course, in Coco's circle, she can do no wrong! That woman can put a lampshade on her head, call it a hat, and within a week, women all over Paris will be wearing lampshades. Ha, ha, ha! Oh, my goodness, that thought is so funny!"

"That is because she is Coco!" Ginger expressed with cool sophistication.

"I noticed a lot of the women at the party had a bit of a tan. It seems like everyone wants that sun-kissed look ever since Coco accidentally bronzed herself on the French Riviera. I spent some time there myself and saw some muscular, gorgeous bare chests on the beach that made me feel tingly all over my body. So many of them were bronzed. Their stomachs ripped like washboards. Oh, my, Lord, it was a sight to behold! Total eye candy, if you know what I mean!"

"Like when the cowboys come into town!" Maggie giggled.

"All-in-all, I had a fantastic trip. Europe seems to be recovering from the pains of war. By the way, did y'all hear the Attorney General finally declared women can wear trousers in America now? Coco will do well with that!"

"Miss Pearl has a pair," Sarah commented. "It's a little strange seeing a woman in pants and pearls."

"I remember wearing those awful corsets! They were painful," Pearl exclaimed. "Now there is even gasoline perfume! In my day ladies always wore rose oil. So much has changed in the last 20 years! The *New Woman* has arrived!"

Happy Harvey was a joy and a thoughtful man. "Sugar pie," "Sugar lips," "Sugar dumplin," or just plain "Sugar" were his favorite terms of endearment for good reason. Harvey's father, who had become wealthy trading textiles on the east coast, had brought his family to San Angelo when he saw an opportunity to become involved in the wool business that was booming in West Texas. His mother, a large, overbearing woman was bossy and rude, constantly telling Harvey what to do. When Harvey was eighteen years old, his father took him into town to spend the day with their banker. "Son," he began, "Today is your day to become a real man and learn about the family business. We are going to open an account for you."

After the papers were signed, his banker led the two men to the entrance of a covert underground tunnel located inside the bank. The father and son went through the tunnel, and in just a matter of minutes, they found themselves inside Miss Hattie's bordello on Concho Avenue.

An attractive girl with long black curls sauntered over to the two men. "Hello, handsome. My name is Sugar," she purred to Harvey. "We've been expecting you. You're coming with me!"

Harvey's father gave him a wink. "Make me proud, son!" he glowed as he patted Harvey on the back. "You're in good hands, Harvey. I assure you Sugar will take good care of you!" A pretty blonde haired girl named Goldie gave Harvey a coy smile and hooked herself into his father's arm. He watched as she led his father down the hallway and saw them disappear into one of the rooms down the hall.

Sugar took Harvey's hand and escorted him into a bedroom with a colorful quilt on the bed. A dark red curtain was hung on the window, blocking the room from the bright sunlight. A candle on the table beside the bed emitted a soft glow, reflecting off the walls. "So, I hear this is your first time, Harvey, or have you already been with a woman without your daddy knowing?" Sugar teased.

"No, Ma'am," was the only thing Harvey could say, bewildered and a little confused. Sugar started taking off her clothes revealing beautiful firm breasts, a long waist, and perfectly shaped hips that were swaying back and forth to a silent rhythm. "Ex…ex…excuse me, Ma'am. What are you doing?" Harvey asked, obviously uncomfortable. His ears were warm, and his forehead dripped perspiration.

"We're going to make Mr. Happy, HAPPY!" Sugar giggled putting her hands below Harvey's belt buckle. "Oh my!" she winced. "Seems like we've got some extra work we need to do for Mr. Happy to get happy!" she exclaimed. "Don't worry, honey, this happens sometimes."

"I don't believe anything is going to happen, Ma'am. Now don't get me wrong! You're a lovely girl, but honestly Mr. Happy only tingles when I see a hard muscled body attached to a tight firm buttocks in a pair of man's trousers, if you know what I mean."

"I think I do," Sugar answered. "I also like a hard muscled body attached to tight firm buttocks in a pair of man's trousers, if you know what I mean!"

"You're the first person I've ever told!" Harvey whispered. "I know my father has different expectations for today, but honestly I don't see this happening. I'm not sure what I'm going to do about the way I feel about men, but I really can't help it!" Poor Harvey was sweating profusely and feeling more nervous and confused by the minute.

"I think my father is suspicious. That's why he brought me here today. You are a very beautiful woman, Sugar, and incredibly sexy, but I'm afraid it's just not going to happen, today or ever."

Sugar was a sweetheart of a gal. "I've got an idea!" she told him. "The springs on this bed are pretty loud. How 'bout I jump up and down on the bed and yell something like '*Ride 'em, Cowboy*' while you yell something like '*Yeah, baby, yeah*'! Then when I give you the signal, let out a big ol' moan. Your father will think everything is hunky-dory, and I can make my money!"

"Sounds good to me!" Harvey exclaimed. "Let's do it!!"

Sugar peeked out the door and waited until she saw Harvey's father emerge from Goldie's room. Since Sugar had entertained Mr. Rochester many times before and knew his routine, she was sure it wouldn't be too long before he ambled down the hallway to the sitting room. Sugar timed it just right. As soon as she saw the door open, she popped back into the room, jumped onto the bed, and started bouncing up and down. "Ride 'em cowboy!" she yelled. "Ride 'em hard!"

Sugar, jumping up and down, made an impressive racket. Harvey was delighted. "C'mon Harvey!" she whispered loud enough for him to hear. "Yeah baby! Say it! Do it now!"

Harvey, totally amused, "Yeah, baby!" he yelled. "Yeah, baby! Yeah!" Sugar was jumping and the bed springs were bouncing and squeaking. Sugar and Harvey were putting on quite a show for anyone within listening distance. "Ride 'em cowboy!" Sugar yelled. "Ride 'em hard!!"

"Yeah, baby! Yeah! Oh, YEAH!!" Harvey cheered.

The next fifteen minutes, Sugar and Happy Harvey made enough noise to be heard at least halfway down Concho Avenue. Miss Hattie raised her eyebrows. "Sounds like your son is having a mighty good time!" she declared with a grin.

Mr. Rochester lit up a cigar, sat back in his chair and smiled. Next came an intense moaning and then quiet. Mr. Rochester puffed on his cigar and proudly announced, "That's my boy! Takes after his father!"

Miss Hattie rolled her eyes. "Uh hum…right."

So it began. Harvey would come to town, go to the bank, sneak through the tunnel to Miss Hattie's, and play "Ride 'em cowboy!" with Sugar while she bounced on the bed. One day she surprised him with a stick horse which he rode in circles around the room. It was fun and made the game more interesting. Sometimes he would put on a baby bonnet and one of Sugar's nightgowns, and Sugar would sing "*You must have been a beautiful baby, you must have been a beautiful child.*" The games were their little secret. Sugar was paid dearly for her services.

The other girls at Miss Hattie's begged for Harvey's affection. After all, with all the commotion coming from Sugar's room, he had to be fun! He always responded with, "Now y'all know Sugar is my girl!" Harvey, with his big heart hated to see anyone disappointed. He felt bad when they pouted as if he had just told them they weren't good enough to get any ice cream. One day he found a solution. "I will give anyone a dollar for a great big snuggy huggy!" he announced. When Harvey started bringing dollar bills for a hug to Miss Hattie's, the girls gave him the nickname, "Happy Harvey." Sugar kept Happy Harvey's secret. Sugar had served him well. The men saw him as an enigma, but to the ladies Happy Harvey was a hero.

Sugar told Harvey on a Tuesday afternoon that she was leaving San Angelo. "I need to get out of this business, Harvey," she told him. "I'm not getting any younger, and I have a sister in Fort Worth. I've got some money saved, and it's as good a place as any to get a new start."

Wednesday morning Harvey rewarded Sugar with $3,000 as a token of appreciation for her three memorable years of personal service to him. "You're my best friend, Sugar. Thanks for everything! I hope you'll be happy. Let me know if you ever need anything."

After Sugar left, Harvey retired his "Ride 'em cowboy" game. It just wasn't the same without her. Sugar moved to Fort Worth where she married a real cowboy and had a couple of girls. When Harvey learned she had married, he thought to himself. "Now she'll be saying, 'Ride 'em cowboy' till death do us part," he thought to himself.

Josephine was another woman at Miss Hattie's whom Harvey befriended after Sugar left. The locals named her "Boom Boom." Harvey figured it was probably because she had a loud booming voice that could wake the dead.

Harvey created a different game to play with Boom Boom. He insisted on a room that overlooked Concho Avenue so that he could open the window, peek through the curtain, and wait until he saw someone he knew. He would then give Boom

Boom a ten dollar bill to yell as loudly as she could, "OH HARVEY JAMES ROCHESTER! YOU ARE ABSOLUTELY THE BEST LOVER IN SAN ANGELO, TEXAS! MORE HARVEY! PLEASE, MORE! MORE!" Harvey paid Boom Boom $100 for each of their sessions plus a handsome tip. Sadly, Boom Boom also moved away to marry a rancher from Ozona, Texas. For months afterwards, Harvey pined for a playmate and was delighted when he heard about the new Parlor opening up on the Concho River.

Harvey James Rochester had received a personal invitation to opening night at Miss Pearl's Parlor which was billed as an extravaganza. The moment he saw pretty little Lucy he knew that he had found his new playmate. In many ways, Lucy reminded him of Sugar. Harvey had invented a new game he called, Little Bo Peep. He saw Lucy as a perfect match and he was right. The first time they were together, he presented her with a sheep's costume, and when he did, she blinked at him with her big brown eyes and proclaimed, "Why don't you call me Babs! That's Ba-a-a-a-bs!"

It was common knowledge in San Angelo that Harvey James Rochester, the wealthy wool merchant, had been a regular client at Miss Hattie's and now was a patron at Miss Pearl's Parlor. Happy Harvey had the reputation for being a ladies' man and a most favored client of the "sporting ladies" in San Angelo. It was no secret that women were crazy about Happy Harvey. The men in town remained curious and never could figure out why!

Visitors from New York

Because of their mutual history with the Santa Rita No. 1, Frank Pickrell and Pearl had become great friends and had developed a trusting relationship. He made it a point to visit Miss Pearl's Parlor every time he went to San Angelo. Because Frank reminded her so much of her father, Pearl considered him family in an Irish kind of way. She shared stories about her parents and told him how the Irish Catholics were looked upon with disfavor in Chicago. He, in turn, told her of his life in Ireland before he had come to the United States. Their stories created a strong bond between them.

Pearl's Parlor was becoming a popular meeting place for the oil industry in San Angelo. The success of the Santa Rita had been impressive, and "Group No. 1" was no longer considered an amateur oil company. Some of the same bankers, businessmen, and lawyers who before had made fun of the drilling efforts in Big Lake were now treating Frank Pickrell as if he were a longtime friend. Pearl knew Frank saw through their chicanery, and it truly amused her to listen to some of their conversations. Funny how the same people who once had been naysayers thought they were successful in convincing Frank they had always been in his corner. When this duplicity occurred, the two friends exchanged looks of understanding, both with enough good business sense to know that silence was more advantageous. Ever since the Santa Rita had come in, it was obvious that San Angelo was next in line to become a Texas oil boom town.

Pearl received a telegram from New York on the afternoon of June 25th during one of Frank Pickrell's visits. "WILL ARRIVE IN SAN ANGELO JULY 7. BRINGING MY SISTER AND COUSIN. STOP. IT IS TIME TO CELEBRATE. MADELINE"

"Mozella! Look! Maddie is coming." Pearl squealed with excitement. "Frank! Maddie is coming with some of the ladies who invested in the Santa Rita!"

"Well, we will just have to show them a West Texas good time," Frank smiled. "You better reserve some rooms for them today. It's getting harder and harder by the week to find an available room in San Angelo!"

When Pearl picked Madeline up from the train station, the two women hugged and jumped up and down like a couple of school girls. "Oh, Maddie, it is so good to see you," Pearl beamed. "So good! Especially now!"

"Victoria!" Maddie exclaimed. "You are just as lovely as ever! This is my sister Elizabeth and our cousin, Rosey."

"Finally!" Elizabeth declared as she gave Pearl a warm hug.

An animated woman in a rose colored dress, a gaudy hat and a big smile reached out to pump Pearl's hand up and down. "My pleasure, I'm sure. I'm Rosey from Joysey!" she intoned in a heavy Jersey Shore accent. "I put up some of the money for the Santa Rita when my husband died and left me a small fortune. Can't say he came by it honest, but that was my Joey! Anyways, I sure am happy to finally make your acquaintance."

Pearl and Ginger took the ladies to the Angelus Hotel. After the ladies had checked in, they decided to have a quick bite and retire early. "Frank has arranged for us to go to the Santa Rita well site tomorrow so you can see where they hit the Big Lime sand."

When Pearl arrived home from the train station, Emma Grace was waiting for her on the front porch. "Tommy Lee's mother has arranged a simple wedding at the ranch, Miss Pearl. We decided to get married on Sunday the 23rd of September. Tommy Lee is fixing up a small house for us to live in. His mother said we can live in their house, but Tommy Lee insists we have a place of our own."

"That is wonderful," Pearl exclaimed as she gave her arm a squeeze.

"It's the absolute bees' knees!" Emma Grace exclaimed. "I'm so happy, Miss Pearl. I've never been happy like this in my entire life! Tommy Lee says we're going to Galveston for our honeymoon. Redbird says it's really nice there."

"She should know. After all, she did grow up in Houston," Pearl expressed. "My dear Emma Grace, I truly am so happy for you and Tommy Lee. He is a fine young man."

"Mother Pearl, you will be at my wedding won't you?" Emma pleaded with her big sweet eyes. "You and the girls are all the family I have."

"Most certainly I will be there, Emma Grace." Pearl answered. "We will all be there!"

"I have asked Sarah to be my maid of honor. Harmony says she will bring her guitar and sing."

"Sounds perfect!" Pearl observed.

"Yes, Ma'am! We are inviting just family and a few close friends. All the family I know is at Miss Pearl's. Tommy Lee's mother really is a kind woman," Emma Grace smiled, "and the cowboys have promised they'll behave!"

The next morning Frank showed up in his new Packard to drive the New York ladies to the well site. Ginger drove a second car, and like always, Mozella packed them a lunch. The scenery was much different from what the women were used to. "This really is the wide open spaces!" Rosey commented. "Are there any real cowboys around here? How about wild Indians?"

"As a matter of fact, there was a woman who lived in this area known as the Rose of Dove Creek," Pearl commented. "Her father was a train robber, and when she was 15, she hooked up with a man named Will Carver who also robbed trains with Black Jack Ketchum, Butch Cassidy, and the Sundance Kid. They were known as *the hole in the wall gang*. Her real name was Laura, but they called her Della Rose.

She ended up spending 5 years in a Missouri prison for robbing a train."

"Holy Camolie!" Rosey exclaimed. "The hole in the wall gang had a hideout here?"

"Yes, Ma'am," Pearl commented. "You were asking about Indians? Not too far from here was the massacre at Dove Creek, quite a sad story. Some soldiers from Fort Concho found a group of Kickapoo Indians and thought they were hostile like the Comanche. The Kickapoo sent out an Indian princess as a symbol of peace, and when they did, one of the soldiers shot her. The Indians attacked and virtually wiped out the entire platoon. It was horrible. Afterwards the Kickapoo headed south to Mexico and escaped."

"Oh my," Elizabeth exclaimed. "That is dreadful."

"West Texas is rich in history, ladies. A man we call, 'Tex', a regular at the Parlor, always has a story to tell when he comes to visit. Tex has been around a long time and he knows about this area. He is very interesting, and the girls just love him!" Pearl complimented. "He has a thing for Maggie. He says he loves her spirit."

"This is all so fascinating!" Elizabeth commented. "Much different from Chicago and New York."

When the cars finally reached the site of the Santa Rita, the ladies were surprised. "After all those months, I guess I was expecting… well, I'm not quite sure what I was expecting." Madeline pondered.

"You should have been here before they set pipe. The Santa Rita rumbled like an earthquake, hissed like a snake, roared like a lion, and then exploded like a fountain of black tea against the bright blue West Texas sky. I'll never forget it as long as I live!" Ginger exclaimed.

"Now what makes her spectacular is beneath the ground," Frank cheered.

"Remember, dear sister, we soon will be getting checks in the mail," Elizabeth smiled.

That night when the small caravan returned to Pearl's Parlor, the Santa Rita celebration officially began. "I can see that working at the Everleigh Club served you well, Victoria," Madeline commented on her tour of the mansion. "You have decorated your parlor with elegant and exquisite tastes, my dear."

Pearl nodded with acknowledgement. "Thank you, Madeline. I do appreciate your saying so. How about I get a chilled bottle of champagne, and we go outside to sit in the gazebo by the river?"

"Sounds like an excellent idea!" Madeline agreed. Arm-in-arm, the ladies walked outside like a couple of old army buddies. When Victoria popped the bottle, both women laughed like they had in the old times.

"Remember when that man drank the champagne out of Gloria's shoe?" Victoria asked.

"My goodness, YES! That man with the King of Prussia. It became a tradition at the Everleigh Club."

"Yes, it did. Actually we do the same thing here... carry on the tradition, I mean. Many a man has enjoyed drinking champagne from a shoe in our parlor. It is Redbird's favorite ceremony, especially for birthdays or any celebration, for that matter."

It was late afternoon, nature had settled into a peaceful state, the land glowed with golden light, and the only sound was the song of a nearby dove. The ladies sat quietly by the river, watching the West Texas sky paint a colorful portrait that changed minute-by-minute as the sun bid farewell to an extra special day. Madeline finally broke the silence. "How are you doing, Victoria? How are you really doing?"

"Oh, Maddie, I miss him so much. It is getting better with time, but once-in-a-while, the thought of Robert overtakes me. I might have gone mad if I had stayed at the ranch. When I am there, everywhere I look I see Robert. The way he would smile and wave at me as he came in from the pasture. The sound of his laughter echoes like a faint whisper in my mind. His smell, his warmth, his love... I miss him so much. It pains me, so I try to avoid thinking about him. There are times that all I want to do is think about him and our times together. Those are the times I read my journals like I did in Chicago when I was missing him."

"I remember that. What about the boys?"

"I am so proud of them. It is funny how even though they are twins, they are so different. Both of them are attending the University in Austin. David is more like his father and will probably end up running the ranch. Michael is the creative one and is studying architecture. They know I have a business in San Angelo, but, I guess you can say, I have protected them from the truth. They are both very independent and strong-willed."

"Like their mother?" Madeline asked.

"Perhaps," she smiled. "How do you like my girls?" Pearl asked, changing the subject.

"Again I have to say you learned well from the Everleigh sisters," Madeline reflected. "I am impressed with your whole operation here."

"I love these girls, Maddie. Sometimes they call me "Mother" and rightly so. It makes me appreciate Ada and especially Minna even more. I will never forget Minna coming to talk to me after that first time Robert left. I have talks like that with my girls now. Like poor little Betsy who would love nothing more than for someone to ride her away to happily-ever-after on a snow white steed or sweet little Sarah who has been through hell and back. Harmony and Annabelle both lost their men in the war. Annabelle is supporting her mother and her sweet little daughter, Julie Marie. They live in a small house in Christoval. She rides the stagecoach down there several times a month to spend time with them."

"I love Ginger's spirit!" Madeline commented. "What's her story?"

"Ginger's mother sold her to a madame in Storyville down in New Orleans, something the Everleigh sisters would never allow! Wait until you hear her sing and hear Harmony play the piano! Maggie and Lucy are a pure delight, and Katie, our little sharp shooter, makes us all feel safe and secure. Redbird has a good business sense and will be ready soon to come into her inheritance when she is 21. She loves to make money like I do, and she is good at it. She has learned well from the businessmen who frequent the Parlor. How about you, Maddie? What do you do all day in New York City?"

"Actually I'm glad you asked. I have a surprise for you from Ada and Minna," Madeline smiled.

"What?" Madeline handed her a small red velvet bag. Pearl opened it to find a simple pearl broach shaped like a butterfly.

"I remember this!" Pearl gasped. "Minna was wearing it the day I left the Everleigh Club. There's a card! *Pearls for our Pearl. Love Ada and Minna Everleigh.* What a nice surprise! It is quite lovely. How are they doing?"

"They are well. I try to see them every other month or so. You heard of course they had to shut down the Everleigh Club after eleven prosperous years. The sisters have worked their way into the realms of high society and have started a poetry circle in New York. Of course, being actresses themselves, they love the theatre. Minna and Ada left Chicago with millions and go by their surname, Lester, these days. They have successfully kept their dealings in Chicago a secret, although there are some men in their sphere of influence who are former visitors to 2131 Dearborn Street. It stands as a mutual agreement that what happened in Chicago stays in Chicago."

"The sisters were always adorned with diamonds and pearls. Minna especially loved wearing those diamond butterfly pins. They must be worth a fortune. Does she still wear them?"

"Most definitely," Maddie answered. "Remember that time Minna was robbed at gunpoint?"

"Yes! Right after we opened," Victoria answered. "It must have been such an awful fright for Miss Minna! The way he pulled her into that small alcove, shut the door, and then stuck the revolver against her ribs! Remember, he was a drug addict? They usually shoot before they think."

Victoria shuddered. "'Off with the junk,' he told her. I believe Ada saved her life by coming into the room when she did. She must have had a premonition. It wouldn't surprise me, the sisters were so close. Can you imagine? She opens the door and sees her sister giving some horrible man her diamonds and then in the sweetest voice says, 'I thought you sent for me.' If she had screamed, the man would have probably shot both of them! It was so clever, he actually thought it was a trick and left with nothing."

"Brilliant! Both women so wise in understanding men and how they think," Maddie exclaimed. "Ada and Minna's loyalty to each other is commendable. In New York, they have managed to hide their past; they always were superb actresses. Very clever those two. The sisters made millions of dollars simply by understanding human nature. Absolutely brilliant! Minna once told me, 'If it weren't for married men, we couldn't have carried on at all, and if it were not for cheating married women, we could have made another million.'"

"America can be the land of opportunity if you are clever, Maddie. I was a rich woman when I married Robert, and I still have all of it. It is unfortunate that our business is the only way a woman of simple means can become wealthy, unless, of course, you marry someone with money. It is rare to see a woman marry someone below or above her station. There always was the exception, but I really do not think I would ever go as far as to tattoo a rose and offer a magnifying glass to make that happen!"

"Suzy Poon Tang! I forgot about her!" Maddie laughed.

"How could you forget about Suzy Poon Tang, Maddie?" Victoria bellowed. "I just told the girls her story a few weeks ago. In fact, it was the day we heard about the Santa Rita coming in."

"You're right, Victoria! I NEVER will forget Suzy Poon Tang! I remember how happy we all were when she only lasted one night. Then there was the man who liked to throw gold coins and let us keep the ones that hit the target. Sometimes he aimed for my belly-button. Other times…well, you know. I became quite good at it! I really do love men. They can be so creative and even sweet."

"How about the banker who liked to watch us climb up a ladder? Never quite figured that one out. I did like him. I suppose it was because it was so easy to make him happy!" Victoria exclaimed.

By now both women were laughing hysterically, tears in their eyes. The two friends finished the last of the champagne, still talking about old times. Finally, Pearl announced that she was hungry, and Maddie agreed. From the house, they heard music blasting. "If I know my cousin Rosey, you can be sure there's a party going on!" Maddie laughed.

Sure enough, there in the Great Room, everyone including Mozella was doing the Charleston to a record that Rosey had brought from New York. Pearl decided to make it a ladies' night and closed her other services for the evening. Tomorrow would be the official Santa Rita party when they were expecting businessmen from all over the world, but tonight Frank Pickrell was the only man allowed in Pearl's Parlor. As far as Pearl was concerned, he certainly deserved it. It was a night for celebration. All those challenges and long months of tenacity had come to this moment. Pearl, Frank, Mozella, and the ladies from New York had been bonded by the success of the Santa Rita No. 1. They drank, sang Irish limericks, and danced all night long.

When Frank left the Parlor around midnight, the party turned into a girl talk session with Rosey taking the lead. She had had plenty to drink and wanted to share. "I loved my Joey, goils, believe me, I did! I just didn't understand why he did what he did! My goodness, both of us grew up in the coal mines and married when we were young. We moved to the city, and both of us started working in a bar. Joey was Italian and could hustle like nobody's business. In fact, he ended up owning the bar, and pretty soon we were doing OK. He moved us to an apartment in Joysey. One day, I sees the lady next door hanging up her laundry. All of a sudden, she's hanging up green striped underwear that looks just like my Joey's. Then I remember she don't have a husband, and the underwear she is hanging up with the clothespins in her teeth ARE MY JOEY'S! That night I ask him if the green striped underwear at the neighbor lady's house is his underwear! He denies it which I kind of expected. Joey always was a crappy liar!" she wailed, tears filling her eyes. Sarah passed her a handkerchief. Rosey put it up to her face and gave it a big HONK!

"Thank you so much, Sarah. So I decides to keep my cool, if you know what I mean. Every night when he comes home drunk, which was about seven nights a week, I start cleaning out his pockets. He never said nothing. I guess it was on account that he thought he might have given his money to the cheap dame next door. I seen him looking for it, and then I just played dumb. After a couple of weeks, I saved up a pretty good stash, so I opened up a savings account," Rosey beamed proudly.

"Did I tell ya' my Joey was a pool shark and had a poker room in the back of the bar? Sometimes Joey would come home with great big wads of money on account he used to run the numbers too. Those nights I wouldn't take all of the money, but I got my fair share. The way I saw it, whatever I didn't get, he'd spend on her. Joey was a sorry, no good, womanizing, cheating scumbag from the deepest swamps in Joysey, and I loved him so much!" Rosey explained, honking into her handkerchief again. "I loved my Joey!" she sniffed.

"My golden moment was at his funeral. Oh, she came all right, with her false eyelashes, shiny platinum hair, skin tight dress with her boobies popping out, a fur Joey probably gave her, red lipstick, and a stick of gum that she popped like a percolator making morning coffee. Cheap, with no class, if you know what I mean. She sat in the back of the church and cried. Can you believe the noive! She even waved at me like she does every time I'd see her hanging out her dirty laundry! How do you think it made me feel, seeing her hang out her bed sheets and my husband's green striped underwear? I just smiled and waved back. It was better if they thought I didn't know. Then I'd go inside and stick pins in a kewpie doll that kinda looks like her that I got down at the Boardwalk in Atlantic City. I guess they both thought I was too dumb to know what was going on!"

"How did he die?" Sarah asked.

"I guess he made the wrong guy mad. Someone shot him in the alley behind the bar. I got the bar, the fancy car, the bank account, plus the stash I had been putting away. I even found a suitcase with $50,000, hidden in the closet behind a loose board when I was cleaning out his stuff. I deserved it! I went through hell those nights knowing he was right next door at her apartment doing whatever. Can you imagine a man who would put his goil-friend in the house right next door?"

Everyone agreed as they shook their heads, "No."

"Oh yeah, I got the apartment house too. Joey won it in a poker game. Joey! Joey!" Rosey yelled shaking her fist at the ceiling. "I guess cuz I got all the money I got the last laugh after all!" Rosey's laugh turned into a sob. "I ain't laughin' now! GAWD! I MISS THE BIG GALLOOT!" Rosey stared at the ceiling. "Joey, if you can hear me, I forgive you! You and your green striped underwear and that crazy dame with the clothespins in her teeth! Damn it, Joey! Just damn it! I sure hope you ain't in hell, but you probably are," she sniffed.

"Aw, that's too bad," Lucy sympathized. "Whatever happened to the girlfriend?

"I don't know, and I don't care! I had her evicted the day after the funeral!" Rosey answered. "She can keep them old green striped underwear. That's all she gets."

"There are good men who you count on, and then there are the ones we love that only show up when they need you," Ginger commented. "I've got one who comes by when he's in town. Good-lookin', sweet talkin', hot lovin', Sam. Only man I've ever known who can make me feel like I might even have a heart. I know, because it jumps when I see him and it aches when we say good-bye. We've got something special that I can't really explain. I know it's the same for him as well, although he'd never admit it."

Although she never talked about it, all the girls knew how Ginger felt about Sam. Redbird took Ginger's arm. "You know, honey, ladies love outlaws."

"Yeah…like little children love stray dogs," Lucy added.

"How do you know if you have a good man?" Emma Grace asked.

"Don't worry, honey. You did all right," Ginger assured her. "It's 3 o'clock in the morning. You ladies ready to go back to your hotel?"

Everyone agreed it was time to end a wonderful day. That night Emma Grace dreamed about her cowboy, and Victoria Pearl dreamed about Robert as well. The next morning all of the girls slept until noon.

A Night on the River

A variety of men went to Pearl's Parlor. There were those who went for sexual satisfaction, but there were other reasons, as well. Some of the older gentlemen were just lonely and simply wanted to spend time with delightful young ladies who were both educated and friendly. Tex, a distinguished older gentleman who was a regular at Pearl's, liked being around pretty women and having a cold beer. The girls loved him and his tall tales. Tex was especially fond of Maggie who held a special place in his heart, probably because she reminded him of his wife who had passed away 15 years earlier. They had never had children, and Tex had never married again.

Fascinated with cowboys and Indians, Rosey had heard stories of the Old West, and now she was actually there. Tex dropped by the Parlor the afternoon before. "Rosey, I have someone I want you to meet," Pearl announced. "This is our Tex. He is the man who told me about the Rose of Dove Creek and the Kickapoo Massacre. He's full of stories and can tell you all about San Angelo."

"Let's go downstairs, little lady, and I'll buy you a beer," Tex smiled.

"Charmed, I'm sure," Rosey flirted.

It was unusual to see Rosey quiet. She was so fascinated with Tex and his slow, deliberate drawl that she only listened and barely spoke at all. "At one time, San Angelo was known as 'the town across the river'," Tex began. "Fort Concho was built across from the town right after the Civil War when a lot of folks were travelling west to start a new life. The fort was established to protect the people from the Comanche and other hostile Indians. There were actually times when the majority of the soldiers stationed at the fort were Buffalo Soldiers."

"Buffalo Soldiers?" Rosey asked.

"Yes, Ma'am, also known as The United States Colored Soldiers.'" After all the slaves were freed, some of them served in the United States Cavalry. The Buffalo Soldiers got their name from the Indians who said their black matted hair reminded them of the sacred buffalo. Anyway, where there are soldiers, there's always a call for saloons, gambling, and friendly ladies. That's really how San Angelo got started. Bart deWitt opened a trading post and named it Santa Angela after a nun in the family. When San Angelo became the county seat, people started moving here. They finally established a post office and changed the name to San Angelo. It's been growing ever since. There are a lot of big ranches around, and San Angelo has had its share of visiting cowboys. When the trains were built, wool trade got real big, and San Angelo grew even bigger."

"Interesting," Rosey noted. "We had a little gambling going on in a room behind our bar in Joysey."

"Back in the 1870's, there was a lady named Maude-Lottie Deno. The locals named her 'Mystic Maude', a professional gambler who gave the men a real run for their money. I actually met her a couple of times when I was a rounder. Men found her brown sparkling eyes and long dark hair enchanting. It was obvious she was brought up in high cotton."

"What's that?" Rosey asked.

"High cotton? People with money." Tex declared. "What impressed me was how calm she was no matter what was going on. A real pro she was. They say her father taught her all he knew about playing cards before he died in the Civil War. She made a good living and supported her siblings with her winnings."

"Sounds like my Grams. She sent many a man away from a card table without his money." Rosey boasted.

"One night in the gambling hall, Maude was working a $50-limit game in the corner. In another part of the room was a high stakes cut-throat game where an Arizona card shark was playing a Texan who had just bet his last dollar. There was more than a thousand dollars on that table!

'*You marked the cards!*' the Texan yelled.

'*You ain't gonna bluff me!*' the Arizona man screamed. They went for their guns, and when the smoke cleared, both men were lying dead on the floor. Everyone cleared the room.

When the sheriff got there, he found Maude sitting quietly in the corner. '*Why didn't you run?*' he asked.

'*I felt safe in the corner,*' she answered.

'*Get out quick!*' he said.

'*Certainly sir.*'

Funny thing… the money on the table was gone!"

"So she took the money and ran?" Rosey asked, nodding her head. "A woman after my own heart!"

"I reckon she did," Tex concurred. "Let's have another beer."

The women in the Parlor were busy making themselves beautiful for the Santa Rita celebration. Pearl had hired two gourmet chefs and some extra help for Mozella. A three-piece combo was setting up to play in the Great Room, and an eight-piece jazz band was hired to play in the speakeasy downstairs.

Late that afternoon, Madeline's sister, Elizabeth, took Heather aside and spoke to her alone on the front porch. "My dear, sometimes I have the ability to know the future. I am not sure why, but I need to let you know I have an uneasy feeling that concerns your wellbeing. Please be careful, and whatever you do, do not go anywhere alone." Heather stared, startled and confused. "Remember what I said, dear. Do not go anywhere alone for a while. I am never wrong about these things."

The party was a huge success. Maggie glided through the room, and with a warm heavy whisper, she assured every man whom she knew intimately that he was the best lover she ever had. Looking mysterious and aloof, Annabelle was dressed in an elaborate black beaded dress, and Sarah wore an exquisite gown that hung low on her back revealing her shapely female curves. Lucy was playful, Betsy was flirty, and Redbird was sexy, wearing a tight fitting, bright red dress accentuating her womanly curves. Harmony radiated elegance in a long flowing white evening gown, and Heather paraded around the room, tickling the men with a large purple plume that matched her own long dark purple fitted satin gown. Heather sang Gershwin, and Ginger, a woman who could smell money when it walked into the room, was a smash hit with her sexy signature song *"Deep Pockets."* There was an abundance of money there that night. *"You got deep pockets, I could tell in a flash, you got deep pockets and a mighty fine... ASK me how I know you are the man for me. Hey Mr. Deep Pockets, are you lookin' for some company."*

Frank Pickrell talked about the oil business with a group of men in the smoking room. Elizabeth and Maddie charmed everyone with their English accents and Rosey was the life of the party, dancing to every song the orchestra played. She even got up and sang several Fannie Brice songs including "Second Hand Rose." All-in-all, the evening was a huge success. The men were especially impressed to hear that Pearl had been a significant partner in the Santa Rita No. 1.

As Frank passed out cigars, Pearl addressed the group, "I must say I am quite impressed with Frank Pickrell's tenacity. I look forward to investing in future projects with Texon as well. After all, who do you know who would climb to the top of an oil derrick and throw rose petals to christen a well? He told the women he would, and he did just like he said. That gesture alone tells me Frank Pickrell is a man of his word."

That evening after everyone had left, the ladies gathered for another girl talk session, but this time Elizabeth was the one putting on the show. "Annabelle, my dear, you have an incredibly handsome young man in a uniform with you," Elizabeth informed her. "He says he loves you very much, and he says he is looking after you and your daughter." Annabelle stared at her unbelievingly. Was this a cruel joke?

Maddie realized that Annabelle was in shock and pain. "My sister has a gift, Annabelle," she explained gently. "Sometimes she sees loved ones who have passed, and she just blurts it out. Please forgive her."

"Everyone here knows I lost my husband in the war and I have a daughter," Annabelle whispered softly.

"He says, 'Remember the lake, the rain…' He is doing some kind of funny dance... He is telling me he liked to dance because it always made you laugh."

Elizabeth was smiling and looking to the right of Annabelle's shoulder as if she could see someone dancing around. Tears streamed down Annabelle's cheeks. She remembered that rainy Saturday on the lake and later her Billy dancing naked around the room, making her laugh. No one else knew about that afternoon, not even her mother. A chill ran through her body like a Texas north wind. "What else does he say?"

"He says he loves you, and he is sorry he had to leave you. He says that he is proud of you… He says when you see orange butterflies to think of him…"

Annabelle managed to smile through her tears. "I already do," she shared. "Every time I see an orange butterfly, I pretend it's Billy saying hello. It just makes me feel better, but I thought it was my imagination."

"Just because we cannot see our loved ones who have passed does not mean they are not here. I know this type of dialogue is uncomfortable for many people. For a long time, I kept my ability to see spirits a secret mainly because people might think I am crazy. However, someone once told me that I have a unique gift and that I should share it. It is appropriate I share it with you fine young ladies. Those who have passed become excited when they know we are aware of their presence. Many times they want to resolve an issue and communicate."

"He's proud of me?" Annabelle asked.

"Yes, my dear. When they are on the other side, they only know love. They do not get involved in our everyday dramas. They only know love."

"I think I understand. Thank you, Elizabeth," Annabelle whispered, breathing deeply and then releasing into the memory of a rainy Saturday afternoon on the lake.

"There is a man with a uniform with you as well, Harmony," Elizabeth observed. "He is waving to you from a train… He is giving me a D… Dennis? Daniel?"

"David!" Harmony said. "It's David!"

"He is handing you a yellow rose," Elizabeth offered.

The Yellow Rose of Texas was his favorite song!" Harmony cried. "He also died in the war. My David was a hero, Elizabeth. He was *my* hero. Last time I saw him he was waving to me from a train."

"No wonder you play it all the time!" Ginger reasoned.

Elizabeth turned and looked at Ginger. "There is a woman with you, young lady. She says she is sorry… She wants you to forgive her… Does this mean anything to you?"

"It's probably my mother," Ginger sighed in a cool unemotional tone, quickly lighting a cigarette. No one at the Parlor had ever seen her cry, and she certainly wasn't going to let them see any tears now. Ginger took a deep drag and exhaled slowly, forming rings that floated in the air. "Didn't know she died," Ginger commented as she took another drag.

"She says she loves you, and she is sorry."

"OK, thanks, I guess," Ginger replied flippantly, holding back her tears.

Everyone was staring at Elizabeth. She seemed to be in some kind of trance, as if she were dreaming with her eyes opened. Even her voice had changed its tenor.

"Do you see my mother?" Sarah asked anxiously. "Is my mother here? She died protecting me from my stepfather. I still have nightmares about that horrible day."

"I do not see a woman with you, Sarah." Elizabeth answered shaking her head. "I do, however, see a young man… He says to tell you it didn't hurt. He says he stayed with you quite a while before he went to the light."

"It's Michael… sweet, sweet Michael!" Sarah exclaimed as she folded her hands over her heart. "The night of our high school graduation we made love and he asked me to marry him. When we came home late my grandfather went crazy and threatened to shoot me. Michael jumped in front of the rifle and saved my life. It was horrible, even worse than the night Mother shot herself. I am happy he is with me! Thank you, Elizabeth."

Then Elizabeth turned and looked at Pearl and beamed. "You have 2 men and a woman with you, my dear. One of the men and the woman have an Irish brogue... they are holding hands... the woman is handing you a red rose... she says she loves you.... she keeps saying the word, 'VICTORY!' and she is very proud of you."

"Those are my parents." Pearl reflected quietly.

"The other man is handing you a pink pearl."

"Robert!"

"He says he is always with you, and he is listening... he likes to talk to you when you go fishing... there is so much love coming to you from this man... he says he is happy you bought the mansion... it was meant to be yours... he says thank you for loving the ranch... he is with you at the springs."

"Thank you," she said warmly and then closed her eyes and imagined her parents and Robert smiling at her. Elizabeth's words made Victoria Pearl's heart feel full.

The room was silent. Elizabeth nodded to Heather who bit her lip and nodded back. After what she had just witnessed, she decided to heed Elizabeth's message.

"Do you see my Joey?" Rosey asked. "Can you see him, Elizabeth? I know you did before when we were in New York."

"Not tonight, Rosey," Elizabeth apologized.

"Okay then." Rosey looked up to the tall ceiling. "I STILL LOVE YOU, YA BIG GALLOOT!" she yelled. Everybody laughed.

"Let's do a women's circle!" Maddie suggested. "It's a perfect night for it; the moon is full! We used to do this all the time in Glastonbury. It will make your souls sing!"

"I used to do this with my mother and had forgotten all about it!" Pearl exclaimed. "When we saw wild mushrooms growing in a circle, Mother called it a 'magic fairy circle', and we sang and danced. The fairies dance behind the magic veil," she would say. "Let's dance with them!"

Together the '*Lady Pearls*' walked quietly to the river. "Take off your shoes, ladies, so you can feel Mother Earth beneath your feet," Maddie instructed. The grass felt soft and cool as the women held hands and formed a circle. "The moon directs the movement of the tides, and the seas dance to her song," Maddie continued. "Like a good woman, she needs not recognition for her quiet strength. Her 28 day cycle is consistent, and she displays herself differently every night. Most evenings, she reveals part of her light, but tonight she is showing her full glory. There will be evenings where she will disappear with the promise of her return. These are the nights that the stars shine their brightest. For these reasons, we call her feminine and are thankful for the opportunity to dance among the shadows of her enchanted light."

As Harmony strummed her guitar and sang: "*Greensleeves was all my joy, Greensleeves was my delight, Greensleeves was my heart of god, and who but my lady, Greensleeves.*"

"I love that song, Harmony!" Maddie chimed. "Do you know who the Greensleeves were?"

"No, I don't believe I do," Harmony answered.

"They were women who brought men womanly comfort. Many times they went with them into battle to take care of their needs such as nursing, cooking, companionship..."

"Women like us!" Maggie exclaimed.

"Exactly!" Madeline laughed. "Some say they got their name because of the grass stains on their sleeves."

"I bet I know how that happened!" Lucy declared.

"Let's all sing it!" Heather suggested.

The women sang and danced as the glowing light of the moon reflected brightly on the Concho River below.

"What a spectacular, magical evening!" Sarah exclaimed. "We might not be able to see our angels, but I know they are here!" and everyone agreed.

Later, when the ladies retired, Victoria sat at the Steinway and filled the house with the sweetness of beautiful piano music. With every note she thought of her Robert and how he loved to listen to her play. Somehow she knew he was with her now, and Victoria's heart and soul brimmed with love.

San Angelo

Pearl wanted to share the story of her life in Texas with Madeline, so for the next several days the ladies from New York enjoyed experiencing West Texas.

"I want to ride in a stagecoach!" Rosey requested.

"There's one that goes to Christoval. "I'll take you to the depot," Katie offered. "By the way, I heard a story about a man named Charlie who used to drive the stagecoach to Sonora. They say he was a whiskey drinkin', backer spittin', wild whoopin' son-of-a-gun! When he died, it shocked a lot of folks. Turns out Charlie's name should have been 'Charlotte' on account *he* was a *she*!

"Holy Camolie!" Rosey exclaimed.

Rosey rode the stagecoach to Christoval while the others drove. After the ladies enjoyed soaking in the mineral baths, Pearl arranged for them to relish the quiet beautiful surroundings of nature and swimming in the natural springs at the Five Star Ranch. "I see now why Texans call this God's country," Elizabeth confessed.

Following several days at the ranch, the women rode the train from Menard back to San Angelo.

"I'd like to see Fort Concho," Elizabeth said as they got off the train. When they arrived at the fort, she immediately focused on a house made of stone at the end of the courtyard and walked with purpose to what is known as, Fort Concho's Officer's Quarters #1. For a moment, Elizabeth stared into the window of the house.

"There is a young girl here... Oh, my word!" Elizabeth began shaking. "I feel dizzy... I...I'm burning with fever... I have the chills... look my teeth are chattering!"

"Are you all right, dear?" Madeline cried, seeing her sister's forehead beaded with perspiration. Madeline took Elizabeth's arm and helped her sit down on a bench on the porch. She pulled out a handkerchief from her bag to wipe her forehead.

Then as quickly as the fever had come, it disappeared. "I believe she died here," she whispered.

"Haunted seems like such a scary word. Oh yes, Edie is here. She especially loves when children come to the fort. She says everything is 'hunky-dory!'"

The women walked around the fort a while until Madeline suggested, "I know! Let's go shopping!"

Pearl readily agreed. "I'll take you to Holland's. They have lovely Concho pearls there. Sometimes the gentlemen like to buy the ladies gifts, and each of the girls from the Parlor actually has a wish list there. Harvey is their best customer!"

That afternoon each of the visiting women bought Concho pearl earrings and ordered a pair of custom made boots from Leddy's. Later in the evening, for the last time, all the women at Miss Pearl's formed another circle by the river and danced barefooted on the cool, soft grass. It was a glorious night beneath the West Texas stars which created a perfect ending to their memorable time together.

"Thank you so much for everything, Pearl! It was wonderful!" Rosey squealed as the ladies said their goodbyes at the train station. "Come see us in New York!"

"Yes, do come see us," Elizabeth concurred. "Your girls are wonderful. Keep a special eye on Heather. I feel she is going to need you especially in the near future."

"I will," Pearl responded with curiosity.

"I love you my friend," Madeline said. "Do come to New York. We can have tea with Minna and Ada and talk about old times. I know they would love to see you!" I would love that," Pearl promised. "Thank you, Madeline. You are a good friend." Pearl stayed on the platform until the train was out of sight. She knew the ladies' visit had made a strong impact on all the girls. It was a wonderful time of bonding among women.

"Come see us in New York!!" Rosie bellowed as she waved goodbye.

Pearl stayed until the train disappeared.

Don't Mess With Texas

For the next few weeks, Pearl kept a special eye on Heather. After what she had witnessed, she was not going to take Elizabeth's words lightly. However, as the days passed and the Lady Pearls settled back into their normal routine, the thought of Heather being in any danger began to fade.

Heather was best known for singing the blues. Her sultry voice and deliberate little pout mesmerized her audience. By the time Heather was finished with her song, men often lapsed into a trance; she held a seductive power over her audience.

Early one evening, one of the customers insisted that Heather sing *"Oh My Man"* for him and gave her a hundred dollar bill. Heather gracefully accepted the invitation. It was one of her favorite songs, and she sang it well. *"Oh my man I love him so he'll never know, All my life is just despair but I don't care, When he takes me in his arms, the world seems bright, All right."* As the saxophone played a sultry solo, Heather closed her eyes and swayed her hips to the rhythm of the music. Then Heather opened her eyes, looked directly at the man who had requested the song, and sang her powerful ending. ***"For wherever my man is, I am his, forever more."*** When she finished, the man handed her another hundred dollar bill. "Thank you, Freddy," she flirted as she tickled his ear with her feather.

Later that evening, Sarah handed Heather an envelope. "Oh my gosh, Heather. The most handsome man I think I have ever seen gave me this envelope and asked me to give it to you at exactly 11 pm. He said he has a surprise for you!"

"Really? Handsome? You say you've never seen him before? Well, let's just see…" Heather opened up the envelope. "Oh, my God! OH, MY GOD!" Heather's voice trembled.

"What's the matter?" Sarah asked. "My Lord, Heather. You look like you've seen a ghost!" Ginger hurried to her side.

Heather couldn't speak. She handed the note to Ginger.

Saw you singing tonight.
Oh my man, I love him so… loved it.
You should have been singing it to me!

See you soon. We have a lot of catching up to do.
Tony

"Quick, get Miss Pearl, Sarah! Get her NOW!" Ginger yelled, pushing Heather out of the room.

The girls at Pearl's Parlor knew the story of Miss Pearl's rescuing Heather from Tony in Chicago and then bringing her to San Angelo. Ginger insisted Heather take a shot of whiskey to calm her nerves. Pearl, however, who was normally in plain sight, was nowhere to be found. Sarah ran into the kitchen. "Mozella! Have you seen Miss Pearl?"

"No, Ma'am! What in the world is wrong with you, Sarah?" Mozella asked genuinely concerned.

"Heather just got a note from Tony that says he's in San Angelo, and we can't find Pearl!"

"This is not good! I knew Tony in Chicago. He liked to cut up women on the Levee and throw them into the river. We have to find Pearl now!"

Heather was crying hysterically. "Oh no, not Miss Pearl! Oh Ginger. Elizabeth was right! She told me to be careful. I didn't even think about Tony! It's been so long since that night I ran away! How in the world did he find me?"

Katie picked up her shotgun and headed toward the front door, "C'mon Rusty."

Tony had been in San Angelo for days watching the girls, watching their routine, and looking for an isolated place on the river. He found the perfect spot surrounded by over growth and brush. Tony took great pleasure in mutilating women and had become good at hiding his deeds. Although no one could ever prove it, Chicago knew Tony was dangerous and capable of heinous crimes. No one ever wanted to make Tony mad.

Pearl was absent because earlier that evening, Tony had escorted Pearl from the stables with a gun in her back. Tony had witnessed her trips to the stables every evening around dusk where she groomed her horse. He had hidden himself and waited patiently. Now Pearl was lying helplessly on the ground at the gangster's mercy, with her feet and hands tightly bound.

"So, you think you're so smart, don't you, bitch? Thought I'd never find her? I guess you didn't count on one of your stupid cowboys showing up in my joint in Chicago running his mouth about a pretty little girl in San Angelo they call *Heather with her feather*. Stupid bitch!! Damn stupid whore! Yeah! You! You're first. I'll deal with Heather later. You Everleigh girls all thought you were so high and mighty. Too good for anyone else! Well, you're just a damn whore!"

Pearl's scalp throbbed where he had pulled her hair. Although Tony wanted to see fear in Pearl's eyes, she was too delirious to be afraid. He pulled out a Bowie knife he had bought in town. "I know you've heard about what I do to whores! I bet you didn't hear about how much I enjoy it. How could you? No one was ever left to tell. I made sure of it because the first thing I cut out is the tongue! It's amazing how much fun it can be cutting and slicing a woman when no one can hear her screams. I always wanted an Everleigh girl, especially since the day they kicked me out of that hoity-toity club. This is going to be fun!"

Tony waved the knife in front of Pearl's face, pressing the cold hard blade onto her cheek. "Hmmm. After I cut out your tongue, should I start with the right ear or the left ear," he jeered. Pearl could sense Tony's insanity and tried to ignore the yellow of his eyes.

Pretending to be unconscious, Pearl could not scream or run away and knew what Tony wanted. She would be damned before she let him see any fear in her face. Closing her eyes with a gentle surrender seemed like her best option.

"Open your eyes, Bitch! Open your eyes, or I'll cut them out!" Tony, the demonic beast, raised the knife in anger. "Open your eyes God damn it! I want to see your fear. I want to see you're afraid! Beg me! BEG ME! THEY ALL BEG ME!! OPEN YOUR GOD DAMN EYES, BITCH!!" he screamed.

BOOM!

The shot rang out in the clear Texas night. Three of Tony's fingers evaporated, the knife blown away with them. Blood pouring from his hand, Tony grabbed his wrist screaming and writhing. Rusty charged Tony, knocking him to the dirt and locking his jaws around his neck. No one could hear the commotion. Tony really had chosen a perfect spot by the river. No one could hear his shrieks.

"Call him off! Call him off!" Tony howled.

"Rusty! Heel!" Katie yelled. The most beautiful crystal blue eyes Tony had ever seen, were aiming a shotgun directly at his forehead.

Rusty, growling at Tony and his bloody hand, went to sit beside Katie.

"You think you can come to Texas and do what you do in Chicago, you stupid thug?" Katie screamed with an angry glare.

With fear in his eyes, Tony begged, "I've got money! Lots of money! Please!"

"What's the matter, Tony? Are you afraid?" Katie mocked cocking her head.

"PLEASE, PLEASE DON'T KILL ME!!"

"You're not in Chicago," Katie replied calmly. "You're in Texas. Someone should have told you, 'DON'T MESS WITH TEXAS', ESPECIALLY HER WOMEN!"

Tony reached for his gun.

BOOM!

The evil was gone.

Katie knelt beside Pearl and untied her.

"Thank you, Katie."

"Can you walk, Miss Pearl?" Katie asked.

Pearl was rubbing her head. "Yes... I believe I'm fine. My head hurts where he pulled my hair," she winced, looking down at her assailant. Suddenly the night was eerily quiet. In one fateful moment, the ferocity of hell instantly shifted into a peaceful, calm ambiance. "It looks like we have a mess here. What do you think we should do?"

"I'll clean up the mess, Miss Pearl. Don't worry, I've done it before. I remember an old-timer in Menard once told me after a neighbor's dog killed some of his sheep, 'Shoot, Shovel and Shut-up!' I'll get Ginger to help me."

"Indeed. Let us not tell the other girls what happened here. It will be better that way. We will just tell Heather, Tony is gone for good. That is all she needs to know."

"Good enough. Let's go back to the house, Miss Pearl," Katie soothed, helping her to her feet. "C'mon Rusty. Good boy!"

"You would have made one hell of a Texas Ranger, Katie! I am proud to know you."

When Mozella saw the two women walking up the path to the house, she ran to Pearl, crying with relief. "Are you all right? Oh, my God in heaven!"

Pearl smiled at her friend with all the strength she had left. "I am fine, Mo. Katie just shot a snake down by the river a ways. Let us have some tea."

Church

With the first week of September, 1923, the dog days of summer had passed, and the people of West Texas were anticipating the relief of cooler days ahead. The Lady Pearls gave Emma Grace a wedding shower, and like always, Harvey and Miss Pearl made it elegant and memorable. The beverage was champagne and the dessert, Mozella's red velvet cake with vanilla icing. The gifts, however, were different from other wedding shower gifts. Emma Grace received perfume, bubble bath, lovely soft monogrammed towels, and French lingerie. "I think these gifts are more for Tommy Lee than for you," Harvey commented after she opened her presents.

The following Thursday, Tex went into Pearl's Speakeasy for a cold beer. Maggie took her usual place beside him and gave him a welcoming hug and a kiss on the cheek. Harmony was playing a soft bluesy tune on the upright piano near the table where Ginger and Annabelle were playing cards. Emma Grace spotted Tex and gently touched his arm. "Mr. Tex, Sir... I was wondering if…well, you know, Sir, my daddy died and…well, you are kind of like family here, and…Tex…would you be so kind as to give me away when I marry Tommy Lee?"

With humble surprise, Tex beamed, "Of course, dear child. It would be an honor." He hugged Emma Grace, his eyes brimming with tears, "An absolute honor!"

"Thank you, Tex," Emma Grace replied warmly.

"Everyone has been so nice. I feel like I have a family," Emma Grace declared emotionally.

Tex felt like telling another story to change the mood and resumed drinking his beer. He looked across the bar where Pearl was sitting doing some paperwork. "Have you ever been to Paint Rock, Miss Pearl?"

"I don't believe that I have, Tex," Pearl answered with a smile. "Somehow, girls, I think I feel a story coming on."

"I've heard of Paint Rock," Maggie said. "Where is it?"

"Paint Rock is about 40 miles east from here a few miles from the confluence of the Concho and the Colorado Rivers. It was named for a rocky bluff on one of the ranches by the river because the rocks are painted with red hematite portraying spiritual symbols with special meanings. At one time this cliff area was sacred ground to the Indians."

"Sounds interesting," Annabelle commented as Ginger proudly laid down her cards and announced, "Gin!"

Pretty amazing place," Tex continued, lighting his cherry tobacco filled pipe. "I've been there before. It's real peaceful out there by the river. That's where I first heard about a woman the Indians called, *The Lady in Blue*.

Maggie sniffed the air. "Oooh, I love the way that tobacco smells.

"The Lady in Blue?" Redbird asked, joining the group. "Who was she?"

"Sounds like one of the girls I knew down in New Orleans," Ginger smiled.

"Quite the opposite, my dear," Tex answered. "In fact, she was a nun!"

"A nun?" Pearl asked. Having been raised Catholic, Tex had her full attention.

By now Betsy, Heather, and Lucy had come in to enjoy Tex's story. "Now girls… I always tell you, fairytales usually start with 'Once upon a time.' But a good Texas tale always starts with, 'Y'all ain't gonna' believe this one!'"

"That's what you tell us," Maggie agreed.

"Well, y'all ain't gonna' believe this one either!" Tex assured them with a smile. "Logic can't really explain it, so I'm just going to tell you what I know. Sister Maria, a cloistered nun lived in a village called Agreda in Spain in the 1600's. 'Cloistered' means she never left her convent. People say that sometimes she got so deep in prayer that she floated in the air!"

"Floated in the air?" Lucy repeated quizzically.

Katie, carrying her gun, and Sarah returned from Sarah's shooting lessons. "What are y'all talking about floating in the air? That's crazy!" Katie exclaimed.

"I've heard about that," Harmony recalled. "It's in one of Miss Pearl's books, *The Lives of the Saints*. I think it was Saint Joseph of Cupertino. He lived in the 1600's as well. He used to float in the air when he prayed."

"All right then," Tex continued. "Here's something that is even more strange! Sister Maria went into a kind of spiritual trance and somehow crossed the ocean and visited the Indians who lived here. The Spanish called them, *Jumanos*. Her trances sometimes lasted for 2 or 3 days."

"But I thought you said she never left her convent," Lucy marveled.

"That's what's so peculiar!" Tex explained. "She never did leave her convent. Maria was confused and confided in the nuns she lived with that she was visiting Indians. She told them what they looked like and described the Texas terrain, much different than what she had seen in Spain. Anyway, a bishop in Spain wrote a letter to the archbishop in Mexico City, telling him about Sister Maria and asking him to be on the lookout for any strange occurrences with the Indians that might verify her story. That bishop passed the letter on to Father Benavides who was in New Mexico. In those days, sending missionaries anywhere was a big deal because they needed supplies and soldiers to protect them. Within a few days of receiving the letter, a group of Jumanos visited Father Benavides and told him the Lady in Blue had told them to find missionaries who would baptize them. Did I mention Maria's nun's habit was blue?" Tex exclaimed.

"Fascinating," Pearl marveled. "Just think of how many months it took in the 1600's for that letter to go from Spain to Mexico City, and then on to New Mexico! Even more fascinating is that Jumanos showed up a few days after Benavides got the letter. Pretty amazing!"

Harmony, engrossed in the story, closed the lid on her piano.

Tex continued. "The story gets even more bizarre! Because of the letter, Benavides sent a few of his missionaries to go with the Indians and check out the Jumanos' story. When they finally got there, over two thousand Indians greeted them wanting to be baptized. Two of the Indians were carrying crosses covered with flowers. Turns out the Jumanos knew about Jesus and other stories from the Bible. The missionaries were amazed because they knew no other missionaries had been there before. The Indians told the missionaries they had learned about Jesus from a Lady in Blue!"

"That really is a tall tale, Tex," Harmony exclaimed.

"It truly is Harmony. The Spanish Inquisition heard about Maria and interrogated her for 11 days."

"Did they let her go?" Pearl asked.

"Yes, they did," Tex answered. "Benavides later went to Spain and spoke in her defense. Her visions perfectly matched the description of the land and the Jumanos, including their tattoos, their flat heads, and a scar on the chief's face. You know how it is said one man's trash is another man's treasure? The Jumanos saw the pearls in the mussels from the Concho River as something to throw away and presented the missionaries with a huge collection of pink pearls whereas the Spanish saw them as a great treasure. The first Spanish mission in Texas was built not too far from here because the Spanish thought they would find a treasure of pinkish-lavender pearls. In fact that's why they chose the name "Concho" which means "shell" when they named the river. Before, it had been called "Nueces" after the pecan trees along the river."

"That is so interesting," Pearl commented. "The fact that the Concho River produces such lovely pink and lavender pearls has always fascinated me. Robert sometimes brought me Concho pearls when he visited me in Chicago."

"They are beautiful, all right. Just like a woman, the longer the mussel shell stays embedded at the bottom of the river the more beautiful the pearl. I always have thought women get better with age," Tex complimented with a glimmer in his eye that actually made Pearl blush. "Pretty is pretty, but beauty is the whole package. The more a woman has met her life's challenges and has known love, the wiser she is. Just like the Concho pearl, a woman's treasures lie deeply within. Looking into the eyes of a good woman exposes her true essence; the eyes always reveal the beauty of the soul."

"That's so nice, Tex," Maggie complimented. "I don't believe I have ever heard you talk like that before?"

"I like the way you think, Tex," Pearl smiled. Tex tipped his hat, their eyes communicating an acumen that only comes with age.

"Real beauty is all about what is inside a woman's soul," Tex proclaimed.

"And real men know it," Pearl answered back.

"Miss Pearl, I have lived a long time. Through the years, I have learned that as women grow older, they become wiser, and their hearts get bigger with age. Anyway, here's something else that is strange about Sister Maria! Her body has never decomposed!"

"What?" Heather asked. "How long ago did she die?"

"1665," Tex answered.

"Wait a minute, that's more than 250 years ago!" Sarah exclaimed.

"No way!" Maggie chirped in.

"I tell you, her body is in a glass coffin in Agreda, and it has never decomposed! People who visit the convent can see it!"

"Now, that's a story," Maggie commented. "You're right. It's hard to believe! I think you topped yourself with that one, Tex!"

"Y'all ain't gonna believe this one!" Katie laughed. "It's a topper all right!

Harmony, listening intently to every word, added, "I love stories about mystics and saints."

"According to Maria, she made over 500 visits to the New World that started when she was 15 years old." Tex continued. "The Indians say that the morning after her last visit they awoke to a blanket of bluebonnet flowers spread across the land, a gift from the *Lady in Blue* to remember her by."

"That is a great story, Tex," Pearl commented. "Although it is hard to believe, I would like to think it is true. My mother told me stories about saints when I was a little girl. I remember Saint Francis of Assisi practiced bilocation."

"Like I said," Tex commented, lighting up his pipe again, "You can't explain it, but you also can't explain it away."

When the West Texas wind blows through the land, it whistles a song of mystery and intrigue. That evening Harmony could not stop thinking about Tex's story. She felt as if the wind were summoning her soul. With crescendo and decrescendo, the low moaning sound was like a woman sorrowfully calling for her lost child. She tossed and turned for hours. Finally getting up and writing, an hour later she had composed: "The Ballad of the Lady in Blue."

In the great land of Texas

In the dawn of the spring

There's a beautiful flower that blankets the plains

It's shaped like a bonnet so lovely a hue

A beautiful gift from the Lady in Blue…

The next day after breakfast, Harmony sang her new song for everyone.

"That was lovely, Harmony," Pearl commented. "Quite lovely indeed. It makes me want to go to church."

"I would like to go to church," Harmony echoed.

"I used to sing at church," Ginger chimed in.

"Yes, let's go to church!" Lucy squealed excitedly.

"It's settled then. This Sunday, we'll all go to church," Pearl announced.

"I, for one, think it's a good idea, you girls going to church and all," Mozella agreed. "I like going."

"Mozella, why don't you come with us?" Ginger invited.

"Thank you, Ginger, but I think I'll pass. You might cause a stir, at least to those who know who you are. But if I go with you, that will only mean double trouble for sure!" Mozella expressed with humility and understanding.

The next Sunday the girls dressed and readied themselves for the Sunday service at a downtown church. "I'm a little bit nervous about this, Miss Pearl," Sarah winced.

"You mean nervous like a whore in church?" Katie laughed.

"Remember the woman at the well, girls? Remember how Jesus loved her and spoke to her. We will be fine as long as we all stick together," Miss Pearl assured them.

The girls looked pretty and fresh in their church dresses. As they were leaving, Mozella gave them a Bible verse to take with them. "*Paul's letter to the Romans says, for in passing judgment on another you condemn yourself, because you, the judge, practice the very same things!*" Mozella hugged each girl as she left Miss Pearl's Parlor. "Remember that real Christians have only love in their hearts, ladies. The mean ones are usually unhappy people or have something to hide."

Miss Pearl made sure they arrived early so they could be assured of a seat in the back. "Hold your heads high, girls," Miss Pearl instructed before they arrived at the church. "Remember no eye contact with ANYONE no matter how well you know them. Church is supposed to be God's house, and in His eyes, you are no less or no better than anyone else in this building!"

Miss Pearl and her girls entered the vestibule and sat in the last row of the church; all of them looked poised and lovely like a sorority of school girls with their hats and gloves. An older woman, smiling sweetly, greeted them with, "I do not believe I have seen you here before, ladies. Welcome to our church."

"Thank you very much," Pearl acknowledged. Another woman, with a grunt and a harrumph, quickly pulled the friendly woman away.

As the congregation sang the first song, "Softly and Tenderly," Pearl sensed Betsy, who was standing next to her, losing control and handed her a handkerchief. By the time they came to the chorus, "*Come home, come home, you who are weary come home,*" Betsy was weeping. Tenderly Pearl put her arm around her. "I am so sorry Miss Pearl," she quietly sobbed. It's just that I miss my family so much. We used to sing this song in church all the time."

"Don't worry, sweetheart, just feel what you feel," Pearl comforted. "We love you, Betsy. That will have to do for now," she whispered softly. "Grab hold and squeeze my hand when you feel your heart hurting again. I am here for you. We are all here for you."

So many times Pearl had heard those same words from Mozella's lips when she had lived in Chicago. "I am here for you." They continued to be comforting.

Oddly enough the preacher's sermon was about the story of the woman who was about to be stoned to death. "*They brought a woman who had been caught in adultery to Him to test Him,*" the preacher read from a red and gold Bible. "The law of Moses commands us to stone such a woman. What do you say? Jesus stooped down and with His finger he wrote something on the ground. Then He stood up and asked, 'He who is without sin among you, let him be the first to throw a stone at her.' Then He stooped down and wrote again. One by one, they walked away."

Pearl smiled. "I just love the way God works," she thought to herself. "My girls need to hear this."

Pearl had grown up in the Catholic Church and had never heard any of the gospel music sung at the service. On the other hand, Heather, Ginger, and Harmony sang every song without a miss. As the congregation sang the closing hymn Pearl and her girls slipped out the back door. They had been the first to arrive and intended to be the first to leave as well.

On the way home, the girls buzzed with excitement. That is all except Betsy who remained silent.

"That felt good!" Ginger announced, as she reached the front porch. Mozella came outside with a pitcher of ice tea.

"Brought back some good memories. Sure wish you could have come with us, Mozella," Ginger complained, hugging her. Because Mozella reminded Ginger of Mamie, the two women had a special bond between them.

"Mozella, what do you think Jesus wrote in the sand to make all those people walk away?" Ginger asked.

"I think He simply wrote, '*Thou shalt not kill,*'" Mozella answered. "That makes the most sense to me."

"Me too," Ginger agreed.

Throughout lunch, Pearl knew Betsy was still in pain. This marked the first time since she had come to San Angelo with Ginger that she had admitted she was homesick for her family. Pearl took Betsy's hand. "Come with me down by the river, honey, and talk to me about what you have on your mind." Betsy tried so hard to make the men like her. Sometimes she tried too hard and came across as being clingy and even needy. Pearl had known a girl just like Betsy in Chicago.

"Oh, Miss Pearl, I have made a mess of my life! I left my family..."

"Have you tried calling them?" Pearl asked. "Do they know where you are?"

"No, Ma'am!! I can never do that! I was so selfish. I really believed the grass was greener anywhere else besides Beckton, Kentucky. I thought I wanted a more exciting life than being stuck on a farm."

"Sometimes pretty girls get opportunities that seem wonderful at the time, Betsy. Don't see it as if you did something wrong. Instead try to see it as a lesson learned. Guilt never serves us well. Just forgive yourself and move on. You're already forgiven as far as God is concerned."

"Now I know that farm was heaven, Miss Pearl, because there was so much love there. I guess I never realized it before. I miss my brothers and my Mama and Daddy so much sometimes it makes my heart hurt. And then there's poor Johnny Wayne. He was so good to me, Miss Pearl. I know I broke his heart. He talked about getting married one day. When I was ten he carved our names in a big tree and made me a grass ring. It's still in my jewelry box in Kentucky."

"He sounds very sweet, Betsy."

"He won't want me now! I don't think anyone will ever want me. I left my home because I thought I wanted to see the world, live in style, and wear fancy clothes. I was so wrong! None of it is real if there's no love. Love is the only thing that's real. I surely learned my lesson about that."

"Does your family know you are all right? Do they know you are even alive?" Pearl asked quietly.

"No, Miss Pearl! I could never tell them what I'm doing! They would be so ashamed of me. I could never tell them. I'm afraid they will never want me around them again. They are good Christian people, Miss Pearl and they wouldn't understand. Am I a bad girl, Miss Pearl? I don't feel like I'm bad in my heart. I didn't know what else to do or where to go. Then when I met Ginger in the train station, coming here seemed to make sense. I had nowhere else to go, Miss Pearl! I couldn't go home! What would I say? I'm damaged goods. Who will want me now?"

Betsy fell into Pearl's arms sobbing. "There, there, Betsy girl. You're going to be fine, I promise. Give it some time. Life has a way of turning around. It always does if you believe. God really is on your side, always has been. He allows us to mess things up so we can learn our lessons. Believe me, I have had my share."

"Cry, Betsy. Let it go. You've been holding it back for too long." Pearl hugged Betsy until she felt her pain subside. "I have an idea," Pearl offered. "I believe you should write your parents a letter, and let them know you're Okay. They are probably worried sick about you. At least they will know you are alive. It is not necessary to tell them what you do here. Just let them know you are safe and well. They deserve at least that. You have nothing to lose. If your parents decide they never want to see you again, you will still be right where you are now. At least this way you will know. We love you, Betsy, but it is different from the love you get with a family. They sound like good people. Let's go inside. I will let you use my best stationery."

Betsy sat at the table in the library. After giving it some thought, she wrote:

September 8, 1923

Dear Mama and Daddy,

I hope this letter finds you well. It seems like forever since I have seen you. Please forgive me for not letting you know where I have been or where I am staying. So much has happened. I just want you to know that I am doing fine, and my health is good. I know you must be worried about me. I have found work in San Angelo, Texas and I am staying with some new friends I have met on my travels. I do not expect you to understand. Just know that I love you, and I think of you every day. Please give my regards to Johnny Wayne, and let him know I'm sorry if I broke his heart. I guess that's all for now. I will write again and let you know how I am doing.

Love,
Betsy

Betsy asked as Pearl walked into the library, "Should I put a return address on it?"

"That will take some courage, my dear," Pearl answered. "Whenever you have a question of the heart, ask yourself what would love do now? In other words, what would you do if there were nothing to be afraid of? That will be your answer."

Betsy put the Parlor's return address in the left hand corner and handed the envelope to Pearl. "Will you please put this with your outgoing mail for tomorrow?"

A warmth passed over Pearl's heart. She had never had a daughter of her own. Now she felt like she had eleven. "Of course, Betsy," she smiled.

"Thank you, Miss Pearl. I feel much better. It's like a huge weight has been lifted," she expressed, giving Pearl a hug. Pearl felt like the heaviness in Betsy's heart had vanished. After she hugged her, Betsy skipped out of the room like a little girl.

As Pearl placed the envelope into the box for outgoing mail, Mozella entered into the room. "You are some kind of lady, Victoria," she grinned.

"I am only soft when it comes to my girls, Mozella. You know how I love my twin boys, but somehow I feel a responsibility to these girls as if they were my own. I really do want them to be happy. Sometimes they seem so vulnerable. I was so much like them at their age. Minna and Ada were always kind to me; there is a strange bond among women who do what we do. It is difficult for women in the outside world to understand us. Thank God, I had you in Chicago. Lord knows what would have happened to me."

"You knows I love ya, Victoria!" she grinned.

The doorbell rang followed by a fierce knock at the front door. "Who in the world can that be?" Pearl quizzed. "It is not even 2 o'clock!"

Mozella peeked out the window. "Looks like we might have some trouble, Miss Victoria. There are four dreadfully unhappy women on the front porch. Three of them look like they just bit into a lemon!" she laughed.

"Let them in, Mozella. I have been half expecting them." Pearl turned to look at herself in a large mirror then applied fresh red lipstick and primped her hair. "This is going to be interesting."

If You Could Wear My Slippers

Although the ladies from Miss Pearl's Parlor sat in the last pew of the church that morning in an attempt to be less conspicuous, Pearl was not surprised when she saw four unhappy women standing on her front porch. Mozella met them at the front door, and Pearl graciously welcomed them inside. "Good afternoon, ladies. Won't you come in?"

It was a lovely afternoon, and the windows in Pearl's Parlor were all open, allowing the delicate white curtains to dance lightly in the breeze. Harmony was playing Debussy's, *Claire de Lune* on the piano, creating serenity in the Great Room. "That sounds lovely, dear," Pearl expressed. "Do keep playing if you will." Pearl knew that Harmony's music might help tame this angry beast following at her heels. She led the ladies into the library where Sarah and Annabelle were reading. "If you will please excuse us, ladies, we will be using this room for a short meeting," Pearl announced with a glimmering smile.

"Yes, Ma'am." Annabelle obeyed as Sarah and she left the room.

"Would anyone like a glass of tea?" Pearl asked.

"Absolutely not!" one of the women spit with contempt. "My name is Gladys Krankalot. This is Hazel Snobgrass, Ernestine Meeny, and Miss Susan Smith. Let me come straight to the point. We do not want you or your kind at our church ever again! It is a house of God!"

"Miss Hattie tried to bring her girls one time before, and we made sure that never happened again! Women like you are shameful sinners," Hazel boasted with satisfaction. "You have some nerve showing up at our service this morning, Miss whatever your name is!"

"My name is Victoria Pearl McKnight. My friends call me *Pearl*. You may call me Mrs. McKnight," Pearl instructed with charm and grace.

"Mrs. McKnight?" Hazel remarked with contempt. "That's a joke. What kind of man lets his wife work in a Parlor?"

"I am a widow," Pearl answered icily.

"Widow or not, we came here today to let you know you are not welcome at our church now or ever!" Gladys screamed.

The third woman, Ernestine, sitting upright with her arms folded up over her breasts, remained silent, only frowning and grunting. Pearl recognized her as the woman who earlier in church had pulled the kind lady away.

"My, but you have quite a library here," Susan commented. *Wuthering Heights!* One of my favorites!" She was younger than the other women and obviously had a much different attitude.

"Yes, I insist that my girls be educated and well read. We read every day, and I personally visit the public library at least once a month for new books," Pearl informed her.

"I am a schoolteacher," Susan told her. "You really have an exquisite place here, Mrs. McKnight."

"You can call me Pearl, Susan."

Ernestine cleared her throat, grunting like an angry bear. Hazel and Gladys threw Susan evil looks. "We're not here to make friends, Susan!" Gladys screeched. "We are good Christian women, Mrs. McKnight. We will not have you in our church with your whores."

Pearl glared at Gladys. If there was one thing she would not tolerate, it was any kind of disrespect to her girls. "If you were a man, within 2 minutes Katie would have her shotgun in your faces escorting you out the door. No one comes into my parlor and calls any of my girls *"whores"* without consequences. Because you are ignorant women unfamiliar with our rules, I will simply tell you to not repeat that word again, Miss Krankalot."

"That's Mrs. Krankalot," she answered.

"How fortunate for you. Is your husband still alive?" Pearl asked.

"Yes, he is! What business is that of yours?"

"Again, how fortunate for you," Pearl repeated with a hint of sadness.

"My husband is alive too!" Hazel bragged.

"I know," Pearl commented.

"And what do you mean by that??" Hazel screamed.

"Why, I saw you standing next to a man in church today. I assumed he was your husband," Pearl backtracked catching herself.

"I'm not married," Susan offered. "Schoolteachers are not allowed to be married. I don't know if I'll ever get married," she sighed.

Ernestine grunted again.

Never having been confronted like this before, Pearl felt herself getting defensive. Although there had been demonstrations parading on the streets of the Levee in Chicago, she had always been protected from any confrontations at the Everleigh House. Never before had she been face-to-face with women of this nature. Ada and Minna paid thousands of dollars to keep the law as well as these kinds of conversations outside the walls of the mansions on Dearborn Street, in Chicago. Mozella had always been an excellent gatekeeper, and Pearl kept to herself when she was in town.

"You know what we do here is not really much different than what you do," Pearl remarked trying to remain quipped. "The only real difference is what we call it. You call it your wifely duty, and we call it survival. Men have needs, and we have made it our business to see that those needs are met in a friendly environment."

"You are all sinners, and you're going to hell!" Hazel snapped.

"I do not understand you women, and I certainly do not understand a church that would refuse anyone to come in and participate. My girls are real people. You have no idea what these young women have been through in their lives. Each one of them is friendly, generous, intelligent, and kind - beautiful inside and out. I know because I am selective with who works here."

Ernestine tightened her arms and grunted again.

"It is simply a matter of biology," Pearl explained presenting her case from an educated viewpoint. "Just like any other animal, man has two basic instincts, survival and procreation. When the two come together, a business like mine develops. Let me ask you a question just so you understand what we do here. How many times can a woman get pregnant and deliver in one year?"

"Just once," Susan said.

"Exactly!" Pearl exclaimed.

"How many times can a man father a child in one year?" Pearl asked.

"Hundreds," Susan answered again.

"That is correct! Because males and females are different in that respect, they each have different needs," Pearl declared. "Women are looking for good fathers who can provide for the offspring, and men are just looking. It is simply a matter of supply and demand. Men need their pipes cleaned and a little female kindness once-in-a-while. We provide both those services, and may I add, the girls are good at what they do."

"That's disgusting!" Gladys shrieked.

"We have a different opinion," Pearl commented. "That is why men come to us. Our job is to make men feel virile and appreciated; we sell female attention and sexual satisfaction. Most of our clients are single men lonely for a woman or looking for a good time. It is actually an honest exchange with no expectations. We are not in the business of stealing anyone's husband. We provide a service, and we do it well."

"Sex is a shameful act that should only be done when a married couple desires children," Hazel avowed firmly.

"That is one of the saddest things I think I have ever heard anyone say," Pearl retorted. "I am not quite sure whom I feel sorrier for, you or your husband. I believe I am sad for both of you."

Ernestine replied with another grunt.

"I am sorry you ladies feel the way you do. Before we walked into church today, I told the girls not to be afraid, and we remembered how Jesus spoke to the woman at the well. Perhaps you are right. I believe your church is not a good fit for us after all. Do not worry; we will not attend your service again. We will look for a church with people who will treat us as Jesus would. After all, is that not what true Christians do?"

Susan, the schoolteacher, listening to Pearl's every word, was impressed with the way Pearl was handling the situation. Ever since Pearl's Parlor had opened up for business, she had been curious to be inside. Now that she was actually here, she realized it was certainly not what she had expected.

"This meeting to inform us that we are not welcome at your church is most unfortunate. The music was nice and actually moved one of my girls to tears. In addition, I am sure your preacher saw there was a healthy increase in the collection plate this morning. I especially appreciated his message about throwing the first stone. Did any of you happen to listen to his sermon? I found it to be both insightful and inspiring."

No one said a word. All three women had that I-just-sucked-a-lemon face again. Susan, obviously disengaged from the others, continued perusing the book titles on the tall oak shelves. By now, Pearl had figured out that she had accompanied the she-pack out of curiosity. "Veronica Franco? This looks interesting!" she commented as she pulled it from the shelf.

"I am sure that you women are not aware that we help support the orphanage in town. The girls often buy gifts for the children. You have made your message quite clear, ladies. We will not be attending your church again," Pearl promised, rising from her chair, indicating the meeting had come to an end. She opened the library doors. All four women stood to leave.

Walking into the Great Room, Pearl saw Redbird, Annabelle, and Betsy reading and enjoying Harmony's music. The church ladies also heard the lovely harmonic tones from the piano; Harmony's performance had protected the girls from the ugliness of the conversation that had occurred behind the library's heavy mahogany doors.

When Pearl saw the young women, whom she had come to love, sitting innocently in the room with the warm breeze blowing softly through the windows, her heart filled with contempt for the women from the church and their self-righteous attitudes. These girls were her family, each one of them precious to her. Her anger was brewing like a tea kettle coming to a boil as the faces of young women she had known in Chicago floated through her mind. Memories of her friends' tragic stories of abuse and abandonment and how people had come to the Everleigh House to sell their daughters dampened her mood even further. She thought of the women who had been kidnapped, drugged, gang raped, and then sold on the Levee after being soiled and shamed.

Like lava exploding from the depths of Vesuvius, Pearl, seeing red, exploded in a rage of Irish temper.

"My girls are not bad girls!" she roared with fury from hell, her voice so volatile it felt like an earthquake was shaking the house. All eyes fixed on Pearl. Harmony's hand stopped mid-chord. The silence was deafening. Pearl's rage froze the women in their tracks. Everyone else in the house slowly and silently entered the room. Until now, Miss Pearl's Parlor had only known Pearl's eloquent speech and calm but firm demeanor. They were in awe as they witnessed this elegant lady transformed into a war goddess. The room was wide-eyed with amazement, except Ginger, who was grinning from ear-to-ear.

"My girls are not bad girls!" Pearl repeated defensively. "Do you think they chose this profession because it was their little girl dream come true? Oh, yes, one day when I grow up, I want to be a prostitute." Pearl shouted with dramatic sarcasm. "What is wrong with you people? How dare you come in and tell us we are not good enough for your precious little church? How dare you!"

Terrorized by Pearl's outburst, the women, unable to move, stared at Pearl. Her outburst glued them to the floor. Hazel had wet herself, and Gladys broke out with a hot flash. Ernestine, the grunter, had unfolded her arms and was holding on to Hazel for dear life.

"For just one day, if you could wear their slippers and have the thoughts and memories these girls have every day of their lives, you would know each one of these women are courageous and beautiful - inside and out. You have no idea what each one of them has been through and how she has survived. Annabelle, my love, tell these self-appointed Christian women why you are here."

"My husband was a soldier in World War I. When I was four months pregnant with our little girl, he was killed in Germany fighting for his country. Billy was the love of my life. We were destitute and met Pearl on a train. Mother takes care of little Julie Marie now, and I send them money. If it wasn't for our little girl, I would be with my Billy now," Annabelle whispered softly.

The church women had stirred Redbird's Irish spirit. She was so angry her shiny red hair looked like it was on fire. "My mother was too pretty for her own good and left us for some man and moved to New York when I was ten. She didn't even say goodbye. Daddy died a few months later with a broken heart. My aunt and uncle moved into our house, and I took care of my brothers. Aunt Gertrude always hated me. One night her son's friend sneaked into my room and raped me."

"Oh, my goodness, that's horrible," Hazel gasped.

"It was obvious what happened. When Aunt Gertrude saw him coming out of my room, she called me a *whore* and kicked me out of my own house. My little brothers were sent away to boarding school," Redbird explained with contempt. "I'm trying to make enough money so we can be together again. Actually, come to think of it, you remind me of my Aunt Gertrude."

"Redbird and I have been best friends since the first grade," Lucy remarked. "I had a brother who died before I was born. My father wanted a son. He and my mother treated me like I was invisible. Our housekeeper, Mary, took care of me. Mother kicked me out of the house after a mean girl put sleeping powder in my drink at a dance and told the chaperones I was drunk. I was sad about leaving Mary and Redbird. I met Miss Pearl and started working here. I was so happy the day Redbird arrived! The girls here are my family now."

Betsy wailed, "I was so stupid! I ran away from home with a man I thought loved me. He left me in the middle of Texas when I wouldn't give him money for a poker game. I hurt a lot of people when I left."

"I found the poor kid in the middle of a train station crying her eyes out," Ginger scolded haughtily. "My mother sold me to a madame in New Orleans for a thousand bucks," she added.

"I thank God every day for Ginger and Miss Pearl," Betsy cried. "I had nowhere else to go, so they took me in."

"Oh, my," Hazel gasped quietly. Ernestine had ceased her grunting, and Gladys shook her head. They had never heard stories like these before.

Pearl put her arm around Betsy. "I believe it is time for you to leave now," she demanded firmly to the women. "You have made your point, and we have made ours. We have no more business with you, and you have no more business with us!"

Mozella opened the door. "*Romans 10:13, For everyone who calls on the name of the Lord will be saved,*" she smiled. The three ladies left without a word. Their sour faces had morphed into faces of bewilderment. Susan stayed behind.

"May I stay for a minute, Miss Pearl?" Susan asked.

Pearl nodded. "Come here, girls," welcoming her Lady Pearls with open arms. Everyone surrounded Pearl forming a close-knit circle. "You are amazing," Pearl praised as she hugged each girl in turn. "I love each one of you as my own."

"Wish I had a photo of those ladies when you roared like a lion protecting her cubs," Mozella beamed with pride. "I believe you woke up the dead!"

"I am not sure where that came from, Mo. All of a sudden, I became so very angry at those women!"

"It wasn't the women who made you angry, Victoria. It was all of it. That fire has been lying dormant in you for years. From the depths of your soul, you were singing for every poor girl who ever got into this crazy business."

"I am sorry those women were so ugly to you, Miss Pearl. I don't like to gossip… however… I happen to know that back-in-the-day, one of those women showed her bloomers to a man after she learned her cousin Florence was sweet on him. Everybody knows she is a jealous woman. Always wantin' sumthin' someone else has. Anyway… it wasn't long after that she married that man! She told everyone her baby was premature. I have never heard of anyone having a baby that weighed 8 pounds after only being pregnant 7 months! Some folks were suspicious..."

"People who point their finger have 3 fingers pointing right back at them, Susan," Sarah commented.

"Like Shakespeare said, 'She doth protest too much!'" Lucy grinned.

"Sometimes men can be easily trapped because they let that thing between their legs do all their thinkin'," Ginger added. "Too bad for him. At least we're more honest about that kind of thing here."

"Satisfaction guaranteed!" Maggie proclaimed.

Pearl faced Susan, who was standing ramrod straight. "What your church lady friends need is a good old-fashioned session with my old friend, Doctor Gedderoff!" she chuckled in an effort to lighten up the mood.

The girls all laughed. "Tell her the story about Doctor Gedderoff," Lucy requested. "It's my favorite!"

"There once was a handsome doctor who specialized in female hysteria," Pearl began. "His name was Doctor Gedderoff. He had a good practice and was in great demand. Although

several doctors practiced this method of sedation, he was popular because he was so good looking and had such a gentle yet effective technique," Pearl told everyone. "He encouraged the women with his deep sexy voice, and he was especially well known for making a woman produce vocal expressions that could shatter glass. Many of the wealthy women in town had treatments two or even three times a week from Doctor Gedderoff. He even had a flier that advertised he made discreet house calls."

"Female hysteria?" Susan asked. "What's that?"

"I learned in Chicago, living in a house full of women, the best way to understand a woman's current disposition is to look at the moon, also on a 28 day cycle," Pearl explained. "The moon changes every night as well. The Mayans actually formed their calendar by the pattern of the moon. Two or three days exist in that 28 day cycle where even the nicest of girls can turn into screaming shrews!"

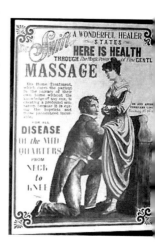

"You mean like Gladys was today?" Susan asked.

"Exactly!" Pearl agreed.

"Well, it seems that one day, somewhere, somehow, somebody discovered that when a woman gets "pissy" or displays a sour disposition, the most effective solution to transform her from a screeching owl to a purring kitten is to stimulate the woman's pelvic region until she starts singing!"

Heather took the cue and belted out her highest note in an operatic crescendo, "*Aaaaaaaaaaaah sweet mystery of life now that I've found you*!" Everyone laughed except Susan, clueless about what was so funny.

"Many times the poor doctors treating female hysteria would get cramps in their hands, working on cranky women. Once-in-a-while, this happened to poor Doctor Gedderoff."

"Poor Doctor Gedderoff," Lucy teased.

"He was a nice man, and the women loved him. Such a nice technique. He had more business than he could handle! I believe he married a rich widow and finally retired."

"Many doctors learned Doctor Gedderoff's famous technique, but alas, their hands cramped too. Doctor Mortimer, an English doctor who specialized in female hysteria, came up with the idea of powered vibration. At the turn of the century, Hamilton Beach invented a vibrator to speed up the process. For years, they sold these appliances in the Sears catalog until somebody complained they were too sexual."

"Probably a man," Ginger commented.

"Although Sears took the vibrators out of its catalog, I happen to know it is still available."

"I have one!" Lucy bragged.

"So do I," Maggie declared. "Zoom! Zoom! ZOOM! The lady Pearls laughed. Even Annabelle and Sarah smiled.

Susan had no idea why the girls were laughing.

"Mozella!" Pearl exclaimed, "I feel like celebrating. Champagne for everyone!"

"I've never had champagne before!" Susan exclaimed.

"My dear schoolteacher, it is certainly time you did!" Pearl assured her.

Within minutes, Mozella and Emma Grace had produced glasses and chilled bottles of French champagne. The bubbly drink flowed. Pearl, studying each face and recalling each story, realized that they were a team united against the hardships of the world. A feeling of peace swept over her heart and soul like a cleansing waterfall.

"I want to propose a toast! Here's to the Lady Pearls of San Angelo, Texas!" Pearl decreed, lifting her glass. "The most wonderful women I have ever had the pleasure to know," her eyes filling with tears of pride.

"Here's to Mother Pearl!" Lucy yelled. "The finest lady in the world. Hip-hip-hooray!"

"Hip-hip-hooray, hip-hip-hooray," they all chanted and drank their champagne.

Ginger stood, and lifted her glass of champagne. "You have made us into a family and given us a place to call home. Miss Victoria Pearl, Thank you."

"Thank you, Ginger... Thank all of you! Play us a song Harmony!"

"C'mon, Heather, let's sing," Ginger summoned. "Let's do 'Basin Street!'" Ginger suggested. "Lord knows, I've got some memories there. *'Won't you come along with me... down the Mississippi...'*"

Redbird swayed back and forth seductively, moving her long slender body to the jazzy rhythm of the walking bass Harmony played. Lucy and Heather joined her, and soon the room filled with dancing, swaying women including Pearl.

"You've got some moves!" Lucy exclaimed as she watched Pearl slowly rocking her hips.

"There might be a little snow on the mountain, but there is still fire in the furnace," Pearl boasted.

Susan, the schoolteacher standing next to Emma Grace, gawked in amazement. She'd had no idea what she might find in Miss Pearl's Parlor, but she certainly had not expected anything like this! She felt like she was in a roomful of sisters, a family who really loved each other. Emma Grace handed her a glass of champagne and introduced herself. "Hi, my name is Emma Grace."

"Hello," Susan answered.

"Not what you expected, is it?" Emma Grace chuckled.

"How do you know that's what I was thinking?"

"I recognize that look on your face because I had that same look the first day I was here."

The champagne gave Susan just enough courage to ask a question that she had been struggling with for quite some time. When the song ended, the schoolteacher walked over to Pearl who was standing by the piano. "Miss Pearl, may I please talk to you about something that has been on my heart?"

"Why certainly, Susan," Pearl answered. "What's on your mind?"

"Miss Pearl…IS SEX BAD?"

The room became quiet for a second time this day. The girls raised their eyebrows, trying their best not to laugh. They made every attempt to help the frustrated schoolteacher keep her dignity. Pearl did everything she could to maintain a calm disposition. Poor Susan looked so desperate, and Pearl certainly did not want to embarrass her. "What do you mean, dear?"

"I've been told all my life that sex is a shameful act and women who like it are bad girls. My mother told me that it hurts a lot, but women have to do it if they want to have children. I figured I wasn't missing out on anything, so I decided to be a schoolteacher."

"My grandmother told me it was like jumping up and down in a wash tub," Harmony giggled.

"Lately I have been having these feelings, Miss Pearl," Susan continued. "I have started kissing my pillow at night and looking at the buttocks parts of men. Sometimes I even look at the front! I have been praying to God for forgiveness and even asked that my evil thoughts be taken away, but it's only getting worse. I am kissing my pillow more than ever! I have been having fantasies about the father of one of my students. His wife died last year, and ever since then, I daydream about what it would be like if he kissed me and held me. I am a sinner having impure thoughts, and I don't know what to do about it!"

Pearl nodded her head at Susan. "Girls, this is our new friend, Susan," she proclaimed.

Susan gave a little wave. "Hello, everyone," shrugging her shoulders.

"When my mother told me about sex, she was most gracious," Pearl remembered. "She told me that when a man makes love to you, it is like dancing in a field of flowers that all open up at the same time," Pearl twinkled. "I learned the hard way that she was right, that is if you are making love to someone who loves you and you love him. Otherwise, it is just a sporting event that can sometimes be fun or sometimes not, depending on your partner."

"Like Joe Bob!" Maggie inserted.

"You are right about that, Maggie!" Redbird added. "That cowboy has some real talent!"

"Personally, I have learned there are three kinds of men," Heather offered. "Those who know how to make love to a woman, those who think they know how, and those who don't care one way or the other as long as they get what they want."

"Look at nature. Every living thing on this planet comes from some kind of seed. Every animal is here because of a male and a female. Some animals include a dance when they procreate, and some are even playful like the squirrels. When sex is performed as an act expressing the most intimate love between two people, it is a beautiful gift from our Creator. The procreative dance can be both playful and passionate at the same time. When sex is sacred, it can be the most exciting experience in the world. My husband Robert and I had that," Pearl remembered tenderly.

"Billy and I had that too," Annabelle added. "Closing my eyes and pretending I am with him gets me through. If it were not for our baby girl, I probably would have given up on life all together."

Pearl tenderly touched Annabelle's shoulder. Annabelle hardly ever spoke, but when she did, people listened. Those who knew her well recognized her silence was due to her broken heart. Men saw her as exotic and mysterious.

"You are right, Annabelle. You can be with anyone you want to be with if you close your eyes," Sarah sighed dreamily. "I like to pretend that Rudy Vallee is singing to me."

"Mine is Rudy Valentino, the Latin Lover," Redbird chirped twirling around the room. "He was so sexy in *Son of the Sheik*.'"

"I fell in love with a Latin Lover who looked just like Valentino. That man could put me on the moon!" Betsy exclaimed. "Unfortunately, it didn't turn out so well."

"I don't know. I like to keep my eyes open and look straight into the eyes of those blue-eyed cowboys," Lucy remarked. "Some of them are so dang pretty! I can never decide which I like better... watching a cowboy walk into a room... or walk out," she grinned. "I've seen some mighty fine backsides."

"Sometimes I fantasize about Rudy Valentino as well, Redbird!" Maggie chirped in. "Maybe it's because of those Sheik condoms we always use. You know they named those things Sheik from that sexy movie he was in."

"I like the Merry Widows myself," Ginger avowed. "They come 3 in a package. Lord, where on earth did they come up with that name?"

"That's easy," Pearl answered. "Women have sex for different reasons when they become older. Sex is so much more enjoyable when you are not afraid of getting pregnant. When a mature woman has a good lover, sex can be better than ever. Unfortunately, sometimes the older men have a more difficult time keeping up. Nature is a little backward as far as that goes. However, a man can become a more sensitive lover with age."

"What are condoms?" Susan asked.

"It's like a balloon you put over a man's happy-stick to make sure you don't get pregnant or some kind of weird disease," Lucy offered, raising her eyebrows and pointing towards the top of her legs.

"Oh my!" Susan gasped.

"During World War I, the soldiers were allowed to use condoms for the sole purpose of NOT spreading disease. Apparently our men in uniform didn't pay much attention when they were told NOT to have sex," Redbird added. "Turns out condoms also work pretty well in helping women NOT to get pregnant, even though technically, birth-control is against the law. In fact just a few years ago, a woman named Margaret Sanger was arrested in New York for passing out brochures on how NOT to get pregnant."

"Oh, my goodness. I have never heard anyone talk of such things!" the schoolteacher exclaimed. "I like it!"

"You know, Susan, in the olden days there were some schoolteachers and librarians who used to make a little money on the side doing what we do," Ginger piped in. "They'd lift their skirts just high enough to reveal those sexy striped stockings the girls in Storyville wore to signal to the men that they might be willing to leave their backdoors open for a price."

"Things have changed so much since my days at the Everleigh Club," Pearl commented. It doesn't seem that long ago that we were riding in trains and horse drawn carriages. Now we have motor cars and even planes!"

"*Let him kiss me with the kisses of his mouth, for your love is more delightful than wine,*" Mozella recited.

"Beautiful, Mozella," Emma Grace chimed. "Is that in the Bible too?"

"It surely is," Mozella answered. "It's in the *Song of Solomon.*"

"*I am my beloved's and my beloved is mine. He grazes among the lilies until the day break and the shadows flee away,*" Sarah quoted dreamily.

"Very good, Sarah, "Mozella praised.

"I read the Bible too," Sarah grinned.

"I will read the 'Song of Solomon' tomorrow," Harmony promised. "It sounds so poetic."

"So sex is not a bad thing?" Susan asked.

"Of course not!" Lucy answered. "I love sex!"

"Me too! It's such a double standard!" Maggie protested "How come when a man wants sex, he's a stud, but if a woman wants it, she's a bad girl? I don't think it's fair!"

"I think I want it!" Susan blurted out. "I want sex!!" she proclaimed in a bellowing voice.

Quickly, everyone focused on the sweet little schoolteacher. "There I said it. I want sex!" Susan repeated with determination.

"I want sex!" Susan announced to the room.

"I WANT SEX!" she bellowed louder.

"I want to kiss a man and feel a man," Susan continued. "I want to snuggle up and cuddle up! I want to excite him and be excited. I want to take him to the 'Land of Milk and Honey,' and

I want him to take me to the Promised Land! "I WANT SEX! I WANT SEX! I WANT SEX, SEX SEX!"

Lucy raised her fist in the air and proclaimed aloud, "YES! THE SCHOOLTEACHER WANTS SEX!!"

Ginger, who rarely even smiled, applauded her with encouragement. Everyone followed suit and gave Susan a standing ovation.

"I WANT SEX!" Susan repeated. "I've never felt so free! No wonder women don't like you. They don't understand you because they don't understand themselves. You're free. They all say you are horrible sinners, but you are free to be sexy because that is who you are."

How old are you, Susan?" Pearl asked.

"Twenty-eight," Susan answered.

"Of course, you want sex, Susan," Pearl exclaimed. "It is perfectly natural that you want sex. God made you that way. To deny it would be denying that you are a woman. Good for you, Susan! Say it again."

"I WANT SEX! I WANT SEX! I WANT SEX, SEX SEX!" Susan repeated arms waving in the air.

"I love men, and I'm not ashamed to say it!" Lucy proclaimed.

"Me too!" Maggie echoed. "Especially those cowboys!"

"I love a Texas gentleman. They always seem to appreciates what I have to offer," Sarah added.

Susan was laughing. "I want to smell a man, kiss a man, feel a man! I want to turn him on and get him hotter than a frying pan!"

The schoolteacher lifted her glass of champagne, "Here's to all of you. Here's to the *Lady Pearls of San Angelo*!"

Everyone in the room held up their glasses and cheered. "To the *Lady Pearls*!"

A Wedding

Emma Grace, sitting at her new vanity, gazed at the reflection of a woman in love. Pearl appeared from behind the blushing bride and gently placed her hands on her shoulders. "You look so lovely, Emma Grace. Tommy Lee is a very fortunate man."

"Miss Pearl. I feel like I'm in a dream! I only wish my daddy could be here."

"I feel like he probably is, sweetheart. And now a crown for our princess." Pearl placed a wreath of pink rose buds, baby's breath, and long pink and white ribbons onto Emma Grace's head. "There! Perfect! You are a beautiful bride! Tommy Lee is a lucky man."

The ranch was buzzing with excitement. Since Emma Grace had chosen pink as her wedding color, the Lady Pearls were wearing various styles of new pink dresses, and the cowboys were all gussied up in clean white shirts and denim jeans. Susan, the schoolteacher, arrived with a handsome widower whose son was in her classroom. Happy Harvey was decked out in a fancy linen cream-colored suit and a pink bow tie. Tommy Lee was sporting a new pair of Leddy's fancy leather boots, a wedding gift from the *Lady Pearls*.

Tex showed up in his best suit. Sarah was to be Emma Grace's maid of honor, and Dusty was Tommy Lee's best man. Four year old little Julie Marie, the flower girl, was wearing a pretty pink dress her grandmother had made and squealed with delight, "Look at my pretty dress, Mommy!" twirling around like little girls do. "Watch me, Mommy! Watch me! I can dance, Mommy! Weeeee!"

Annabelle gazed upon her daughter like loving mothers do, "Just like a pretty ballerina, sweetheart." Annabelle's mother smiled at both of them the way grandmothers do. Annabelle squeezed her mother's hand. "Thank you for making the dress, Mother. It's adorable."

Tommy Lee's mother, Marybelle, gracious to everyone, had made pink dresses for all her girls. Her husband, Jed,

Tommy Lee's father, was dressed in his best white shirt and a cowboy tie. Although there were some flirtatious looks and smiles being exchanged, the girls and the cowboys behaved themselves. Mozella was wearing a new hat and had baked her signature fresh bread for the occasion, just for Emma Grace.

For the last several months, as a labor of love, Tommy Lee had been refurbishing the two bedroom cottage on the ranch that had once served as his parent's first home. With every nail driven and every brick laid, he had fantasized about being married to Emma Grace. There was a lovely view of Dove Creek from the front porch, and a majestic old oak tree stood in the front yard.

Tommy Lee and his mother had decided that the shade of the trees beside the water would serve as a perfect setting for their wedding. His friends had arranged wooden benches in a circular pattern facing the creek to catch the soft autumn breeze, blowing gently through the red, orange, and golden-colored leaves. Nature was singing her song for the happy couple.

When the guests were seated, the preacher stepped to the bank of the creek and turned to face the small gathering of friends and family. Tommy Lee stood to the right. Dusty took his place beside him. When Harmony strummed her guitar, Sarah emerged from the cottage, holding a bouquet of pink and white roses. Little Julie Marie, serious and composed, stepped out next. Everyone smiled as she carefully dropped the rose petals one-by-one from her wicker basket onto her path to the preacher.

Tex had never had children and had been deeply touched when Emma Grace had asked him to give her away. He proudly stepped out of the newly finished cottage, escorting the lovely Texas bride, wearing a simple flowing white dress with a pink satin sash. The flowers in her hair gave the illusion of a lady in the king's court. Tommy Lee's heart swelled with love when he saw Emma Grace come out of their new home. That same beautiful smile that had been etched in his mind since the night he first saw her was beaming at him now.

Watching as the young couple exchanged their vows sent a warm feeling over every heart in the audience. Some, including one or two cowboys, found tears in their eyes. Pearl thought of the perfect synchronicity and series of events that had brought everyone at the wedding to this perfect moment. As she considered the faces of her girls watching Tommy Lee and Emma Grace, she contemplated what each of them was thinking. How many women dream of marrying their Prince Charming one day? What happens to a woman when she loses hope of ever finding, "happily ever after?"

As Pearl watched Tommy Lee put the ring on his bride's finger, she felt blessed to have had Robert for as long as she did. She affectionately gazed upon little Julie Marie in her pretty pink dress that fanned out when she twirled. All of these women were at one time filled with childlike innocence like hers. Life's journey had brought them to Pearl's. The Parlor was an opportunity for these girls when options were slim and offered a temporary haven, a sense of belonging and a financial solution that paid substantially better than anything else they could ever find. Mozella was right. She had been one of the lucky ones, and, in that moment, Pearl silently prayed for each of her girls.

"I now pronounce you man and wife. You may kiss your new bride." Like a beacon of happiness, Tommy Lee kissed his beloved Emma Grace. As the young couple turned to their friends and family, everyone cheered and applauded. They were cheering for love. They were cheering for life.

Tommy Lee's uncle brought his fiddle, and a few other musician friends had brought a banjo, a harmonica, a couple of guitars, and an upright bass. There was barbeque, potatoes, beans, greens, tomatoes, and corn as well as contributions of favorite recipes from some of the neighbor women. Tommy Lee's aunt made a wedding cake. The bride and groom fed each other in the traditional way symbolizing they would always fill each other's needs. It was a great day. Everyone there was ecstatic for the newlyweds.

The evening before, Pearl had invited Emma Grace to watch the sunset in the gazebo and gave her the talk her mother had given her. "Making love to a man that you love, Emma Grace, is like dancing in a field of flowers that all open up at once..." she began. That afternoon after the wedding, Pearl had managed to take Tommy Lee to the side. Handing him an envelope with a $100 bill, she smiled, "Here's a little something for your honeymoon."

"Thank you kindly, Ma'am."

There was another reason Pearl wanted to speak privately to Tommy Lee. She had a strong feeling that he could use a little education before his memorable evening with Emma Grace. "By the way, Tommy Lee I need to ask you something. Have you ever grown a garden? Do you get the soil ready before you plant the seeds, or do you just throw them down and hope they'll grow...?"

Early that evening, the young couple said goodnight to everyone and retired to the cottage. While Tommy Lee made a fire in the fireplace, Emma Grace prepared herself for her wedding night. Pearl frequently advised, "Remember to always be clean girls. A gentleman appreciates a clean lady." She took a luxurious bath with lavender oil to relax and put on a hint of French perfume and the lovely white gown from the *Lady Pearls*.

"It will be wonderful," Annabelle told her. "Just follow his lead after he kisses you, and you'll know what to do."

Presenting herself to her new husband, Emma Grace emerged from the bathroom. She was full of butterflies. Within 3 minutes, her beautiful white gown was on the floor. That evening in a small 2 bedroom cottage in West Texas, Emma Grace and Tommy Lee danced in a field of flowers that all opened up at once. At the same time, the new bride was basking in the pure ecstasy of her womanhood, Tommy Lee put a little baby boy inside her. The lovers had become one in body, heart, and spirit, and a tiny little soul secretly rejoiced in its new beginning of life.

Time to Go Home

By the fall of 1923, business was prosperous at Miss Pearl's Parlor. With the discovery of the Santa Rita Number One, San Angelo had indeed turned into an oil boom town. Wealthy men, judges, lawyers, and oilmen became regulars at the Parlor, a favorite place to discuss business deals. A deep sense of trust among its patrons captured the essence of, "What happens at Miss Pearl's Parlor, stays at Miss Pearl's Parlor."

Pearl liked to celebrate the girls' birthdays in a special way. Mozella baked their favorite cakes and decorated the Great Room in some kind of theme. Parties were always good for business, and the girls were treated like the *princess of the day*. Redbird turned 20 on October 9th, 1923. Her Aunt Gertrude had never acknowledged her birthday. In fact, most of the girls had never had a birthday party before they had come to Miss Pearl's. Happy Harvey loved parties and usually bought the girls a gift from Holland's Jewelers. Last year, it had been bracelets, and this year it was a piece of jewelry with a Concho pearl. This particular afternoon of Redbird's birthday Harvey arrived, honking the horn on his brand new red, shiny 1923 Jewett Roadster. Rusty received his bag of look everybody   , and Redbird opened an exquisite pendant made from a freshwater Concho pearl. "Thank you so much, Harvey! It is absolutely lovely," she exclaimed, hugging his neck.

"Now, Redbird, you know I love you!" he gushed as he clasped the gold chain around her neck. "Only the best for my Lady Pearls! Love the new dress! That yellow looks fabulous with your stunning red hair!"

Sarah's, Aunt Katherine came wearing a pair of brand new bright red trousers and a matching cloche hat. Susan showed up with her student's father, and Clarissa arrived with Julie Marie. "I have a party dress for you, Julie Marie!" Harvey exclaimed. "And a new Madame Alexander Doll!"

The little girl squealed with delight! "Thank you, Mr. Harvey."

"Let's go put it on!" Annabelle, taking her daughter's hand.

Mozella arrived with the mail. "You have something here from Houston!" she exclaimed and handed Redbird a white envelope.

"It's from my Uncle Donald." For the last two years he would occasionally send a check, probably out of a guilty conscience. This time it included a letter:

> September 22, 1923
> Dear Linda,
> I am sorry the way things turned out for you and your brothers. Your Aunt Gertrude died a few weeks ago. Seems like she choked on a chicken bone best the doctors could tell. I don't want the house. It was always Gertrude who wanted to stay there. The house would have been turned back to you anyway when you turned 21 as well as the rest of your father's estate. Now that Gertrude is gone, the house is available to you and your brothers. Your father left you and your brothers his half of the business. The company is doing well, and I work long hours. I have a flat in town where I spend most of my time. Again, I am sorry for the way things turned out. Working hard is all I know.
>
> Sincerely yours,
> Donald Donovan

As she silently read the letter from her uncle, Redbird's face showed her surprise. "What is it, Redbird?" Lucy asked.

Unable to speak, Redbird handed her childhood friend the letter as she sank into a nearby chair. "Great God Almighty, Red! You're rich!"

"May I see that?" Pearl asked. She read the letter and smiled. "Looks like you are going to Houston, Redbird." Now she knew how Minna Everleigh had felt when Victoria Pearl announced she was moving to Texas to be with her cowboy. Knowing that the girls in their profession didn't last many years past 28 years old, she insisted her girls educate themselves, save their money, stay clean, have impeccable manners, and maintain their beauty. The ones who did had a much better chance at life than the ones who let the business use them up and throw them out onto the street when they were 30.

"I can hardly believe it, Miss Pearl. I am going to be with my brothers again!" Redbird cried with tears of happiness.

"Houston!" Harvey exclaimed. "I love Houston! I'm going with you! We'll need to redecorate and get that nasty old hag's energy out of there! This is exciting!"

"What's exciting?" Emma Grace asked, coming through the front door with Tommy Lee on her heels.

"Redbird is moving back to Houston!" Lucy exclaimed.

"That's wonder… uh oh!!" Emma Grace quickly put her hand over her mouth and ran to the washroom behind the kitchen.

"She's been like that ever since we got home from Galveston," Tommy Lee commented.

Mozella and Pearl grinned at each other. "Looks like you're going to be a daddy, Tommy Lee! Congratulations!" Mozella announced proudly, heading toward the kitchen to take care of Emma Grace. "*Corinthians 16: Let all that you do be done in love!*"

"A daddy?" Tommy Lee repeated, looking just as Redbird did a few minutes before.

"What's been goin' on here?" Maggie asked as she and Tex rounded the corner.

"Redbird is moving back to Houston and Tommy Lee and Emma Grace are going to have a baby!" Pearl announced.

The other girls appeared in the Great Room. "We are celebrating wonderful news!" Harvey exclaimed. "Redbird is getting her big house back, and I'm going to help her decorate! Tommy Lee just found out he's going to be a daddy!"

"This is fabulous!" Harmony exclaimed.

When Emma Grace reappeared, with Mozella following behind her holding a glass of water, Tommy Lee took her arm. "C'mon baby. You need to sit down. Emma Grace, I believe I love you more than air!"

Emma Grace smiled so sweetly at her husband, it brought tears to Pearl's eyes.

"I love you too, Tommy Lee. You are my life. Mozella says we're going to have a baby. She said she can see it on my face."

Tommy Lee gently put his hand on her stomach "We're going to have a baby?" he whispered.

"Psalm 139, "You made all the delicate, inner parts of my body and knit me together in my mother's womb," Mozella quoted with a happy laugh.

"My Lordy God in heaven… I can't believe it!" Betsy cried, her eyes as big as saucers. Standing on the front porch behind the etched glass door was a tall, handsome man holding a bouquet of pink roses.

"What's wrong, Betsy?" Sarah asked.

Mozella opened the door for the stranger. "May I help you?"

"Yes, Ma'am, I've come to see Miss Betsy Ann Smith, please."

"Johnny Wayne, what in the world are you doing here?" Betsy exclaimed as she ran to the door.

"I've come to take you back home, Betsy Ann. I've built us a house on the farm. Your Mama showed me the letter you wrote. They were really happy when they finally heard from you. Everyone's been worried sick about you! Now, go get your things. It's time to go home, so we can get married and have babies and all."

Betsy and Johnny acted as if they were the only two people in the room. Happy Harvey pulled out his handkerchief and wiped his eyes.

"I can't go with you, Johnny Wayne," Betsy cried. "You don't know what I've done. You don't know where I've been. I've known men…"

"It don't matter, Betsy. I love you, and it don't matter what you've done. No one in Kentucky needs to know anything. It's none of their business. I know your heart. I know you better than you even know yourself! Always have. Now go get your things, so I can take you home. There's a train leaving in a few hours."

"Miss Pearl?" Betsy implored with a confused look on her face. "What should I do?"

"I think you need to do just what Johnny Wayne asked you to do. Go upstairs, and get your things together. I believe it is time for you to go home, Betsy. This is what you've been wanting. Looks like God has answered your prayers," Pearl assured her with a tender smile. "Now hurry up! This young man has been waiting long enough."

"I'll help you!" Lucy exclaimed.

"Me too!" Sarah echoed.

"Would you like some sweet tea, Johnny Wayne? Mozella, why don't we put these pretty roses in a vase. Harmony, I think it is time for some music! We have a birthday, a baby, and a happy reunion to celebrate!"

"Yes, Ma'am!" Harmony declared. "C'mon, Heather and Ginger! Let's get this party started. *There's a yellow rose in Texas, that I am going to see...*" Ginger and Heather quickly chimed in while Lucy grabbed Redbird from the chair to doseydoe. Tex danced with Maggie, and Happy Harvey twirled little Julie Marie. Susan sang, and Annabelle danced with her mother while Katie encouraged Johnny Wayne to clap along with her. Tommy Lee and Emma Grace went outside to the gazebo to get some fresh air and watched as Rusty chased a squirrel.

Soon Betsy came downstairs with her bags packed. "I'm sorry I'm going to miss your birthday party, Redbird." Here's your birthday present. Thank you for being a good friend to me when I was such a cry baby."

Redbird opened her gift and found a ceramic red cardinal bird. "It plays music, see?" Betsy demonstrated turning the small key on the bottom.

"*Fur Elise*! I love it! Thank you, Betsy!"

In tears, everyone said their goodbyes to Betsy. All knew that this was the last time they would ever see their sweet

Betsy, Pearl more than anyone. "Good luck, Betsy," she cried, holding her an extra minute before releasing her forever.

"Thank you for everything, Miss Pearl. I will certainly miss you," Betsy sniveled.

"Ginger will drive you to the train station. Go on now. You don't want to be late. Take good care of our Betsy, Johnny Wayne."

"Yes Ma'am I will," he assured her as he held the car door.

"Goodbye, Miss Pearl. Goodbye!" Betsy waved and Pearl stayed on the porch until the car finally disappeared down the road.

Redbird's birthday party was a great success. That evening after all the festivities, Mozella and Pearl sat on the front porch like they did every night. Pearl thought out loud, "Lost two of our Pearls today, Mozella, perhaps even three. Lucy will probably go back to Houston with Redbird."

"I'm sure she will," Mozella agreed. "Especially if Harvey goes."

"I've been thinking about doing some traveling, Mo. I want to visit Madeline and get a taste of the big city. I would love to see Ada and Minna and go to the theatre. I like the fact that their socialite friends in New York have no idea how they made their millions. They were always good to me."

"Yes, Ma'am, I believe you should go."

"Ginger has a good head on her shoulders. The two of you can certainly take care of things at the Parlor while I am gone."

The two friends sat in silence like only best friends can, listening to the night sounds of nature play in perfect syncopation and watching the lights from the midnight sky reflect off the Concho River. Finally, Pearl broke the stillness. "We've been friends a long time, Mo. You are my rock. Lord knows where I would be if it were not for you. If I had stayed at the ranch, I probably would have withered away. I miss Robert so much. I miss my cowboy. The Parlor has given me a sense of purpose. Today was a magical day.

Mozella looked at her friend and smiled. "'*Ecclesiastics 3: To everything there is a season, and a time to every purpose under the heaven. There's a time to weep, a time to laugh, a time to mourn, and a time to dance.*' What do you want to do in this moment, Victoria Pearl?"

"Well, I guess I have already wept, laughed, and mourned today. Let's go dance!"

The two friends meandered down to the river where together they sang, "*Meet Me in Saint Louis, Louis, Meet me at the fair*" and danced by the light of the Concho moon.

1926 – Epilogue

The Santa Rita No.1 had changed the way the oil industry looked at West Texas. San Angelo was already the number one wool trading center of the world, and with the new oil boom, San Angelo had grown and become even more prosperous.

Since boys will be boys and men will be men, Miss Pearl's Parlor continued to generate a sizeable income. Because of the abundance of money flowing with the boom, San Angelo boasted a new club in town called Rainbow's End.

By 1926 many events had transpired:

Tex had passed away and left his entire estate, including the ranch, to Maggie.

Sarah and Maggie both married cowboys and moved to the ranch where they raised their children and remained lifelong friends.

Redbird was reunited with her brothers and moved with them into the big house where they had grown up. She invited Lucy to move in with her and work as a buyer in their import business. She also offered Mary, Lucy's surrogate mother, a position as housekeeper and cook. Happy Harvey made the house in Houston a unique showplace. In 1925 Uncle Donald died, and Redbird bought out her cousin, enabling her to assume the family business her father had worked so hard to build. Within the first year, she increased the revenue of the company by 30 percent. Lucy spent most of the time travelling abroad on buying trips, and often, Harvey went along.

Emma Grace and Tommy Lee had had a little boy, Daniel, named after Emma Grace's father, and she sang "Danny Boy" to him when she rocked him to sleep. They were expecting another baby around Christmas.

Betsy and Johnny Wayne had had a little girl named Ginger Anne, and Betsy was pregnant with their second child. The couple kept her past a secret for the rest of their lives.

Annabelle bought a house in Christoval, Texas where she opened a small grocery store and raised her daughter Julie Marie. Her mother helped her run the store.

Heather went to Hollywood and began working as an actress in the film industry.

The Everleigh sisters arranged for Ginger and Harmony to join the Ziegfeld Follies in New York where they performed for a year. Ginger became a recording artist and sometimes ran the Parlor when Victoria Pearl took trips abroad. Harmony remained in New York where she became a popular concert pianist and entertainer.

Texas Kate and Mozella stayed in San Angelo and continued working at the Parlor. Mozella's brother Duke moved to San Angelo from New Orleans and became the new piano player. Everyone called him "Professor Duke."

Pearl continued to support the orphanage in town and maintained her high standards at Miss Pearl's Parlor. Between her business, the ranch, and her oil investments, she became a multi-millionaire. She continued mentoring the ladies who went to work for her. Her nickname became "Mother Pearl."

Susan, the schoolteacher, quit teaching school and married her student's father who had lost his wife. A year later, they welcomed a little girl and named her Victoria Pearl.

In 1923 San Angelo became the center for the West Texas oil boom. Also in 1923 the towns known as Texon and Best were established near Big Lake, Texas. Boom Boom, who had formerly worked at Miss Hattie's, opened a successful business of "sporting women" in Best, Texas and did well in establishing a "friendly reputation" for the town.

One day, a banker friend brought a distinguished visitor into Pearl's Parlor. "Welcome to Miss Pearl's Parlor, Mister Hilton," Pearl stated as she offered her hand.

The man kissed her hand in a gentlemanly fashion. "Thank you, Miss Pearl. You can call me Conrad. I have heard great things about your business. I am having a difficult time trying to find a place to stay in San Angelo."

"Let me make some phone calls," Pearl offered.

"Thank you. I can't seem to get a room anywhere in this town. Maybe I should build a hotel in San Angelo," he commented. "Seems like a nice place. The people are certainly friendly."

"It is a nice place, Mr. Hilton. Perhaps you should," Pearl answered with elegance, grace, and style.

"Pearl" music CD available at cynthiamusic.com

Alfred Cheney Johnston

Alfred Cheney Johnston was born in New York City on April 8, 1885. Around 1916 Alfred Cheney Johnston's photography was brought to the attention of Florenz Ziegfeld, founder of the Ziegfeld Follies. After seeing examples of his portrait photography, Ziegfeld invited the young Johnston to become official photographer for the Follies. Cheney had one stipulation to accepting Ziegfeld's offer. He required that his name be included as a byline below every one of his photographs. It proved to be an excellent business move because Johnston's byline brought him other commercial work for film companies and advertising agencies.

Ziegfeld promoted his shows as "Glorifying the American Girl," and it was Johnston's job to capture Ziegfeld's vision on film. Johnston's portraits of Ziegfeld's girls became world famous. Just as his mentor Charles Dana Gibson created the "Gibson Girl," Johnston went on to create the "Ziegfeld Girl" which became the next standard of beauty for a new generation of Americans.

Cheney Johnston had a lucrative career with the Follies until the stock market crash of 1929. Alfred Cheney Johnston died alone in 1971 survived only by his cat and the remains of thousands of portraits from a faded era which had made him famous.

It is an honor to have been given permission to use the photographs of Alfred Cheney Johnston. His exquisite work has brought my characters to life, and for this I am extremely grateful! ~ Cynthia Jordan

Cynthia Jordan was born and raised in Redondo Beach, California. In 1983 she wrote Billboard's #1 Country Hit Song of the Year, *Jose Cuervo (you are a friend of mine)*. In 1984, she married Dennis Buckingham, a Texas oilman/cowboy and moved to East Texas where she began a ministry for children. In 1998 Cynthia relocated to Nashville where she composed and produced 11 CDs of ambient piano music. There have been over 4,000,000 downloads of her piano music worldwide. In 2005 Cynthia moved to San Angelo, Texas and created *Ahh Radio*, a radio show programmed to inspire and help people relax. She wrote the books, *Butterfly Moments* and *If This Was Heaven*. *Pearl* is her first novel and theatrical musical. To learn more about Cynthia Jordan and to listen to her music including the songs written for the musical, *Pearl*, visit cynthiamusic.com.

"The kingdom of heaven is like a merchant looking for fine pearls. When he found one of great value, he went away and sold everything he had and bought it." ~Matthew 13: 45-46